Mrs. Campbell Praed

The Scourge-Stick

Mrs. Campbell Praed

The Scourge-Stick

ISBN/EAN: 9783337031589

Printed in Europe, USA, Canada, Australia, Japan

Cover: Foto ©Andreas Hilbeck / pixelio.de

More available books at **www.hansebooks.com**

The
Scourge-Stick

By

Mrs. Campbell Praed

" . . *I have seen my little boy oft scourge his top,*
And compared myself to 't : nought made me e'er go right
But Heaven's scourge-stick "

London
William Heinemann
1898

TO

MY SON

BULKLEY

BOOK I

" How unbecoming it is for one that is mortal to entertain proud aspiring thoughts: for presumption, when it has put forth the blade, is wont to produce in fruit an all-mournful harvest of woe."

WRITTEN BY ESTHER VASSAL:

AND I Esther—not of the City and the Conventions: but Esther of the Wilderness, whose languid pulses beat youth's measure anew to Nature's piping: whose tired heart throbs again in passionate answer to the pæan of victorious Love: and whom the old art-crave has fierce in grip once more—why should not I, Esther Zamiel, scribbler, write yet another book: my last book: my *reallest* book: which shall be my own story?

For the magic of Philotis is upon me.

Spring spreads abroad her pleasant odours: the birds are mating: roses play the wanton to bees and butterflies: the orange blossoms in the harem-garden are dropping from around the young fruit: the fig-trees are green, and the vines are putting forth leaves and have tender grapes.

Softly through my closed jalousies steals the glad Southern sunshine; and with caress as gentle as a lover's kiss upon the cheek of his sleeping mistress, the warm wind from the Mediterranean plays upon my face. It bears upon its breath the wooing murmur of palm leaves, the fragrance of mimosa, the dreamy break of tideless waves upon the shore, and thrills my senses again with the dear scents and sounds of this well-loved Blue Land.

And memory harks back—back to the Enchanted Days.

A dream within a dream: what else? So little has changed. The very carnations and freesias and anemones, set about in the same green pots of the country as those we bought long ago in the market at El-Meriem, might be the flowers of bygone springs. It is the old gay life of Philotis which rolls on down below—the carriages coming and going in front of the hotel: the Neapolitan singers trolling the same old love-songs they used to sing before the Grand Duke's windows: the voices of the Arabs, squatted outside among their embroideries: the laughter floating up from the drinking-fountain: the Muezzin's solemn call, " Allah is great: there is no God but Allah!" . . . Long silent chords vibrating in the oft-repeated melody. . . . All as it was before —in the Enchanted Days!

3

I have taken out from their locked place and looked over
back-time note-books and journals. Truly I was a writing-
woman from the beginning. How stupid it was of me to mistake
my vocation and to fancy, as I did at first, that I had it in me to
be a great actress!

My real story opens upon the day when I played *Claudia*.
That was the fork of my Y of life—I quote *his* phrase. So I
will start from that grim afternoon when I went in at the stage
entrance of the Regency Theatre, before making my appearance
as the leading character in Dr. Quintin Glaive's new play.

It was so curious to see my own name in big letters on the
red posters outside the theatre—

> *Claudia* .   .   .   . MISS ESTHER VRINTZ.

Esther Vassal! Esther Zamiel! Esther Vrintz! Are you
bewildered by this triune personality? Well, wait a little while
and you will understand.

Before I stepped inside the stage-door, I turned and stood
still, looking down the foggy street and up at the murky sky.
There was one ragged rift in the leaden mass through which the
sun gleamed for a few seconds before the rift closed again—a
blood-red sun, savage and sinister, like the threatening eye of
some malignant fate. In that glance upward, it seemed to me
that I was putting forth an appeal to destiny.

For weeks I had been straining every nerve in preparation for
the great ordeal, and now at the critical hour I lost hold of myself. Everything appeared unreal, and I myself most unreal of
all. People walking were as grey ghosts, and cabs and omni-
buses showed monstrous outlines through the mist. To this day,
the uncanny impression of that halt at the stage-door remains
vivid as death. Something cold stung my face: a flake of snow:
to me most dire omen. For from childhood I have had a superstitious dread of snow, and have always felt that whenever anything
disastrous should happen to me, there would be snow falling or
lying white. It used to come into my bad dreams. Mother was
buried in a snowstorm. Father died when snow coated the
Vasques Hills: and when I was married . . . Of that, however,
I will tell later.

But I knew that now I must brace myself to the work. I
must not let such fancies overcome me. I must collect my
faculties. I must be brave and confident. I must triumph.

The people in the passage waiting for the doorkeeper to hand
them letters and telegrams looked at me oddly, and that brought
me back to the actual world. A lady passing out at the moment

nodded and said, "Good morning : I wish you luck." She was a "principal" in the evening piece ; and I, who till to-day had been a "super," felt the novelty of being thus addressed by a "principal," and found comfort in the incident. Then several of the others wished me luck also, and the stage doorkeeper smiled benevolently and raised his hat. The stage doorkeeper's countenance was as a weather-glass of theatrical favour, so I took courage, and that horrible dazed feeling lifted.

There was one telegram for me, which I opened and read going up the stairs. It was from Agatha Greste, daughter of Frank Leete, the dramatic critic, now on her way to Ceylon, wishing me success. As a man came down by me, I suddenly remembered the theatrical superstition that it is unlucky just before going on to meet anybody on the stairs, and was not grateful when he called out cheerily—

"Well, Claudia, how do you feel?'

"Oh, I am terribly frightened."

'So am I ; it's a good sign. Look here ! you were upset over that dress rehearsal. Don't worry about it. We old stagers know that a bad dress rehearsal is often a good sign, and don't mind a little bit. Just you let yourself go ; and good luck go with you."

My foolish superstition—was it foolish ?—made me wince notwithstanding the kindly words. This man was one of the older members of the company, and was always sympathetic and encouraging to beginners, but in the play he took the part of *Claudia's* evil genius, and his ironic blessing followed her through the acts like a curse.

The leading lady's room represented then my notion of an earthly paradise. To-day, by grace of Dr. Glaive, I was for a few hours to be in possession of this paradise. I had caught glimpses of it on my way up and down the stairs ; and in the leading lady I saw my ambition personified, and envied her, as those on the lowest rung of the ladder envy the successful climbers. But I had never spoken to her, and probably till I was cast for *Claudia* she had been unaware of my existence.

My paradise was charming with chintz hangings and bright light. A long cheval glass reflected me ; a couch and easy-chair awaited me during the intervals ; and there was a dressing-table draped in muslin, with brushes, toilet implements, pins, and cosmetics laid out by a careful hand ; and best of all, a neat dresser standing at smiling attention. The place in its freshness, refinement, and quietude brought me a luxurious sense of having reached my goal, and I had to force myself to remember that this was but as a vision of the Promised Land, which I had as yet not earned the right to enter.

Then again came that numbing dread, paralysing brain and limbs.   The dresser made me drink some champagne, which she said Dr. Quintin Glaive had sent.   There was, too, a loose bunch of white roses, tied with ribbon and bearing a card on which was written, "With Dr. Quintin Glaive's compliments and good wishes."   This thoughtfulness surprised me, for, indeed, just then, there was no one in the whole world, or out of it, whom I held in such terrified awe as my "author."   I had had no dealings with him, except in the way of business and at rehearsals, and he had seemed to me severely critical, and on the whole unsympathetic.

Those rehearsals ! . . . Queer bits of scenes and grim touches of humour start out as from a dream.   I see the great dim theatre, feebly lighted by two or three gas jets, and the weird effect of the boxes draped in white sheets, while the galleries yawned in cavernous blackness, and the stalls looked ghostly in their holland shrouds. . . . Then on the stage, actors and actresses with hats on—why do actors always wear their hats, I wonder, when they are rehearsing?—and carrying little oblong manuscripts of their parts, strutting, gesticulating, or else waiting at the wings studying, while the manager, standing in front of the T. light or walking up and down, watched and admonished.

I seem to hear him. . . . " Chesney, Chesney, that won't do at all. . . . Will you try to remember that in the play you are supposed to be a gentleman ?   Come, now, this is how it should go "—stepping forward and demonstrating. . . . And then the laugh when Chesney, who was an irreverent youth, replied, " Just as you like, Mr. Carter-Blake ; but Dr. Glaive told me to be natural."

And Dr. Glaive's voice would float across the footlights from the front row of the stalls, where he used to sit when he looked in at the theatre after his morning consultations.   Perhaps we had not known he was there. . . . Then the lines would all fly— Oh, can you imagine what it is to lose your part altogether from sheer nervousness !   " Word !—word ! " you murmur agonisedly ; and either the prompter will not give it, or you are more hopelessly put out by the wrong cue.

Dr. Glaive was truly alarming—dryly sarcastic to the men when they annoyed him by their misconception of his meaning ; politely painstaking with the women.   There was an old lady who played elderly plutocratic lead, and who couldn't make herself vulgar in just the subtle way he wanted.   I don't know why one meaningless phrase in the play sticks, "That has nothing to do with *us*." I can hear Dr. Glaive's courteous expostulations, "The *us*, Mrs. Ferrers. A good deal more should be made of that *us*. Say it as if—as if you were the editor of *The Times*, you know." Then to me gently reproving in the midst of my love scene, "I don't like it, Miss Vrintz. . . . Please, Miss Vrintz, try that again. . . ."

How they echo, the trivial sentences, through the long years !

I have never been able to understand why Dr. Glaive offered me the part of *Claudia*. Mr. Leete told me that he had been attracted by my voice in a recitation he had heard me give at a party—Mr. Leete got me that engagement—and that in appearance I realised his conception of his heroine. He had said also that he was pleased at the absence of dramatic trick in me, and that he wanted to make an artistic experiment.

I was enormously flattered, and even Mr. Leete was overwhelmed at the magnitude of the opportunity. There wasn't an actress in London who would not have welcomed it. Dr. Quintin Glaive was the playwright in whom, at that time, the critics were most interested. He was a kind of John the Baptist to Ibsen, though of course it is only last year that Ibsen began to be talked of; and in those days no one could have dreamed of quite such a flying in the face of dramatic conventions. It did indeed seem extraordinary that this fashionable dramatist should have chosen for the title-part in his new play a poor, unknown girl, living in one room in Bloomsbury, and earning twenty-five shillings a week in a curtain-raiser, and with not a penny in the world besides. A half-foreign orphan girl, with no friends to push her—not counting Mr. Leete, and he didn't consider me fit yet to be pushed—with no theatrical training, no stage experience to speak of, nothing of any kind to commend her. Why, it was simply a marvel.

Not to me. There's a saying that a river, a strong man, and genius carve their own way. *I* was genius. Jove knew it : and the Fates had given me my chance.

That is what in my crude egoism I said to myself.

Was it quite fair on a poor, ignorant girl to make her the subject of an artistic experiment ? And would Dr. Glaive have made the experiment if he could have seen how my whole life would be affected by it ?

Besides Dr. Glaive's flowers, there was a magnificent Covent Garden basket of roses, lilies, and orchids from Mr. Hector Vassal

—a pretty courtesy, and quite the sort of offering for a millionaire. Yet in all my clammy excitement there came over me an odd instinctive feeling about that costly bouquet : it was like my feeling about Mr. Vassal himself.

This too, however, I shall have to write of later.

Then began the making up and dressing ; and then came the low rumble from the theatre as it filled : the quavering of the orchestra : the dull sound at the wings of the curtain rising . . . And then my call. . . .

.   .   .   .   .

Alas ! alas ! The glory was departed from me, and my paradise was forfeit—perhaps for ever. I had failed ; failed absolutely and irretrievably. The first two acts had been an exhibition of reckless incompetence ; the third act was collapse ; the last, despair. It was ruin complete, and the murder of my career. There was no consolation in the reflexion—if at the moment I had been capable of reflecting — that Dr. Glaive's blundering confidence in his experiment and my own overweening self-conceit and ambition had been its murderers.

I stood, a frenzied, hunted thing, in the leading lady's dressing-room, waiting for what should come.

Presently the stage-manager knocked at the door and asked, pushing it ajar as he spoke—

" Miss Vrintz, will you take your call ? "

From the theatre sounded the shrilling of excited voices. . . . Was it possible that they were hissing the author ? Why had they not hissed me ? The curtain had fallen in a silence, ghastly, deadly, more appalling than the loudest roar of denunciation.

" No, thank you, I'd rather not. . . . Unless {Mr. Carter-Blake says I must."

" Oh, no ; you are to do as you please," and he shut the door and went away. After a little while there was another knock, and the dresser went to the door.

" Mr. Leete, to see Miss Vrintz."

Again, as the door opened, came echoes from the front, and the hoarse roar of pit and gallery, where they were shouting now " Au—thòr ! . . . Au—thòr." The dresser turned to me, " Will you see Mr. Leete ? "

I nodded, and she held the door open for him and then went out.

Mr. Leete stood still for a few moments, as if uncertain how to address me. He has told me since that I seemed terrible to him, in my white make-up and stony calm : and that his task would have been much easier had he found me in hysterics. The big man looked at me with moist eyes, and his voice was smothered in his great beard and moustache as he spoke with his head down, nervously stepping forward and taking my two hands. I hardly realised then, but I know now what it must have cost him to come.

"What can I say to you?" he exclaimed.

"The truth."

I took away my hands; his touch only hurt me, and sympathy was a mockery.

"You'll have to write the truth in the *Sentinel*. Let me hear it now."

"The truth!" he repeated, giving me a frightened glance.

"The true truth. I think I know it. But grind it in; and for God's sake don't pity me."

I understood by his startled expression that he was not prepared for this mood of savage desperation. I had always been so quiet, so shy—except about my art.

"Very well. Perhaps it *is* the kindest thing to tell you straight out that you have made a miserable failure." Having taken the scalpel he used it unflinchingly. "An unmitigated failure. Esther, I feel a brute—yet you have asked me for the brutal truth."

"Quite right. But there's such a thing as failure with a glimmer of possibility in the future. Is there a gleam? That's what I want to know."

He hesitated. "You must recollect," he said, "I always told you that the part of *Claudia* would tax the resources even of a great artist. I never expected you to grasp it."

"No; but you expected——"

He paused, then answered deliberately, "Well, I expected that your conception would show originality—that though technique might be deficient, there would be spontaneity, passion—in short, some flash of genius. There was nothing of the kind.

"It passes my understanding," he went on in an exasperated tone, "when I think of your reading of *The Duchess of Malfi*! Allowing for want of experience, for being stage-struck allowing for everything, there should still have been moments."

He made a few agitated steps, and clutched his beard and moustache after a way he had when he was excited. I waited.

"There! if you will have it,—there wasn't a redeeming point. The whole thing was hopeless."

I didn't wince at the death-probe. I had known the truth all along. Throughout the play I had never held the audience for an instant, and had felt it. I had never struck one spark. It had been mouthing and miming in the dark—putting out my whole strength against a stone wall. I cried out something of this to him, thanked him for his candour, told him I knew it was the best thing for me that he should be honest.

"Upon my soul, I believe it is," he answered huskily. "It may be saving you years of untold suffering. You are not like the rest. You have got an ideal. And if there's a pitiful thing on God's earth, it's an artist with an ideal and no power to realise it."

"That's true," I answered. "My father was like that."

"Yes, your poor father thought he could compose a great opera, and he was just a fifth-rate musician! It's in the blood."

Again Mr. Leete walked up and down, and at last stopped before me, dragging at his beard. They say that one notices trifles when one is dying, and this trick of his was what impressed me most just then.

"Look here," he said; "you told me you only wanted to be put to the test. Well, you have been tested. Abide by the result. Give up the stage and try some other way of earning a livelihood. Go out as a governess."

"I couldn't parse a sentence or do a rule-of-three sum. I'm totally uneducated on the ordinary lines, and I hate children."

"That's bad! Well, you wouldn't do badly in drawing-room recitation. I daresay that I could get Glaive to help you along. I'm not much in the way of party-giving ladies myself — in Belgravia anyhow. But Glaive knows a lot of them."

I shuddered. The poems of Adelaide Anne Procter, and the *Song of the Shirt* at suburban entertainments! For I could never look in Dr. Glaive's face again.

Mr. Leete gave a groan when I said that.

"I'm greatly to blame for this. I encouraged your high-flying aspirations. I've been a romantic fool."

"If it was being a romantic fool to trust generously to my faith in myself! yes, I suppose you were one. You'll be wiser another time, Mr. Leete; and so much the worse for some other poor girl who has got the real stuff in her."

"I wish you wouldn't kiss the rod so meekly," he exclaimed. "You make me hate myself."

"I . . . *I* kiss the rod!"

"Think it out," he said, "and above all things let us be practical. I have your welfare at heart. If it's only because you're a friend of my Gagsie. And she's gone off to Kandy, and heaven only knows when I shall see her again! I should have it on my conscience if I didn't try to stop you from running after a will-o'-

the-wisp. You are a delicate thing and not fit to stand up against disappointment and rebuff. If I've been rubbing in the salt, it's to harden you."

"Of course," he went on, "no one has a right to pronounce definitely. It's possible that you may prove all the critics, myself included, mistaken, and that in years to come you may take rank in the profession. But I'm bound to tell you my honest opinion—that of an old critic, who has watched the rise of scores of actresses—and it is, that if you remain on the stage you'll have to make up your mind to a low place. Always supposing that your professional advancement would come through the legitimate channels."

"I don't quite understand what other channels there could be for me besides what you call the legitimate ones."

"You are not a child," he answered, "and you must have had your eyes opened in the theatrical world. If not, the sooner they are opened the better for you. You have seen leading ladies who can't act a stroke, pushed forward by managers and puffed in newspapers—attracting a public that they've got round by advertisement, good looks, trick of manner, dressing, some style and fascination—the Lord knows what; but it's *not* legitimate art."

His meaning became dimly apparent. Perhaps it was curious that my eyes had not been opened wider during the year and a half in which I was a "super" at the Regency. But somehow my nature hadn't, so far, assimilated notions of that sort.

"You've got the good looks, and a—it was said by a man I don't like—a power of attracting. You might work a career in that fashion if you chose. Certainly if you did choose, Gagsie and I would wash our hands of you, but that's not the question. Anyhow, no matter how you might recoil from the thing, it's a danger you ought to realise. You'd find the temptation horrible—good women have told me so. It begins so insidiously — cheap outlay at the start; just looking pretty and making yourself agreeable, and the inducement of opportunity to prove yourself. Esther, you are a brave, true, proud girl, but, like every other woman, you have your weak side. Do you think you are strong enough to play the waiting theatrical game honestly—no fear and no favour—to the end, which will probably mean the bitter end—defeat?"

I couldn't answer him. There was a reckless streak in my nature of which sometimes I felt afraid. If the devil had come to me the night before, mightn't I have sold my soul for success?

Mr. Leete put his heavy hand on my shoulder in a rough fatherly way.

"My girl, as I said, let us be practical and look at things as they are, and not as we want them to be. My sincere conviction is that you'll never get higher than a step or two on the ladder. To reach beyond that, will cost you years and years of drudgery. To-day's failure will throw you back. I've done you harm; Glaive has done you harm—I've told him so. Oh, it's a sickening business grinding on in the ruck. You haven't the health or the grip for it. The profession is a grand one for those who have the capacity to mount; but you have seen enough as a 'super' to know what the other thing means."

Then I lost my self-control, and lifted my arms wildly as I cried out, "What it means! To grind on till one has lost youth, health, hope, enthusiasm, even ambition—and still to grind on! God help me! Yes, I know what it means."

Frank Leete cried out too as I let my arms drop again.

"My heaven! That's good! Why couldn't you do that sort of thing on the stage. Tell me just—why?"

I laughed—how grimly!—repeating "Why?"

Presently I asked, "Have I killed the play?"

"Oh no, the play will be seen again."

"But *I* shall not."

"It doesn't really matter much to Quintin Glaive," said Mr. Leete. "Playwriting is only the recreation of his leisure hours, and he has made his name and can command the market. By the way, he told me to ask if he should come round and see you. He spoke very nicely about it all. You had better see him."

"No! The cannons of Balaclava sooner!" I gave Mr. Leete a message for Dr. Glaive that I was sorry to have been such a disappointment, and that I would not trouble him any more. Then I asked Mr. Leete to go.

"I'll put you into a cab," he said, and pressed my hand in affectionate and remorseful good-bye. But I told him that I wanted to be alone and to slip out unnoticed. Besides, how could I afford cabs now?

"If any one speaks to me I shall go mad," I said; and added, "You see, I've got to act my little part this evening."

He lingered just a minute while I put away in their box the paste ornaments I had been wearing and which had been my mother's—worn by her on the stage also. She, too, had been an unsuccessful actress, a little unknown Jewess of Philotis, who had played in the theatre there, and had fallen into ill-health, and soon after her marriage had given up her profession. Doubly inherited failure was born in me.

Mr. Leete shook my hand again, promised his interest in

getting me on for a country tour, if I still remained bent upon the theatrical life, bade me sup with him at his house on the morrow, which was Sunday, to hear the news from Agatha Greste, his daughter, and talk matters over with his wife.

I answered vaguely that I would try to come; but in truth, I felt little appetite for the discussion of my failure with Mrs. Leete, who was a worthy person, but a poor comforter in misfortunes, which she was apt to regard as the result of arrogant self-confidence.

. . . .

Quarter of an hour after Mr. Leete had gone, I was dressed again in my ordinary clothes, and had left the leading lady's room, from which henceforth I was outcast. With a thick gauze veil and a waterproof hiding completely my face and figure, I had passed unobserved through the stage-door, and was waiting in the open portico of the theatre for an omnibus to go by.

The world was quite white, for snow was falling in thick noiseless flakes, and the unlovely alley leading to the stage entrance seemed transformed, with all the projections of the mean houses drawn in dazzling lines; while the roar of traffic was deadened and the shapes of vehicles and people appeared even more phantasmal than they had done three hours before. Now for the first time since the beginning of the performance, I became conscious of being sick and faint, so that I could hardly drag along my limbs. There was no omnibus of the familiar colour in sight; and secure in my shrouding veil, I turned within the portico and sat down on a stone ledge abutting from the wall, behind a pillar upon which the placards with my name conspicuous, still hung. These formed for me an appropriate screen from the little crowd of persons who had collected there, waiting like myself for omnibus or cab.

Some of these seemed in no hurry; they were men—critics and literary and theatrical people, who were discussing the play. The feeling of dizziness left me at the sound of my own name uttered by one of a small group which had gathered beside the very pillar that sheltered me. I knew by sight two of the men in this group. One was a novelist; the other, dramatic critic for an important paper. There were two or three besides, whom I did not know.

"Oh, damn the play!" one of these was saying. "That will do well enough when it's cut and pulled together. It's not the play. It's the actress!"

"I'm not talking of the actress for the moment, but of the

English drama," said another. "Esther Vrintz, or anybody else —genius or duffer, what does it matter? Everything nowadays is sacrificed to construction. That's part of the theatrical shibboleth. It's the system of dramatic upholstery that's at fault. Give us psychological upholstery instead. Why don't some of you novelists turn dramatist and upset the whole modern apple-cart—go in for real realism—of the heart and not of the garments. For I loathe that machinery which makes for 'points' and works up to a 'curtain.'"

The man who spoke was leaning against the pillar with his profile towards me. A tall man, loosely built, lean and square, in an overcoat that hung on, rather than was moulded to his spare bony frame. I saw the outline of a long, straight nose, with mobile nostrils, a nervous-looking mouth under a small moustache, and a peaked chin with a cleft in it, not hidden by the short silky beard trimmed to a Vandyke point. It was an odd mixture, the face, of sensitiveness and power. Somehow the man put me in mind of a worried lion; perhaps because there was a touch of the lion in the shape of his heavy brow and rather massive head, and in the backward wave of his mane of short hair, which turned up at the points and grew in a peculiar way upward from the temples that I observed when he took off his hat to a lady passing. The eyes were a very clear grey, with lashes much darker than hair or beard, and had a melancholy particularly intent expression, heightened by the close knitting of the rather shaggy brows above them. Altogether there was something in the appearance of this man which fixed itself on my brain, and during years afterwards I never forgot the face.

Do you believe in mind currents which attract or repel certain persons to or from each other? I hadn't thought much about such things then, and yet even then I seemed subtly conscious that something went from that man to me, during those minutes, when the skirt of his coat almost touched my cloak as I crouched in my niche behind him—something that in my dazed misery and the blur and desolation of my failure gave me an odd sense of warmth and support. His voice too affected me; it was deep and musical, and his manner of speech had a peculiar force and incisiveness. A queer fancy darted through my mind, that whatever this man said should be accepted by me as a pronouncement of fate. Always I have had a fantastic leaning to this kind of divination by straws of circumstances.

"Quintin Glaive had given a push or two to the apple-cart," said the first speaker. "But he must have been mad to imagine that girl could touch the part of *Claudia*."

"She is really a doosid pretty little thing," said a dandified mustachioed man, with a disagreeable accent. "Small, but a fine shape of a woman, and moves well. I believe she would fetch the town if she was taught to dance and put into burlesque."

"I don't know which was maddest, Glaive to offer her the part, or Frank Leete, who seems a friend of hers, to let her accept it," said the novelist. "But one can't beat the heroic audacity of these mimes. No doubt she thought herself a born immortal."

"Ah, that divine courage of egoism!" said the Man of Destiny. "We've all had our turn of it, and should be compassionate for the failures. If no man had ever believed in himself, the world would be pretty barren of achievement. Well, it was too painful an exhibition for me to care to watch it closely; and yet—I am not sure——"

"You don't mean to say that you think she'll do—in spite of this."

"Not on the stage," he answered decidedly. "But I shouldn't wonder if she did do something some day."

"Some day is a long day—and what?"

"That's beyond me. But those eyes *must* mean inspiration of some kind—they're magnificent. It's a curious type."

"At any rate," said the critic, "however heroic her audacity may have been, she put nothing heroic into her failure. The thing was sheer collapse from the middle of the first act."

"But there was something heroic in the look of dumb desperation she threw round the house," said the Man of Destiny. "It was the passionate despair of absolute incompetence."

"Yet Leete was declaring at the Roscius that he meant to make something of her."

"He'll never make an actress. . . . Why didn't she let herself go, and trust to her eyes and hair, and those extraordinarily fascinating dimples to carry her through?" the Man of Destiny exclaimed with a sort of angry abruptness. "She impresses me distinctly as a bit of womanhood, but *that* for the actress!" He gave an expressive squaring-back movement of his shoulders. "As woman pure and simple I fancy she would be convincing."

"Frank Leete assures me that it is as the actress, unfortunately, and not as the woman, she wants to convince."

"Advise him to tell her that she has mistaken her vocation," the Man of Destiny answered. "It will be kindest. For the stage she is simply hopeless. Far better that she should fall in love, marry, and cultivate babies instead of dramatic art. Perhaps, after all, the meaning in those eyes may be merely crudely feminine."

Ah, heaven! it is a bitter thing to be a woman! I remembered what Mr. Leete had said about the channels which were not legitimate. Had women, then, no vocation but one? There was a note of pitying suggestiveness in the voice of that Man of Destiny. He too might have been thinking as Mr. Leete had thought. He was not like the others, though to him, too, I was just—"a bit of womanhood."

It seemed as though another part of me, something which was myself and yet not myself, had been listening to and noting the dialogue—noting it as though not I, but another miserable actress who had failed were its subject. I had sat so still, so numb, and yet so intensely alive. The sensation resembled that of taking chloroform, when all that happens seems to take place in another room. Now I came suddenly to myself, and the pain of that coming to was like the sticking of a knife into a limb no longer anæstheticised. I had cast my die, and Fate had decreed against me. As I rose, a gasping sound, which I could not repress, escaped my lips. The Man of Destiny turned, and his eyes fixed themselves upon me full. They were strange eyes, deep, bright, and intensely melancholy. But it was impossible for him to see my face through my veil, for which I was thankful.

"I beg your pardon," he said, mechanically making way for me as I walked blindly through the group and out from the colonnade into the street and the snow. People jostled me, and I had the feeling that they weren't real people at all, but fiends let loose for my torment. I went along quite a distance before I even thought of an omnibus, and was standing still, shivering, when a policeman asked where I wanted to go, and hailed one which was passing. I shrank and shivered in the corner of it, looking out over the conductor into the street, where the things I saw struck me with a ridiculous acuteness, and fixed themselves indelibly, so that even now I could tell what were the flowers that day in the window of a big florist's —there were sheaves of mimosa which reminded me of Philotis —and then I have a vivid memory of a man with a barrow roasting chestnuts; and I particularly noticed a row of hearth-rugs outside a second-hand furniture shop, illuminated by flaring gas jets, and I remember thinking that a hearth-rug at six and elevenpence halfpenny must be good value for the money.

They put me down near Gower Street; and I remember, too, as I walked, scrunching the snow underfoot in savage wrath, and thinking to myself, "Oh, if I were only some superhuman giant, and could trample down those creatures who jeered from the gallery, and strike murderous blows at the fine folk in the stalls who had tittered during my great scene.   What did they know about pain ? If I had but the power to make them scream with my agony !   If I could only hurt somebody ! "

There were three flights of stairs to my room, which was dark except for the gas on the landing.   The fire was unkindled, and the encrusting snow made a white dimness on the window-panes. I lighted the jet within, drew the curtains, took off my wet cloak, and made myself tea with a spirit-lamp.   I was determined that I would not think, if I could help it, till after I had played in the evening piece.

I had to start off again almost immediately, but the tea and the food I forced myself to swallow, did me good, and I no longer felt faint.   I knew that I must nerve myself to my task.   I must not break down until the theatre was over, and then I might cry all through the night, and all through the morrow, and all through the next day till half-past six, if it so pleased me. .

.   .   .   .   .   .

Again I passed through the stage-door.   This time nobody wished me good luck.   As usual, people were standing near the rack reading their letters, and I heard the ring of laughter and caught a scrap of the talk.   " Why, gracious, my dear ! she was too feeble for anything ; she simply———" Then as the speaker suddenly saw me, there was an audible " H—sh " and quick bending over correspondence in the effort to appear absorbed and oblivious.   The stage doorkeeper had no smile for me now.   He, too, was intent over the sorting of his letters and telegrams, and pretended not to see me.   Oh, I don't suppose they meant to be unkind ; theatrical folk are not, as a rule, given to exult over a comrade in misfortune.   They just wanted to spare me and themselves the embarrassment of allusion to the afternoon's calamity.   Anyhow, it didn't matter.   No pin-pricks could hurt me now.

The door of the leading lady's room stood open as I went by, and I had a mocking glimpse of my forbidden paradise, and could see the dresser making her preparations.

The " supers'" dressing-room was ever so high, and I shared it with three others.   As I stood on the threshold for a few moments unnoticed in the buzz of talk, with what poignant bitterness the contrast struck me between the dainty restful chamber below and this comfortless little barrack, with its pervading air of commonness and its noisy occupants, whose underbred voices jarred more sickeningly than they had ever jarred before.   I realised forcibly just then that the dramatic profession is in itself a social system, having its aristocracy, its middle-class, and its democracy. These women were of the condition to which "supers" of a London theatre mostly belong—the fixed quantity that has found its level, the ruck of which I must in future form a part.

That was how the thing hit home. Till to-day, I had never looked upon the supers' dressing-room as anything but a mere passage to the queen's apartment. It was horrible to think that night after night, during long year after long year, I must go forth to my work from just such a place as this and from among such companions.

There were three of them standing with their backs to the door, arranging their dyed hair and making up their faces in front of a long shelf which had drawers underneath, and looking-glasses between wire-guarded gas jets on the wall above.

To-night all the sordid details of the room seemed to rise up at me, and they fixed themselves in my brain as the things in the street had fixed themselves while I had sat in the omnibus, so that I could make a catalogue of them now. The dingy washing-stand in the corner, with the paint worn off it; the two or three cane-bottomed chairs; the make-up appliances set before each glass on a soiled towel or bit of newspaper; powder in saucers or large shabby boxes; flabby, stained powder-puffs of different sizes; pots of vaseline; sticks of cosmetic; rouge and grease-paint; pencils of black and blue lead; the human effluvia mingling with whiffs of sodden drink from the dresser's breath— she was not a pleasant specimen, this particular dresser; how different from the one in the leading lady's room! But then, could one expect the supers' attendant to be the same order of handmaid as the dresser who, during a course of years, had been trained to the requirements of the leading lady?

I had opened the door softly, and as I did so a shout of coarse laughter caught my ear, and my own name.

"My goodness! Vrintz was a frost this afternoon. Didn't I say she'd be too dire for words?"

"Serves her right. I can't stand the conceit of these 'ten minutes' actresses, who think themselves Mrs. Siddonses."

There was a glance sideways between wisps of hair, and a lull as I went to my own corner. The girl who had last spoken turned effusively to the dresser. "Get us another bottle of stout, Bessie, there's a darling."

"All right, dearie," returned the dresser, and went out.

"So the notice has gone up for this bally old farce," I heard another of the women say, as she stood back to see the effect of the lines she had been drawing under her eyes. "Well, it doesn't matter to me. Gascoigne will take care that I'm in the next piece. Thank Heaven *I* don't aspire to be leading lady all at once;" and though I wouldn't look, I felt the spiteful glance upon me.

If the notice was up, I suspected that my engagement, like the farce, was coming to an end. Should I get another? And if not, how was I going to live?

Presently there came the familiar sound outside the door, "Beginners, please!" and I had to go on.

.   .   .   .   .   .

I made up my fire when I got home, and sat down on the floor in front of it, for I was shivering and shaking. Now I knew myself to be alone with defeat; and that grim fiend I had been trying to keep at bay, clutched at the nerves somewhere in my chest: and the tightness and pain threw me into a sort of gasping convulsion, so that I literally writhed on the floor where I had laid myself when the paroxysm took me.

Oh my God! what had I done that I should be crushed in such agony of despair. No physical pain could be worse than this suffering. Why should the one supreme good upon which my whole soul had been fixed be wrenched away from me? It was not as though I had wanted anything wicked. From the time that I was a little girl, every instinct in me seemed to have been pushing on in the crave to be a great artist. Where was the wrong in that to be punished so cruelly? And if it were wrong, why had God given me the instinct of art for my inheritance? Frank Leete was right; the crave was in my blood; and failure was in my blood too. Don't I remember how we found Father lying in a red pool and the score of his opera torn into little shreds round him! He had been artist enough to know that he could never be great. And I was artist enough to know that the man of the profile had spoken truth, and that I could never be great either.

Looking back upon that anguish of despair, it all seems such crude, such exaggerated emotion. But that was my way. I have never felt deeply about more than two or three things in my life; and those have pierced down into the roots of my being.

No wonder I thought God cruel—if indeed I had then a definite belief in any especial God. For all faiths had meant pretty much the same to me in my bringing up—a Roman Catholic or a Protestant church, a Jewish synagogue or an Arab mosque— just as it came.

And it wasn't either that I was ambitious in the worldly sense.

Though I did even then realise that there was in me a streak over which I have always vaguely puzzled. An exaltation of sense—I cannot quite phrase it—a susceptibility to certain finer forms of emotion, and an immense yearning for fulness of life : a yearning which was nevertheless mainly spiritual and which seemed to affect me mostly through Nature and in my passionate determination to excel in art. Oddly enough, the human merely repelled me ; it appeared gross, and I had a dislike to it at close quarters. For I don't think that I was vain in the ordinary girl's way ; and it never entered my head to try and attract admiration. I only cared about being pretty in so far as I might approach in outward similitude the splendid creatures of imagination I wished to impersonate.

These analysings of my temperament are the after translation of what I was then merely feeling, and, maybe, are inartistically discursive. But they occur, so I let them stand.

I don't know how long I lay there in front of the fire ; it had died to ashes, and my gaspings had ceased, when after a bit I knew that I was hungry. My supper was on the table—my landlady always put that ready. Only some scraps of cold meat, bread, and a glass of milk, which I took ; and then I noticed on the table a letter that must have been left by special messenger, for it had no stamp. There was not any need of the embossed address on the flap of the envelope to tell me whence it came. I knew that Mr. Vassal, the rich man who had sent me the basket of hothouse flowers, was the writer.

I could not take in the meaning of the letter at first. Not till I had read it over twice was I sure that it was genuine.

No, certainly, it was not a hoax, for I had already received from Mr. Vassal two notes. One had been about a dinner at Richmond that he gave for the Leetes and Agatha's *fiancé*, Captain Greste, just before the marriage, and to which he had invited me. The other—some trivial matter which also had relation to Agatha—yes, I remember, it was to ask whether a certain wedding-present he had thought of would be acceptable.

So that my associations with Mr. Vassal had been of a kindly nature, and there was nothing to account for the faint feeling of repulsion I had towards him. Well, yes, there had been something. One evening at the Leetes', when Mr. Leete was reading aloud a play that had been submitted for his approval, and I, was feeling rather interested and excited over it, I looked up and caught Mr. Vassal's eyes fixed upon me, and their expression somehow made me frightened and uncomfortable. I did not know why at the time ; I do know why now.

That Mr. Vassal should be in love with me ; that he should

wish to marry me was more marvellous and incredible than that
Dr. Quintin Glaive should have thought me fit to play *Claudia*.
This was the letter :—

"—— GROSVENOR STREET,
January 14.

"MY DEAR MISS VRINTZ,—You may be surprised at the
subject of this letter, and you may perhaps think that, in writing
it, I am presuming too [much on an acquaintance which has
offered but few opportunities for intimate interchange of thought
and feeling. You may never even have suspected that in those
opportunities I have learned to love you and to form the wish,
very close to my heart, that you should become my wife.

"May I dare to say, without seeming brutally unsympathetic
or disparaging of your talent—which was to-day too severely
taxed by want of experience and a part of immense difficulty—
that I am selfish enough to hope the critics' verdict may dis-
courage you from continuing your stage career. For, unflattering
to my vanity as is the reflexion, I am afraid that were the verdict
as favourable as your theatrical well-wishers hoped, you would
not pause to weigh such worldly advantages as might be involved
in my proposal. But in the event of failure to realise your artistic
expectations, I would ask you to consider, does the alternative I
offer, hold nothing in the way of compensation for your disappointment ? You will at least acquit me of undue self-confidence. I
am aware that I am dealing with a nature singularly guileless and
elevated in aim and motive. Were this otherwise I should not
be so greatly attracted by you. I should not see in you the
woman whom of all others I most desire for my wife and the
mother of my children.

"Esther, this is what I ask—that you will accept me as your
husband. I do not presume to anticipate that you can love me
at once after the romantic fashion in which you might love a
younger man. But I indulge the hope that if you will give me
the right to try, I shall be able to rouse in you a feeling not wholly
incompatible with my own ardent devotion. Of this devotion I
will not now say much, for I fear that effusive protestation might
jar upon your sensitive reserve, and injure the cause I most
earnestly long to plead in person.

"I anxiously await your decision. Will you let me see you
to-morrow ? Yet rest assured, my regard for you is so great
that I would not unduly press or worry you : and whatever may
be your mood, I will respect it. May I request the favour of an
early telegram naming the hour most convenient for me to come.
I am—yours with deepest affection,   HECTOR VASSAL."

As, after long years, I re-read this letter, I wonder within myself whether its studied self-repression and formal courtesy were the result of consummate knowledge of woman's nature, or of an instinct of self-preservation which forbade a loosening of the curb, lest shock and antagonism should follow. In any case, the effect was well calculated. I had no key to the disposition of the writer. He was a stranger; and if it seems curious that I should not have shrunk from this closest of all relations with a stranger, it must be remembered that I had gone through a mental and moral cataclysm, that I was bruised, quivering, and bleeding, and in the extremity of desolation, and that almost any hand then stretched out, would have brought a sense of stay and refuge. Then, too, the fact that the letter had come at a moment of crisis, seemed in itself fateful, and I was in the mood to yield myself unquestioningly to guidance which had the semblance of destiny.

Thus after I had read the letter three times, and had sat for perhaps a quarter of an hour with my head in my hands, staring at the dead fire, and with my brain a chaos and my whole being an ache, I took my blotting-book and spread out a telegraph form upon it.

I thought I would write the telegram at once, and ask the landlady to send it at eight in the morning, telling myself that I should sleep better for having made the decision. So in a reckless impulse, I set down the address.

Then something stayed my hand, and for the first time the immense importance of the step I was about to take, came over me. It was the confession that I was beaten; it was good-bye to the art life for ever; it was—oh, something strange, dreadful —and yet vaguely alluring.

To be the wife of a man extremely wealthy, and to live in state and luxury; to be freed from everything that was sordid and degrading; to be loved . . . The image of Mr. Vassal with that disagreeable look in his eyes rose up, and I fell to shuddering, for I understood sufficiently what marriage meant, to know that I should be selling myself body and soul.

But, it was the lot of almost every woman!

The shudder of repulsion didn't last long enough to deter; the vision of the future didn't paint itself luridly enough to appal. Both were over-swept, as by a wave, with the recollection of Mr. Leete's warning and condemnation. And following his words, came back those other words, the pronouncement of destiny, ringing through the silence in their deep incisive cadences, over and over again. . . . "Mistaken her vocation." . . . "Never make an actress." . . . "The despair of absolute incompetence." "It's true; it's true," I wailed out into the empty room.   The echo of that man's voice rang the fiat.   I wrote a telegram.

"To Hector Vassal, —— Grosvenor Street.—Come to-morrow at three.   ESTHER VRINTZ."

I slept the dreamless sleep of exhaustion.   In the morning when I awoke my telegram had gone.

At three o'clock Mr. Vassal came.   I wonder if I can describe him just as he impressed me then.

He was a particularly tall and largely-built man, spare and upright, always extremely well dressed and well groomed; and at that time, I had never seen him without an uncanny sort of orchid in his buttonhole.   He varied his flowers, but, to the end of his days, they were without exception rare and peculiarly coloured, streaked and spotted, and of the kind that is forced abnormally. I used to think later that his taste in this direction gave a clue to certain phases of his character.

His face was striking and distinguished—massive features; a determined chin, smooth-shaven; blackly marked brows; eyes prominent, weary, indifferent, yet intensely alive and masterful; a sallow skin, smooth for his age, the only lines then being two furrows from the nostril to the corner of the mouth, and a slight triangular mark caused by a puffiness beneath the lower eye-lids; a big mouth; strong lips, half hidden by a heavy grizzled moustache; long, yellowish teeth; hair grey-black and closely cropped; a dent in the bridge of the nose; the neck a thick column which put one in mind of the busts of Roman emperors. That was his type.   Agatha Greste, who had odd fancies, used to say that he was a reincarnation of the Roman period.

When he talked to women, his manner was elaborate though quiet; but in the company of commonplace people he would have moods of bored endurance; at other times he would say cutting, cynical things—now I am drawing on later experiences and impressions.   One had the feeling with him of forces in leash—ferocious forces, perhaps, and that anything terrible might lie under the outer calm.   If I had thought the whole matter out then, I might have remembered that Frank Leete, who, with all his Bohemianism, was the properest, kindliest, and yet most frankly human of men, never spoke of Mr. Vassal without some slight constraint, nor seemed perfectly at his ease with him.   To be sure, Mr. Leete often dined with him in Grosvenor Street or at the Roscius, and always seemed pleased, and a little flattered, when asked; for Mr. Vassal's bachelor dinners were, he told us, famous.

He would recount to us the dishes, over which he would wax eloquent, and the names of the guests; but he would put off Agatha's closer inquiries by one of his mock worldly-wise sayings —perhaps quote Erasmus, I think, to the effect that we should choose our friends for the service they do for us; and observe that it would ill become him to criticise the mental feast when the physical one was so superexcellently good. But all the same, I got the impression that he did not wholly approve of Mr. Vassal's dinners or of the conversational tone of his guest. I had asked my landlady, who was a dressmaker, to let me see Mr. Vassal in the parlour where she took orders from her customers. She had looked inquisitive and a little distrustful when I made the request, but seemed satisfied when I told her that it was an elderly gentleman, a friend of Mr. Leete's, who was coming to call on me. But she only lighted the fire as he arrived; it was just sputtering cheerlessly, and gave me cover, as I poked it and put on more coal, for the embarrassment of the greeting.

Mr. Vassal, quite composed and magnificent, and more Roman-emperor-like than ever, though in a frock-coat instead of a toga and the purple, was examining a monstrosity in coral under a glass case on the centre table. The contrast between us—between the dingy dressmaker's room with a dummy in a ball-gown covered by a sheet in the corner, the wax flowers, the family Bible, and the photographs of upper servants on the walls, between all this and the mansion in Grosvenor Street, which I had seen in passing, with powdered footmen hanging about the steps —struck me as bewilderingly comical, and I asked myself whether this interview were part of a fairy story or a nightmare.

"Yes, it is extraordinarily cold," Mr. Vassal said in his well-bred way, as though the scanty spitting fire were a concession to unusual weather. Then he added when I had left the coal-scuttle and had taken my seat on the horse-hair sofa, "It was very kind of you to telegraph to me." He put himself into the one slippery arm-chair, laying his hat and stick beside him, and removing his left-hand glove. The silver-mounted stick, the unobtrusive perfection of his clothes, the orchid, and a faint perfume mingling with the after whiff from expensive cigars, struck pleasantly upon my senses, and seemed a testimony to the reality of that new world the doors of which he wished to open to me.

One or two more superficial remarks passed, and it was a relief to find that he made no allusion to the disaster of the previous afternoon. Then silence fell. I was shivering inwardly, and I could not look at him, but watched the fire crackling and belching thick smoke through the layer of cheap coal.   All the time, I was uneasily conscious of his gaze, and at last was forced by a kind of fascination to turn my eyes upon him, for, from beginning to end, he had always a fascination over me, even when it was the fascination of hate.

He was bending forward and looking at me from under his black brows with the expression that had repelled me in Mr. Leete's drawing-room.   Somehow it did not now repel me.   Was this because I was half-way to the devil's market?   Oh, why didn't I stay in the temple and do penance, and wait upon my goddess till it should please her to turn her face to me?   But I had shut the door of my temple behind me, and baser influences were playing round.   I seem to know all this now; but then—how could I tell?   I was half-frightened at some uncomprehended spectre of the future: half-intoxicated by the immediate thought of empire over this man, who, in his own fashion, was so powerful.   And as I met his eyes, that look in them lowered before mine, and his face became moved and softened into an expression of anxious expectation.   I knew it was doubt of my answer that was thus shaking his self-confidence, and the knowledge gave me a shock of wonder and of awe at this mystery of love which could so change the nature of a man.

Looking back now upon that scene, it becomes all a blur of confused emotion.   I have in my mind the sense of struggle against that shapeless dread : the sense, too, of almost pleasant self-surrender.   I remember a thrill of intense strangeness and loneliness.   I remember getting up from my chair and going to the mantelpiece, where I leaned my head, sobbing like a lost child.   I have the consciousness of that tall, strong form close beside me, of the faint perfume of the clothes, of the indescribable physical and mental atmosphere that seemed to surround it, and which, till the very end, affected me.   I can hear now the voice deepened with subdued fervour, and appealing in its tenderness.

" Esther, I can't bear to see you cry.   Only let me take care of you, and no one shall ever be unkind to you again."

Ah, that was what I wanted—some one who would take care of me, and wrap me round in sympathy and affection, and cover me from failure and derision and despair.

So it was settled that I was to be Mr. Vassal's wife.

BOOK II

" Oh, Jove! why hast thou given us certain proofs to know adulterate gold, but stamped no mark where it is most needed, on man's base metal?"

EXTRACT FROM
A LETTER
WRITTEN
BY
FRANK LEETE
TO
MRS. GRESTE:

Now for a paper talk with you, dear Gagsie —a poor ghost substitute for the real thing. You remember Sterne's remark about "the apparition of the fifth instant (for letters may almost be called so)?" By the time this arrives, you will have settled down in Kandy—which sounds comic, but which I, alas! find unrelieved tragedy — and I shall be realising in even fuller measure than now what it is to have lost a daughter. Yea, and more than a daughter! Secretary, proof-reader, fellow-critic at first-nights, literary co-worker, friend, companion! A daughter is a human accident; a true companion is a human miracle. And when both are combined—oh, then Providence in one of its nasty little ways steps along with the husband. And it's " Bless you, my children." and down goes the curtain, the lights are out, and all is ended. "Oh Provvy, Provvy! It's all the fault of Provvy," as Jeremy Bentham says.

Concerning first nights. Felix Ffolliott's opening on Saturday turned out a brilliant function—all but the play, which, as it happened, was *not* the thing. Talk of construction! It has no beginning, no middle, no end. Nothing happened all through; and of the two leading motives, one of them is quite too weak, and the other quite too unpleasant. And the writing! Well, I don't know what English is coming to, or criticism either, to judge from the next morning's papers—except with the much-abused old public, who, take my word, simply *won't go.*

What can one do but shrug! Only a few days ago I saw it placidly stated in a newspaper that no literary man in England had tried stage-writing since the days of Sheridan. In Sheridan's time they said the same; but one wonders what Goldsmith, Sheridan Knowles, Bulwer, Miss Mitford, Shirley Brooks, Tom Taylor, Reade, and a few other inferior people were if they were not literary. Truly, it is amusing to hear Ffolliott, who does not, in the literary sense, know a play from a palimpsest, publicly deploring the want of authors equal to his genius. Oh! the deadly ease with which a poet might retort on the tragedian, whose ear can't tell him the difference between ten syllables and twelve. But better shrug! I wanted your support badly that night, for I hadn't the courage of my convictions: got talking to Ffolliott afterwards at the Roscius, and slurred my notice.

I've wanted you too, abominably, in the Esther Vrintz affair. Truly, for startling developments and human incongruities, every-day life beats the most blood-and-thunder melodrama. Prepare for a shock of astonishment—Vassal the millionaire is going to marry Esther the actress! But I will relate from the beginning, as the storytellers say, for, like Elia's Bridget, "I must have a story, well, ill, or indifferently told." *Claudia* duly came off: and, by the way, your Brindisi telegram arrived in good time at the theatre. The poor girl made the direst failure. We were all wrong, and those readings of *Camiola* and the *Duchess* meant nothing. I never witnessed a more pitiable exhibition; and I can tell you, it took a stringing up of nerve to go round after-wards and convince her—she asked me straight—that she was hopeless. I did my best to persuade her that she would do no good on the stage. It was the honestest, and certainly I thought then the kindest course, though I felt like the slayer of the one ewe lamb.

For if you can't be great—why then, as Hamlet says, "the rest is silence."

It's a queer thing that consuming passion for artistic success, when, as in her case, it is unallied with the capacity. There weren't two opinions among the critics about that—as you'll see from the batch of papers I asked your mother to post to you— no, nor on the part of the "Great Big Stupid" either.

I really believe that in our poor Esther, this passion has swallowed up every other sentiment and feeling. She lived and breathed on that hope, and when it was taken from her, the very life seemed wrenched out too. She knows no more of the world as it is, or of men as they are, than a year-old baby.

Gagsie, my dear, I'm glad it isn't you that Vassal fell in love with. No doubt it is a fine thing to be the wife of a millionaire, but will it be a fine thing to be the wife of Hector Vassal? That's where the shoe of responsibility pinches. For it was under my roof that he first met her: it's I who got her on the stage: and it's I whose brutal plain-speaking gave her no choice than to accept his offer; though, as a matter of fact, I don't suppose there are a dozen unmarried, penniless women in London who wouldn't jump at it. Anyhow, I find comfort in the reflection that it was not I who put it into Quintin Glaive's head to cast her for the part of *Claudia*.

All the same, the thing worries me sorely. Why, I cannot exactly explain—that is, according to the enormous importance it assumes. I have never since the days of callow youth lost sleep o' nights because of a girl who was no kin to me. For there is not truly any obligation upon me to concern myself so deeply over poor little Esther's future—no tie of consanguinity, nor even the bond of a long friendship with her father.

I had not common patience with Vrintz's egotistic vapourings about his music, which always ended in collapse, for sheer want of pluck and faculty. I couldn't stand the way either that he bullied his wife, who was a feckless creature, but I am sure had stuff in her, if only he had allowed it to come out. Yes, there is really no reason, except that you are fond of her, why I should make myself miserable about the girl's marriage—at which, too, as I have said, most Belgravian mothers would rejoice for their daughters. But I do make myself miserable for all that. I suppose it is the ineradicable folly of the male, who is bound to run tilt against windmills for the sake of a pretty woman. In fact, several times lately, when thinking of Esther as I walked home from the Roscius, haunted by her appealing eyes, I've imagined myself into the heroic mood—felt quite ready to encounter giants in the shape of theatrical managers, and rather anxious to see a few dragons lying round from whom one might rescue distressed damsels with this valiant little arm and this good sword.

And the funny thing is, that after I've catalogued her eyes and hair, and soft skin and nice red mouth all made for kisses, I can't for the life of me analyse the damsel's particular charm, which is distinctly independent of these things. I'm not sure that it does not lie in the contrast between those magnificent brown eyes with the red glint in them, out of which Melpomene illusively gazes, and those helpless baby lips which are so unutterably pathetic when they quiver in disappointment, and so fascinating when they break out, which is seldom enough, in a downright girl's laugh. Do you remember the gladsomeness of the child that day when we picnicked at Burnham Beeches, and when I told her that Glaive was pleased with her recitation?

Well, poor Esther! there's not much laugh in her nowadays: and upon my soul, were I Vassal, and as confident as I ought to be, if I were about to marry a girl of nineteen, that I was the right sort of husband to teach her to play high jinks with life discreetly, I'd want to shake all the Wertherian nonsense out of her first of all : then hug her as soon as I'd done laughing at her tragedy airs, and

finally put a lollipop into her mouth to keep her from scolding
me.   But when I watch old Hector playing the elderly and opu-
lent lover—and he does it with quite becoming dignity—I sometimes wonder within myself, whether I ought not to pull out that
good sword from its sheath, and make an onslaught upon the
dragon right down through its golden scales.

There are nasty stories as to his treatment of the first Mrs.
Vassal, and—well he hasn't been a patron of the drama for
nothing.   Ask your husband, who has been a young man about
town, what they say of Hector Vassal in the clubs.   We had a
little discussion on the subject, Greste and I—who am an unsuspecting devil, and loth to think ill of my friends—in connection
with that Richmond dinner, which Greste wanted me to refuse.

Do you recollect what a point Vassal made of our bringing
Esther?   If I had had the least notion! . . . Well, one might
spend a lifetime in moaning because one has just not happened
to seize the psychological moment!   Anyhow, the affair is settled
now, beyond even a dramatic critic's jurisdiction.   And I can but
maintain that, when everything is said and done, it is a fine thing
to be the wife of a millionaire.

Besides, old Hector is genuinely in love with the future Mrs.
Vassal, which is a very different thing from being in love with a
ballet-dancer.   My first impression after the engagement took
place was—and you know the saying, "Always mistrust your
first impressions, for they are generally correct"—that if Esther
will only be human and spontaneous, and allow herself to enjoy
life without analysing her emotions, and forget that she ever had
artistic cravings and morbid sentimentalisms, she may reform the
rake and bring out whatever good there is in him—even Lucifer
was a fallen angel—and be, in short, as happy as most people
who are contented with the moon and don't cry for the sun as
well.   But Esther is Esther, and I doubt if she'll e'er be graced
so far.

By the way, it has struck me as a curious exemplification of
the man's enormous egoism that he should cherish the Arcadian
dream of making poor little Esther Vrintz fall romantically in love
with him—at his age!   Or is it the overweening confidence in his
manly charms, induced in even the breast of a sexagenarian by
the possession of much gold and the flattery of a
woman? . . . Who would credit old Vassal with romanticism!
But there's no folly to beat old folly!

The men at the Roscius are still agape, for nobody expected
Hector Vassal to play King Cophetua.   For myself, apart from
romanticism, I should have guessed it as the very rôle he would

choose.   He'd always want to be boss of the matrimonial show, and that might not have been so easy, if he had gone in for a Vere de Vere.   Moreover, he is a bit of a cynic, and a millionaire can afford to despise the question of pedigree.   For there is really nothing against our Esther except that she is the daughter of a bandmaster, and was a super at the Regency.

Besides all that, too, Vassal has an object in view outside the matter of personal attraction.   I could have prophesied that before the second year of his widowerhood he would be leading a new bride to the hymeneal altar, for reasons apart from love.   The grievance of his life is that he has no son, and the property is entailed and must go to Robert Vassal, which would be the bitterest drop in old Hector's cup of death.

You know the story, don't you, how Hector Vassal was engaged to a pretty girl, the wedding-day fixed, and everything ready, and how his younger brother, who had been in India, turned up and eloped with the lady.   Robert Vassal, the *Views* man, is the son of these two, and for this nephew, the offspring of his betrayers, Hector Vassal is supposed to cherish an undying hate, quite on the good old melodramatic lines.   You see what a duty poor Esther will owe to her husband and to the millions, and Heaven help her if she fail in it.

Oddly enough, Robert Vassal and his uncle met in Glaive's box at the *Claudia* performance.   Robert was there for *Views*, the dramatic critic—Fox, you know—being down with bronchitis. Hector Vassal looked his nephew unflinchingly in the eyes, and walked straight out of the box: it was deucedly uncomfortable for the rest of us.   I have been wondering whether that chance meeting did anything to precipitate his matrimonial intentions.

Yes, he's a bit of a cynic.   I'll tell you of a little episode that occurred that Sunday.   It was just after Esther had accepted him, and perhaps that's the reason, when I come to think of it, why it made an impression on me, for the matter itself is hardly worth mentioning.   I was not feeling easy about the girl.   I had asked her to come to supper, and had left the Roscius in the afternoon, thinking I'd walk round to fetch her and cheer her up.   I hadn't gone half way when I met Vassal, who told me that he had been calling on Esther, and that he wanted to speak to me about her, and persuaded me to turn back with him to the club.   As we were passing down in the fog, a miserable starved woman stepped from under a lamp-post, and whined for a shilling.   Vassal looked at her in a cold-blooded way.

"Why should I give you a shilling?" he asked.   "You'll only go and spend it in the gin-shop."

"And what would you do?" she said with a croaking laugh, "if you were cold, and hungry, and wretched? Wouldn't you go and drown it all in the gin-shop?"

"Yes, I should," he answered. "You are a sensible woman, and here's half-a-sovereign for you. Go and get drunk."

It was the tone in which he said it that jarred. And then a few moments later, in the Roscius smoking-room, he was discoursing, in his quiet deliberate way, upon the advantages to a man of mature experience in wedding with youth, beauty, and innocence, and of providing an interest for declining years in the calm joys of domestic life. And then he informed me that he had arranged to marry Esther Vrintz.

He has bought her—that's what it comes to. Bought her in the hour of her abasement, when pluck failed her, and she could not stand up against her beating. And I'm the wretch, the false friend who should have lifted her, strengthened her, and helped her to new courage for a fresh fight. And I just didn't. I hit her instead when she was down. I be-rated her and trampled upon her, and when, on the marriage-day, the parson asks me, "Who giveth this woman to be married to this man?" and I answer, "I do," I shall feel no better than a slave-dealer handing over a helpless maiden into captivity.

She doesn't love him—not in the very least. But then how could a girl of twenty love a man who is at least thirty-eight years older than herself. I should say that she is half afraid of him; half magnetised by him. Do you know, that as I watch them together, I can't help being reminded of the snake cage in the Zoo, and of the poor little rabbit mesmerised by the snake's eyes and waiting for the deadly spring. It's a nightmarish fancy, but I can't get over it; she has just that pathetic, quivering, dazed look. Yet I am bound to say that there's no fault to be found with his manner to her; and that when he makes his offerings, it is rather with the suggestion of a knight doing homage to his liege lady than of a sultan decorating his latest favourite. Fancy poor little Esther Vrintz hung with the Vassal diamonds! I should like very much to know what Robert Vassal thinks of it all; but I hear he has taken his annual holiday from *Views*, and is with his wife at Philotis. The marriage is to come off immediately—quite a private affair. Esther is staying with us, at Vassal's request; he asked me that Sunday in the Roscius smoking-room if I would father her for the occasion. Of course, I told him that would have been my business under any circumstances. I got her off her last week's engagement at the Regency, which was a very simple arrangement with Carter-Blake, who was electrified

when I explained the position. A delicate system of indemnifi
cation for our trouble has been already inaugurated in the shape
of enormous hampers of game and garden produce from Grisewood and Tregarth, with the result that we have abandoned the
high teas of suburban economy, and so marked an advance has
taken place in the health of our weekly bills, that your mother
and I, like Francis Jeffrey and his bride, now trust in Providence,
and have hopes of dying before we get to prison or the work
house. For my own part, I confess that the last woodcock of
the season, with forced asparagus and strawberries to follow, are
not dainties to be sniffed at. Your mother and the bridegroom
expectant have fixed up the matter of the trousseau between them.
I, acting on Esther's behalf, have tried to work a marriage settlement. But our millionaire demurs; he prefers that his young wife
should not be monetarily independent of him. There speaks the
cynic again. No doubt on broad lines, Wisdom is justified of her
children. I don't like it, but am not in a position to press the
point. I thought it my duty to lay the matter before Esther, and
she absolutely forbade me ever again to allude to it. Oh, you
women! what unpractical, ridiculous, divine creatures you are!

Now I have delivered myself, and leave your mother to give
you all other news, social and domestic. . . .

BOOK III

" I only know myself as a human entity; the scene, so to speak, of thoughts and affections; and am sensible of a certain doubleness, by which I can stand as remote from myself as from another. However intense my experience, I am conscious of the presence and criticism of a part of me which, as it were, is not a part of me, but a spectator, sharing no experience, but taking note of it, and that is no more I than it is you. When the play, it may be the tragedy of life, is over, the spectator goes his way. It was a kind of fiction, a work of the imagination only as far as he was concerned."

WRITTEN
BY
ESTHER
VASSAL: FROM the years when I was quite a little girl, I used to have at odd times a strange, starved, excited feeling which made me want to say poetry, to act some great emotion, to listen to grand music, or else to write — to write out my very soul. And the poetry, the acting, the music—when I could get to the Catholic Church at Philotis and hear the organ—or the writing down of my crude passionate fancies, would take away the restless gnawed sensation, and I would feel as though I had eaten soul-food and were filled and satisfied.

But the satisfaction was never for very long. Always, the soul-craving would come back; and in the old days at Philotis, when Father was sick, gloomy, and estranged, I don't think I could have borne my loneliness but for the dream-life I managed to create for myself side by side with everyday existence. I used to intoxicate myself with all kinds of glorious imaginings about the future, when I should have become a great actress; and as I wandered among the pine woods above El-Meriem, the wind through the pine branches, the gurgling of hill torrents, and the murmurous break of the sea, seemed all part of the dream, and I would feel impelled to scribble down my fancies in those flimsy-leaved copybooks with chequered rulings that I bought at the French stationer's in the Square Casphar, on afternoons when Father led the band which played there twice a week.

I have been looking over those old copybooks, and there are bits in them which set me weeping scalding tears of sheer pity for that lonely, emotional, idealistic child, who was such a strange mixture of earth and heaven. But there's nothing in the pages that fits into place here. Journals are such ghosts of things, they tell so little and suggest so much.

So I'll just go on autobiographically, culling from the old notes here and there.

.　　.　　.　　.　　.　　.　　.

How curious it is, that flashing conviction one gets at moments —through the word, the look, the movement, the glancing present—of a link with some far distant past, gone before it is even recognised.   Not so much is it the sense of having lived this very thing before, which I have heard people say is what they feel— as an overpowering consciousness of causes dating ages back, and of mystic relation with the forces shaping destiny.   This seems a grand way of putting what is I believe a common enough experience, but that was how it seemed to me ; and one day its indescribable vividness startled me into the vain effort to break off my engagement with Mr. Vassal.

He had been talking in a rather more intimate manner than usual about his first marriage, and the embittering effect it had exercised upon his life.   Certainly the union had not taken place under auspicious conditions.   The girl to whom he had been engaged, and whom he truly loved, had been false to him, and had run away with his younger brother a day or two before that fixed for the wedding.   In a fit of rage and wounded pride, Mr. Vassal owned, he had almost at once married another woman. " A Delmar," he said, as though that explained everything.   I had asked Mr. Leete before about the Delmars, and he told me they were a great, old, and very poor Catholic family, with a streak of eccentricity running through them ; and that he had always heard of the first Mrs. Vassal—she had been dead barely two years—as a cold, proud, bigoted, and most unhappy woman. He looked at me earnestly when he said the words "most un- happy"; and I wondered if he could be wishing to put me on my guard ; but it did not seem loyal to Mr. Vassal, who was to be my husband, and was very good to me, to question a third person about his private affairs.   Mr. Vassal himself I should never have dared to question.   Besides, what did it matter now that I had chosen my fate?   Only, Mr. Leete's manner gave me pause ; and I had at the moment a sort of foretaste of that dreadful feeling which came over me while Mr. Vassal was talking.

There was nothing to account for it in his words or look, except indeed that suggestion of masked fierceness which struck unpleasantly at times, and may have caused the shrinking sensa- tion when he came near me, which I could not help, and for which I blamed myself.   For I have often thought since with surprise how particularly kind and gentle Mr. Vassal was during the short period of our engagement.

He had been speaking of the grief his childlessness was to him, and how bitter the thought that his property would even- tually enrich the son of his greatest enemy—the man whose treachery had practically destroyed the best years of his life.

" It turned me into a hard materialist and made me despise

women," he said. "I'm not referring to the late Mrs. Vassal, whose greatest fault was that she bored me. And then one couldn't stand the house being filled with priests, and it seemed simplest to leave her, as much as regard for appearances allowed, to enjoy their society undisturbed. I don't excuse myself," he went on; "no doubt it was all very sad and very bad, but the blame rests on the man and woman who broke my faith in human nature and poisoned all my best impulses.

"For I'm not the callous pleasure-seeker the world takes me for," he went on. "Let a real emotion grip me, and the whole strength of my nature becomes concentrated upon it. I've loved well; I've hated well. The one thing means the other; it is merely a question of polarity. Now you know, dearest," and he kissed my hand as he spoke, "the priceless boon I am taking from you. It is you who are giving me back my youth, and re-making what is left of my life. You restore the happy hopes those two robbed me of—the hope of home, of dear companionship, of a son to sit in my place and supplant the son of my enemy."

His voice dropped as he said the last words, and he seemed himself to become conscious of the note of implacable aversion in it, and to be anxious to remove its impression. He got up abruptly, and his manner changed and became restrained as usual.

"There! I've given you what few people have ever had, a glimpse of my true self, and perhaps I haven't raised my character in your estimation. But remember what I said. Love and hate are convertible terms, and you are the angel who is to work the miracle of transmutation."

Presently he took leave of me, and in a dazed way I returned the good-bye, for it was then that the supernatural hand seemed laid upon me, and that the warning flash of past and foreknowledge filled me with sudden fear. I cried out as he was leaving the room, hardly knowing what I said—

"I can't do it! Oh, I can't do it."

He came back at once, standing over me, tall and strong.

"What is it that you can't do?" he asked.

"I can't marry you. Oh, don't make me; it would be of no use."

"Why would it be of no use?"

He spoke quietly, even tenderly, but at my resistance a flame leaped into his face changing its whole expression; and as he caught my hands in his firm soft grasp I had the feeling, deepened in after years, of a force in him which, if there ever came to be a struggle between us, would paralyse me into cowed submission. I fought against it now in desperate jerks.

"Because I shouldn't be anything that you want. . . . I'm frightened of what may come of it. . . . I don't love you."

"I know that," he said; "but I mean to make you love me."

And I seem to see the gleam in his eyes, which my fancy likens to that in the eyes of some fierce pinioned thing; and again I feel the shudder. . . . Why did I not know that the shudder which ran through me then at his caress was a sign from God's Servers warning me against marrying Hector Vassal?

For truly I believe that at each of life's crossroads, God's Servers stand ready to point out the better way. But we, like dumb beasts, which have not yet attained man's higher faculties, have still to reach unto soul-sight and soul-hearing; and until through love and pain our spiritual senses have been awakened, we may not see the arresting hand nor understand the guiding voice. I have learned that it is good to love, that it is good to suffer, and that, as it is written, "Even when the gates of prayer are shut in heaven, those of tears are open."

.   .   .   .

I can't write about those days before my marriage. They say that in some Eastern countries the girl-brides are given haschisch, and that is how it seems to have been with me; for everything is confused and phantasmagoric as in an opium dream, the inner blending unreally with the outward, while through it all, ever vividly present, the magnified and distorted image of Mr. Vassal shows like some unnatural representation upon a shadow-sheet. Through all, too, there comes back upon me the sense of impotent revolt and of growing dread. Once I planned to run away, but my penniless condition made that impossible, and I distrusted my own impulses. Then I wrote a letter to Mr. Vassal, a pitifully foolish outpouring of my heart, beseeching at least for delay. That too was but the helpless beating of a caged bird against the bars. The jailor brought sugar and stroked the bird's plumage, but the cage remained close shut. He said the letter was sweet and maidenly, that he loved me all the more because of it. Then he took the sheets out of his breast-pocket and burned them in my presence, bidding me forget they had been written. He said that once I was his wife, once I had plunged into the irrevocable—the phrase struck chill— I should smile at my girlish tremors and be glad in the happy reality which he would not let me renounce.

Had Agatha Greste been near, I think I could have told her everything, and she being married and loving her husband, would have understood, and would have helped me to understand. But Agatha was far away in Kandy, and there was nobody else. How could I confide in Mrs. Leete, who was never tired of praising Mr. Vassal and of congratulating me upon my good fortune?

   .   .   .   .

If only the human drama could be divided like a stage-play into acts with dead blanks between! If the curtain might have fallen when the marriage ceremony was over, and we stood waiting for a few moments on the church steps, the central figures, as it were, of a closing tableau!

Alas! in life there are no drop scenes.

It was strange that this day, too, snow should be falling. Thick and fast the flakes drove, starting painful thrills of association. There rushed into my memory that first picture standing out from the mists of childhood, of my mother's coffin borne through the door into the great white rain. And then a later picture of snow-covered hills and stone pines painted on a blue sky, and the ground white-flecked in the shadow of tombstones, where they were laying Father to rest. . . . And then, more startlingly distinct, the scene outside the theatre and the group of men in the portico. And I felt once more the icy chill and the stab at my heart as the man of the profile had spoken the words of destiny. . . . "She has mistaken her vocation." . . .

Mr. Vassal's voice awoke me.

"My dearest, you are shivering with cold. Why don't they come up at once?" and he spoke authoritatively to the servant who was signalling the carriage. He hurried me down to it. The leave-takings had been done; he had arranged everything. We were to drive straight to the train, and there was to be no breakfast. Mrs. Leete had kissed me in the vestry, and had cried, just as she had cried at Agatha's wedding. She wore the same dress, too; but how different my wedding was from Agatha's! Mr. Leete had looked at me with a strange expression in his eyes as he had mumbled a blessing from under his big moustache. Now he pressed heavily forward and gripped my hand as Mr. Vassal led me to the brougham.

"God bless you, Esther," he said again, and added, "Take care of her, Vassal; remember she is only a child."

"It's hardly necessary to give me that injunction," said Mr. Vassal with a low laugh, which vibrated unreally. But everything was unreal, though so curiously vivid, that day. Mr. Vassal paused to express in rather formal but elaborate terms his gratitude to Mr. and Mrs. Leete for their "great kindness"; and taking his seat beside me gave the order to drive on.

Then as he leaned back, wrapped in his sable-lined coat, it seemed to me that his form dilated with pride of possession, and it was my master who took my hand—my master claiming the thing he had bought. "Mine now," he said; "mine to have and to hold and to cherish! Mine till death parts us!"

By-and-bye we were speeding along alone together. Our compartment had been specially reserved, and Mr. Vassal's servants had laid out furs and newspapers and different luxuries of travelling, including a most dainty luncheon. That broke the first strangeness. Mr. Vassal waited on me, and made me drink champagne and eat, remarking what a much better arrangement this was than the wedding-breakfast Mrs. Leete had been anxious to provide in St. John's Wood.

"It is a relief to get out of those surroundings," he said. "Kind, good people! I must be for ever grateful to them; but of course one prefers his own atmosphere."

And indeed he seemed now to have a different air, more self-assured and still more Roman-emperor-like than in the Leetes' little house, where he had adapted himself with a grand urbanity to their simple ways, but had clearly conveyed that they were unaccustomed and uncongenial. This of course had not struck me so much there as now that I saw him with obsequious servants waiting his commands, and, as he said, in his own atmosphere. I realised what a personage had married me.

At the first stopping-place they came and took away the luncheon, and got Mr. Vassal something he wanted, and then we two were left to ourselves.

.   .   .   .

Alone together, as the train rushed through the falling snow and the darkling afternoon . . . alone together, my master and I—husband and wife, bound to each other so long as we both should live!

And the actualities of marriage came for the first time close to me, looming shapeless but overwhelming. My eyes were drawn to my master above the furs he had put round me, and I found his eyes fixed upon my face with that look in them I had seen before.

At my glance he moved abruptly to my side.

My left hand was lying bare in my lap, with my new wedding-ring upon its third finger. He kissed my hand, and kissed the ring, and played with the ring—my master!

"A little loose," he said. "I thought of that yesterday, and chose a guard." It was a spring serpent in diamonds with ruby eyes, that coiled twice round my finger. . . .

And my master's eyes seemed to me like the snake's eyes, . . . or like those of a wild beast lying in wait for its prey. . . . And my master's encircling arms were like the snake's coils.

Rushing on . . . rushing on ! . . . And the gusts of snow blurring everything—blurring the gaunt trees, the red lights, the ghostly houses . . . blurring thought . . . blurring sensation.
Oh, that pitiless snow !   Oh, that veiled, distant moon !

Rushing on still.   Now in my master's brougham, drawn by my master's horses.   Over the noiseless snow, past pale hedges, by sodden fens and sedgy pools.   Now through lodge gates and down an avenue of eldritch oaks and elms, with the wind making a dismal groaning among their knotted limbs.

There was a little oratory leading out of the sitting-room next my bed-chamber.   It had a window to the east, with an altar below, and on the altar an ivory Christ.
In the wintry dawn upon the morrow of my marriage-day I crawled to the foot of the altar.   And the frozen sun, as it broke against the east window, shed a dimmed glory upon the crucified Christ, but no ray of divine pity pierced the blackness of my despairing soul.

BOOK IV

" Words are the physicians of a distempered mind."

WRITTEN SEVEN YEARS LATER BY DOCTOR QUINTIN-GLAIVE: I AM asked to fill up the gap in Mrs. Vassal's story, and to tell of the circumstances which brought us into closer relation.

It was in the December of '72 that I was suddenly summoned to Grisewood Castle to see its mistress, who was dangerously ill.

I had not hitherto been on terms of intimacy with the Vassals, though not long before, Mrs. Vassal had consulted me as to the state of her lungs, of which I had not thought favourably. I had also found her nerves overwrought, and her general condition unsatisfactory. Besides this professional intercourse, I had met her casually from time to time at formal entertainments in London; and from the occasion of my first meeting with her, in especial after her marriage, she had inspired me with the deepest interest. This was not only because of my connection as the author of *Claudia*, with her trial and failure in the Regency Theatre, but the circumstances of her marriage had aroused both my curiosity and compassion, Mr. Vassal being a man of whom I had little reason to think highly. Then, too, the woman herself appealed as no other woman has ever done to my sensibilities, alike of man, artist, and doctor. I don't know whether I am out of the common in this respect. Certainly, I have wondered much that Mrs. Vassal did not, during her London career, excite more general admiration. It may have been that she was not a prominent figure in society, at any rate at that time, so that beauties of a far inferior order, but with greater claim to notoriety, were quoted before her. Or it may have been that she was of that subtly refined type which impresses only the less commonplace order of man. In any case, she was to my thinking—and perhaps I am not altogether commonplace—exceptionally lovely, with her small flower-like head, her wonderful brown eyes, delicate aquiline features, and that curious exotic charm so noticeable among the Jewesses of Philotis—the charm which is inseparable, I fancy, from some Eastern strain of parentage—that subtle blending of the fate-doomed immortal with the mutable feminine. So that it is as though the wing of trouble overshadowed a lovely maiden's head : as though the hymn of the Furies echoed faintly in certain vibrant modulations of a girlish voice : as though the terrible inspiration of a Cassandra shone from out eyes meant to languish in tender love-glances.

In truth, what struck me most in her was that grievous suggestion of arrested development, as of some odorous tropical blossom blighted before it could open and shed forth its perfume : or of a rich stream issuing from a fount of rare virtue, and turned to ice near its source by the touch of untimely winter. For my experience of Esther Vrintz, the actress, slight as it had been, made me certain that her emotional nature was once vividly alive, and that she had cherished an intense ambition. This chill petrifaction of a woman was not the girl I remembered. Her very voice had changed in timbre, had lost those flute-like notes so indicative of passionate feeling, which had greatly influenced me in giving her the part of *Claudia*. Thus I found myself wondering on every occasion that we met, what had so altered her. Though she had failed artistically, she had certainly made a success from the mundane point of view ; there was round her as much of pomp and paraphernalia as would have made most women happy, and which, even in the case of a nature above the ordinary, might have proved a basis of reconcilement with conjugal in-felicities. Might not hers be, therefore, I asked myself, one of those other-worldly temperaments to which marriage must repre-sent either heaven or hell—as her own favourite heroine, the *Duchess of Malfi*, puts it : and life under certain moral conditions, an unendurable degradation? Alas! through what Valley of Humiliation could she have passed to bring that look of dumb misery into her eyes, and to quench all the hope and joy that by right of youth were hers? I longed inexpressibly for her confidence, but how could I think that she would ever reveal to me the pain she kept sedulously hidden from the world? Yet, though she told me nothing of her inner feelings, it is not im-possible to read some few scattered pages of a life that interests one, even though it be written in a dead language hidden from the world?

I had watched her progress as far as my limited opportunities would allow, and had seen that she made no success in London. No doubt her lowly origin was against her, and she was too deficient in social ambition, too unused to fashionable ways, too self-absorbed and timid, and worse than all, too unhappy, to shine either as guest or hostess. I could not judge of how she got on among her neighbours at Grisewood—probably ill enough

—but in London, those great houses I knew, mostly kept their doors closed, or opened them to her doubtfully: and at the few parties at which I met her, she seemed morbidly shy, or else in a kind of dream, and had a cowed dog-like way of glancing at her husband, as if waiting for a cue; which was unpleasantly suggestive, though I must admit that Mr. Vassal's ornate courtesy in public showed no justification for the terror and repulsion some instinct made me divine in his wife.

This was during the season or two following their marriage when as I said the Vassals did not go out a great deal, and not at all into literary or Bohemian society, which would account for what has always puzzled me a little, the fact of Mrs. Vassal never having been brought into social contact with Robert Vassal, her husband's nephew and heir, also now a member of the young Tory party, and coming into some small prominence in Parliament. Here, too, she had failed entirely in what was expected of her, there having been no sign of a son to inherit Grisewood and Tregarth. I felt sure that the secret canker gnawed, and was probably, I thought, the cause of all the wretchedness.

Grisewood Castle, the House of Bondage, as later I sometimes called it, is an imposing, many-turreted edifice, approached by a long avenue of gnarled and ancient trees, and set among venerable cedars. A majestic but dreary abode, and, from its low-lying situation, not the healthiest that could have been chosen for one so frail of physique as Mrs. Vassal. From its sombre look, I could well have imagined it a "house possessed with ills": and the vague legend hanging round it, of a malediction upon the later Vassal branch, which had somehow, it was supposed, not altogether fairly, dispossessed the rightful stock, lent itself to the sinister effect of the castle exterior on this bleak evening of my first arrival there.

The great place was full of servants, but there was no one else to give any attention to the sick woman, if one might except the local doctor. I learned that he, in conjunction with Mr. Wargrave, the rector—Mrs. Wargrave was away—and Mrs. Vassal's maid had decided upon telegraphing for me. Mr. Vassal, they told me, had started on a yachting trip just immediately before his wife had been taken ill.

Never did there seem a being so forlorn as this mistress of a grand castle and of a millionaire's fortune.

I found her condition greatly aggravated, if not mainly caused, by a severe mental shock she had evidently sustained. I did not discover the precise nature of the shock, but from certain facts, which in the exercise of my profession had come previously to my knowledge, and from her utterances in delirium, I concluded that it was caused by some painful revelation concerning her husband.

I spent the greater part of the night by her bedside, and fragments of her wandering talk detach themselves, and stand ineffaceably written on my memory. Pitiful babble, in which broken bits of her life pieced themselves incongruously, and gave me the clue, for which I had once wished, to her secret misery.

She seemed to recognise me.

... "Why do you come here? ... No, no. I don't want you to do anything. Let me alone. ... Listen! What's that? ... Au—thòr! ... Au—thòr!" Her voice pitched itself to a quavering semblance of the hoarse shout from pit and gallery at a first-night. ... "Don't you hear? ... Why don't you take your call? ... They are not going to hiss *you.* ... Ah!" She shrieked wildly, "Save me ... save me. ... There ... It's going to spring. ... Oh, for God's sake, keep it away. ... Down by the curtain there — a long black snake. ... And there's another! ... And here! Oh! On my finger! ... See its eyes—its cruel glittering eyes. ... Take it away—take it away. ..."

She tore the ring from her finger and flung it on the floor. "Bury it in the snow. ... Oh, fall thicker, thicker ... faster, faster. ... Cover it. ... Hide me from him. ... Oh, don't let him come—don't let him come. ..."

She had cowered back into a corner of the bed panting with terror, and then she uttered a plaintive moan.

"It's no use ... it's such a difficult part. ... Oh I can't do it. ... No, that goes flat; I know it does. ... Music! ... They've missed the cue. ... '*Claudia, is this death?*' ... Death? ... Oh, word—word. ... *Thy heaven's doors are my hell-gates.* ... That's not it. ... Why don't they play up? ... How can I remember without the music? ..."

> "'How horrid in the sight of God
> Are those grey locks which seek
> Fictitious youth! How horrid those old eyes,
> All wrinkled round. ...'"

"For I mistook my vocation, you understand."

The wide uncomprehending eyes gazed solemnly into my face.

"And you know, when you feel the despair of absolute incompetence, there's nothing for it but to make a vow before the altar. ..."

Then again a fit of shuddering, and the voice sinking to a horror-stricken whisper.

"'The snake's eyes shining through the snow. . . . Oh, save me ! . . . Don't let him touch me ! . . . I hate him. . . . Oh, God ! how I hate him ! . . . And all the time to be so wicked ! Shame . . . Shame ! Oh, it's horrible. . . . *I* was a young girl too once. . . . Destroyed . . . all destroyed. . . . And he laughs ! He *can* laugh ! . . . Devil's laughter ! . . . All one pollution . . . The cue— *Claudia's* cue. . . . No, that's something else. . . . Word ? . . . Oh, why *won't* they give the cue ? . . .

. . . "There's the doctor . . . Pah ! how badly you smell . . . you doctors and your drugs. . . . And the long glittering serpents . . . and the poor women . . . and the wretched—wretched girls ! . . . I know I must die. It has bitten my arm. . . . Oh, how you stare ! . . . No, I won't drink ; it's poison. . . . I must die. . . . And the snow will hide me away and cover me up. . . . I shall never make an actress—that's what he said ; and there's nothing left for me to do. . . . It was he who brought the snake. . . . But I'll pray . . . I'll pray at the altar. . . . The Christ is there. . . . There *must* be a God who will punish wicked men. . . . He laughs— they're all laughing. . . . That's hissing. . . . Don't you see the gallery is full of snakes. . . . I tell you I *will* be great. . . . And I will laugh too . . . laugh . . . laugh. . . ."

The hollow peal rang out like a ghost's merriment. And so all through the night till the morphia I injected began to take effect, and dawn brought an interval of unconsciousness.

It was some time after that—when she was convalescent— that I had a talk with her, which, though I could hardly then have imagined it, materially influenced her life.

I had been called down a second and third time—now by Mr. Vassal, who had returned to Grisewood on being informed of his wife's illness, and had shown all due concern in regard to its progress. There was nothing in his manner, suave, deliberate and self-contained as usual, to confirm my suspicion of a harrowing scene before his departure. He received my remarks upon the case with becoming solicitude, but when I alluded to the origin of Mrs. Vassal's attack, and spoke of the necessity for guarding against a recurrence of mental trouble, he looked me straight in the face with his cold prominent eyes, and said without any sign of discomposure, "That is perhaps less easy than might be supposed. You are a man of the world, Dr. Glaive, and you must know that it is not always possible to wrap one's womenkind in moral cotton-wool. And your professional experience of the neurotic temperament must no doubt have shown you that a sudden worry is apt to produce an effect quite disproportionate to the cause."

She winced as at a painful recollection, and her imploring eyes, with no restraint in them now, gazed into mine, while a sudden flush reddened her pale cheek.

"There's something I wanted to ask you," she began faltering. "I couldn't ask Mr. Sergison. . . . I was delirious, wasn't I? . . . I must have said things." . . .

The red went out of her face, and her voice sank to a whisper.

"How could I bear it if I had let people know. There was the nurse, too, you see. . . . How could I bear the spying and whispering and prying? Can't you understand how dreadful it would be? . . . Tell me—not anything you can help—which it would hurt me to speak about. . . . I shall know—For you are wrong—It is so much better not to speak of some kinds of trouble. But tell me if I said——"

"Nothing, believe me, that you need distress yourself about. Your wanderings were all disjointed and incoherent: and the first night, when you were most delirious, the nurse hadn't come: and I was in the house, and sat up with you. And surely I needn't tell you, that whatever a doctor might learn in that way, would be as sacred as though it had been spoken to a priest in the confessional."

An expression of relief crossed her face, and the surface agitation calmed, though I could feel that it was still surging beneath.

"Thank you," she said: "if people don't know, that's all that matters."

She looked away from me into vacancy, and closed her lips tightly, resolved, apparently, to say no more. I could not bear to watch her, and got up and walked to the window, standing there, and noting unconsciously the funereal plumes of the great cedars as the wind swayed them, and trying to compose myself into the attitude of the physician. But this was difficult. Presently I came back to her and spoke impetuously.

"You said that was all which mattered—people knowing. There's everything else to matter. Your own life, and whether it mightn't be best for you to face the thing—whatever it is, out straight, and find a means of escape. For your trouble will probably kill you if you can't rouse yourself and rise above it."

She shuddered again at the thought, I supposed, of laying bare her sorrows.

"Oh, no, no: don't speak of it. How could I escape? . . . There's nothing I could do."

She would not even admit the suggestion of practical counsel, and my own inability to give it was certain. For that, a clear comprehension of the facts was necessary. I could only ask if she had no man-relation or close woman-friend in whom she might, as the first step, confide fully.

"I haven't a relation in the world," she answered. "And as for a woman-friend, I can't think of one closer than Mione Arathoon." And she gave a dreary little laugh, which I half echoed, for Mrs. Audley Arathoon did not then seem the person one would cast for that part.

"Let us talk of something else," said Mrs. Vassal, resuming her forced quietude. "I want to know if I shall live to be old—I mean in the ordinary course of events."

"No, you will not live to be old if you go on spending your winters here. How many have you spent already?"

"I have been married seven years."

"And how old are you?"

"Twenty-seven."

"Listen," I said, "I am going to lecture you, and you must bear with me patiently."

Then I made some fatuous exposition of the duty of the physician in the matter of plain speaking.

"There's no reason why you should die. You have youth and vitality, and all the material advantages. If you could find a real interest which would prevent your mind from fretting away your body, also if you could winter out of England, you would gradually get quite well. Now I want you to make some engrossing work for yourself."

"That's the worst of being rich," she answered, smiling faintly. "There's no work one is obliged to do."

"Surely," I said, "the possession of riches implies responsibility;" and was again angry with myself for seeming a prig.

"Yes, I know what you mean. But you see I wasn't built that way. How can you expect a poor girl, who was the daughter of the bandmaster at Philotis, and lived on twenty-five shillings a week in a Bloomsbury lodging, to play the part of an English county lady properly. I've tried it, and have made a disgraceful failure—almost as bad as the *Claudia* failure. Ah!" she exclaimed, in an outburst of emotion, "Looking back to that performance at the Regency makes me feel bitter against you, Dr. Glaive. For," she added, in answer to my expostulatory ejaculation, "don't you see that if you hadn't put me into *Claudia*, we shouldn't be sitting here now, talking over my ruined life?"

That was the fear which for a long time had haunted me. I told her this, saying, "At least I can put forward the odd claim upon your confidence that I have been the means of destroying your career."

"My career!" she replied in a tone of melancholy derision: "that is such a big word, and so inappropriate. For you know as well as I know in my heart, that I should have failed just the same whenever the test came. I hadn't got in me the capacity to succeed: and it's absurd and wrong to reproach you. Besides, it wasn't you who changed my life for me." Her voice vibrated in deeper cadences, as though she were thrilled by some acute recollection. "I might have gone on, and failed again and again, if it had not been for something I heard by accident that day—the opinion of another person, which decided me. . . . No, *you* are not responsible. And perhaps I should not feel bitterness, but gratitude towards you. Yet," she exclaimed, "there's never a day nor a night in which I don't regret that baulked career. To look back upon what I was then—upon the enthusiasm, the ambition, the belief in beautiful things—it's like looking back through midnight murk to the glory of yesterday's sunrise."

She had leaned forward from her reclining posture, her chin raised a little, her eyes shining and absent. Now she drew back in an embarrassed manner, as though half ashamed of her poetical fervour.

"It's stupid, isn't it, to talk like that? I don't know what makes me have the impulse to tell you things. In all these seven years I've never spoken out to any one."

Moved to the quick by that struggling appeal for encouragement even against herself which I had discerned in her jerky manner and the painful questioning in her fixed gaze, I implored her to trust me, to give herself outlet for once, and to let me be her safety-valve. She listened to my reasonings and entreaties with the same dry shining look in her eyes and with a tremulous working of her features.

When I had ended, there was silence for a few moments, in which the very air seemed heavy with restrained emotion. Then she cried suddenly and passionately—

"Well, if you think it best. . . . You shall be my safety-valve. I will try to speak out, and after to-day I will be silent and endure my lot. Perhaps talking to you might help me a little. Doctors ought to understand something about people's dreadful thoughts and feelings, or else what use are they? . . . But other people's couldn't be as bad as mine! . . . The utter blackness and desolation! And your body doing everyday things . . . and then suddenly in the midst of them the ghastly horror seizing you. . . . A supernatural kind of horror that would drive one mad if it lasted. . . . I can't put it into words . . . as if your soul were separated—alone—shivering in awful space. . . ."

She shivered now, and went quavering on with the morbid egotism peculiar to such cases as hers, only that I could never bring myself to regard her quite as a "case."

It seemed to calm her when I explained that this sense of shadowy horror was a symptom familiar enough to the nerve specialist; and as I discoursed upon physiological and psychological connections, and described certain other sensations to which she had not referred, but which she recognised as part of her condition, she smiled gratefully, as though I had given her a clue through the mental labyrinth in which she wandered.

Now that the reserve was broken, she seemed even to have a difficulty in controlling the flow of self-revelation, sometimes repeating herself, and continually showing by the pucker in her brow and the clouded expression of her eyes how great had been the strain under which she had previously walked the ways of ordinary life. I let her talk on, only now and then interrupting her with a word of sympathy and reassurance.

" . . . Yes, it is all very well to say that I should feel differently if my nerves and brain were properly nourished . . . the neurotic temperament—that's what you doctors call it. . . . But you know it is not only that. . . . It is that I am—what I am; that my life is what it must be. . . . I have made it so and can't alter it. . . . No, it can't be altered. Do you think I haven't thought it all out ? . . . There's no use in worrying over that. . . . The thing is to meet it like a woman of the world. Of course there are many women placed in positions more difficult than mine. It's I—myself that make my hell. Don't you remember—

> ' Hell hath no limits, nor is circumscribed
> In one self-place ; for where we are is hell,
> And where hell is, there we must ever be.'

" I recollect ranting that to myself in the pine-woods at El-Meriem . . . we had a home there, you know—El-Meriem isn't far from Philotis—when I was a girl."

Oh, the organ-stop pathos of those words "when I was a girl !"

" . . . But the trouble is that I'm not like other women. . . . And I've tried so hard to live the life—to care for things that—and I cannot. . . . It turned to nausea—loathing. . . . I'm tired—tired of struggling. . . . Do you believe that one can be taken possession of by a spirit of hatred ? . . . It is so terrible to hate . . . a person . . . who is very near—so that there can be no getting away. . . . As if you were chained to some strange soulless thing that is stronger than you, and fascinates and compels you, and yet fills you with rage and revolt. . . . That's how I've felt ever since I married. . . .

"And I've prayed—in there"—she signed towards the oratory, . . . "cried aloud in my despair . . . but never any help came. . . . You see I married wrongly—for the sake of money and position and to escape from my failure. . . . And at the beginning I did not try as I ought to have done. . . . I did not try enough to conquer my rebellious feelings. I let the . . . aversion get the better of everything . . . of all that was gentle and tender in me. . . . And then the feeling towards me seemed to change and become dislike . . . a kind of mocking triumph in making me obey. . . . And there were reproaches that seared like hot iron . . . because . . . you know . . . I am very proud. . . . And it is degrading to take things—money, luxuries—one's very food and clothing . . . and not to give the payment that was agreed upon. . . . And then to be taunted with the humiliation. . . . Besides, you know . . . he wanted to have a son. . . . And I was like Hannah and besought the Lord, and He heard me not. . . . Sometimes I have a dreadful feeling about the curse on this house . . . for you know the story, don't you? . . . how a Vassal, not quite rightfully or legitimately of the family—I forget . . . forced the heiress into marrying him. She was not quite right in her head . . . and he got to hate her and starved her to death, they say. . . . And ever since a curse has rested on the house. . . . I feel it . . . as though the place were reeking with all the revengeful thoughts of years and years back—till the air is like a pestilence—the old hate breeding fresh hatreds. . . . For doesn't it seem to you possible that a very strong wicked feeling might take invisible form and infect weak people by its own poison? . . . I am glad that I have no child to be cursed too. . . ."

A fit of dry sobbing stopped her. She had been speaking fast, with little pauses between the agitated utterances, sometimes so low that I could hardly hear her. The tragedy of those broken, allusive sentences overwhelmed me. I longed to give her some sign of my deep sympathy, and yet was afraid to say anything lest my own emotion should choke me and make me seem unresponsive, thus checking the stream of her difficult confidence. . . . I put out my hand and timidly touched hers; and presently she went on again, her voice gaining strength.

"It's because you are a doctor, and different from others, that I let myself go like this; it's not because I want advice or words of pity. . . . I don't want you ever to remind me of to-day. . . . You said it would be like speaking to a priest in the confessional. . . . I know what my life must be. . . . That day . . . when I had the shock of knowing . . . and I ran out into the wood . . . I thought my marriage could be broken . . . I did not know what I was doing . . . I wanted to be alone . . . to breathe pure air . . . to escape from this evil house. . . . And he brought me back, and I was forced to obey. . . . Then I asked him to let me go, and he would not . . . he said there should be no scandal. . . . And what would be the use ? . . . the harm is done, and never, never can be undone. . . . I have made my lot, and I must abide by my making. . . ."

The despair in her tone gave me the most miserable sense of helplessness. Though human misery had often before now been bared to me, this misery affected me as none other had done, for its root seemed not so much in the actual facts of Mrs. Vassal's life as in the inner springs of her being ; and it was indeed canker of the soul. Putting stress upon myself, I avoided the more tragic aspect of the matter, and, from the professional standpoint, urged upon her the necessity for giving occupation to her mind, if only as a means of physical relief and intellectual discipline. Thus gradually I got her to talk more composedly, and upon more general topics. I spoke of her old interest in the drama, and asked her if, merely as an artistic study, it might not be possible to revive it.

She shook her head.

"I suppose," she answered, "that I am morbidly self-absorbed ; but I cannot take up things in the abstract. I seem to need the stimulus of personal emotion to rouse my faculties. . . I read a good deal, but the more scientific books are outside me ; and I find works of imagination mechanical and artificial. Plays seem very wooden to me now ;—always at the critical moment the scene closes and the curtain falls, and the real life of it all has to be woven out of what is unsaid and undone. . . . Often as I sit in a London theatre I wonder to myself that the drama ever appealed to me as the highest form of art."

" Music then ?" I said.

" A certain kind of music ; devotional music in especial affects me horribly. . . . I say horribly because it makes me so sad. . . . But I can't express myself in the language."

I asked her if she had ever thought of writing, adding that I myself knew no more engrossing pleasure than the creation of a world of one's own with the pen. My suggestion seemed to take some hold on her. She thought for a moment or two, and I saw by the expression of her face that her mind was working backward along healthier channels.

" You make me think of my girlhood," she said presently,

"and of how I used to scribble things at El-Meriem. I always
had a fancy for writing, and kept a kind of journal of my ideas
and feelings—you can imagine the sort of girl-nonsense. . . .
But I dropped all that when I married."

"Why not take it up again now?"

She drew herself together with a little shudder.

"I didn't mean in the purely introspective sense, though
I believe it would be better for you to write down morbid
imaginings than to let them prey upon your brain. I was thinking more of my own early method of training memory and
observation, and of getting a firmer touch in character-drawing;
for you know it's my pet private conviction that in me a novelist
has been spoiled by the doctor. That may or may not be true,
but in parenthesis let me add, that I am certain my early efforts
in fiction have helped me as a doctor to a better understanding
of human nature."

I told her of theories I had about the craft—since then far more
ably set forth by Robert Louis Stevenson—which would involve a
course of preparation as systematic as that to be gone through
by the painter or sculptor: the student of fiction looking upon
the world around him as an atelier, and before attempting any
sustained work, making many rough studies, and filling as many
note-books as the art student spoils canvases.

It was a favourite theme of mine, and I enlarged upon it,
for I found it was taking her a little out of herself; till a message
came from Mr. Vassal that the carriage would soon be round to
take me to my train, and that he requested the favour of a few
words before I started. I got up and took my leave of Mrs.
Vassal.

"You will pay attention to my prescription for your mind
as well as to my prescription for your body?" I said, after
impressing upon her certain medical injunctions.

"Yes," she answered; "I will try."

"Map out a novel or drama," I went on. "Or better still,
do not map out, but make studies of life as it presents itself
to you individually; and if you feel cramped by your own
personality, think that there is a good deal, if not everything,
in the theory that the artist is not much more than a sensitised
plate for the receiving and giving forth of impressions. So write
from the deeps of you, and be not afraid."

"I am certain," I said, "speaking as the physician, that you
will find relief and help from the outlet; and speaking as the
artist, I am certain, too, that you will do good work. I couldn't
have been so far out in my estimate of you in the beginning,

though in *Claudia* I handicapped you too heavily. Frank Leete
has never ceased to reproach me for that."

She gave again that dreary little laugh which so went to my
heart, and repeated, "I'll try;" then added, conquering her
reserve by an effort, for I had seen already that she repented her
burst of confidence, and that the flood-gates once closed would
not easily open again, "I am sorry that our talk has ended.
And I want to thank you; you have done me good. I will
remember all that you have said."

"And you will rely on my friendship—my discretion—my
most earnest wish to be of use to you in any way that is possible?"

I felt my voice tremble; she too seemed greatly moved, and
I saw the tears gather in her eyes.

"Thank you—thank you," she said hurriedly. She put her
hand in mine, and the convulsive pressure of the little thin
fingers sent a strange quiver through me.

"Good-bye, Dr. Glaive . . . I wish . . ." she faltered. "I seem
unresponsive. . . . But indeed, I am very unhappy."

"I know it; and I can do nothing—only preach to you and
physic you, neither of which are of much good. Well, you will
write to me sometimes, and tell me how my two prescriptions
work?"

"Yes—thank you."

The door closed upon me, and I left her, praying inwardly
that my sympathy might have lightened her burden a little. At
least I had the satisfaction of seeing that the tense look upon her
face had relaxed, and that her eyes were softer and more natural.

I did not go again to Grisewood Castle, and my next meeting
with Mrs. Vassal was not for some time afterwards.

 How did I ever for a moment imagine that I could stand up against Mr. Vassal? Perhaps it was my talk with Dr. Glaive which gave me courage. But it is hopeless. When he looks at me with that concentrated gleam in his eyes, the old terrified fascination overcomes me, and I am like an exasperated bird fluttering between the claws of a great, soft, fierce cat. I hate him, and yet I am afraid of him. I'd fly to the ends of the earth to escape from that look in his eyes, from the touch of his big white hands; but I cannot. I am rooted before him by this strange force of mingled attraction, repulsion, and dread.

They say that the soul has lived and will live on through æons; they say that love is of the soul, and endures through eternity. But, is not hate more powerful than love, stronger than the very soul itself?

It is wrong of me to write this. But I am a wicked woman. My heart is bitter and my mind is evil; and God, who is Love, can have no commerce with hate.

Why was I made after such fashion? Why have I been chained in this yokeship of living enmity? Why is not my lot as the lot of other women who have husbands dear and honoured, and babes at their breast, or lovers for whom the world would be well given?

And what is the meaning of all which is written about love—the love of man for woman; of parent for child; of brother for sister; of friend for friend; of saint for sinner? This mighty river of human affection, which poets tell us will soften the hard rock, and make the desert blossom! This spiritual sun, which will pierce the heart's darkness and wither noxious thoughts and cause the soul to send forth shoots to heaven? I have read of these things, but I do not know them.

Why should my life alone be arid, my heart alone unlightened and unwarmed? Or is it all nothing but a mocking lie, a pretty fable, a tinselled robe which civilisation has shaped in place of the fig leaves?

So, often I tell myself as I look round upon the London world; as I see the girls exhibited in the marriage-market, and the wan tricked-out creatures in the gaming-rooms at Homburg; as I catch the indefinable look on men's faces when they have dined freely and the mask falls for an instant.

But at other times—maybe on a clear spring day, when quivering sunbeams shoot down straight from heaven through the crinkled leaves of nut branches; when the violets and wood-anemones are lifting their modest heads, and the may-bloom is out and the lilies of the valley breaking their sheaths; when the birds are cooing and calling to each other, and the wind rustles inarticulately through young foliage, and the whole earth seems filled with pure fragrance and tender mystic murmurings. Then all the old El-Meriem dreams come back to me enriched and glorified, and I believe in love.

Then I wonder in my soul if the divine dove will ever descend upon me, the symbol of a new baptism and of a hope eternal.

Foolish fancies, which shrivel and shrink beneath the sombre flame of Mr. Vassal's eyes.

But it is a relief to have them out. Yes, Dr. Glaive is right. The moral canker was spreading poisonous humours for need of outlet.

There seemed to me a savage inappeasable animosity in Mr. Vassal's gaze when I dared to meet it after the wild words which broke from me in my desperate revolt.

I can't remember what they were, but I told him that I hated him, that I wished to go away and never to see his face again.

And then I must have flung at him some reproach which struck home. He had listened so far without moving a muscle; now the set ironic look relaxed in a spasm of rage. He lifted his head, drawing a long breath, as though fury were bracing his frame, and came closer to me. The scorching gleam from his eyes was more than I could bear; his domineering personality overpowered me; and it was as though my passion of aversion were thrust back by his grim might and held me in one long throe. I lifted up my arms with the helpless instinct to shield myself. His soft strong fingers seized my wrist as in a grip of steel. Yet there was no brute energy in the grasp, and his voice when he spoke scarcely rose above a whisper, though each word cut like a knife.

"That's a damnably vulgar thing to say. But what can one expect out of the slums of a theatre? It would have been too much to suppose that you could meet a situation with dignity. God! you shall not say things of that sort to me. I'm your master, understand, and you'd better ignore what you find unpleasant. I give you the opportunity, and so much the worse for you if you don't take it. Just listen! You've got to behave decently. There's to be no talk, mind—no scandal—no running away, and none of those heroics. You failed on the stage ; don't try it on in private life. You've got to do what I choose ; and let there be an end of this injured wife business, once and for ever."

He took away his hand. On his lips was the smile with which I've seen him watch a beaten dog quail. I turned dizzy and sick ; the room reeled, and the flame of the fire and the flame in his eyes leaped towards me. I felt myself falling, and everything became black.

When I came to myself I was on the sofa, and Mr. Vassal and Tremlett, my maid, were beside me. Tremlett was sponging my forehead, and Mr. Vassal held a restorative to my lips.

.   .   .   .

I don't care whether Mr. Vassal ever reads what I am writing. Why should I care? If he were to read it, and it made him so angry that he were to cast me out from his house, that would be the best thing, not the worst, that he could do to me.

But I need not even conjecture what effect these self-communings of mine might have upon him. He is not the sort of person to examine his wife's private papers. If by chance he were to pick up this book and run his eye over the page, he would take a cold-blooded pride in letting me know that he had not turned the leaf; and I can imagine the sarcastic suavity with which he would recommend me to pursue my literary labours if they afforded me any satisfaction, but would beg exemption from the privilege of criticising them.

That is exactly what he did say once, not long after our marriage, when he handed me back a letter of many pages—surely I ought to have learned by that time not to write letters—containing my whole ecstatic philosophy of life's woes, and a fervid appeal to him not to confound my faith in things spiritual by a too strenuous enforcement of his own carnal code.

Often have I wondered whether there is anything good in the universe in which Mr. Vassal believes. That he should look upon religion as a mere form does not so greatly surprise me, for all my life creeds have somehow seemed to me but as so many different sorts of vesture to be varied according to climate, temperament, and social conditions, the spiritual body within remaining ever the same. In the worst darkness of my doubt and despair, I have tried to find comfort in that spiritual reality which my inner senses have ever dimly discerned, though the shape of it is hidden from me. But for Mr. Vassal the Spirit has no existence ; and it is this division, as between two kingdoms of nature—this dead wall of matter—which gives me the feeling of moral alienation indescribable. For him, beyond the flesh there is nothing—God a fetish, more or less poetic as the scale of civilisation rises or falls; the Church a useful State institution; the clergy liveried officials for the suppression of independence among the lower orders, to be outwardly supported with honour and observance, but merely as part of the masque and pageant. And for the domestic sanctities! I've heard him speak of marriage as a legalised method for the production of heirs and the preservation of family property. And love—no, I won't quote his definition.

I am roughly epitomising his private views as they have been at various times delivered in the billiard-room after dinner to such intimates as Mr. Arathoon and Mrs. Raphon, his sister; to Mione, Audley Arathoon's wife, and others broadly tolerant. Sometimes, too, I have listened to Mr. Vassal's talk across a London dinner-table. I believe he is considered a clever talker, but I have observed that rich men usually receive the attention of their audience. Occasionally he says startling things in a soft, deliberate manner; more often he looks bored, and gives an impression of reserved power. With a certain type of woman, whom I don't frequently meet, he has the air of Cæsar unbending; with another he is the sedate epicurean; with a third—such as Addie Heseltine, our neighbour's daughter—he is a blend of Sir Roger de Coverley and Dean Swift. It seems to amuse him to play a part adapted to his background. Not in order to make an effect —Mr. Vassal would never do anything so common!—but as a kind of emotional stimulus. I have heard him declare that the only saint worthy of being canonised would be the person who invented a new sensation; and once when he had lost an enormous sum of money on the Stock Exchange, he announced, in a complacent drawl, that it was the first time he had ever known the enjoyment of gambling.

From that point of view I can understand his interest in the drama. How he must have laughed at my poor pretensions to be an actress—he who is so accomplished a performer on the social stage, and who can suit himself with the ease of a consummate mime to a change in the mental atmosphere.

For instance, the Mr. Vassal of Grosvenor Street and the Mr. Vassal of Grisewood and Tregarth are, as I know from observation, two separate personalities. I can never help admiring my master at Grisewood when we are entertaining our country neighbours, and the Bishop, and Dean, and Canons of Woodchester—there is a flavour of the clergy in our severe Grisewood functions, and the Bishop always comes to us for near confirmations, church openings, and the like. Then when we have house-parties for the Hunt Ball, and in the shooting season, Mr. Vassal is again a study in decorous geniality. Equally admirable, too, is he at tenants' dinners, and among the miners at Tregarth when he visits his Cornish estate ; and he can be evangelically agreeable to our portly parson Mr. Wargrave, and that serious Christian, his wife.

If I am crudely flippant, remember that I am still unpractised in literary portraiture. There is also a certain grim humour, which I am sure Mr. Vassal would himself appreciate, in the notion of his supplying me with a character-model. For I am following on Dr. Glaive's suggestion, though so far, I fear, to little profit. I have tried to map out a novel, but all is dim and chaotic, and my attempts at composition are laboured and lacking in inspiration.

As regards the fight against circumstance, my illness, or the cataclysm in my conjugal relations, seems to have strangely deadened my power of resistance, even my power of feeling. Or it may be that I am living a little more outside myself, and do not kick quite so hardly against the pricks.

.   .   .   .

We have a party in the house for the Hunt Ball. It is made up of our usual set at Grisewood—the Cotherstones from the other side of the county; the Heseltines from Fincham—he is master of the fox-hounds; a pretty rich young American and her husband who have taken a place near for the hunting; a couple from Devonshire, some men, a stray girl or two, and Mione Arathoon and her husband.

I don't care for the Arathoon family, which seems linked with the Vassals in rather an odd way, for Mr. Arathoon is only a great London solicitor and Mr. Vassal's legal adviser, and Mrs. Raphon, his sister, who keeps his house, though very handsome and dressing splendidly, is just a little under-bred. Mione tells me that she was supposed to be in love with Mr. Vassal, and very angry when he married me, but that apparently does not prevent the two from being great friends. There is some sort of kinship between the families. I think, but am not sure, that Mr. Arathoon's mother was a Vassal. And then Mione, wife of Audley Arathoon, the solicitor's son, is of the Delmars, and so distantly connected with Mr. Vassal's first wife. Mione is an heiress in a small way, and I have always wondered how she came to marry Audley Arathoon, for she frankly despises her father-in-law and aunt by marriage. Audley is a barrister and has good manners.

Mione interests me, she is so flinty, and frivolous, and shrewd, and yet somehow I can't help fancying there are depths beneath, if one could only sound them. She has fluffy red hair and the complexion that goes with it, and romantic velvety eyes that seem out of place in such a worldly person. She says she likes coming to Grisewood because it's a rich house, and her idea of perfect happiness is to have quantities of money and everything about her as luxurious as possible, and also because Mr. Vassal mounts her, and she can't afford to hunt as many days as she would wish from her own little hunting-box.

. . . .

How like a dream it all is! The arrivals, the inane civilities, the great hall in which we receive our guests, with its carvings, portraits, suits of armour, Indian gods, blue porcelain, screens, palms, stands of flowers, and all the rest; the flames of the log fire leaping up in the half light and making gleams and shadows among the groups—stiff at first, till the servants bring in lamps and tea, and there comes the clatter of cups and the fuss of handing scones and muffins. Mr. Vassal, the genial country squire, is saying just the right thing to everybody—discussing county matters with old Lady Cotherstone, inquiring from her what the various house-parties are to be, and the latest views of "the Duchess" about the organising of a political fête which is agitating the neighbourhood. I hear him in snatches, here and there, deploring my recent illness and the lung delicacy which will prevent me from going to the ball; explaining how anxious he is to make my imprisonment in the house as little irksome as may be this winter—he has had Quintin Glaive the specialist down, who has advised a warmer climate for future winters, though it was not thought desirable that I should risk the long journey at present so late in the season. But next winter he will arrange that I shall leave early for the south—Cannes, Biarritz, or perhaps Philotis. . . .

Philotis! A lump rises in my throat; and I stand dazed by the rush of ghost-memories. . . . And then somebody speaks to me. . . . It is Mione, who has just come in with Mr. Littlewood; and I notice that at sight of him Addie Heseltine blushes uncomfortably. Not long ago Mr. Littlewood wanted to marry her; and when she refused him, he went to live in the forests of Yucatan, and scraped buried monuments and took to archæology and to photographing ruined cities.

Mione's flutter and chatter are all part of the dream. She is covered from head to foot in a sealskin coat. . . . "I'm too abominably untidy. . . . We've driven over eighteen miles. Such a run!

. . . I ought not to kiss you ; my cheek is freezing.   Chocolate ?
thank you. . . . Audley ? . . . But *where* is he—just ?   That's what
I want to know.   I'm quite uneasy about him.   I think he must
be sitting in a ditch. . . . Of course he was out.   And if you
had seen the wretched horse he was riding, rear this morning
when our second man mounted him, you wouldn't wonder I'm
uneasy. . . ."

Mr. Vassal asks if Audley is looking out for a hunter, for
he thinks he has heard of a good bargain ; and young Lord
Cotherstone joins in. . . . He knows a man who wants to sell his
horses . . . Rathdowney—a splendid lot. . . . And the master, Mr.
Heseltine, who is always drawn by shorthorns and hunters, but
is mostly silent on other topics, wakes up to declare that Rathdowney is a regular horse-coper, and that selling his hunters is
a dodge to get rid of them. . . .

More arrivals and new civilities, and fresh tea. . . . And the
dream-medley of babble. . . . Mione sipping her chocolate and
entertaining Addie Heseltine close to me with reminiscences of
recent doings. . . . She had been rushing round . . . had been in
Norfolk for a family wedding . . . a sixteen-mile drive to church
and no foot-warmers . . . had suffered atrociously from the wicked
behaviour of Audley's sister's youngest hope . . . " A three-year-
old bridesmaid dressed like a ballet-dancer." . . . " And fancy the
brat holding out her skirts and doing a *pas seul* and then flopping
down on the bride's train at the ' Wilt thou have this man ? ' " . . .
Then . . . "The women didn't approve of me ; and the husband ·
of one of them told me what they said : playing it rather low
down, wasn't it ?   Well, of course I know I'm not pretty ; but
I'm effective.   Every woman can be that if she chooses ; it's only
a question of putting on your clothes and setting your hat at the
right angle."

Oh yes, Mione is quite right ; she is effective.

How curious it is, this froth and spray of life ! . . . And I suppose that for every one of them—even for Mione—there are bitter
ingredients seething in the brew beneath.   But does nobody
think of them ; does nobody care, as long as there are good things
to eat and diamonds and county balls and splendid runs ? . . .
The fancy becomes vivified in my brain—my poor brain, which at
moments, seems as empty and unreal as the froth and spray itself.
The lights and fire-gleams and glints of silver and china, and
people's faces and the bits of colour in their clothes seem to detach
themselves, and to be as so many dancing bubbles tossed up on the
billows of life-experience—past mingling with present in confused
glimmerings.   For a second, there is a queer incongruous flash giving

me back the supers' dressing-room at the Regency—the women with their dyed hair making themselves up, and one of them saying, "When the gag's too strong, it just guys the whole show." . . . Fancy remembering that theatre slang all these years, and thinking of it now. . . . The whole show! What is this but a show! . . .

I feel a hand on my arm. Prim, majestic Lady Cotherstone has come up to me. . . . "My dear Mrs. Vassal, you look as if you were going to faint. I cannot think that you ought to be standin' about, worryin' after us all, though Mr. Vassal tells me that Dr. Glaive prescribes amusement and cheerful society. But I know what it is to receive a party for the first time after recovering from an illness; and I am going to make you take me upstairs and show me my room; and I shall feel more comfortable when I have seen you into your own for an hour's quiet rest. Leave Mr. Vassal to look after the others; he doesn't need any one to help him. What a difference between the old school and the young! Cotherstone hasn't the faintest notion of a host's duties. If I could only persuade him to take your husband as a model! But it seems to me that the young men of to-day expect their women-kind to do their manners for them as well as their religion. . . ."

. . . .

The dream-scene changes. . . . There is the long dinner-table with its decoration of orchids—we are famous for our orchids—and its array of plate. The dining-room is hung with tapestry in deep dull tints, and the gay dresses and bare necks and diamonds shine out against it. Every one is talking and laughing, and all seems glitter, froth, and colour, the pink coats of the hunting-men making vivid plashes that are accentuated by the black garb of the London men and the clergy. It is a large dinner-party, for near neighbours have been asked to meet the house-party, and the Dean and a Canon and their wives have come over from Wood-chester.

In the drawing-room the women's comments and condolences upon my ill-health are like thin string trios and quartettes after a full orchestra, Lady Cotherstone's deep middle notes dominating, and a bounteous matron in a tiara taking up the refrain.

. . . For Mr. Vassal's sake, it is so important that I should run no risk . . . his anxiety . . . etcetera.

"Oh, *so* touching!" bleats Mrs. Wargrave, nodding her smooth serious head with its flat plaits and bands curved over a benevolent forehead, and smiling her deprecatory smile.

. . . "Young women are so careless about their health till gout and other things begin to happen . . ." from Lady Willoughby.

. . . "Mr. Vassal was saying that it all came from an imprudent walk in the wood on one of those bitter days . . . How unfortunate that he should just then have started to join his yacht ! . . . Mandour, wasn't it, where he went ? . . . . Oh, too fascinating by Mr. Vassal's description ! . . . A real bit of the old East within five days of London . . . quite close to Philotis, where people are all going now for the winter, since *Views* began to praise up the place. . . .

. . . "And what a wise thought of Tremlett to consult with Mr. Wargrave and have Dr. Glaive telegraphed for. . . . Mr. Vassal seems to have such confidence in Tremlett. . . . Oh, it's a great advantage in one's maid being an old family servant." And so on. . . .

Doctors and ailments, gardens, bric-à-brac, and village bounties! Don't the dowagers and clergy-women ever tire of these things !

"Such a touching little shop with its little plate of sweets in the window and string of reels. . . . And there was a small shrubbery at the back of the house . . . quite a touching little wilderness. . . . And the baby buried and got rid of! Such a mercy ! . . . A wee cosy grave in a warm corner of the churchyard ; and the mother free to begin the world again, and *so* grateful to the Ladies of the League !"

That's Mrs. Wargrave explaining things to Lady Cotherstone, who is President of the Woodchester Rescue and Reformation League. . . .

Oh, sickening ! Why don't they leave the poor women alone, and begin by reforming their own brothers and sons — and husbands ?

Mione makes some queer little cynical remark about the girls in the Westminster slums, and then says that she thinks a mission should be started for the rescue and reformation of unfortunate women of society with incomes under fifteen hundred a year, who are expected to keep up appearances. "It's a moral impossibility," says Mione, "though I know a woman who manages a brougham, and Worth dresses and diamonds—not old-fashioned family jewels, but beetles and doves, all sweet new Paris designs, genuine and of the first water—on less than a thousand. . . . And she gave up dyeing her hair—it used to be golden when I first knew her, and now it's dark brown—because she doesn't think that sort of thing 'quite nice in the mother of a little family.' . . . And it's all done on Irish rents ; and we know what *that* means."

Mrs. Heseltine looks shocked, and changes the topic to homeopathy, and Mione retires to examine a photograph and talk gowns with the pretty American. The men straggle in, and two or three, who make for the dowagers, stand at attention while homeopathy holds the field, till Lord Cotherstone gives a dash as though he were going to open a gate for a lady, pulling the lapel of his pink coat and stammering slightly.

"It all c-comes of sleeping with your window shut, Mrs. Vassal. L-liver and the east wind, and that sort of thing. I've been t-touched myself, you know. Upon my honour, when I've had a good night—liver all sound, and slept like a t-top with a bit of the window open, I declare I don't look more than twenty-five. And when it's an east wind, and I'm stewed up—t-touched in the liver and chippy, you know . . . well, on my honour, I m-might be forty-five."

Oh, how absurd and grim it all is! One might fancy that coffee—"strong coffee made in the French way—it *must* be in the French way . . . black and *very* clear, with a *tiny* dash of brandy,"—as says Lady Willoughby of the tiara in her treble staccato—one might fancy that this, and aconite, and belladonna are a cure for diseased souls! And there's a sort of devil's chorus to the drawing-room comedy, "Lies—lies—all lies!" it runs. . . . And through it Mr. Vassal's voice horribly distinct—his well-bred country-squire voice.

"Tiresomely short of foxes, ain't we? I doubt the stock holdin' out. . . . A capital run the other day . . . two rings round Swinton and Nunneloe. . . . Oh, bad, bad yesterday: the country very deep, and the Master dreadfully disappointed at not killing."

. . . Then Mr. Vassal again, to Sir James Willoughby. . . . "Do you really think we ought to grant the licence? Isn't it playing up to the brewing interest?"

And . . . "Yes, Mr. Dean, you are quite right. It is certainly our duty as landed proprietors to face the responsibility. But really in my humble judgment this depravity of the upper classes is an exaggerated matter—a sensational cry of the Radical press. Of course vice exists: let us sorrowfully grant the fact. But *has* our class the monopoly of vice? The *Woodchester Independent* might as well accuse us Woodfordshire squires of being a dissolute set—eh, Master? because morality in the shoemaking villages is at rather a low ebb. . . ."

I set Addie Heseltine to the piano. Her music has tears in it; and Mr. Littlewood places himself at the angle of the instrument and gazes unutterable things. But Addie won't glance his way, and I am sure that she is thinking of the curate whom her parents have banished from Fincham. How can she want to marry a curate, I wonder! . . . She plays a waltz by Chopin, and then some Schumann bits. . . . By-and-by she stops: and the buzz of voices begins once more: and at intervals, detached phrases sound above the confused hum . . . Mr. Wargrave's robust laugh and strident tones.

"A fine row the hounds made on Saturday, Master, giving tongue down by the osier bed near the churchyard. You quite spoiled my funeral. . . ."

The two Gainsboroughs look down from the yellow brocade wall—those sweet serene Gainsborough ladies, whose muslin draperies fall so graciously, and whose eyes are so limpidly pure, that sure they can never have peeped down into the tragedy below life's bubble and froth. . . . Or was it that though those Vassal wives had bad husbands, too, and many a gnawing grief, they knew how to preen their heads proudly and to use their rouge-pot and hide disgust under a smile? . . . If I might but call them down from their gilt frames and ask them their secret!

. . . Night has brought an interval in the raree-show, and the performers are taking their rest. All but one. . . . The fire casts strange flickers upon the buhl furniture of my bedroom, and draws dancing gleams from the silver boxes and bottles and ornaments upon the tables. But through the leaden hours my wide eyes watch the glimmering rays till they die and dawn replaces them. It is during vigils such as this that I feel the superstitious dread, the horror of desolation, which Dr. Glaive told me is due only to unstrung nerves and a bloodless brain. But no material explanation will do away with that consciousness of unseen presences and of being delivered over to the powers of darkness.

I know when the ghostly terror is coming, by a sensation of clammy cold that deadens my limbs while my mind remains acutely alive. Any distant sound swells into the rhythmic volume of a corps of soldiers marching to the beat of drums. . . . Then, too, I lose the sense of weight and size, and my pillow becomes a universe and the canopy of my bed realms of space.

Great waves of light pass over me, to be followed by waves of darkness. Sometimes unknown faces start out of the void with lightning vividness, gaze for a moment, and melt away, to be succeeded perhaps by a whole processional pageant in which grotesque phantoms move along in regular order and bewildering rapidity. . . .

This feeling that the world around is no more than a painted picture, a sort of magic-lantern illusion flitting across a white sheet, becomes a grisly oppression, never lifting. . . .

. . . .

. . . I am alone. The house is strangely silent; the carriages have driven off with their freight for the ball—young men and maids, old men and matrons, pink coats and black. satins, velvets, and diamonds and clouds of tulle. They bade me good-night in the hall. Mione gave me a kiss; and last of all, in presence of the whole party, Mr. Vassal came deliberately towards me, wished me pleasant dreams, and raised my hand to his lips.

"What an adorable manner! and what an angel to devote himself to us when he would so much rather be doing Darby and Joan with you!" whispered Addie Heseltine, who ran up to beg that I would not stand in a draught.

I went back to the empty drawing-room; it was full of ghosts. The hall-door fell to with a muffled bang, and the roll of carriage wheels died away down the avenue. The high-headed Gains-borough women smiled at me out of their frames their arch superior smile. They too, no doubt, had gone gaily off to county balls in their time, disdaining to be sick or sorry.

"You an actress!" the sweet mocking lips seemed to say. "And la! you cannot play your part as bravely e'en as we played ours. And you must mope and weep and tear your hair and take to bed, because, forsooth, you hate your husband! 'Tis vastly fine to sulk; but was it for love or money, tell us, that you sold yourself? And since the bargain please you not, to break it were mighty easy. Go, then, and cease from vapouring. Thou hast no little ones, as we had, to cry shame and call thee back. Thou hast not given to the house an heir. Go now, this very night. Be free, forsaken, and hungry. Live in a garret, an it suit thee better than a castle. What should hinder thee?"

What should hinder me?... Nothing... nothing but my deadly weakness. Nothing but the dense spiritual blackness which closes me round like a wall and shuts out the way.... Nothing but the power of my master....

.   .   .   .

... I have been sitting here for a long time. There is only a heap of grey ashes on the hearth. The fire has gone out, and I did not know it. Another fire warmed me.

For, while I was brooding in loneliness and great heaviness of soul, a wonder came to pass. It seemed that in the stillness of night and the gloom of dejection, a miracle was wrought—a Pentecostal quickening, as though there had come the rushing mighty wind from heaven, and the descent of the cloven tongues of flame.

I have known within me, dumbly, inexplicably, helplessly, that I had something of the art-gift. But there was neither sound nor language in which it might find utterance.

And now, at last, my fancy has spoken, as the voice to the Hebrew of old spoke, saying, "Take up thy pen and write."

My fancy has become a thing of life. A crude misshapen thing perchance, but it has a lusty cry; and I love this bratling of Sorrow's begetting.

.   .   .   .

I have told no one of the saving grace which has fallen upon me: yet it is under the support of this new hope that I have taken courage and looked my fate in the face: for it is clear to me that in my work I shall find the solace of dark hours, and the torch to light my steps along life's difficult path.

After seven years of torpor, the old mysterious cravings have seized me once more; and the artist nature, with its sweet pain and tumult, is awake and clamouring. My work is at once the cry of my starved-soul for bread, and the manna with which heaven feeds it.

I am very grateful to Dr. Glaive.

Nevertheless it is strange that his two or three letters to me have not roused responsive chords; and beyond asking him the names of some books which might help me in the cultivation of a literary style, I have said very little to him about the work. Nor have I any impulse to set him up as the high-priest of my temple of art.

Why is this? . . . Sometimes I have dreams of an absolute artistic sympathy, but I get no realisation of them here. It may be that the impulsive outburst of confidence after my illness has brought its reaction: it may be that the laws of affinity are arbitrary and do not admit of reasoning.

I have been a great deal alone. There have been long frosts, and Mr. Vassal has made lengthened visits to London—or else-where—for I know nothing of his movements. Once he brought Mr. Arathoon, the elder, down with him, and I believe the two spent a whole day in the library going over family documents. Mione, who has paid a short visit at the Castle once or twice, gave me to understand that there was hope of a legal loophole, by which the entail might be evaded: and afterwards, that negotiations had been set on foot for a compromise with the heir.

I have an instinctive dislike to Mr. Arathoon. Is that, I wonder. because he dislikes me? It is not easy to discover Mr. Arathoon's sentiments, but upon the fact of his aversion for me

I feel no doubt. He is a fair, handsome man of the Jewish type, with a thin nose slightly beaked, and a long silky beard with hardly a trace of grey, which is so fine that it scarcely hides the lower part of his face. His eyes are light grey, expressionless, and singularly hard and opaque, so that when he looks at you full, which is not often, it seems to be through thick glass. He is a man of culture—that is his own phrase—and a great lover of music; and it is odd to hear him singing love-songs in a well-trained mellifluous voice, and to remember that his profession lies mainly in the searching out of man's baser motives. He has got a foreign streak in him—I don't quite know whence : and among the politicians, journalists, and artists of note whom one meets at his house in Chesham Place, there is a good sprinkling of distinguished Frenchmen, Germans, and Russians. He is a gourmet as well, and has composed a cookery-book.

I am amused sometimes at hearing Mione talk about her father-in-law. "Caliban intended Mr. Vassal to take Mrs. Raphon off his hands." Mione has a trick of giving irrelevant nicknames. "I suppose you know," she went on, "that my aunt by marriage once cherished an ardent passion for your husband. Perhaps she does still—how can I tell? There *are* persons outside books capable of sustaining that sort of thing, though I am not one of them. Oh !" she exclaimed in whimsical despair, "I often look at Audley and ask myself 'Why? . . . Wherefore in a mis-guided moment did I imagine that I was in love and condemn myself to become an Arathoon?' . . . Let me warn you, Esther, never to expect a good turn from old Arathoon or his sister. They are of the tribe which always pays back a grudge with compound interest."

Mione has related to me the story of Rhoda Raphon's unfor-tunate marriage : of a bubble company in which Mr. Raphon had been scapegoat, and Michael Arathoon, Mione hinted, not scathe-less, but undiscovered : of the Raphons' complete loss of fortune : of the mysterious suicide of Mr. Raphon, and of Mr. Arathoon's generous offer to his half-sister of a home. But Mione scoffed at the notion of her father-in-law as a benefactor. "Caliban disin-terested ! Why, he never did an unselfish thing in his life. You may be certain that he cheated the Raphons, and that there was something he was afraid would come out if he let her loose on the world. Then he wanted a housekeeper, and it is respectable to have a sister presiding at your table. Besides, she is handsome and agreeable, and it's a cheap way of getting out of responsibili-ties, which is a consideration to a rich pauper like my father-in-law, whom common decency compels to provide an allowance for an only son. He doesn't love Mrs. Raphon, I can tell you," said Mione. "He says he wouldn't mind a handsome demon, but that he is bored with a handsome fool. Mr. Vassal would have been an ideal brother-in-law, putting the social advantages on one side, for you see, Caliban knows all his secrets, and there could have been no inconvenient questions asked about the Raphon scandal."

Mione communicated to me the result of the search among the Vassal papers. "They can't do anything. There's not a legal needle-eye for even my father-in-law to wriggle through ; and if there had been one the size of a pin's-point, you may be sure he would have managed it. Robert Vassal will not hear of terms. Audley tells me it is Mrs. Vassal who holds to her son's rights and refuses to be bought out."

I should like to learn more about Mr. Vassal's heir, whose name is never mentioned at Grisewood. Perhaps it is not strange, though it seems so, that we have not once met in London, for naturally people would have avoided asking us together, knowing of Mr. Vassal's animosity; and if we ever happened to be in the same room at a large party, it is not likely that any one would have pointed him out to me. I have heard that he is a literary man and the editor of *Views*, and occasionally I buy a number of that weekly journal, and wonder which of the articles are written by him. I know that he wrote the novel which ran through the paper last year and was much criticised. I got it afterwards from the library, and it seemed to me extraordinarily powerful. There were scenes in it which throbbed and *ached* with feeling—vivid, and unlike anything I have ever read. Then philosophical and psychological bits, intensely sad and full of subtlety ; then other bits almost fantastic, with a kind of wanton sword-play of metaphor and quaint conceits. When I think of that book and of the volume of poems by Robert Vassal, which I have read also, I shrivel into myself with shame at my own presumption. But there are simple as well as complex harmonies, and I tell myself that I must pipe my own poor tune to the time my leader beats, and to no other. These words, which I found in a beautiful American book not long since, bring me reassurance :—

"*If a man does not keep pace with his companions, perhaps it is because he hears a different drummer. Let him step to the music which he hears, however measured and far away.*"

I have heard, too, that Robert Vassal has lately been elected a Member of Parliament, and is one of a rising little camp of new-time Tories.

Mione Arathoon tells me that she is second or third cousin to Mrs. Robert Vassal, but has never really known her—I imagine partly on account of the Vassal and Arathoon intimacy. They are both, curiously enough, of the Delmar stock, to which the first Mrs. Vassal belonged. Through Mione I heard that the Robert Vassals had been dreadfully poor, till he had made his way in the literary world and had obtained the editorship of *Views*. This seems hard indeed, when he or his son must eventually succeed to Grisewood and Tregarth. Mione told me also that she had met Mr. and Mrs. Robert Vassal last winter at Philotis.

"It was at the Hôtel Cosmopolitain. They had taken the Villa Dépendance in the Cosmopolitain garden. You know it?"

I answered, "No." For they had not finished building the hotel when I went away from Philotis.

But memory thrust forward a vivid picture of grey-green slope and zigzag white road, losing itself in the dark green of fir-thicket —of a fringe of pine-tops against the blue, of a shadowed ravine cutting the hills, of a pile of glaring masonry and trellis of scaffolding, of newly turned earth, and young palms, and gold-dropping mimosa. Memory even gave back the cooing of a wood-pigeon in an ilex grove and the scent of tea-roses from the garden of an adjacent villa. Oh, blue sunshiny dreamland! Land of youth, of freedom, of hope!

Mione went on.

"He is an odd jerky person, Robert Vassal, with eyes that don't seem to be seeing you when you are talking to him. I should have known he was an author; they've all got something queer about them—a kind of latent energy that you feel would boil up into any sort of nonconformity on the least provocation."

I asked her to tell me of Robert Vassal's wife and the boy.

"His wife! She is queerer than he is. You know she is supposed to be a little wrong in her head, to put it mildly—though nobody says much about the matter, and he manages to keep it all dark very cleverly. But Father-in-law, who knows everything about everybody, told me that for two years after the boy's birth she was practically insane, and that most husbands would have shut her up. But he didn't. He looked after her, and she got better. Now she only has occasional mad fits. He didn't show up more than once or twice at Philotis; they told me there that she was pretty well. . . . A tall, lean woman with a Grecian nose and a head like a cameo. The washed-out, greyish-yellow, run-to-seed, aristocratic type—the Delmars came in with William the Conqueror, or thereabouts, you know. So ghost-like!" Mione gave a little shiver. "Pale yellow eyes, pale yellow hair, pale yellow skin—I used to call her the Yellow Woman—with something in her way of looking at you that forces you to think of her afterwards whether you want to or not. She reminded me somehow of a big sickly yellow orchid thing we used to grow in the stove-house, which had a very strong scent."

Strange! Mione's exaggerated description has made this woman a definite human fact to me, and she has been vividly in my mind ever since; it's almost like an uncanny possession. I asked Mione whether she had ever talked to her.

"Yes, once. She used to sun herself in a sort of gravelly place with bamboos round it, in the Cosmopolitain garden, wrapped up in shawls, not reading or doing anything, but just watching him with her bright yellow eyes . . . such extraordinary eyes, like a mad cat's. He had a habit of walking up and down with his book, as if he felt restless and uncomfortable, and I am not surprised. . . . Then, every now and then, she would call to him, in a deep sort of organ-note voice, 'Robert!' And he would go back and settle her wraps or something, and sit by her a bit, and then begin walking again. I couldn't help noticing them, for my chair was fixed on the slope just above. He was as attentive to her as though he had been a well-paid courier. They were supposed to have been very much in love with each other."

In love with each other! That's better than owning Grisewood and Tregarth, and the Vassal diamonds and the rest. Well, they are not to be pitied after all!

"She had money, I believe," said Mione, with the little cynical gesture—an uplifting of her chin and crinkling of the lids over her soft eyes that I associate quaintly with a peculiar after-dinner laugh of Mr. Vassal's. "It couldn't have been much, or she wouldn't be a Delmar. Indigence and eccentricity are the only Delmar inheritance I ever heard of. In fact," pursued Mione, "I'm the one sane and practical Delmar there has been for generations. They all go shaky on something—religion, or railways, or love— or any fad that happens to fall handy! . . . And I'm the only Delmar, too, who ever had twopence—that's by a fluke, through a maternal uncle. . . . From that, and the way he looks after her, it seems as though the romantic-attachment part of the story was true. There is a fascination about her even still—I remember when I was a tiny child, I used to hear of her as 'the beautiful Miss Delmar,' and there are all the remains, though, of course, now she is a specimen of the 'once-have-beens.' . . . Enormous will-power! That woman would do anything she had set her soul on. No doubt she set her soul on getting possession of him, and did it. Haven't you noticed that man-geniuses are always weak on the side of their feminine relations? They're either very much married, or very much the other thing. I prefer them myself when they're the other thing. Robert Vassal is very much married."

I made Mione tell me everything she could about Mrs. Robert Vassal.

"Well, she interested me in a haunting kind of way; and I was abominably bored at the Cosmopolitain, and thought I'd like to know them. So one day I walked down the bank and introduced myself—as a distant Delmar connection, you know— and made some nice speeches about her health, and the table-d'hôte food, and that sort of thing. I chose my opportunity when he had left her for a morning—and I don't wonder he wanted a change—so that she shouldn't fancy he was the attraction. . . .

"Oh! she is certainly very odd. There she sat with a port-folio, and some bits of paper in her lap—I never saw anything so funny. The papers were all covered with queer geometrical sort of drawings, and new moons scattered about, and signs of the zodiac—I know those because I once went to a fancy dress ball as Night, and they were embroidered in silver at the bottom of my skirt, though, as you can't see them, what they had to do with Night I don't know. . . . I asked her if she was doing Euclid problems, and she shook her head.

"'Perhaps you wouldn't believe,' she said, 'that I was clever at mathematics once, and used to help my husband a great deal in his literary work. He wouldn't be the famous man that he is if it hadn't been for me. He says so, and I know it's true. But now I'm broken down, and I lead a retired life. . . . And I've got a reason,' she said, 'for not making new acquaintances : they're dangerous to *him*.'

"If you could have seen the look she gave me. I began to have cold shivers. . . . But I didn't intend to be beaten, so I pretended not to notice the hint, and smiled, and condoled, and agreed that her husband was a very famous person indeed. But I put up a silent prayer that she wouldn't question me on the grounds of my belief; for, between ourselves, that novel of his is altogether too high flown and incomprehensible for my taste. And as for his poetry ! Well, I never know what people do want to write poetry for. As if there wasn't quite enough of nonsense in the world in the love-making line, without adding that. . . . But I really was curious about those queer drawings—fancied they might be embroidery patterns—and I asked her what they were for.

"'It's a hororary figure,' she said; and I was just as wise as ever.

"'You see,' she went on, fixing me again with her crazy look, 'Saturn is lord of the ascendant, and rules the sign of Venus. She's evil aspected in Leo and Cancer, which denotes misfortune for him'—that was her husband—misfortune in the months of— I'm sure I forget which. . . . My dear! such gibberish! There was something about a cusp—whatever that may be; and somebody's sixth house, and somebody's lady of the eighth house. . . . And I said it was extremely interesting, and quite exhilarating in these hard times to hear of anybody with eight houses, or even six—only I hoped for his sake they weren't on agricultural property. But I told her that the lady sounded rather improper— especially if he had one in each of his houses—and that if it was a riddle, I should like very much to know what it all meant. . . .

"'You mustn't tell *him*,' she said. 'He doesn't like to see me doing it. . . . But it's for his sake. . . . There's an Influence coming into his life . . . that's what it means, and I want to guard him against it. . . . It's not you,' she said, staring at me with those uncomfortable eyes. 'You're not the kind of person to influence *him*: though you *are* a Delmar. But, no doubt, you take after your mother. Her family lived in Woodchester, I have heard'—which was a ladylike way of reminding me that Grandfather retired from the iron trade into domestic affluence— with aspirations—and aspirates. To the last I bear solemn witness. . . . Oh, dear! didn't I just feel inadequate! and I told myself that I'd better go. 'What a strange talk we are having,' she said. 'I hope I haven't said anything disrespectful of your mother's family. I have always understood that she was a very charming person. But I am quite sure *you* are not the Influence.'

"I said I was sorry that I wasn't the Influence, because perhaps my wits might be improved if I were; and then I toddled up the bank again. Next time they settled themselves by the bamboos, I only ventured to bow; and he glowered at me as he took off his hat. I always thought that I was the cause of their hiring the Dépendance, which they did soon after, and as its garden is separated from the hotel grounds, I never saw her again: and that was the beginning and the end of my attempt to scrape acquaintance with the Robert Vassals. I was rather sorry," Mione added. "I should have liked to get at the inside of that woman, for I believe there's some sanity in her madness, and I'm sure she'd have amused me; and perhaps I might have amused her. I should have laughed her out of her nonsense.

Think of spending one's life casting hororary figures, and suspecting every good-looking woman of being an 'Influence' one
has got to guard one's husband from.   It's sad—when there are
always gowns and Guardsmen to shake one out of the dumps.
The thing that jars upon me is that she makes herself such a
frump.   Do you observe that's a failing with clever men's wives?
... And now that crinoline is buried in the past, and you can
always buy yourself a curly toupet, there's no excuse for unbecoming invalidism.   Bless the being who invented tea-gowns!
They make it so easy to manage picturesque floppiness.   Now I
feel morally certain that in domestic privacy Mrs. Robert Vassal
wears a red-flannel dressing-gown with white woollen feather-
stitches meandering about—judging from her shawls.   It annoys
me when a beautiful woman doesn't make the best of herself." . . .
And then Mione wandered off on the philosophy of marriage, a
subject she is rather fond of. . . . "A pretty woman who can't
keep her husband on his knees adoring, is too stupid to exist.
The two best safeguards against Influences are Worth and the
Cookery-book.   It's always the nice virtuous domestic wives who
are tyrannised over or neglected—the wives whose maids make
their gowns and who screw down the cook.   Nobody—not even
a genius—wants his wife to wear home-made dresses and economise
over the eggs for the puddings.   The first necessity of a modern man
is to dine decently ; the second, to be envied by his fellow-men ;
the third, to be amused.   Who could envy a man when he owns
a frump?   Feed your husband ; flatter him ; flirt, and let him flirt.
... Those are my tactics with Audley, and I'm quite satisfied
with the result."

I brought her back to the Robert Vassals by inquiring about
the boy.

"Oh, he wasn't at Philotis.   Probably left behind at school.
But somebody told me that he's a splendid British bulldog sort
of little chap.   How did they contrive it?   On the principles
of two negatives making a positive, or the other way on—Vassal
and Delmar!   My good gracious! what will *his* children be
like?   It's certain that the third generation will give the Lunacy
Commissioners something to do."

Then a softer note came into Mione's voice.   "I don't wonder," she said, "that you feel rather bitter over that boy."

"I have not the least feeling of bitterness.   Why should I
grudge another woman the happiness of being a mother?"

"Well," said Mione, becoming flinty again, "that's a happiness
that, personally, I never hankered after.   I've no leanings towards
the young of the human species, which is just the most tiresome

in the animal kingdom. You can't for interest compare a baby with a kitten or a puppy. But then, you see, by Provvy's merciful dispensation, as Frank Leete would say, I am not required to provide anybody with an heir."

.   .   .   .

I am almost happy to-day!

Curious that I should write these words—I to whom joy has been so long a stranger.

But I am not old yet. And the sun is shining, and the air is dreamy and sweet and melodious with the scents and the murmurings of coming spring. The crocuses and the little fat aconites are pushing up their heads through the yielding earth, the birds are softly twittering, and my heart is glad in the gush of running sap and budding things—glad in the thought that life is not all barren; that though love may be an illusion, marriage a mockery, and motherhood a vain yearning, there remain the service of art and the striving after spiritual beauty. And my heart is glad more than all in the sense of a trial made and of work done. For this morning I wrote the last page of my story.

Now I am confronted by a practical difficulty. How am I to get my book published, or even read by a publisher's reader, without letting the publisher, at least, know who I am? And I can't write under Mr. Vassal's name; that is absolutely out of the question. I will go unfriended and unknown before the bar of the public, as Esther Vrintz went. I will be judged without favour, as Esther Vrintz was judged. Perhaps I shall fail, as Esther Vrintz failed. But something tells me that I shall not fail.

I have thought of taking counsel with Mr. Leete. I can trust him to help me and not to betray my secret. He loves a literary mystery. A long time ago he himself published a novel anonymously—it was a failure, and once only in a burst of confidence did he allude to the subject, which is a sore one. And have I not already proved his lively faith in untried genius! So I have written to ask if I may talk to him about a literary matter I am interested in; and if—for I believe Mr. Vassal is staying in Grosvenor Street—he will choose a date when there is no first performance at any of the theatres, and beg Mrs. Leete to take me in for a night. I remember his ways. He never goes to bed before four in the morning, and does not rise till afternoon; and he is in his happiest mood when he has dined and is sitting in his den with his cup of black coffee, a liqueur, and his pipe.

Ah, it makes me think of the time when I read Massinger to him and dreamed of being a new Rachel! How well I seem to know the little dark room, its walls covered from floor to ceiling with books,—books exude everywhere in the Leetes' house, on the stairs even, which have a dado of them and are narrowed in consequence,—the table a litter of papers, proofs, pipes, and photographs of dramatic celebrities adorned with straggling inscriptions in black ink written with a quill pen, and the wee shabby copy of Pope close to hand. For it is a peculiarity of Mr. Leete's that he always carries about a copy of Pope for the consolation of a dull hour. I have heard him recite the *Rape of the Lock* from memory; and he is proud of having translated *The Essay on Man* into French—he is an accomplished French scholar—which was a great production. He read it aloud to Agatha and her *fiancé* and me, and I am sure never quite forgave Captain Greste for saying that he thought the English version dull enough. How well, too, I know the look of Mr. Leete as he leans back puffing clouds of smoke, and clutching spasmodically, as he gets excited, at his great beard—a trick of his, while he discourses on dramatic criticism, the Elizabethans, Alfred de Musset, Victor Hugo, and the rest. And every now and then he kindles to such a pitch of boyish enthusiasm that I feel just a hundred years old beside him. Is it the air of Bohemia, I wonder, which keeps people young? I said something of this kind to him, and his kind eyes grew moist, his face saddened, and he quoted Henri Mürger.

"'La jeunesse n'a qu'un temps,' even in Bohemia!"

Then we got talking back to old times, and to *Claudia*, and to my failure; and he stooped forward and patted my shoulder with his fatherly hand and gave his big mellow laugh, saying—

"Well! well! At any rate, none of us critics would dare to give you a bad notice for the 'Mistress of Grisewood.' It's a big part, and takes a lot of playing, and there's no fault to be found with your rendering."

"There's every fault," I cried out. "I play it very badly. And——" I had to choke down a sob and a great longing to take his two warm hands and feel one of them on each cheek—just for the sake of the dear old Bohemia and the girl who is dead and buried—and to tell him that I would give all Grisewood and Tregarth and the Vassal diamonds to be Esther Vrintz once more in her third-floor room in Bloomsbury. But I didn't quite make a fool of myself.

"Mr. Leete," I said after a moment or two, in which he looked at me with a look he might have given to Agatha, his daughter, "it's all right . . . and the part's a big one, and I'm glad I'm not an utter duffer in it. . . . But—it wants variety, you know. And I've got the old artist crave on me again. I failed as an actress, and now I want to try as a writer, and I want you to help me."

Then Mr. Leete laughed his great tender laugh again, and one hand went up to his beard, and he took the pipe out of his mouth with the other, laid the pipe on the table, and stretched out the hand to me, his face crinkling up with delight.

"Where's the manuscript? Give it to me," he exclaimed. "You want my opinion ; it's a novel of course, and you've got it with you. Go and fetch it for me."

I told him that I did not want him to read my novel in manuscript, or at all, unless it were a real success. I explained the whole thing to him and my reasons for secrecy, and made him give me his promise that he would under no circumstances divulge my true name.

He swore by all his gods, and they are many. "You are quite right," he said. "There's nothing I enjoy so much as a literary complication. Command me, if not as your critic, then as your slave."

"After all," I answered, "I don't want very much. I am going to send my manuscript to Brock & Son, and neither they nor any one else in the world except yourself, is to know who has written it. I have signed it by my mother's name, 'Esther Zamiel.'"

Mr. Leete nodded approvingly. "As a *nom-de-plume*, excellent."

"I shall beg Mr. Brock for a candid opinion. Now may I have any communications from Messrs. Brock addressed under cover to you?"

Mr. Leete seemed disappointed that his part in the affair was to be such a passive one, but he agreed readily enough.

"And I don't fancy," he said, "that if Vassal comes to know of it—which he will do sooner or later—he can call me out for conniving at that sort of clandestine correspondence."

As for my prospects, he was full of hope and encouragement. He had always felt certain, he said, that I should do great things somehow and some day. It could never have been intended that my artistic individuality should be merged in a grand marriage. I was an artist, and would always be an artist, always belong to dear Bohemia, let Philistia claim me never so loudly. . . .

Ah me ! Poor Esther Vrintz ! . . .

Then he added : "And suppose that your book does take

London by storm, and that old Brock, whom I know slightly, should worry me with questions about Esther Zamiel, what am I to say?"

"Say that you knew her father, who was a disappointed musician, and that you helped her on to the stage, where she was a failure, and are helping her now in another line of business. Very likely she will be a failure in that too, and then nothing will matter."

.   .   .   .

My manuscript has been a month in the publisher's hands. I have written again. And now Mr. Leete has forwarded me a note in which Miss Esther Zamiel is requested to call upon Mr. Brock.

BOOK V

" Look into thine heart, and write."

WRITTEN
BY
ESTHER
VASSAL: I HAVE seen Mr. Brock. Yes, what Mr. Leete says is true. I am artist to the very fibre of me, and I thrill with exaltation, doubt, and pain. I will tell of the interview.

Mr. Brock is elderly, with rather long, grey hair, the stoop of a man of letters, alert eyes, and an eager, genial manner which seems frankness itself—and which yet, now I come to think of it, commits him to nothing. He was seated before a large writing-table, on one side of which, stood a row of electric knobs with names printed on them, and below these several speaking-tubes, one of which was conspicuously labelled " MS. Room." There was a high bookcase behind the writing-table filled with books in new bindings, and on the top of it, the bust of a great novelist, for whom Brock & Sons published. On the wall hung an engraving of another dead and gone author, a famous woman, whom Mr. Brock's father introduced to the reading world. The house keeps up its traditional policy of fostering unknown talent : that is why I chose it.

On Mr. Brock's table were packets of business papers neatly docketed, some pages of manuscript, a pile of what looked like ledgers, and a bundle of proof-sheets of the new number of *Brock's Magazine*, which he seemed to have been reading.

The card on which I had written *Miss Esther Zamiel* lay upon the blotting-pad. As I entered, the publisher rose and held out his hand.

"Miss Esther Zamiel," he said, and pulled forward an arm-chair to which he waved me, seating himself again at the writing-table, "I am extremely obliged to you for having granted my request for an interview."

His keen eyes ran me up and down. I had put on my plainest clothes ; but perhaps he thought that my dress was not quite appropriate to the struggling literary aspirant, for there was surprise in his expression. Something of the old terror of the footlights came over me and shrivelled me into stiff reserve. I answered mechanically and sat still, waiting for him to speak. He hesitated, arranged his papers before him, and fidgeted with the card; and all the time I could feel his eyes shifting on and off me.

"Miss Zamiel," he began presently with an air of embarrassed candour, "I was anxious to see you and to have an opportunity in conversation with you of forming my own judgment independently of my Reader. That was why I asked you to come, and yet I feel that I ought to apologise for doing so, for I have nothing definite to tell you."

He waited, but I said nothing.

"The truth is," he went on, "your letter interested me, and the reports I got of the story you were good enough to submit to us interested me still more. They have also surprised me, for they are not the kind of reports we usually have of a young lady's first novel."

A pause.

"Your manuscript has been through the hands of two of my Readers. I had better tell you at once that their reports are not quite favourable. They differ; but though opposed in certain details, coincide upon the main point. Both speak of talent, power, originality; yet — in short, you asked for an honest opinion. If you wish it I will read you some extracts from these reports."

I said that I should like to hear them.

Mr. Brock selected a volume from the pile of ledger-like books near him and opened it. I saw that it was labelled "Reports," and that on each page was pasted a smaller page of manuscript with the heading of the firm. Mr. Brock turned over the leaves.

"Here it is . . . *From Nadir to Zenith*—Of course," he said, "that title would never do. Too astronomical, and not taking. And perhaps I ought to say now that, as a rule, we don't care for one-volume works—especially by unknown authors. They don't pay the expense of advertising—however, we can go into that question later. My first Reader sums up the book——"

Mr. Brock hummed over the opening sentences.

. . . "Pity that a certain amount of good material . . . vividness of impression . . . feeling for the beauties of Nature—in parts, force of description—should be so entirely thrown away. The subject is objectionable." Here followed an epitome of the plot, which Mr. Brock skipped freely. . . . "Handled with the crude amateurishness of an hysterical schoolgirl . . . revolting from the utter absence of artistic reserve. . . . It is true that the book might attract a class of readers, but so do the reports of the divorce court . . . h'm! . . . h'm! . . . It offends against the laws of probability; but what is worse, it offends against the canons of good taste and morality."

Mr. Brock turned over the page, and with accentuated delicacy refrained from meeting the eyes of his shocked and wounded listener.

"You will pardon me, Miss Zamiel. I trust that you will not be too deeply hurt by the sharpness of the criticism. I thought it best that you should hear it without any softening down. The second Reader takes in some respects a different view."

Mr. Brock began again.

"*From Nadir to Zenith* is daring in its originality and in its unconventional treatment of a world-worn theme." . . . Mr. Brock paused to run his finger down the lines. "Here we have again an abstract of the plot. I need not trouble you with that . . . h'm ! . . . h'm ! . . . Here we are." . . . "It is in parts crude, in parts repulsive, but the power and passion of the book are undeniable. Passion indeed forms the motive of the work, and some of the love-passages are so realistic that to the prurient mind they might give a suggestion of animalism." . . . Mr. Brock gave a deprecatory murmur before he proceeded.

"The almost painful conscientiousness with which these are made to accord psychologically with the delineation of a debased character, might, however, in the case of the thoughtful reader, remove that impression. . . .

". . . So unconventional is the treatment, so masculine the sentiment, that but for the feminine prefix and other evidences of origin, one might almost believe the book to be the work of a man. . . . In its present form it is impossible. Three volumes are crammed into one in a manner savouring of melodrama, and certain details, set forth with an amazing and even childlike candour, require careful toning down. To be acceptable to the public, the entire work needs recasting and expansion. My belief, however, is that there is a touch of genius in the author, and that she will in time make a distinct mark. I strongly advise you not to lose sight of her."

"And now, Miss Zamiel," said Mr. Brock, closing the book, "I come to what I wanted to say when I asked you to oblige me with an interview. I'm going to be quite frank with you. I cannot publish your story in its present form, nor am I quite disposed to accept as final either of the judgments which I have read to you. I am going to ask a favour. Leave me the manuscript for a little while longer. Unfortunately, the Reader on whom I place entire reliance has been absent from England during the last month. He returns shortly. I should like him to read your story ; and if he thinks·well of it, to give you his advice as to the remodelling of it. There is no one in England better qualified to give such advice, as you would at once admit if I might tell you his name. That, you will understand, is not possible. Candidly, I don't want to lose sight of you ; and I ask you this as a favour, because it is of course quite possible that the final verdict may be discouraging."

"Yes," I answered vaguely. I got up from my chair. "It does not seem to me that there is any favour in what you ask, Mr. Brock. I am very glad that my manuscript is to have another chance. Besides, you might have kept it ever so much longer without saying anything to me."

"We should probably have done so, had you not written a second time. I am very much obliged to you, Miss Zamiel, and I promise you that you shall have our answer at the very earliest opportunity."

I thanked him and went away. Mr. Brock conducted me himself to the door of the outer office, and it struck me afterwards that this might be an auspicious circumstance. But then I was dazed, hurt, astonished. The sentences of the Readers' reports kept repeating themselves in my brain. I had followed Dr. Glaive's advice, and had written out of the deeps of me. What is there in me to call forth such comment as that which I heard ? How can I have offended against the canons of good taste and morality ? . . . I who have never known love. . . . I walked on, my cheeks crimson, tears starting from my eyes, and yet moved to the core and treading on air. The woman in me bled : the artist rejoiced. Had not the Reader spoken of a "touch of genius" !

FROM
ROBERT
VASSAL
TO
JAMES
BROCK: My dear Brock,—The east wind has travelled like wildfire through the whole of this miserable machine, till I have become an incarnate Cough and a walking Inflammation. And that is what one gets from a return to one's native land! And you call me unpatriotic! Patriotism is a quality no more: it is a vice in everybody who is not Irish, and an advertisement in all who are. Which means that I did not open your bundle of MS. till yesterday.

Good boy Barham, with his eternal cant about the moralities, is out of it this time, though I grant you that a certain toning down of style and revelations will be necessary before you introduce your Unknown to Mrs. Grundy. I'd stake a good deal, however, on the woman being as pure-minded as a Greek Venus— always supposing that a Greek Venus was ever endowed with mind, which we know she wasn't. Tryon is nearer the mark in his criticism. The author of *From Nadir to Zenith*—Heavens, what a title!—will certainly make her mark, as he predicts. No, distinctly and emphatically, don't let her go. There's money in her, which appeals to the mercantile element in you ; and there's genius too—a rare combination. She wants delicate handling, and she mustn't be allowed to get it into her head that she is improper. Excuse me for saying that I think you made a mistake in reading her those reports. A touch of self-consciousness might make her immoral. At present she is naked and not ashamed— an Eve of novelists.

Tryon is right : the book is impossible in its present shape ; it needs recasting, and might with advantage be spread over two or three volumes—two, I should say, for a prentice hand ; it takes workmanship to make a second volume in three interesting. I believe that with toning down, pulling together, and drawing out, there's stuff in the story for a big success, though nobody knows better than yourself that the appreciative faculty of the British reading public is almost as incalculable a quantity as that of the playgoing public. In fact, you never know where to have 'em ! If you think that Esther Zamiel is of the sort to take kindly such help and advice as I can give her, I will gladly fall in with your suggestion of an interview, provided always that my incognito be strictly preserved.—Faithfully yours,

ROBERT VASSAL.

By the way, I don't know why you should take it for granted that Esther Zamiel is a pseudonym. Esther!—"whom the king married and made queen . . . and the two dragons are I and Haman "—of the tribe of the critics—" And their cry was great ! " Zamiel—of the Rabbis—a name, I fancy, I have seen in Philotis. Many thanks for your inquiries after my wife. She has been much benefited by her sojourn in that City of Delight.

WRITTEN
BY
ESTHER
VASSAL:
I want to remember every word that the Reader said to me.

There were two men in Mr. Brock's office when I went in. The publisher greeted me in his bland alert manner: the other man was standing at the farther window, his head a black blur against the light, a manuscript in his hand. He just looked up for a moment, then began reading again. "I have to thank you a second time for coming, Miss Zamiel," said Mr. Brock. "I congratulate you on the interest your work seems to have aroused; and I hope that you may feel disposed to give attention to my Reader's suggestions, and that when remodelled I may have the pleasure of publishing your story. I ought perhaps, however, to tell you that you will need all your courage, for you have to do with a critic who is considered mercilessly truthful."

The man at the window looked up again sharply, as though he were annoyed. I seemed to know in a queer intuitive way that the publisher's words had jarred. A touch of that other-world presentiment which I have had before, made everything seem at once vivid and unnatural for a moment. I can't analyse the feeling—it's a thing by itself.

I said that it was the truth I wanted.

Then the other man spoke, as if he were quoting from the pages before him, "Oh, ye men, are not women strong? Great is the earth; high is the heaven; swift is the sun in his course. . . . Great is truth, and mighty above all things! You will note, Brock, that I have been studying the Apocrypha."

He stepped sideways from the window, claiming attention. The other-world grip tightened on me, and in the daze it made there was the shock, sharp and insistent, of a past association. I had listened to that voice; I had seen that profile before.

Presently I heard Mr. Brock say, "Now I am going to leave you to your fate." He made a gesture with his hands as though he were shaking off all unpleasant responsibility. "Unfortunately, Miss Zamiel, I can't present your critic by name. For obvious reasons, a publisher's reader and a professional slayer of literary hopes is anxious to keep his incognito. But allow me, 'The Reader . . . Miss Esther Zamiel.'"

The man bowed, impatiently I fancied, and said, as the door closed on Mr. Brock and his periphrases, "Miss Zamiel will understand that there may be young authors less ready than herself to sacrifice vanity to truth."

And now that he had come closer, and that he looked at me, it all flashed back—the falling snow, the gloom of winter afternoon, the great pilasters of the theatre, with their flaring red posters, the group of men in the portico. I heard again those incisive tones—Fate's fiat for me—felt again that stab of despair. I could not speak. I could only stare at him wildly; and he exclaimed with a frown of annoyed surprise, "You know who I am?"

"No," I answered, recovering myself; "I don't know your name. I have only seen you once, and that was long ago."

"But you seemed so startled—so shocked. . . . Where did you see me?"

"It was at the theatre—outside, after a matinée."

"A matinée! . . . But what of that?"

"I was an actress, and I had failed dreadfully . . . and you were present at the failure. . . ."

"There must have been a great many others present also," he said.

"Yes. . . . But it was something you said—I heard you say that I had mistaken my vocation, and that I should never do any good."

He knitted his forehead as if searching for a clue that he could not find.

"I am very sorry if I hurt you. . . . I wish I could remember. . . . I seem to have a glimmering. . . . But it's of no use. I suppose I have seen a good many young actresses—who failed."

"It is nearly eight years ago," I said ; and then the thought occurred to me that if I were to proclaim myself Esther Vrintz, I might as well proclaim myself Mrs. Vassal. Somehow the sight of him swept away pretences, and I had almost forgotten that I am masquerading under a pseudonym.

"Please don't try to remember me. I had much rather you didn't. Only it is strange that, after having heard you say that I should not succeed as an actress, I may now have to hear you say that I shall not succeed as a writer."

"Yes, it is strange," he said thoughtfully, and his eyes seemed to search my face still.

"Won't you sit down?" he added abruptly, pushing forward

the leather arm-chair, and himself taking Mr. Brock's place at the writing-table. He turned over the manuscript he held, which I now saw was my own. "I am not going to say that you will not succeed as a writer."

Again I had the sense of mind-currents playing between us, just as on that day when I was crouching against the pillar in the theatre porch and listening to his talk, only it was intensified many degrees. And indeed ever since this meeting in Mr. Brock's office the impression has remained. Perhaps it is the peculiarly bright ray his eyes give out when they are fixed upon one which causes the fancy. They are sad eyes; there's something repressed in them. But they are kind; and the mouth, that is so sensitive and worried-looking, becomes quite different when he smiles.

" You know George Lewes's admirable saying, that in criticism everything depends upon the point of view. I may criticise you according to a low standard, or according to the highest."

I said something about wishing to aim at the best things. My own words seem to matter so little; it is his which I should like to keep as a possession.

"Good! Tell me," he asked abruptly, "are you working for money?"

Something of the puzzlement which had been in Mr. Brock's face was in his, and I noticed a quick glance at my neck, and remembered a valuable pearl set in a brooch, with which my lace scarf was fastened, and that the lace itself is old and particularly good, like all the Vassal lace.

I told the Reader, that if he thought I was fit for it, I wanted to work for Art.

"Oh, Art!" He laughed and gave a little upward movement and turn of his head. It is a fine intellectual head, so much stronger than the lower part of the face, with the hair growing rather curiously straight back from the forehead and curling at the points.

"I am not sure that Art didn't thrive much better in the garret days than be-dinnered and be-diamonded in modern London. Hunger, you know, is medicine for immortality! . . . May I read aloud a bit of your manuscript? That's how I shall begin my criticism. And remember, it is to be the highest standard. *We* want to write for men and women who have thought and suffered—not for the penny million."

My heart beat quick with pleasure at this coupling of me with himself. Presently it beat quicker still, but in dread and shame.

"Listen to this," he said.

He read aloud several passages from my manuscript. They

are bits which, now that I go over them in cold blood, make my cheeks tingle. While he went on it seemed to me that my secret soul in all its folly and presumption was being laid bare as under a magnesium light. My glowing metaphor, my romantic sentiment, my fervid dialogue, became vulgar twaddle and jingling melodrama. Every now and then a delicate irony from him, or a pointed illustration, would accuse me of slipshod English— or worse. Once he gravely inquired what had been my artistic intention in regard to a complication of plot ; and alas ! I had had no "intention," but had written at the spur of fancy. He reproved a tendency to inartistic commingling of the Romantic and Naturalistic methods, quoting a line from Ruskin and delivering a warning against the irreverent adaptation to modern life of situations dealt with in the Greek tragedies. . . . There are many kinds of torture; this is one of which the recollection makes me start from sleep o' nights, as Mr. Leete's Elizabethans would say, smarting and burning as though the lash were stinging yet.

"I have been very hard on you," he said at last, laying down the manuscript; "but it was with a purpose. I thank you for your brave patience. Don't hate me for plying my trade ; and is it any consolation to know that I only do this sort of thing for those I see are worth it ? Try to look upon me as a surgeon, who to do his patient any good must probe deep."

"Tell me if I am quite hopeless," I cried desperately. "You said it once before in my hearing ; say it again to my face ; and if that's the truth, don't gloss it with soft words just because you are sorry for me."

"And why should I be sorry for you?" he asked abruptly, bending a little forward and looking at me with an interested expression. "Even supposing I didn't think much of your chances as an author, why should I pity you? You don't need to work for money, so that it can't be a matter of vital importance. You must have all the ordinary interests and pleasures of a woman of the world ; and there are better ways of amusing oneself than by the writing of novels. . . . Unless," he paused, and I fancied that he was endeavouring on outward indications to construct a theory about me—"unless it is that you are alone in the world, deprived perhaps of some dear companionship, and that you are counting on this work to supply what is lacking in your life?"

"Yes, I am alone in the world."

I spoke from my inner sense of things—not considering, as I have done since, the false impression my words might produce. But how, as Esther Zamiel, could I have replied, except evasively? How convey the truth without conveying also the fact that I am an unhappy married woman? Yet I have been wishing all the time that there were no petty deceptions between us. While I am talking to him, there comes over me a feeling I have never had in my life before—a feeling of having gained mental foothold, and of standing with one able to comprehend my inner self on a platform high above the worldly conventions. That is as it should be. Where Art reigns, the ordinary-man-and-woman conventions should cease to exist. He is just "the Reader" to me. I don't know his name; I don't want to know it. I am his pupil; he is my teacher.

"Surely you can understand," I said, "what it is to be stifling for the need of expression—the need of a larger life?"

"I know the need well, and have suffered severely from it; but a man has outlets difficult for a woman to find. Well, I have learned so much about you without any telling from you. It's all written here"—he touched the manuscript with the palm of his hand. "Here I see the yearning for things unutterable; here I see the curse and crown of genius."

"Genius!"

"Yes; you have power, originality, sincerity. I venture to believe that you have genius."

Did I cry out in my rapture and astonishment, and was it that which made him rise and stand for a minute, looking down on me with radiant and yet mournful kindness?

"It's a big word—genius! Think! You may be great; that thought should keep you humble. But I observe with gladness that though you have artistic pride, you have not artistic vanity. If I handled you roughly at first, it was because I wanted to test you; so that I might, if you would let me, help you in mastering the craft. I have found fault with the form; and the form, remember, is everything, and is nothing. It is the spirit that giveth life. Remember, too, that the spirit manifests itself through form, and that form may be moulded into symmetrical beauty. That is where I, as an elder craftsman, may be of use to you. The art of the novelist has to be learned; it is a mistake to suppose that the fine taste which leads to perfection of form comes by intuition. At the same time I realise a responsibility. I should dread the quenching of the spirit by a too strenuous insistence upon technicalities. If I were to become, to some small extent, your teacher, I should not approach you again in the carping attitude of this morning. I want you to rewrite your book according to the new lights, and to send it to me feeling certain of appreciation, and that my suggestions and corrections would be just those which a more experienced workman might offer to an enthusiastic beginner, in danger of assaulting the canons of intellectual Grundyism. One wiser than I has said that though genius may sometimes need the spur, it as often requires the curb."

" I will do everything that you say is right, if you will tell me where I am wrong."

He looked pleased, and still standing, or else walking to and fro in the narrow space between window and fireplace, he began to discuss the manner in which my story might be improved and expanded. He advised me to brood—for a week, a month, six months—exactly so long as it might take me to get grip of the subject.

" Then, put aside the old manuscript, and write—write what comes to you. Remember you cannot describe vividly what you do not *feel* vividly. Get your keynote, make your atmosphere, and be fearless, and trust in your own sense of art. If it doesn't carry you along, it's worth nothing. . . . And if you come to a *crux* and want advice or sympathy, don't hesitate to write to me; I shall take the deepest interest in your progress. Next to doing good work oneself, the greatest artistic joy is in watching others do it. A letter addressed to 'The Reader' under cover to Mr. Brock will always find me, and shall be answered without delay."

I got up to go. Some instinct of shyness kept me from holding out my hand. He made me a low bow. I could not help saying—

" If you only knew what new hope you have put into my life, you would understand why I find it hard to thank you."

" Don't try," he answered abruptly. " Besides, I do know. Do you think I have never been hopeless and lonely and in want of encouragement? There's no need to thank me. Do that when London is talking about your book—though," he added, " I shall have done nothing to deserve your thanks."

<table>
<tr><td>

FROM
JAMES
BROCK
TO
ESTHER
ZAMIEL:

</td><td>

Dear Madam,

Presuming your work *Naamah* to make three volumes, I beg to offer you, on the signature of the agreement, fifty pounds (£50) in cash, and on the publication of the book fifty copies free of charge.

</td></tr>
</table>

I beg to remain, very faithfully yours,

JAMES BROCK.

*From the Same
to the Same.*

Dear Miss Zamiel,—Tone down ; *tone down* ; TONE DOWN. —Yours faithfully, JAMES BROCK.

*From the Same
to the Same.*

Dear Miss Zamiel,—I cannot thank you too much for the extreme kindness with which you receive the suggestions offered you.

I appreciate the difficulty, as also does the Reader, of giving effect to them so as not to lose the unity of the story. It seemed right, however, for me to place before you the different, and indeed opposite, opinions of two Readers, one judging much by impulse, the other by reason. I knew you would get from the two together a view in advance of what the two schools of critics would say, and so be beforehand with them by obviating any objections which appeared to you legitimate. I think the process of temptation is always difficult to show without begetting a feeling of repulse in the reader's mind, if the mind be healthy. This is the point I am most anxious about.

However, I now leave the matter with you, in gratitude for your patient forbearance.—Yours very truly, JAMES BROCK.

*From the Same
to the Same.*

Dear Miss Zamiel,—I send you a line to say that I am *amply* satisfied with progress so far.

I have just received the *Piccadilly Gazette.* A grand notice ! —Yours very truly, JAMES BROCK.

... OF course, the more absorbing interest of the story lies in the psychological analysis of Naamah's character, and of the effect upon a virginal nature, at once singularly elemental and singularly complex, of a loathed bondage to legalised sensuality. Profoundly painful as the study is to me—and that for reasons much deeper than any mere rule of conventional propriety—I cannot say that I would alter or omit a single line. You must expect to be misunderstood. Stupid people believe that evils are mitigated, if not cured, by not being talked about. Prurient people believe that sensuous passion can only be treated from the motives that would actuate themselves. Of course, I do not know how far your object was, as I need not say it might legitimately be, artistic purely, or how far it was also social and moral. But the book has set me thinking on the workings of popular philosophy and fashionable practice. The inculcation of theories which are afterwards found not to square with the facts of life, of creeds which will not bear examination, doctrines which will not stand the test of experience, destroy I am sure many characters and wreck many careers. Add to these, the dreary, witless, vulgar flippancy which is supposed to constitute the best social tone, and wonder if you can, that a girl with any mind or heart or soul breaks out into extravagance or vice. Your book afflicts me. But my consolations are two. In the first place, fashionable society, which alone lives like that, is a very small portion of the human race. In the second, people will find out sooner or later that the only security against morbid misery, the only existence worth leading is the double life of the intellect and the affections. I observe with pleasure that your Leonore does not care for reading. That is as true a touch as Iago's contempt for women.

The frivolity of the social life described and the tragedy which is being enacted behind the scenes reminds one of the

Venetians in Browning's poem who amuse themselves by night and by day.

> "... *till in due time, one by one,*
> *Some with lives that came to nothing, some with deeds as well undone,*
> *Death stepped tacitly and took them where they never see the sun.*"

.   .   .   .

I read your chapters last night at a very advanced hour, after the House had done its work. The hour was appropriate to a story so full of ominous suggestiveness, but was too late for me to do more than scribble you a rough impression of the effect produced. I have now some criticisms to make and some faults to find. ... [Here follows a list of corrections.]

.   .   .   .

... Pardon me if I make a suggestion. You have painted your Naamah pure, forgiving, and—passionless. Can you not infuse a few warm drops into the current of her blood?

I am afraid that human sympathy, except in the case of a small canting section, will always be with the Magdalen rather than with the woman who leaves it to be supposed that, after all, her coldness has been the safeguard of her purity. Could you not by a stroke or two of your pen let us at least guess that under different conditions, in a more congenial atmosphere, under the touch of a master-hand, the marble statue would have breathed, and that the spark of passion would have been kindled?

If, however, you as an artist are content to leave the appreciation of your work to the comparatively small number of minds capable of discerning the spirituality of the ideal, you are certainly justified. When therefore I say that Naamah might be improved by a little "warming up," remember I say so from the point of view of Mr. Brock's public—the public which demands that the ideal should be debased slightly, as the Mint puts alloy into pure gold to make it current. ...

.   .   .   .

You have seized and expressed my meaning. You have animated the statue. . . One passage only I should like to expunge. . . .

.   .   .   .

... I am going to give you a little lecture in parenthesis. Whether of my work, or your work, or anybody's work, never believe in being too good for the public. It may take a little while to educate it, but "the Great Big Stupid" always understands in the long run. One can never be too clever, except by being obscure—the crying sin of a whole crowd of writers, who use obscurity of language to veil obscurity of thought.

And now—another parenthesis: and to answer the difficulty at which you hinted. You will be less dependent upon mood when you grow master of your work. Mastery comes from knowledge ; and knowledge only from reading and experience. Originality is idle without it, and cram is poor substitute.

. . . Cultivate knowledge, not of society, but of books, whose strange fascination grows like no other. Oddly enough, there is no diet for imagination like knowledge when it is not mere formal cram.

I understand what you say about those "partings of the way" —those Y's of life—which belong both to the intellectual and emotional life. Several years ago I myself came to one such. I was then older than you are now. Up to near that time, I had read practically nothing but French novels and poetry, and was absolutely without the invaluable power of attention. I had worked half-heartedly, and wanting the spur of actual need, at a profession I loathed. There could not have been a more wasted life, or one more unhappy or discontented. I had broken down after my father's death, and other severer trials ; and for more than two years was practically non-existent. Then that came about which obliged me to take myself in hand, and I did begin to read. A naturally good memory helped me to conquer indolence and inattention, and I *forced* myself to know. . . . Never had life so harlequinesque a change ! In health : in power : in happiness—in everything ! Imagination, starved as I say for lack of knowledge, seemed to grow with my reading. I am not of the way of thinking of Schopenhauer, who looks upon truth that has been picked up from books as a meretricious sort of thing. Books are worth to me all the society on earth excepting that of a few real and kindred souls. There's a chapter of autobiography. I don't ask you to forgive it, irrelevant as it seems. It means, cultivate knowledge for your own gift's sake —and especially now that, as I glean from sundry phrases and allusions in your last letter, you feel yourself at one of life's cross-roads.

.   .   .   .

Why do you make your prominent men-characters sceptics or atheists? If you can't stand an orthodox Churchman—I speak artistically—why not go in for a Roman Catholic? Atheists and sceptics—c'est toujours perdrix. I think you will see with your artistic eyes what I mean. Darwinise Max if you like, but give him faith in something. . . .

.   .   .   .

I had to hurry off the proofs of your last chapter this morning, and regret having given myself no time for explanation or apology in regard to my fussy little interpolation. It was suggested by a remark of my wife's, who occasionally looks over proofs for me, and by a chance, lighted upon that delicate awakening passage— a passage which naturally appeals to the feminine view of things. I gave the marginal criticism for your consideration merely as embodying the idea of the conventionally brought-up Englishwoman, and not because I agree with it. On the contrary, I think I hold with you; but it occurs to me that in some matters your method of generalising is rather of the masculine order.

Still another autobiographical parenthesis. You speak of apathy of the mind and soul, and of an "awakening" crisis. I have gone through one of those crises to which you allude, and at the root of them lies a mystery apart from causes material and mental, for it is above and beyond both, and it comes of the spirit. And again I say unto you—Work.

Do you not agree with me that the truest definition of genius is chronic incapacity to harmonise with its environment? The contrasting types of the two women of genius in your story realise this notion—antithetically. Strange how in the region of things invisible, as in the universe visible, the law of duality reigns. Genius as an abstract quantity distinctly comprises the dual attributes—body and spirit. Leonore, secondary figure as she is, and notwithstanding her indifference to books, must be classed under the heading. Naamah is genius of the reflective order in its poetic and spiritual aspect; Leonore represents intellectual-material genius, and expresses it in action and feeling rather than in what I must call the literary tendency. Your psychology seems to me correct in making these two women—the one all brain and spirit, the other all brain and passion—fall in love with a poet who combines, as every genuine poet must, the three elements, passion, mind, and soul. Your analysis of the poet's temperament interests me curiously. But it occurs to me that just as poets are differentiated from other men, so are poets differentiated from poets. In your poet, for instance, there is more of the traditional artistic weakness and inconsistency than, say, in a Victor Hugo; and there is more strength and steadfastness than in an Alfred de Musset. One might add that there is in some poets an extraordinary power of the nobler loving, that underlies and overarches perpetually all their merely artistic phases, and also a depth of religious feeling—I speak of the Nature religion, not the religion of creeds—which causes continual turmoil and conflict—the battle of the two beings within one.

Yes, I wish I could help you by throwing a flash from the masculine understanding upon that question of the poetic temperament and its emotional complexities. But alas! I cannot see a way out of the horrible problem which for generation after generation has made the relation of man and woman, thus crowned and cursed, an agony rather than a glory. Yet I think I do feel some truths about the poet nature—its strength and its feebleness; its fret and fervency; its fatal battle of soul and sense; its moth-like flutterings towards an unrealisable ideal; and the torturing lack of unity in it, which makes its heaven-in-hell and its hell-in-heaven.

But surely the final word should not be given to the pessimist, or in very truth there is no God. Surely, if there be a law spiritual, the ineffective beginning should shadow forth the glorified End.

Do you picture the poet in youth, under the magic touch of first love, glowing with the enthusiasm of a boy-Shelley, pure, noble, full of passionate faith in God and Woman and Man—full of ecstatic belief in the eternity and oneness of marriage?

Then picture the overthrowing of his altar, the discovery that marriage is not a fulfilment of the monogamic Ideal, but only a fragment of a vast, so to speak, polygamic scheme. Picture him brought face to face with that insoluble riddle of the artist nature, the inappeasable hunger for perfection : forced to know, with a poet's unerring intuition, that the highest good is to worship one woman ; and yet to realise that he is doomed to worship a kind of mosaic of complex womanhood—doomed by the arbitrary will of the Demi-urgos, having not yet found the greater God. For you remember how the Greeks used to figure to themselves that in the sombre darkness behind Zeus, there loomed another stronger God, the Ultimate Fate—in Whom, I confess, lieth my hope.

Some words you have written, embolden me to express a nebulous fancy that neither man nor woman are fit yet for the monogamic ideal. . . . I theorise on abstract lines. There is scarcely a man or woman at this stage of evolution fit to be trusted with the entire life of another. The race is not developed enough. Man will wreck woman by unfaithfulness of the spirit or the letter: woman will wreck man by jealousy, ill-temper, a hundred woman's weaknesses.

Yet, I cling to my half-doubting faith in the ultimate Zeus, the Larger Beyond. I tell myself that all is not pessimism ; all is not defeat. I tell myself that the martyrdom of the many may mean the redemption of the few : that to pass through the gateway of an unspeakable agony, behind all the conventional gods, may be a nearer reaching towards the mystery of the universe, and a way opened for the race into higher being. I cling to my trembling hope that here, or hereafter, the Love-goal may be won, the twin-soul recognised, and the passionate progress close in peace ineffable.

. . . Will the drafts of faith be honoured?

Forgive this rhapsody. I have again burst my bonds of critic. Perhaps I had better make the clean confession that I myself am half a poet.

WRITTEN
BY
DOCTOR
QUINTIN
GLAIVE: THE next occasion upon which I met Mrs. Vassal was at a dinner-party at the house of Mr. Arathoon in Chesham Place, at which she and her husband were present. Already I had received a note from her, desiring me to call in Grosvenor Street the following day, as Mr. Vassal wished her, she said, to consult me about her winter plans.

This was in November, very soon after the publication of *Naamah*. The book was making a sensation. I had got it in the natural order of things from the library: had at once discovered the authorship, and had, I must own, felt deeply hurt at Mrs. Vassal's silence on the subject. But when I saw her, the ever-renewed charm of her personality, her pathetic smile, and that air of aloofness from petty interests, which made her unlike other women, worked their spell, and I ceased to resent her want of confidence, attributing it to its rightful cause—the shy pride of a sensitive nature, and reactionary reserve after her impulse to self-revelation.

I noticed a certain change; and fragile as she still seemed, it was on the whole for the better, though the brightness of her eyes and the vivid, pink flush on her cheeks made me suspect lung mischief, and resolve within myself that if I had any voice in the matter, Philotis, or some such Southern place, should be her winter abode. Beyond this, her face had lost something of its old brooding unhappiness, something too of that strained quietude of feature, which had been in such unnatural contrast with the wild frightened expression, at moments, of her eyes, always to me sadly suggestive. I could easily guess that her literary work had been an outlet for morbid energies, and that her nerves were in a healthier condition than when I had seen her at Grisewood.

The frightened look only came back when Mr. Vassal spoke to her. Yet on the surface, there was nothing in his manner to call it forth. He was coldly suave, indifferently elaborate: in fact, he gave her rather more attention than society usually demands from a seven years' husband who has grown tired of his wife, but is too well bred to make the boredom apparent.

There was something in this man which, long before I began
to take a special interest in Mrs. Vassal, repelled me so greatly
that I had avoided his company, and after the first, had refused
the invitations he sometimes sent me to his bachelor dinners,
famous as these were in the matter of viands, wines, and witty
conversation. The wit was of a flavour not to my liking; and
though I am a man of the world, and I hope, neither prude nor
prig, that first entertainment offered no inducement towards a
repetition of the experience.

It gave me a curious impression of having leaped centuries,
to certain Roman banquets of Imperial times. We only wanted
couches and garlands of roses and ivy, and a myrrhine cup or two
for a theme, and Syrian dancing-girls and nightingales' tongues
and a few other such trifles ! And was not there Loseley Allard
paraphrasing the Parasite, and delivering paradoxical epigrams in
defence of the noble profession of dining-out—and some other
matters ; while grosser echoes floated from a still further past on
the after-dinner talk. One does not need to dive deep for ancient
instances. We have refined the outward forms a little ; but is the
inner man less of a brute than in the days of a Caligula or a
Commodus ! And now as then, the gold-gods take the reserved
places, and no doubt the moon wails yet over the calumnies
of scientists and philosophers—if there were eagles' and vultures'
feathers lying handy, to bring one within hail of her.

Yes, it forces itself—the parallel between that dead empire in
its pride, luxury, and wantonness, and the pride and luxury and
wantonness which meet us day and night in this great, vile, magnificent London.

It forces itself—the similitude. Not in point of moral de-
cadence only, but in the grip and grandeur of the race : its
combativeness, its resistless stretch for dominion : its civic pomp
and pageantry and forensic brilliance : its intellect, glitter, and
dash, and its gropings too after a philosophical interpretation of
life's problems. Here and there, a stern grappling with these on
Stoic methods : more widespread, the gentle Epicurean tendency
to garner in the beautiful and to lull discontent with a sort of
mental haschisch. Then, too, the nation's despairing satire ; its
hard materialism ; its deification of Reason ; its derisive railings
against the old myths and the dethroned gods. And side by side
with all this, the melancholy of honest thinkers : the feverish
worship of vain idols : the cult of superstition—for as Novalis
puts it, " Where there is no God, there are ghosts."

While over this seething mass of sensuous and intellectual
elements there broods palely the divine Ray : the dawn in

humanity of spiritual knowledge. And so it seems to me, that here, now, in this city of corruption, outshining wandering lights, and putrescent gleams, there is shed the irradiating influence of an other-world truth, just as in imperial Rome, reeking with vice, fetid with the stench of blood, some earnest souls caught, eighteen hundred years ago, the distant glory of the Star that rose above Galilee.

One might in truth be tempted to believe, in moments of fantastic wondering, that those old Romans have reawakened in the flesh after their bodiless sleep of nigh two thousand years, and are walking our streets, pleading in our tribunes, legislating in our Senate House, dancing and miming in our theatres, rioting and wantoning in our pleasure-palaces. Think of this, as you stroll down the long gallery in the Uffizi, filled with the statues of dead Romans : or nearer still, go through the Roman court in the British Museum, and there among the busts you will find men and women whose type you met last night in some London drawing-room. But Mrs. Vassal never struck me as being of the type of imperial Rome. She had rather a touch of the Greek— of the Pythia of the Delphic Grove ; the priestess of some Ionic temple set against a background of turquoise sea and grey slope.

I have always been grateful for a certain intuitional faculty which I consider one of the essentials towards successful practice as a physician. True that the intuition has failed me on occasions, mainly where my own feelings have been involved ; but on the whole I have been able to rely fairly upon these flashes of inner vision, which, piercing the corporeal mask, seem to reveal the incorporeal being with its salient emotions and desires, in a manner that is often extremely painful and rarely creditable to human nature. To-night, three people appeared thus illuminated—Mrs. Vassal, her husband, and Mrs. Raphon our hostess. Why the latter I hardly know, unless it were that as I watched her greeting of the Vassals, my interest in Mrs. Vassal made me divine at once that she was the object of Mrs. Raphon's bitterest dislike and jealousy. I had already scented drama in the past relations of Mr. Vassal with this handsome fervid lady—unusually handsome to-night, in a ruby velvet gown, and coronal of diamond stars, which set off her brilliant complexion, magnificent sweep of shoulder, and languorous Southern eyes. I noticed the glances she cast from time to time at him, and they contradicted, on a certain inductive process of reasoning, any casual-observer theory as to Mr. Vassal's indifference towards his wife. It became clear to me that Mrs. Raphon suspected, as I myself did, the smouldering rage of baffled desire underlying his frigid urbanity, and that it roused in her emotions, too complex to be more than guessed at as being of a somewhat correspondent order.

Jotted down in my commonplace book, I find a quotation trite enough to make me suppose that it owes its admission to reflexions upon the Vassal situation.

"Love and hate," it says; "attraction and repulsion in the human creature, are practically equivalent forces."

I have often thought that, presuming spiritual electricity to be governed by the same laws as physical electricity, a series of experiments to determine and regulate the relative polarity of wedded pairs might be productive of interesting results.

I had entered the drawing-room almost simultaneously with the Vassals, who were the last arrivals; and, till we were seated at dinner, was not able to make out the different guests. The Arathoon parties were always a mixture of law, art, politics, and finance; and to-night, the Vassals and Mrs. Audley Arathoon seemed the only social ingredients not to be thus labelled. Perhaps I should except the very mundane mother of a girl-novelist pretty and quaintly serious, who was proudly bear-leading an ephemeral sensation in the way of poetesses—a provincial poetess, the freckled, sandy-haired, and altogether incompatible embodiment of certain Sapphic inspirations. I made notes of the trio with a view to extracting from them minor comedy characters for a drawing-room scene, but somehow have never put them to use.

Besides these, there were a Law-lord and his lady; an un-married member of the Cabinet; a famous painter; the French correspondent of a great daily paper, himself a man of letters; two pretty bright women whom I did not know; a celebrated Eastern traveller, and four or five others with whom I was more or less acquainted. But though the company was sufficiently amusing, I found the dinner dull. Mrs. Vassal was some way down on the same side of the table, so that I had not the pleasure of watching her; and the poetess, who was my fate, did not interest me one jot.

After dinner, when we men joined the ladies, I noticed from the door that Mrs. Vassal was sitting a little apart, and that she looked nervous and uncomfortable. It seemed to me that her glance in my direction was appealing; and I began my progress towards her, not altogether a rapid one, owing to the flutter and movement brought about by the men's re-entrance. In my slow course, however, I found out the cause of her discomposure. Passing a knot of women who had paused apparently in the dis-cussion of a rather engrossing subject, I saw in the hands of one of them a new library volume. Two others lay on the table by her, and I read the title *Naamah*. No doubt Mrs. Vassal had felt embarrassed at being forced to give an opinion upon her own book.

My way was blocked by the portly form of a financier who was hanging on to Mr. Vassal, with Audley Arathoon in tow.

"Fifty-four thousand pounds to be paid into Court before two o'clock! And none of the Syndicate knew it! Is that the way you do business in the City?"

"My dear sir, I ain't a Parliamentary lawyer," languidly replied Audley. "What's going to happen?"

"The thing won't float, that's all;" and just then the man of letters, who had taken up a volume of *Naamah*, accosted Mr. Vassal.

"This is the book I was mentioning to you at dinner. It's a curiosity in its way, as the work of a woman."

Mr. Vassal looked at the book, and entered its title on his tablet. His wife was watching the occurrence; and when I spoke to her, turned with a start and a scared look in her eyes.

"Mrs. Vassal," I said in a low voice, "I guessed your secret when I read *Naamah*. But without that, I should know it now by the expression of your face."

"Oh, you will not betray me?" she implored. "I could not bear that Mr. Vassal should find me out."

"I think he will certainly do that if he reads the book. As far as I am concerned, of course you are absolutely safe."

My tone must have conveyed that I had been wounded by her reticence, for she said hurriedly—

"Forgive me for having told you nothing about it—after all your kindness, too, in advising me. But I had so little confidence in my work. And perhaps I was superstitious—you know that's a weakness in me—and you were connected with my first failure."

"At any rate," I said, "you have not failed this time. Listen."

By a glance I directed her attention to the group, of which Mr. Vassal and the man of letters now made part, and to the remarks being uttered by a distinguished-looking, white-haired lady—the wife of the Law-lord.

"Oh yes, terribly clever—deplorably clever for a woman, and for one so young. You can see from several things in the book that she must be young, and that her experience of the world is limited, in spite of the strong views she takes. I couldn't bear the story on that account. It made me quite miserable to think of a woman of her age being so morbid. Why, she ought to write about cream and honey, first love and constancy, babies' kisses and conjugal bliss."

"Talking of kisses," observed Audley Arathoon, "did you see that an unfortunate man was fined eight pounds for kissing a girl?"

Mr. Vassal, who had been turning over the leaves of *Naamah*, gave his indescribably mirthless chuckle, murmuring—

"Poor devil! He might have kicked his wife to death for that."

Mrs. Vassal turned on me her eyes, which were full of tears.

"I suppose that I am morbid, and so the book is morbid?" she said.

"Yes, you are morbid, and the book is morbid. Perhaps that is hardly to be wondered at."

And it came into my mind suddenly to say, "I wish that you could love some one."

"Love some one!" she repeated.

"It's the one real educator," I said. "But I suppose that I ought not to wish that for you."

"No," she replied. "You ought not to wish that for me. Certainly I cannot wish it for myself. It's the one thing I should dread."

"Your work will suffer. This book would have been better— powerful as it is—if you had ever loved. I should like to tell you what I think of *Naamah*," I added impulsively.

"Tell me," she said. But at that moment Mr. Vassal brought up the man of letters, whom he presented to his wife; and when I approached her again, the mother of the girl-novelist was discoursing animatedly close by, and my own novelist-incognita was listening in amusement.

"Here is another view of the literary profession," she said to me with a smile. "You must pay attention to it."

I have heard it asserted that Mrs. Vassal had no sense of humour, an opinion I never shared. I think that under happier domestic conditions she would have been quick to seize the lighter side of things, and that a joyous trait of her nature would have expanded like a flower. In obedience, I lent my ear to a blonde, fashionably dressed lady, with restored bloom and an air of sprightly appeal, who gave the impression somehow of having furnished insufficient material for an elaborate mould.

"Well, after all," she was saying, as she smoothed down and contemplated a piece of rose-point on her gown, "Rosalind is so solid, that perhaps it is a good thing for her to have a frivolous mother who enjoys life."

"I enjoy life too, mamma," said Rosalind.

"Oh, but you enjoy it in such a fearful way. I should die if I lived Rosalind's life; and I suppose she would die if she lived mine. Rosalind likes histories and type-writing and things—May I tell the story of the type-writer? It's something quite new and wonderful, you know; and you can print your own books with it. . . . Well, we were staying in a country-house and I was in the morning-room, and suddenly we heard a sound of whizzing and whirring; and Lord Alec said, 'Good gracious! what's that? Has the water-pipe burst?' And then Lady Alec said, 'It comes from Rosalind's room.' So I went up to see; and there was Rosalind type-writing—a sort of sewing-machine business on a thing like a piano; and a treadle going——"

"No, no; not a treadle, mamma."

"Well, never mind! If I am to be corrected, I won't go on. I asked Rosalind what was the matter, and she said, 'Oh, it's all right, mamma;' so I went back and told Lord Alec, 'Rosalind says it's all right; she's type writing.' Then every one in the house insisted on marching up to Rosalind's room, to see what type-writing was like; they'd never heard of it before. . . . Oh, it's a dreadful thing to have a literary daughter. And she believes in palmistry too. May I tell the story about the literary breakfast? It was at Venice——"

"No, Rome, mamma."

"Rosalind, if I'm to be interrupted, I won't go on. . . . There was the man who wrote about beetles and dancing dervishes, you know—he died just afterwards. And when the palmist looked at his hand, she said, 'I see nothing——'"

"No, no, mamma; she told somebody else——"

"Rosalind, I'm certain she said 'I see nothing.' And afterwards when she talked about it to Lord Alec—he was there too—she said, 'How could I tell him what I saw? His line of life was cut short, and I knew he was going to die.'"

Miss Rosalind had been signalling with her eyebrows across the room to the poetess, by whom Mrs. Raphon was endeavouring to do her duty.

"Mamma, we shall be late."

"It's a literary party," the elder lady announced lugubriously. "Is anybody here going on? Of course you are not, Mrs. Vassal; I do wish you were literary. Rosalind, *will* there be any one at the literary party for me to talk to?"

"No, mamma, they'll all be lions roaring."

"Well, I do hope there'll be some idiot for me to talk to;" and she turned plaintively to me, "Are *you* going, Dr. Glaive?"

There was a little ripple of laughter which pleased me, for Mrs.

Vassal laughed too, as simply as a child—Oh, yes, this work was doing her good. The lady who had caused the laugh appealed to me once more.

"What have I said? *Are* you literary? I must say I never feel comfortable in literary society. They ask me what I *do;* and what I *think.* And they wear high dresses in the evening—brown silks and cameo brooches and their heads flat. Now don't they, Rosalind? You can't deny it."

"That was one phase of literary society, mamma. To-night there'll be diamonds and Parisian gowns."

"Well, I do hope there'll be *somebody* for me to talk to—some human being, I mean."

Then in the general break-up which followed, Mrs. Vassal rose too. I had no opportunity for a long time of telling her what I thought of *Naamah,* my visit next day being purely professional; and shortly afterwards she went back to Grisewood to make preparations for wintering at Philotis.

After leaving Chesham Place that evening, I dropped in at the Roscius. I found the supper-room crowded, several strangers having been brought in, and among them Robert Vassal, the editor of *Views.* He was not a member of the club, probably because his uncle belonged to it. He was sitting beside Frank Leete, the dramatic critic, whom I spotted, and seemed to be delivering himself pretty freely upon the wrongs of English authors.

"We're suffering from two running sores," he was saying—"the little host of doctrinaires—Paravel's at the bottom of it—he started the school of literary priggism—who write biographies and lay down the law about everything; and then there's the shameful class of writers who steal our ideas because their own fields are barren, and live by robbing their fellows. They ain't all playmakers— How are you, Doctor?" Leete gave a mellow guffaw.

"What about dramatic critics?"

"My dear fellow, who *would* be a dramatic critic if by God's outside mercies he *could* be anything else? . . . *You* can; and are. . . . As for those others, with them I acknowledge no fellowship; they're beyond man's tribunal; and they're not even worth the Almighty's shot—created like black beetles for contemptuous annihilation."

I asked after Mrs. Robert Vassal.

"Fairly well, thank you. I'm taking her to her old quarters at Philotis, and shall stop there for a month or two while the House is up—I can't stand England"— he went on, talking fast, as though he wanted to get away from an unpleasant train of thought, and

I guessed that one of his wife's nerve attacks, as he called them, was worrying him.

"I'm a nuisance to myself—temper awry, brain bothers, sheer incapacity for work! I want solitude and the desert. Aversion for friends—another symptom, and loss of interest in every mortal thing."

"What's the reason of it all?" asked Leete.

"Want of a sphere; growing old; twopenny halfpenny accidents that wouldn't damage anybody else; the humours of Westminster; tiresome contributors and exacting editors. . . . What are you doctors for, Glaive? Physicians, I have found in vain—one, after another, you included. . . . I was made to drink all things and no fluid, turn by turn; was commanded to avoid all men, and to cultivate company; to work hard and not to work at all; to travel and stay at home; to abstain from flesh and to eat nothing but meat; and now, I'm beginning to see fancy shapes, and to make studies of suicide. . . . By the way," and he turned suddenly to Frank Leete, "there's something I want to ask you. Who is Esther Zamiel?"

Frank Leete's guilty start convinced me that he was in Mrs. Vassal's secret.

"What on earth has that to do with you?" he exclaimed; and added, "By Jove, I forgot. You read for Brock?"

"Not in a regular way now. I haven't the time. But he generally asks my opinion when Barham sends him a particularly venomous report."

"What do you think of Esther Zamiel?" asked Frank Leete, transparently evading the original question.

"I confess that little lady takes my fancy. She has got plenty of good stuff in her. But who is she?"

Frank Leete smothered a laugh between his big hand and his big beard. No doubt he, like myself, saw a certain grim comedy in the situation, which had brought Mrs. Vassal into unconscious relation with her husband's hated heir. I trembled for Frank Leete's discretion, but he maintained it honourably. Bending forward as though he were about to make a mysterious communication in the most solemn secrecy, he whispered loudly behind his hand.

"A poor little actress who made a mess of things. That's all I can tell you."

"Made a mess of things!" repeated Vassal, with a pucker of his brows. "She was wearing sixteenth-century Flemish point, and a pearl worth a good deal of money."

Frank Leete gurgled on behind his hand.

"You can buy wonderful things in the Palais Royal."

"You don't buy that lace in the Palais Royal, nor that pearl either."

"Upon my honour," said Leete, "I can't tell you anything more about her."

The dramatic critic bustled out of his seat. "Excuse me, my dear fellow, but there's Bonham beckoning to me. I can't lose this opportunity of extracting the truth about a little matter I'm concerned in. Bonham is a devil of diplomacy you know up to 2 A.M. And then if you can get him well on the other side of a whisky bottle, I assure you his revelations are surprising."

"Frank Leete doesn't know much about Esther Zamiel: or doesn't mean to say what he does know," remarked Vassal. "It's the last with you too, I conclude; for I notice that you doctors *do* know most things."

I shook my head.

"It's not the type. No, it's not the type," he exclaimed, as though he were contradicting an assertion. "I've had some correspondence with her over her book," he went on. "She is very interesting. I should like to get at her history—if she has yet developed one."

The qualification struck me, for it seemed to echo my own feeling in regard to Mrs. Vassal. In spite of the dramatic conditions of her life, her own drama was still embryonic.

The little incident of this meeting and the conversation with Robert Vassal impressed me even at the time as a curious link in the chain of circumstance. Later on it assumed a more significant suggestiveness.

WRITTEN
BY
ESTHER
VASSAL: I HAVE been thinking a great deal about what Dr. Glaive said—that my work would have been better if I had ever loved.

Of course, looking back I see that I have never really loved any one in my whole life—never any one but myself. If I have shown kindness to others, it was because I felt it my duty, not because I cared. Round about Grisewood, there are a number of people—commonplace, wholesome, fussy, good people, like the Heseltines and Wargraves, and Lady Cotherstone, from whom there seems to flow a stream of general benevolence and affection—towards their families, their friends, the villagers—towards almost everybody, in fact, who comes their way, except sinners and vulgar persons. But I am not like them. I don't have any gushes of affection. The stream has either been frozen within me, or the source is not there.

Partly, perhaps, because I have not been educated in loving. There was Mother—I was fourteen when she died. It seemed sad and strange to lose her, but that was all; I soon got over it. And Father—Well, I never troubled much about loving Father: it wouldn't have seemed natural.

I wonder if I am one of those elfish creatures—a sort of Undine who has got to find her soul in love.

Mother talked to me before she died about the defects in my character: and one of the things she said was, "The greatest fault you have, Esther, is that you don't love enough. Never be afraid of loving. All the blessedness that ever comes to us women, comes through loving: and all your trouble in life will come through not loving enough."

Poor Mother! my memory of her is as of a flower that withered slowly for want of water. Child as I was, her words set me thinking. I wrote them down, and the account of her last days, to which death gave a dramatic value. No doubt this was greatly due to the instinct of the writing woman, but it was my tendency in those days when my whole mind was set upon being a great actress, to dramatise everything, even Nature and Death.

While I have been shut up here at Grisewood with a cold which has delayed my departure for Philotis, Addie Heseltine has driven over pretty often to see me. She plays dreamy music, which puts me into a writing mood, and counteracts the effect on my nerves of her enthusiastic eulogies of Mr. Vassal as a husband, from the Woodfordshire social point of view. And between times, she discourses upon her curate-romance and the Littlewood complication.

So I have been taking notes of the curate-romance as a study of tame emotion.

"You see things have come to a crisis," Addie said. "I can't keep Mr. Littlewood dangling any longer. He has been very patient and devoted for years, and it comes to a question now either of his going away altogether or staying as my husband. . . . I'm in a bad hole, dear—a worse hole than I've ever been in before. . . . And you see, too, I *ought* to marry. I can't go on wasting my youth and losing my chances. . . . Oh, it is all very well for you to smile, and I know you think it dreadful to look upon marriage as a profession, though——" and Addie stopped and went red, and I knew what had suddenly occurred to her. . . . "But that's what it comes to. Poor dear Father can't live for ever, and Mother will be jointured, and we shall have our portions, and tiny ones they will be. There are ten of us, you know, counting the boys and the married sisters. . . . And so I've written to Harold Milward, and I've told him all about Mr. Littlewood. That's one comfort—Mr. Littlewood knows every-thing, and Harold knows everything too. I got his answer to-day—Harold's. There wasn't a word of clergy-shop in it, except that he prayed God to guide me in my decision. But he says that he can't hold out the faintest hope of ever being rich enough for Father to consent to our marriage. . . . And then Mr. Littlewood takes it all so sensibly. He says that he won't talk of love, but of community of interest—that's such a nice way of putting it—and that I shall help him with his monuments and his hiero-glyphics, and he will help me with my music, and love will come in time. 'I'd go back to Yucatan,' he said, 'and stop there, if my going would insure your happiness with the man you love. But if I went, what would remain to you? You can't marry the man you love, and there's only a blank left in your life with a man who loves you taken out of it.' And you know, dear Mrs. Vassal, that's perfectly true."

I could only assent.

"I should like to get away from Woodfordshire," Addie went on. "Oh, how I wish you could take me to Philotis with you.

It seems impossible to make up my mind here.   I feel as if I were in a hothouse, or like a fly in a honey-pot.   I can't escape from the thought of Harold. . . . You never saw him, Mrs. Vassal—that was the year you were away.   He was very ugly, with great square shoulders and a heavy face and kind eyes, and a true look—oh, not half so polished or clever or such a man of the world as Mr. Littlewood. . . . It was all Father's fault too. He *would* ask Harold to dinner, and what could you expect?   I used to think what a comfort it would be to have some one always to depend on—who wouldn't fly out at trifles, and grumble at the dinner, and be in a sulk because there had been a bad run —though I don't think Mr. Littlewood is bad-tempered, and I'm sure I've tried his temper enough.   But Harold is so firm, and strong, and gentle.   And I knew that the parish work was utterly distasteful to him, and that he had been forced into the Church. Yet the old women always had their wine, and their Bible read to them. . . . And, oh dear ! I must settle something, for I can't stand Mrs. Wargrave's sympathy. . . . 'This is terrible, dear Addie'—and don't you know her funereal look?   Really, when Mrs. Wargrave begins to gush over one of the rector's funerals, I always think, what a pity it is that she won't be alive to enjoy her own !"

And then Addie laughed in a way that didn't suggest a broken heart.

Oh yes ; Addie is wavering.   The curate is away in Birmingham, and Mr. Littlewood is not going to Yucatan, but means to hunt with the Woodchester pack this season.   I counsel and plead on the side of youth, love, and romantic poverty, and Addie looks at me curiously and says—

"Ah, if we poor girls could only all be as fortunate as you are.   There doesn't come to many of us the chance of millions, middle-age, and Mr. Vassal."

Yesterday Mr. Vassal came unexpectedly into my sitting-room and asked me for some tea.   He held in his hand the second volume of *Naamah*.

"Hast thou found me, O mine enemy ? " my shrinking heart cried.

"You need not have been ashamed of your bantling," he said ; "but on the whole you are wise not to own it.   I see that you have shocked some of the critics ; it would be a bore if you scandalised the parsonesses and squiresses."

I poured out his tea ; he drank it, his eyes fixed on me with an inscrutable look.   I said something ; it does not matter what. How had he discovered me?

"That did not require any abnormal cleverness. I was recommended the book at the Arathoons', and you don't suppose that, after having lived with you for seven years, I could fail to recognise you in it? Besides, I had observed that during the last few months a new interest absorbed you, which made you forget yourself—and me. I knew it must be an artistic interest. Of course, under other conditions, I should have suspected the usual intrigue. But that hasn't developed yet."

My indignant exclamation made him laugh.

"Yes, I know the phases—curiosity, disappointment, weariness, repulsion, reaction. They generally culminate about the fifth year. Then sooner or later comes along the lover."

Again I felt the helpless rage of a trapped creature, and the mockery of his smile maddened me. He tapped *Naamah* with his smooth white forefinger.

"This may take the lover's place. I always told you that you had the capacity for a grand passion. The mistake I made was in imagining that *I* could arouse it. Let this be your safety-valve. Go on writing. You have my full approval. Will you give me another cup of tea?"

BOOK VI

" Love, like death, comes to the soul but once."

PHILOTIS ! The name weaves a spell. It is Memory's password to the Blue Land.

Here now, as I lie in Philotis dying, I look over my little old note-books — limp-covered, square-ruled, bought in the Enchanted Days at the French stationer's in the Square Casphar, where I used to buy the same kind when I was a child.

Do you know that odd, living magnetism which inanimate things sometimes give forth—things which have been wept over, joyed over, to which one's deepest and dearest emotions have clung ? Then you will know, too, how the sight and touch of these little books stir in me throbs, reincarnate, of the dead rapture and the buried pain ; how, as I look at the scrawled pages, I seem to be looking into the face of a ghost—a ghost who has the very aspect of mortality, but whose hand I cannot clasp, whose lips I may not kiss—a ghost with terribly sad eyes, between whom and me there is silence—still always silence.

Philotis ! I linger on the word ; it breathes—love.

And I love the place, though I am dying of it—love it with a youthful fervency and with impassioned thrills of association, bound up in sea and sky and hills, in trees and flowers and the sound of the wind, in the faces of the people and the appearance of the streets.

It is so beautiful, and nothing seems ever here to change. The sky is always that softly luminous blue, with the jagged aloes, the tangled palm-fronds, the glistening fir-needles, drawn in different shades of green upon it, as upon an immense turquoise. And then, the blue of the sea ! Deeper turquoise than the sky ! That rich clear Mediterranean blue—except in the bay, close to shore, where the water lies in curious zones of colour— here a ribbon of intensest emerald, there a weed-streak of reddish brown ; here, in the shallows, a stretch of foam-flecked purple, and where the sun touches it, of delicate opal whitening to silver. Then, standing forth against the infinite sky, the blue mountains —Sralta and the snow-tipped Katka range—shadowed, mystic as the hills of a dream.

Sometimes I sit in a boat and look back at Philotis. The mountains rising behind seem to spread arms around it—the Vasques hills, their summits fantastically serrated, barring the western side of the harbour; and to the east, the long lone promontory of Cape Feurd, with the lighthouse on its hump. Then, as the boat sways round, the islands show at the harbour's entrance, Rassem and Médiane, the surf breaking over their black tapering points, and making a shining line upon the sea's blue. Tier by tier the city rears itself, like a great white amphitheatre, glittering in the sunlight, built up from the bay. Grey volcanic-looking ridges back the olive-groves and pine-woods and melt into the misty hills. Villas and gardens and lovely Moorish palaces, embedded in palms and bamboos, spread out in the curve ; and on the level, white houses, red-tiled, flat-roofed, and the domes of many mosques, some of which are Catholic churches.

It is sad to think of Philotis as a conquered city, though there is a curious picturesqueness and a dramatic contrast in this blending of West and East.

Down by the strand lies the French town, all garish boulevards and arcades, with its new cathedral and opera-house, and the square, where still plays the band that Father used to conduct, and where all the motley life of the place gathers.

From the square, lead tortuous stair-streets, climbing up the Arab quarter to the overhanging citadel, and to a very ancient mosque, sacred yet to the creed of the Faithful. It is like some city seen in a dream, for indeed, all that old girl-life, when I knew the Arab quarter well, seems a dream now. The houses nearly touch each other, and are painted grey and green and greenish-blue ; some few are bright blue, and in the windows of these you may see looking out, women with uncovered heads and painted faces, their eyelids and eyebrows darkened, wearing fancifully embroidered jackets and narcissus flowers in their hair.

Such quaint bits ! Beautiful Arab doors, brass-studded, and lintels of carved stone with gorgeous tiles let into the wall above ; here and there, an open door, giving the glimpse of a Moorish courtyard, of slender pillars and graceful arches embossed in red and green and gold. There is so much of that soft green colouring everywhere, even in the jars outside the native pottery shops, some large enough to hold one of the Forty Thieves. How quaint, too, is the life of those narrow streets ! The droves of donkeys driven by bright-eyed Arab boys ; the white figures in yashmaks, threading their silent way ; the melancholy Arabs in grey-hooded cloaks and white bournouses passing along ; the hideous negresses ; the copper-coloured gipsies ; the Bedouin women, with their olive faces and silky hair, and the cabalistic blue mark on their foreheads and chins.

And then the vignettes in the windows! The embroiderer at his work; the hooded Arabs and turbaned Jews seated cross-legged by their wares; the weaver, his threads spread out, stooping before his wheel; the negro basket-plaiter; the players at chess and dominoes; the devout son of the Prophet, in his bed droning the Koran; there, a Muzzabeet from the desert wrapped in his carpet-cloak; there, a group of tattered men and veiled women pausing with their loads of vegetables from the market, round three blind Arab troubadours—fine-looking fellows, with chiselled features and short beards, and sightless eyes, upraised as they chant in monotonous recitative, and sing choruses to the beating of tom-toms.

These are the pictures in the Arab quarter, now as then.

Away by the hotels and villas it is quite different. The roads are white, and send out a blinding glare, and the shadows under the umbrella-pines are almost black. The cloying Arab smell has given place to the scent of flowers. In the ravines the broom is yellow; the mimosa buds are changing from green to gold; the narcissus is out in the meadows; roses fling themselves on the walls in a laughing caress, and the yuccas hang their creamy bells; trails of mesembryanthemum drop down stone parapets; the orange groves have blossoms among the ripe fruit; the pepper-trees toss forth red clusters; the fir-woods are a tangle of under-growth—wild rosemary, lentiscus, and sea-lavender, and white heath, with here and there a thin-stemmed forest pink.

. . . .

Back through the years to the mood in which I wrote at the beginning of the Enchanted Days.

. . . It is so new, so old, so strange, so familiar. . . . I am not the Esther of Grisewood, pining in a dank dungeon of morbid despair. I am a liberated Esther, enwrapped by the divine glamour of youth, in whom hope and joy are reborn. For the magic of Philotis is upon me.

Faintly intoxicating blows the breeze. The glitter of sunbeams on the sea; the hum of insects; the rustle of leaves; the scent of roses—all bring a delicious sense of irresponsibility. I laugh softly to myself in very lightness of spirit. A thousand frolicsome fancies seem let loose within me. I have the consciousness of unseen presences, of whispering voices. I love to bask in long luxurious reverie, and my very lassitude becomes beatific. Thus I lie for hours on the couch before my window, lulled by the breath of an unknown happiness. I watch the lateen sails scudding across the bay, the roll of the breakers over Rassem's rocky snout—he looks like some strange primæval monster rising from the deep—and the play of the clouds on the Vasques hills. Then comes the Muezzin's call, "Allah is great; there is no God but Allah;" while, as though in gentle mockery, following upon it, sounds the chime of the convent bell. And gradually the sea reddens and the shadows grow darker, the horizon line more misty, and the mountains deepen to purple against the glory of the after-glow.

And it is as though a gracious spirit brooded upon the waters, while in the hush of a mysterious expectancy Nature awaited his coming. And my sleeping soul is stirred by the hovering nearness, and the fountains of my heart are unsealed.

Oh, that I were as other women are, and might hear the voice of the Beloved as he cometh up from the wilderness :—

"I am come into my garden, my sister, my spouse. . . . Open to me, my sister, my love. . . . At our gates are all manner of pleasant fruits, new and old, which I have laid up for thee, oh my beloved. . . . Arise, my love."

Oh, that I might arise and answer and open to the Beloved.

.   .   .   .   .   .

The train crawls slowly along to El-Meriem, between hedges of prickly pear and aloe, with here and there a row of gum-trees, their wind-blown bark hanging in shreds like beggars' tatters. Across the white road, which lies parallel with the line, one sees an occasional auberge or orange-farm. Odd figures and processions move along the road—strings of panniered mules led by Arabs; files of women, who, as the train passes, pull their veils hastily over their faces, leaving only a loophole for one eye to peep through; withered negresses laden with garden produce, and sometimes a whole Kabyle family, the bigger children on donkeys, the mothers wrapped in white haiks, fastened by barbaric pins and chains, which hang on their breasts and foreheads, carrying babies slung between their shoulders. Then the plain widens into orange groves and fields yellow with narcissus, and from it the mountains rise abruptly behind El-Meriem. It is Sralta which towers yonder, snow on his crown, his base black with firs. Then a range of naked grey peaks bristle down from the great Katkas, the gorge of the Mestral cutting it, and the Mestral river, a green ribbon, white-spotted where it foams in the shallows, winding through the valley between dwarf bamboos and oleander trees, and losing itself among the coast hills on the way to the sea.

.   .   .   .   .   .

There is a small village perched on the brow of a hill a little

way inland from El-Meriem.   Its attraction is an old mosque and
Marabut's tomb, the resort at certain times of many of the Faithful.

Yesterday I went to this place, which is called Kassis.

It is a very quiet spot, almost deserted except on pilgrimage
days ; for even the Arab houses are many of them empty.   Once
it was a fortified town, and is still encircled by the grey ruins of
a fortress wall.   For a little while, some public works close by,
made it more French than Arab, and so the hillside was planted
with olives, and there was an attempt at growing vines.   But the
ground was stony and unprofitable, and after the works were
done, the French population dwindled, and the Arab one did
not come back.   That was before my time.   Now there is still
less sign of active life at Kassis.

Even the Cours with its plane-tree built round by a stone
bench in the middle, and its café, outside which is inscribed the
obsolete legend, " On casse croûte à toute heure," is silent and
almost empty.   The French quarter lies, as the way is here, on a
lower level than mosque or citadel, and behind these, rise desolate
spurs of the Katkas—grey crags, bleak and naked, except where,
low down, there is a straggling patch of olives or a tiny red-
roofed cabin with whitewashed walls and slits of windows, or a
clump of cypresses—dark blotches against the grey.   A mule,
with gaping paniers, comes clattering down the narrow street
leading up from the Cours, and bestriding it, an Arab, bare-legged
and tattered, yet with that mysterious dignity stamped upon the
meanest mendicant among the Prophet's children.   Perhaps it lies
in the impassive features, on which the word Fatality seems written ;
or, maybe, in the folds of the bournous or haik, that, to their last
shreds, fall back with something of classic grace.   The street is
only a rough stair of cobble-stones, the houses over-arching, and
the upper storeys resting on sapling pillars.   They have doors
mounted in dull brass, and benches are fixed underneath the
projections.   But the doors are mostly closed, and only a few
Arab children crawl about the benches—bright-eyed, clear-skinned
rogues.

Now and then, passing along to the mosque, one may see
a ruminative Arab or a pair of veiled women ; but all the interest
of the town seems to have centred round the native coffee-house,
where are squat groups of Arabs drinking the thick black beverage
of the country ; and two are kissing each other with comic
solemnity.   They turn to look at me as I go by, and make a
remark ; but I know Kassis of old, and am not afraid to walk
through its streets alone.   Here is a long stairway with white
balustrades, where women in yashmaks and bearded turbaned

men are going up and down. The stairway leads to a little garden enclosure, in which grow palms and twisted cactus plants; and two sides of it are walled in by the mosque. Beggars whine and cringe about the stair and against the outer wall: a white-bearded mufti comes out of the building and paces the path, absorbed in meditation. Through an open doorway there is a glimpse of the Marabut's tomb, with the yellow and red flags hanging about it, and of figures bowed on the floor around. Rows of slippers stand at the entrance. Close by, on a stone pedestal, is perched an emaciated saint, who nods his hideous head, and murmurs toothless thanks for the coin I place by his side. Do I not know that saint? Here he had his habitation when I was a girl at El-Meriem, and now he must have grown into almost a part of the stone.

Down a small flight of steps there is another court, and another great door, through which I may not pass, and which gives a new vision of prostrate figures and of more women in yashmaks going in and out. It is not permitted me to enter, but I may wander on through a narrow white passage, and I may examine the old doorway and the tiled fountain in the wall. And now I am in a second small quadrangle, with green-tiled arches and spiral pillars, and a fountain trickling into a marble basin where the votaries of the Prophet are washing their feet. Beyond lies a peaceful little burying-ground, where the graves of the muftis are open to the sky. Just a grassy plateau, with a low parapet wall on three sides, and some old slanting cypresses framing a wonderful view of grey hills and distant snow-capped mountains—majestic Sralta nearest—of olive-clad slopes and curving white roads; of the green valley of the Mestral, widening down from the beetling bluffs of Tourmestral; and far away, the glittering roofs of Philotis curving round its blue bay, and, with the lighthouse of Cape Feurd, a pale spot on the horizon.

I sat myself on the parapet, in the farthest corner, where the graveyard wall makes an angle with the wall of the ruined fortress. It is on the brink of the steep. In the wall are jagged gaps, and a little below, on a green ledge, grow more almond-trees, blown slantwise like the palms and cypresses, and which are putting forth bloom.

Down beyond Kassis the tops of the olives make a grey-green, billowy bed. When I bent forward, I could see all the expanse of country and the sea afar. But when I leaned against the wall, it was almost as though I were in a dead world; for then only the barren hills, the ruined citadel, and the grey stretch of olives were visible. The wind swept across the plateau from the snowy mountains, and it seemed to have a voice different from the voice of the wind in other places, and to be telling a sorrowful tale of long past things and people, of dead loves and buried hopes. The silence and deadness and greyness of it all gave me an uncanny impression, which was intensified by the sight of those veiled, wraith-like forms flitting past the entrance door on their way back from the mosque. I shivered with the chill of this ghostly feeling, and got up from the niche, intending to find a more sunny seat : then stood still, wonder-struck, for at that moment the Reader came into the burial-ground.

Yes, it was the Reader. I knew his profile and the backward poise of his head. I knew his worried, intent expression, as he stopped, not seeing me, and stood gazing out on the view. Presently he came quite close to me, still blindly, and I gave an exclamation. He started ; a light of sudden astonishment flashed from his eyes, and, raising his hat, he stepped forward, holding out his hand.

"Miss Zamiel !" he said : and I too started at the sound of the name which was not mine. Somehow, here, in this Moslem burial ground, we seemed to meet for the first time as man and woman.

"I am so glad to see you," he went on. "It's a funny coincidence. Though I don't know why—for since, by the malignant irony of Fate, Climate has begun her games, Philotis naturally results."

"It is not so much of a coincidence as far as I am concerned," I answered, "for I know this place very well."

"Really !"

"I was born at Philotis. My father died at El-Meriem."

"You were born at Philotis ! Then that accounts——" He was looking at me intently. "You have eyes like some of the Philotis women," he said abruptly, and added, "Please forgive me ; but the thought came into my mind at the moment. and I couldn't help saying it. It puzzled me, for I don't recollect ever having seen it before—that peculiar reddish-brown—out of this place. There was a child in the tram to-day with eyes that colour."

His evident fear lest he had been too personal made me laugh, and he gave me a quick startled look. When I asked him the reason he replied—

"Do you know that your laugh sounded quite girlish, and out of keeping with the tragic impression I had got somehow of 'Esther Zamiel' from that one meeting of ours in Mr. Brock's office. It must be the vivid setting of Philotis that makes the difference. . . . And so you have been here before ?"

"My mother was a Philotis woman." And I told him how

we had left Philotis when I was a little child, and had come back after Mother's death, and had then lived at Philotis as long as Father was alive.

"And no doubt you have people here of your own, and that's what brings you back again?" he said.

I told him that I had no people of my own in the whole world, and that I had been sent here for my health.

"I'm sorry to hear that. And yet you look better than when I saw you that day in Mr. Brock's den."

There was a little silence I had sat down again, and he was leaning against the wall, with his foot on the parapet, prodding the ground with his stick. I caught his eyes fixed upon me, and I think he would have liked to ask me more questions. I daresay that he wonders about me—who I am, and because I seem rich, where my money comes from. Presently he said, "May I sit here?"

He placed himself on the parapet facing me in the angle.

"You see," he began again suddenly, "I was a true prophet. I told you that you would succeed."

"I owe it to you, for I couldn't have done anything if you hadn't helped me. And I've never been able to thank you properly for your letters. They gave me just the help and encouragement I needed so badly."

"Did they do that? I'm glad. Well, I liked writing the letters; though I often fancied, when I had let my pen run away with me, that they might bore you; and I liked yours in return. I missed them ever so much when they came to an end."

"And I—I thought that perhaps you might have written—perhaps after——"

I stopped, for it seemed as though I were taking his personal interest too much for granted. After all, it has been nothing but a literary association, though in his letters he told me a good deal about himself, which must be what makes me seem to know him so well.

"After you had become famous! So you did mind a little my ungracious conduct, which is admitted without benefit of clergy. But, you see, after all, I was only the Reader to you; and my work ended when the reviewers began theirs."

I fancy he must have been subtly conscious that his words rebuffed me, for after a minute he added more genially, "Yes, I wanted very much to know how you took success, and whether it made you any happier. Has it?"

"Happier! Oh yes—for the joy of the work."

"Why," he said, "you are not old enough to feel, as I do, that work—real work—is all that's worth living for when afternoon draweth nigh. But your success must have made a difference in things generally."

"I don't know—I don't care in that way. No, it has not made any change in my life."

"Is it that you too want to get away from publishing and shilling books, and Mudie and puffs? And do I find another out-of-date person who agrees to loathe publicity? I'm not at all sure, though, that it's a healthy sign in a beginner, this indifferentism."

He seemed puzzled, and I fancied a note of rebuke in his voice. I wanted to explain to him that there was no affectation in my indifference; for, in truth, to win praise as Esther Vrintz would be very sweet to me. But of what use is it to Mr. Vassal's wife? Of what use, too, to let the Reader know who I am, though I can hardly doubt that he would keep my secret? Still, it would be a jarring note; and this relation, which is unlike any other, and is the most poetic thing in my life, would be brought down at once to the common-place level.

So I answered nothing. We shall meet again, and he will learn to know me better. Then something made me say—

"How could you tell, that day at Mr. Brock's, that I was unhappy?"

"Oh, it was easy enough to read that—in your book, in your face, and by one or two things you said. Somehow, before I saw you, I had got you into my mind as a poor girl—poor in the money sense, I mean—on whom Fate had not smiled."

"And afterwards?"

"Well, afterwards I came to see that I had been wrong in some things, not in others."

"Are all authors so kind? And do you often help struggling writers as you helped me?"

"I try—when I get a good chance. But I don't often manage to do it so nicely."

"Why?"

"Well, for one thing, they are not usually so satisfactory as you from the literary point of view. And they don't always take criticism so kindly. As for the kindness of authors, I know— what I know of it. Dickens cut and altered and edited me in my beginnings, asking my permission as though he were the tyro and I the master. And I could tell you of others—— So, my dear Miss Zamiel, I should be less than worthy in my own eyes if I didn't at least try to do to others what others have generously done by me."

"I wish that I could read some of the books you have written," I exclaimed.

"How do you know that you have not done so?"

"I don't know . . . very likely. Mr. Brock gave me to understand that you were a great author."

"Brock flattered me. Think of me, however, if you like, as half a poet, which is a long way from being a whole poet. No, no; I'm not going to give away my incognito just yet: there's such a charm in it. So we'll let my immortal works slide for the present."

He did not speak for a few moments, but demolished with his stick a tender little sucker of mesembryanthemum which hung over the wall. I had a half impulse to stop him; it seemed so cruel: but I only picked up the soft fleshy thing with its pink bud as it fell at my feet.

"I suppose it's as good a thing as one can do," he said.

"Oh no, no." I was thinking of the mesembryanthemum. He looked up at me quickly.

"What? Not to help others?"

"That!—Yes; but it would be no use my trying. I want so much help myself."

"Now, there's just where you might give help—in taking it from people, and so bringing about an interchange of sympathy. There's nothing so good for one as that."

"It's difficult," I said, "for people who are shut up in themselves."

"Don't I know it? I should have been a much happier man if I could have thrown myself more on my fellow-men—been more objective, in fact. But that's the curse of us writers—the subjective mania. We must needs turn our minds into private dissecting-rooms and lock the door upon our nearest and dearest, while we scrape our sensations bare and gloat over their mechanism: or we take out our emotions and put them into a pickle-bottle, and spend our time in gazing at them. And then, some of us write a novel or a poem in which we describe them. Oh, you needn't laugh. You are as bad an offender as any—worse, for you take yourself so deliciously seriously: and some of us, who have got a gleam of humour, don't—always.

"Perhaps," he went on, "you fancy that your *Naamah* is somebody absolutely new and original whom your fancy has created outside you. But she isn't. They're your own nerves that you were scraping: and your own—I won't be so daring as to say your own experiences, but your potentialities of experience."

I used to wonder sometimes, when I was sending him the

bits of my book, whether he understood. He *did* understand. And his eyes, when they looked straight into mine, gave me a feeling as though he were searching down right into my soul. They made me speak from the inner *me*.

"But then reserve may be a sort of safeguard—if confidence between you and the one—those nearest you, is impossible. . . . It must be impossible when one's reallest thoughts and impulses are in rebellion against the conditions of that very nearness. . . ." I spoke stumblingly. "Surely," I exclaimed, "that's the cruellest thing that can be."

"The cruellest! It's hell upon earth."

He said the words with repressed vehemence: and again it was as if some subtle air-current carried a mind-vibration from him to me. I can't describe the feeling in any other way. He was looking down, and again slashing savagely at a mesembryanthemum trail.

"Oh, don't," I cried involuntarily.

"Don't?" he repeated. I pointed to the torn, bleeding shoot, and we both laughed.

"It was temptingly juicy, and I wasn't thinking. I shouldn't have supposed that you were sentimental in that way. You'll be telling me that you are a ragamuffin-champion and beast-lover —not that that isn't a good thing—and an anti-vivisectionist into the bargain, which is what some people think all nice women should be."

"Then I'm afraid I'm not a nice woman in that sense, practically, though I am sure that I am theoretically. But it has never come into my way to get up enthusiasms about crêches and broken-down cab-horses, or against vivisection either. I know it's a great fault in me that I'm not in the least philanthropic."

"Yet you couldn't bear to see me slaughtering a flower."

"I don't know why. It seemed inconsistent somehow with what you said about helping people."

"Oh, I'm a mass of inconsistencies. But never mind. Why should *you* have said what you did? That seems inconsistent . too; for at anyrate you have got your life in your own hands— more, that is to say, than most of us. You told me that you were alone."

Then suddenly his eyes moved down from my face—perhaps there was something in it which betrayed me to my ungloved left hand lying on my lap. I saw that he noticed the wedding-ring on my third finger, and that now he understood. He gave a little start and drew back rather stiffly.

"No," I said, "I am not alone: not in the way you meant."

"Of course I might have guessed that you were married."

He looked away at Sralta. The furrows in the mountain's side were deepening as the sun lowered ; and I had a pang in thinking that our talk must soon come to an end.

"It was unaccountably stupid of me, and I ought to beg your pardon," he went on with a certain severe courtesy. "I had no right to lead up to anything so personal. I quite understand that you may have some good reason for not writing under your own name. Naturally to me you will always be ' Esther Zamiel.' But perhaps I am wrong, and that *is* your name : only you are not *Miss* Zamiel?"

"No, it is not my name ;" and I added, "If I am just Esther Zamiel to you, you are to me only the Reader."

"That's quite fair, isn't it? Though—" he pulled himself up—"No, it doesn't matter."

I wonder if it was an instinct of delicacy which kept him from telling me his name—the feeling that, since I wanted to withhold mine, he would not put me in a false position by disclosing his.

"No, it doesn't matter," I repeated.

"In fact, as I said, the incognito has a charm of its own. I shall be immensely interested in your literary career, and I hope that we may always have that very pleasant meeting-ground. Are you working now? But I suppose you are. Do you remember what George Sand says in one of her letters, 'One must have a passion in life, and the profession of writing is nothing less than a violent and indestructible passion.'"

Then he became "the Reader," which he had not been all through our talk till now. I told him about a story Mr. Brock had asked me to submit for his magazine, and we discussed the plot, and he advised me as to its treatment.

As we talked, the sun dropped slowly, the sky became softly golden, and the desolate greyness of Kassis was changed into a rosy flush. Truly in that tender glow there seemed to me something symbolic of the art-comradeship which may henceforth irradiate the greyness of my life, while the wall that closes in our meeting-ground shuts out also sex and circumstance and all the ordinary worldly conventions. Is this the reason why, when he talks, and even when he looks at me, there comes over me a sense of dreamy harmony and of satisfaction such as I have never known in any human companionship?

The shadows of the cypresses in the graveyard grew quite black, and out of the glow there crept the chill of sunset. We both got up. I had yet to drive to El-Meriem, and my doctor's orders are stern against exposure after the sun has gone down.

So we walked back through the tiled quadrangle, past the open mosque and the Marabut's tomb, and down the flight of stairs, along the Arab streets to the Cours, where the carriage stood.

As we waited while they were closing up the landau, a French child stepped forward and gave me a bunch of violets. She was a clean, pretty creature, with appealing dark eyes : and something made me stoop down when I took the flowers and give her a kiss. I don't know why I had the impulse, unless it was because I felt happy. I don't care much for children, though sometimes I have longed intensely for one of my own—not because of Grisewood and Tregarth, nor from the wish for an heir to dispossess the nephew whom Mr. Vassal so hates; but because I have had the feeling that warm arms clinging round my neck and a baby's head against my bosom would soften my hard heart and teach me the meaning of love.

I had that thought now as my lips touched the child's cheek, and was filled with a strange emotion, so that I knew, when I looked up, meeting the Reader's eyes, that mine were bright with tears.

"Take care," he said kindly, as I gave the little thing some money. "You will have the whole small population of Kassis down upon you with nosegays, and you won't get to El-Meriem before sunset. Are you at the *Europe* ?"

"Yes— And you ?"

"Oh, I keep to the old-fashioned *Poste*. It's only for a night or two. I have left my wife at Philotis, where we are in a villa."

He helped me into my cloak and settled my furs.

"I shall be back at El-Meriem almost as soon as you, for I am on the tramp, and shall make a short cut by the traverses."

That was yesterday. I wonder if I shall see him in the town to-day.

El-Meriem has become a modern French town, and at the first glance I hardly seemed to know it. Yet if one looks for them, there are all the old picturesque nooks still. For the French part is only an adaptation, or rather aggregation, skirting the Arab city, leaving its heart untouched. The Cours is in the French part, and has a huge palm left in the centre, and a stone fountain, and there are plane-trees planted all round, with rough benches underneath them. Cafés and green-shuttered porticoed buildings line the Cours ; and here are all the hotels in the place, except the new half-English *Europe*, which is built higher up the hill than even the Arab town. All the inhabitants of El-Meriem seem to be coming and going through the Cours—Arabs in white hoods, bare-legged and idly sprawling: others squatting beside pyramids of oranges, making no effort to attract passers-by, and with always that strange look of fatality upon their Biblical faces. There are Jews in rich dark greasy clothes, and handsome fashionably-dressed Jewish women, while some wear the hard unbecoming black head-dress of the Jewesses here. There are soldiers in full red trousers striped with blue, high boots and blue embroidered jackets; Arab boys in red fezzes and ragged garments frolic on the edge of the fountain basin and pelt the dogs which come to drink: and here a file of stately Bedouins march along, and at the moment, in odd contrast, two fat Frenchmen look up from the *Petit Journal* and exchange a laugh.

The market-place, close by, is full of picturesque bits too. The oranges and yellow pumpkins and strings of capsicums make bright spots of colour among the piles of vegetables and fruit. Here one sees an even greater confusion of callings and nationalities—Arabs, Jews, Kabyles, Bedouins, Spahis, and Zouaves; bourgeois Frenchmen and French women, and veiled beings with yashmaks parted to show one roguish eye intent on purchase. Here a pair of ancient Moors in brown gowns sit cross-legged conversing, and there, before a café, is another, making jokes that seem out of keeping with his patriarchal mien; and there is the Arab barber shaving his customers. Ah! what a familiar scene is this market-place to me; and how often I used to come here in the old days with our servant Barbe to lay in provisions!

Up in the old town there are two mosques,—El-Meriem, like Kassis, has the memory of its sacred Marabut: and there is an Arab cemetery on the slope, to which on certain days a long straggling procession of white-veiled women may be seen winding among the palms and oleanders and olive groves. Near the Cours there was once another mosque; but it is a mosque no longer: and where the Moslem used to prostrate himself towards Mecca, the Christian now kneels before the Madonna and Child. It is all out of harmony: the slender Moorish pillars and tiled arches clash with the tawdry pictures of saints and the images of the Virgin; and dignified Arab simplicity with artificial flowers and guttering candles. But, in spite of these jarring elements in the association of two faiths, I have always loved and been deeply moved by this mosque-church. To-day, the dim lofty place, the organ music, and march of priests down the aisle, brought me a soothing sense of peace and healing, and had upon me something of the effect of a mediæval pageant belonging to some past existence, now altogether faint and unreal.

Is it possible that I have ever been a child at El-Meriem?

Long after the service ended, I stayed kneeling before one of the side altars which has a great, white, thorn-crowned Christ, reminding me of the Christ at Grisewood. But that other Christ had never shed any blessed balm upon me when I had crawled to His feet in sharpest pain and direst dread. To-day as I knelt beneath the mystic Light—to-day that I am not unhappy, but am filled with dreamy content—I had the sense of a Divine Presence, of a spiritual haven. All the time that I kneeled, the remembrance of Kassis blended in a vague way with my mood of half-religious exaltation : and vividly near, seemed a ghost-like companionship which has been hovering since yesterday. Fragments of conversation float in my memory—thoughts, explanations which I wish now had been made, but which I have a dim fancy were understood.

This feeling of an unseen, sympathetic fellowship was with me even more strongly as I came down from the cathedral steps into the everyday world I used to know. After the dusky solemnity of those echoing aisles, there seemed something visionary in it all—the brilliant sunshine, the heterogeneous crowd, the fantastic contrasts of the Cours. Through this masque of Eastern life a procession of the creed of the West was passing—a procession of priests, the crucifix upraised, and of acolytes in crimson habits chanting to the rhythmic movement of the censers. Then came a following of white-capped nuns, and behind them a gathering of peasants—men in blue blouses, weather-beaten women, and sturdy brown children, the faces of all hushed into devotional gravity. Here was more than just the dramatic clash of two civilisations. The human element, refined almost from its grossness and squalor, somehow appealed to me with a pathos and deep meaning which I had never before found in it, and seemed to lend the scene a symbolism of deeper meaning and higher beauty. It is an unwonted experience to me, this human thrill, this sense of being no longer apart from the everyday crowd, no longer quite bound about by the circle of my own emotions. Only the last day or two have I had that feeling of touch with the common interests of humanity, that feeling, which made me want to kiss the child at Kassis, and which stirs in me an inexplicable sympathy with the sorrows and joys around, as though it were the throbbing of a new life within me.

How is this, I wonder!

As I walked along the broad path towards the fountain, I came face to face with the Reader: and he turned and paced beside me, asking if I had caught cold from the late drive of yesterday.

So we got into talk, and sat down on one of the benches under a palm. As we sat there and were looking up at Sralta and at a great ragged cloud resting on the mountain's brow, a sunbeam bursting through a rift in the mass brought into sudden distinctness the fortress perched on one of the grey crags which beetle over the Mestral gorge.

"Do you know that place?" he asked.

"It is Tourmestral."

"Yes, I know; but have you ever been there?"

I told him that as a girl I had often wished to visit Tourmestral, but that for a long time the way had been impassable by a great landslip, and I had never been able to go. There was only the zigzag path we could see now faintly drawn on the side of the precipice.

"They call it the Road to Paradise," I said. "But it was too far off and too steep for me to climb it alone."

"The Road to Paradise!" he repeated. "Ah, that is a path one does not climb alone! Though I have done so," he added with a laugh. "I made a tramp to Tourmestral last year."

I asked him to tell me what had happened to the Château, and what Paradise was like when you got there.

"It is the most fascinating old Moorish palace you can imagine, crammed chock full of eighteenth-century and Empire properties! You know it used to be a Moorish stronghold, and was called Bab-el-Mestral, which, as you must know too, means Gate of the Mestral. But the French drove away the Moors and rechristened it; and the castle, which had been the summer palace of the Dey, was bought by a Marquis de Cayrol not so very many years ago. His wife died there, and he took a hatred to the place and would not go near it again. Now he is dead as well, and it belongs to his son, whose sympathies are more with Paris racecourses than with remote Moorish ruins. You see I have been working up its history professionally. There's an interesting library at the Château. I wish we might go some day and explore it."

I wondered what my doctor would say to that "mad scheme."

"Well, I suppose it is rather a mad scheme for you just now. But there's a fair carriage-road in the daylight, and we should not be condemned to mount by the Chemin du Paradis. It wouldn't do for you, however, to think of the excursion till late spring. The day I went, I was nearly snowed up."

Presently he said, "I saw you in the church just now, and wondered if you belong to Rome."

"No; I sometimes wish that I did."

"And I too," he said seriously, "sometimes wish the same thing. It's a fine historic institution, and there's a certain poetic grandeur in one's notion of the voices of many ages echoing through that vast dim pile. Besides, its very fetters give a delusive idea of security. I have moments when to put myself into a sort of moral or intellectual prison seems to me just the most desirable thing—if it were possible."

"I don't ever want to do that."

"Naturally! You've nothing yet to guard yourself against. . . . One goes through the phases." . . . (I am taking up his words as I recall them). "It's all a kind of seesaw rebound. At a particular time of life materialism has one in grip; then comes the turn of unquenchable spirit. The spiritual view of things always seems the most convincing in the long-run. . . . But we pen-talked something of this in relation to the poetic temperament, didn't we? I remember writing you a rhapsody, of which later I repented."

I asked him why he had repented of it, but he did not tell me.

"Our affinities, even on paper—perhaps because they were on paper—seemed pleasantly comradesque," he said; "and I suppose that accounts for the rhapsody; I can't account for the repentance. . . . You must realise as well as I," he went on, "that in art and in emotion and in religion, which is only a blending of art and emotion, there is always a further beyond—a fearsome region where the limbs totter and the knees fail, and a man cannot answer for his actions or his feelings when he gets into it. That's where one realises his helplessness to cope with forces, not so much outside as within himself—forces stronger than will or reason."

"But you give me the notion of a strong man," I exclaimed impulsively. "I should never have thought of you as being tossed about in that way."

He made an abrupt backward gesture.

"You don't know me in the least—how should you? I'm weak, deplorably weak. There's a confession! When it's a case of reaching a certain pitch of feeling—I've only reached that pitch once in my life. . . ." He paused and prodded the ground with his stick as he had prodded the mesembryanthemum at Kassis.

. . . "You'll think of course that it came through being in love with a woman—especially after what I wrote in that concatenation. . . . But that wasn't it exactly." He hesitated again and then plunged on.

"'The thing that frightened me was being brought face to face with all the terrible and magnificent possibilities of a splendid love. . . . I'm not speaking of the ordinary love, but of the kind of passion that totally transforms a man or woman. It was a shock to me to realise the sort of heaven or hell that might be the key to. . . . There's where my weakness comes in. I've a holy horror—except of course professionally—of the grand crisises of life I once wrote about—no, we won't be pedantic and talk of 'crises.' I should always want to double back round the fork of the 'Y.'"

He turned off the subject jerkily.

"You women-writers never rightly gauge the weakness of the male artistic animal. You nearly always turn us out prigs, sentimentalists, or monstrosities. Your poet in *Naamah* is a masterly prig, though you've done him so sincerely that we accept his priggishness kindly. And your man of muscle is a beef-fed sentimentalist—the Agnostic lover—and your cynical husband is a refined monstrosity. A man would have made him grosser in some ways and yet less repulsive."

"A man," I answered, "would not have seen him with the woman's eyes. No man can see another man from the woman's point of view."

"'That's true—indisputably true as regards the marriage relation. But, my dear friend"—(there was a certain whimsical humour in his smile as he leaned towards me)—"I don't believe that artistic temperaments, about which we talk so much, are a bit different from other people's temperaments. I suppose I've got one—I don't know! But we like putting things off; we don't like being kept in order; we hate being bored; we expect the world to dance to our tune—and we excuse ourselves by our 'temperament.' . . . That for your private ear; it wouldn't do to utter such heresies openly."

We both laughed. Close by, a hideous black man tried to draw our attention to a performance in which he twisted his flattened nostrils and protruding lips into the likeness of various birds, beasts, and reptiles. The Reader noticed my gesture of distaste and said—

"Let us move on. These negroes are a nuisance."

He threw the man some coins, and we walked to a bench on the other side of the square. Here a quaint, big-eyed Arab child, with henna-dyed hair and thin little brown hands—what is it that is so appealing in Eastern hands?—one holding together the folds of its grey striped garment, the other a bunch of flowers, came up and offered me the nosegay. I took it, saying something to the little thing which drew a jesting remark from the Reader.

"Have you any children?" he asked suddenly.

"No."

"I have one—a boy—a jolly little chap. He's just going to Harrow. *He* hasn't got the artistic temperament, bless him!"

"Then he won't be an author?"

"No. If there's one thing he has a holy abhorrence of, dear fellow, it's the craft. No authoring for him! The bar or the army. Seems a queer choice of alternatives, but such has he decided."

The Reader's face lightened curiously, and his laugh was very soft and tender. I can see that he cares deeply for his boy.

"We had thought of having him over for the holidays; and he'd have been a splendid chum for me in my tramps—when we weren't wanted at the villa."

There came over his face that indefinable shade of melancholy, and I wondered.

"But," he added, "his mother didn't like the notion of his crossing alone when the gales were on."

The Muezzin call reminded me of the hour, and I got up. We strolled together out of the Cours, and up the hill, along a road bordered with ficus-trees on one side, and on the other by a low wall, against which leaned the ragged Arabs, their Scriptural faces silhouetted upon the wonderful blue, to which no blue on earth can be likened.

"I am taking you out of your way," I said.

"Oh, one can't walk too much in this place. When I get away from my desk I'm like a giraffe on the loose. I wish," he added abruptly, "that you'd let me talk over your new work with you, as you get on with it. Seriously, give me time to read. mark, learn, and inwardly digest, and I believe I could help you as well as anybody else."

Why, who could ever help me as he can? . . . I told him this, and how gladly I accepted the suggestion; and then I was moved to say—

"I should like to make something out of my life through my work—if it isn't too late."

"How can that be?"

"Ah, you don't know what it is to have failed in everything you have undertaken. It's owing to you that I haven't quite failed in this. You showed me the way. . . . That is what makes you seem different to me from other people."

As I looked at him, I saw an expression in his face which I could not quite understand, but which filled me with gratitude and gave me a new impulse of trust in him. As though I needed any new impulse! Have I not trusted him unhesitatingly from the beginning! . . . It was partly pity that was in his face, and a vague protecting tenderness. I think my look must have made him feel that I was grateful, for he spoke out impetuously.

"You! a child!—to talk of failing in everything! Why, you *are* a child—a little unformed child. I can't help speaking unconventionally. As you say, I'm different in my relation to you from other people, and I'm utterly glad of it. . . . Yes, you're a child, in spite of *Naamah* and the critics. You have looked upon one side of life from behind nursery bars. It's perfect nonsense for you to speak of things being too late. . . . You, so young, and so——" he waited a moment—"and with the promise of a brilliant career before you."

"Oh, but I am not young at all," I answered. "I have been married eight years. I am nearly thirty; and for a woman at that age, it is too late for many things."

He laughed.

"I am certain that you have not grown any older since the day you left here—ten years ago, didn't you tell me? Or else your fairy godmother was waiting for you on the pier when you landed, and touched you with her magic wand—for, you know, Philotis is an enchanted garden."

Ah, yes! that is how it is! Philotis is an enchanted garden!

... HAVE you any idea how unconsciously winning you were in those early days, when we were "the Reader" and "Esther Zamiel" to each other? And do you realise in the least how the mystery and the fascination of your beauty worked alike upon the half-poet and the whole man, so that at one moment I would dream of you as pure soul, an ethereal Influence with whom to soar into the realms of the gods; and at another I would be tormented by an inconsistent and most human longing to provoke the play of those unsuspected dimples which were always so chary of exhibiting themselves—particularly that one especial and enchanting dimple which was a pointer to the left curve of your upper lip, in one especial and enchanting smile. That was a little Nyanza, that dimple, waiting for the adventurous explorer to come along; the others were only dints which your fairy godmother made with the tips of her fingers when she stooped over your cradle at Philotis and marked you with the fairies' sign! And did you know, that by some queer racial freak, you had got a dash of the gipsy, dear—whence else gat you that free grace of tread, that startled-fawn poise of head, and the delightsomeness to you of green woods and running rills and wild things and earth-frolic? And did you know that that curved upper lip of yours, which pouted the wee-est bit when you smiled, and caught back upon your pretty teeth, was then—for all its tragic droop in sad times, and its look of pathetic futility—just the ripe-pomegranate, kissable lip of a passionate, laughter-loving child? No, you never realised in the very least your vivid, troublous, and altogether un-English charm.

And though I aimed at an Arthurian chivalry in the matter of respecting your reserve, how impossible it was not to construct theories about you, not to piece together scraps of your talk and stray allusions that you made, and draw inferences therefrom; —or rather to fail in drawing any inference that was satisfactory. For this puzzled me—that while of a surety, the pleasant land of

Bohemia was no unknown country to you, and you had undoubtedly wandered in the streets of that picturesque city of Prague, you yet seemed to have somehow acquired a knowledge of English provincialism and clericalism, nearly as complete in its way as Miss Austen's own. Then, too, how impossible not to speculate upon what grim experience might have befallen you, which, while leaving you with the bloom of maidenhood almost unbrushed, had yet inspired that vehement revolt in *Naamah* against things that are, and had brought the fateful look into your eyes.

Do you remember the morning at El-Meriem when you spoke of having failed in everything, and of its being perhaps too late to mend your life? And can you recall the moment when your big mournful brown eyes looked straight into mine, with the appealing trust of a lost child who has found a protector—the moment, which now thinking back upon it all, seems to me the critical moment in our joint relation?... What would you have said then, could you have known of the rush of bewildering emotion which swept over me, and of the longing I had to take your slim hand in mine, and then and there vow an eternal comradeship, a life's devotion in return for your confidence?

Too late! How the phrase from your lips moved me! Yes, too late no doubt for me and for millions of other men and women who have missed their supreme opportunity. But for you who had never come within touch of life's truest realities—I was convinced of that—for you—beautiful, rare, exquisite, aflame and athrill with undeveloped capacities, created to give and take blessedness, to love and to be beloved! That you should utter over yourself the knell, " Too late!"—It seemed pitiful.

My mind was torn with these thoughts and with wonderings about you—Esther Zamiel, who nevertheless was not Esther Zamiel—as I climbed the olive terraces behind your hotel that afternoon, haunting the place where you were staying, in the half presentiment and the dim hope, that a kind Fate might bring us together again. A benignant Fate indeed! All hail to the dread Sister! She was in a tender mood that day.

And so thus thinking, I tramped the lonely pine forest, which grew denser and more lonely the farther I got from the town. You know the rift in it,—of course, well—where one comes on that grand view of Sralta, rearing his flattened hump of naked rock above the dark mass of pines, as though it were some primæval altar, while the smoke of the charcoal-burners rising from the hill-furrows seemed clouds of incense before a shrine. And you know well too the cleared spot beyond, and the rough footpath bordered by lentiscus and sea-lavender leading to a tiny house set about with old fig-trees.

Ah yes, you are familiar enough with that quaint abode—the red-tiled roof and gable with a cross upon it; the narrow terrace and its balustrade of perforated brick, and the oranges hanging over the wall; and the extinguisher-shaped summer-house at one end, purple with bougainvillea! Even at that first glimpse I associated you in an inexplicable way with this little dwelling. I pictured you dreaming your early day-dreams on that sunny terrace. In imagination, I could see you gazing out over the balustrade towards the hazy sea and the unknown world, your tremulous face kindled, your eyes shining, and your chin up-lifted in that impulsive movement you make sometimes, which shows the curves of your beautiful throat. . . . And then. . . . ah, was not Fate good to us that day? . . . Did not I see a slender form in a long furred coat pacing slowly from the summer-house? And was it not indeed Esther Zamiel who came down the steps to the path where I was waiting? And you did not seem to think it at all wonderful that I should be there. Nor did it seem to me at all wonderful that you should say, as you did, simply, " I came to look at this house; we used to live here when I was young." And then do you remember how we stood together under the olive-trees; and how still it was—not a grey leaf swaying; and the queer crooked boughs showing so black against the moveless foliage. And how dreamily sounds floated up from the distant town—the tinkle of mule-bells; the hammer-strokes of workmen at the forge; the cathedral chime; and near by, the woodcutter at work and the soft cooing of pigeons?

And do you remember, too, what a strong scent came from the narcissus patch, and how, as you leaned against the terrace wall, you idly gathered some daisies and said that they weren't like English daisies—those sweet El-Meriem daisies, with their pink tips and their fat yellow hearts? And you said, too, that the anemones would very soon be out, and the asphodels in bloom; and we agreed that the asphodel is a disappointing flower, and has no right to its poetic traditions. . . .

How pleasant it is to call back those trivial things!

And do you remember our walk—our never-to-be-forgotten walk? How I asked you if there were not some *gourbis* close by; and you shook your head and said you did not know; and how presently a melancholy Arab came strolling along in ragged dignity, and you ran down and questioned him in Arabic. And how mock-indignant you were when I made a jest of your Arabic, declaring that it was mere argot; and how you retorted and challenged me, and I was obliged to own up to my own educational deficiencies—for I couldn't speak Arabic then. It was almost —not quite—a revelation to me, that light-hearted girlish aspect of you. Yes, you said the Arab had told you there was a *tribu* across the ravine, quite near, only that we must beware of the dogs.

And did I not catch at that inadvertent "we" of yours; so that you were obliged to come along and continue to be my interpreter?

And in what happy comradeship we set off! And were you as blithe and rejoicing in it as I was, I wonder? Yes, I think you were. Do you remember how at first you would not have me carry your cloak, till you were forced to yield it up, as we cleaved a way through the fir and undergrowth across the ravine? And how, as we mounted again, I made you sit down and rest, because you were panting? There was such a soft pink flush on your cheeks; and you talked so gaily, calling my attention now to this thing and then to that; and I found something infinitely touching in this capacity of yours to get pleasure out of Nature's trifles; and you seemed to me like a flower expanding in air and sunshine. . . . Do you remember the ladybird that settled on your neck? —Shall I ever see a lady-bird in the woods without again seeing you, and the pretty gesture with which you preened your head and drooped your lashes, as you tried to watch the insect meandering from your neck to your shoulder?—while I in my turn watched you, and admired the fashion of those golden dark rings fringing the nape of your neck, and the satiny sheen of the coil, which I fancied your maid must spend a long time in brushing to make it so glossy.

And then you looked up at me and laughed, and asked me if I knew the superstition that when a ladybird alighted upon one, something good was going to happen? . . .

Ah, my dear, my dear! Has there any good come to you through me?

WRITTEN
BY
ESTHER
VASSAL: SOMEHOW, I can't think of him now as "the
Reader," but as my friend, my comrade, the only
real friend and comrade I have ever had—except
Agatha Greste; and she married and went out
of my life so soon, that I can hardly count
her as a practical reality.

We seemed to make a leap forward in our friendship—to
become companions rather than master and pupil—two days ago
when we went to the *gourbis* together.

It was so odd that he should have been there when I came
down to the roadway from visiting my old home—just there
waiting for me, exactly, I could have fancied, as though Fate had
sent him.

And yet in that expedition we didn't talk much or very
intimately—till, at least, quite the end. It was the sense of
growing things, the wind in the branches, the sunlight flickering
on the bark, the sound of the birds and insects—all sorts of
outside and trifling circumstances, and the wonderful *feeling* of
it all, which seemed to bring us near to each other. I hadn't
much chance either of talking gravely while we ploughed our
path down and up the ravine. And there, when we got to the
top, lay the native encampment, with a ring of prickly pear
marking it round, and all the dogs running out and barking
at us. But he quieted them. He must have a nice way with
dogs and children, for the mob of half-naked copper-coloured
little creatures that followed the dogs, only played at being
frightened.

Then came out a brown girl with flashing eyes, and wearing
silver haik-pins and anklets, and bracelets that tinkled, tinkled as
she moved. She carried a brown baby; and when I talked to
her, could only giggle and nod. But she was content to chatter
to the Reader, crying at intervals, "Makash! Makash!" when he
was obliged from sheer shame, as I told him, to bring forth a few
halting words of Arabic. For now it was my turn to play the
critic, and to tease and exult over him, so that we all made merry
together like a pack of school-children on a holiday. But how

could any one help being glad of heart in this smiling Blue Land?

The women spread a clean mat on the ground inside the prickly-pear hedge, and other brown mirthful beings came out of the huts. They wore barbaric jewellery, and some of them held brown babies. They clustered round and examined my dress and trinkets, making soft gesticulations and infantile sounds of curiosity and delight. It was so lucky that I had some chocolate and a ribbon, and some trifles that I could give them as little presents. The Reader made me translate and interpret, for though he declares that he can read scholarly Arabic—which I take private leave to doubt—he says that Arabic argot is beyond him; and often I felt embarrassed, for I could not tell him quite all that the women said.

Then we looked into the *gourbis*, where were the skins drying which are to be made into water-bags. and the great pottery jars filled with grain, and the balls of wool for the weaving of bournouses. The kùss-kùss was cooking for the men's evening meal, and I tasted it first, and the Reader after me, and the woman with the heaviest bangles and anklets told us that Suliman liked the kùss-kùss best when it had meat in it, but that was only four or five times a year; and as for wine!—But that was forbidden by the Prophet. Then she stroked the fur of my coat and kissed my hand, which was a great honour, for she is the wife of Suliman, and Suliman is chief of the tribe.

Far back in the dimness of the *gourbi* were some raised yellowish patches, each showing two gleaming red spots, and those were the eyes of roosting fowls. Suliman's wife dived among them. She wanted to make a present in return for that five-franc piece of the Reader's, which insures meat for Suliman's kùss-kùss to-morrow. The brown woman laughed, the fowls cackled and cluttered, and one new-laid egg after another was brought out and put into the Reader's hands, to his great embarrassment, till I made a bag for them with my pocket-handkerchief, and so we carried them away.

When our merriment had come to an end, and we were across the ravine again, the words broke involuntarily from me, "I have been so happy." Again he gave me that pitying look.

"Aren't you ever happy at home?" he said.

Then all the light went out. Home!... In my mind's eye rose a picture of gloomy Grisewood against its background of mournful cedars and sagging grey sky, a picture, too, of my master's face with its cold, tired eyes and the lines about the nostrils. My breath caught in a strange little gasp.

"Home!" I cried wildly, impulsively, scarcely knowing what I said. "This is my home. I love this place. It makes me feel young and good and happy."

"Oh, you poor little thing!" he exclaimed. "Why shouldn't you be always happy and always at home? . . . For sure, home is where loving hearts dwell together in peace and oneness." . . . Then he added hastily, "I beg a hundred pardons, but—you interest me."

"Why?" I asked impulsively.

"I don't know. Your book interests me, *you* interest me. . . . And somehow I have felt all along that your life was a very lonely one, and very sad."

"Yes, it is sad," I answered. "And yet one needs so little on this beautiful earth to make one happy."

"Nothing but the liberty which God has given to the wild things He has made," said the Reader with a laugh, in which there was a note of bitterness; and he went on—

> "The birds that live i' the field
>   On the wild benefit of Nature, live
>   Happier than we; for they may choose their mates,
>   And carol their sweet pleasures to the spring."

"I know every word of that part," I said. "Once I had the presumption to dream of playing it."

"You! Ah, I forgot that you had once been an actress."

Presently we said good-bye. He told me that he was going back to Philotis that evening.

.   .   .   .

In the great Square Casphar there sounds continuously the drop, drop of multitudinous footsteps and the Babel of many voices. At this hour in especial it is thronged with the polyglot population of Philotis. For it is the hour when the band plays—and oh! how many times as a little girl I have sat on this very bench and have watched and listened and waited till the concert was over, and it was time to take train back to El-Meriem.

For old sake's sake, I often come down now to hear the band play. I know hardly any of the English or French people here, and no one takes any notice of me; and in the intervals, if I get bored with the familiar sights, I read or scribble. Tremlett is always with me, but one can't talk to one's maid. I can't, at any rate, talk to Tremlett in the way I have heard women talk to their maids. I dislike Tremlett, but she performs her duties so faultlessly, that if I wanted to do so I should have no excuse for sending her away. Besides, Mr. Vassal would be annoyed; it was he who chose Tremlett for me. She is the daughter of an old butler at Grisewood, who is dead, and Mr. Vassal thinks very highly of her as an entirely trustworthy person.

It is an interval between the pieces, and I have been studying the crowd. Such a curious crowd; every nationality, one would fancy, represented in it. There are men in Greek, Turkish, and Armenian dress; Jews in greasy gaberdines; French, English, and American residents, and English and American tourists. There are smart cavalry officers in uniforms of blue and red, and picturesque Zouaves and Spahis. There are gipsies and negroes and Moors; there are Arab women waddling along in trousers of a fulness that varies according to the rank of the wearer. . . . How funny that is ! . . . Then there are smug French shopkeepers and their wives; there are widows in weeds, and consumptive people in Bath chairs, and children and bonnes and grisettes. Sickly little Arab girls with their hair dyed red are pretending to kiss the hands of passers-by as they beg for coins. Here comes along a dirty Arab man carrying a load of skins newly flayed. All the dogs in the square rush at him and are driven back by the crack of his long whip, only to rally again. Out there at the end of the square streams a great band of gesticulating Arabs. Is it a political *émeute* or a rising among the Christians? Nobody takes any notice, and the band begins to play once more. It is merely a rush to a cheap auction that has been opened a little way off.

. . . I remembered that I had something to call for at the Arab jeweller's in the stair-street which leads to the old town. So Tremlett and I joined the band of shrouded figures which are always going up and down. At the top of the stairway stood several handsome, bold-looking girls in embroidered jackets with painted faces. I know them for the girls who sing and dance, and who, legislation ordains, shall have their dwellings marked in blue figures. I have a curious feeling about these girls. They don't look good, yet it is certain that they don't look unhappy. One can tell by their faces that they have never knelt in remorse and regret before maidenhood's desecrated altar. They have not been tormented by morbid fancies nor spiritual yearnings which have proved only a vain shadow. If there be any satisfaction in material pleasure, they must have discovered it. At least they must *live* their lives ; and in the strange by-ways of emotion through which they have passed, who can tell what sweet-smelling blossoms they may have gathered !

I got what I wanted at the jeweller's, and, turning out of the shop, saw the Reader coming towards me. The bright, interested look, which I have learned to know, illuminated his face as he greeted me. How good it is to call up that look!

"You are going into the old town," he said. "I wish you would let me come with you. I am now studying colloquial Arabic, and shall shortly resume my original attitude towards you—of critic."

This was a merry little expedition too—almost as merry as that to the *gourbis*, though there was all the time a disagreeable consciousness of gaunt, unsympathetic Tremlett stalking behind. I wonder if it struck her as odd that I should be in so gay a mood, and I wonder, too, what Mr. Vassal would have thought could he have followed us and listened to our chatter.

How quaint it all was—the irregular houses leaning together, the white-clad forms, the glimpses of Moorish courts and dim interiors, of great cool mosques and fountains and bowed worshippers. Then the fascinating suggestiveness of streets and windows! Here was an athletic middle-aged Arab carrying another Arab, who was old and fat, upon his shoulders, and just behind them two priests in cassock and shovel-hat; and after them a drove of donkeys laden with lentiscus faggots, and then a negro bearing a load of charcoal on his bent head, and butting his way through the crowd, shedding his charcoal as he went; and every now and then a group of stately Moors, who might have been posturing for an illustration in a pictorial bible. We sat on a bench and drank Arab coffee, and many a veiled woman passing, looked at me through the peep-hole in her yashmak, and laughed and nodded as her slippers flapped on over the stony way. Then we visited the shops and bought brass pots and kùss-kùss spoons with coral handles, and embroideries and charms against the evil eye, and many other odds and ends. And the Reader teased me again about my Arabic argot, and rebuked me once more for being a sentimentalist. That was when I had given a lettuce to a starved donkey and some goodies to a row of Arab boys, who were flattening their noses against the window of a French confectioner's at the foot of the old town.

"Now what is going to be the result of this injudicious benevolence?" he said. "The next nice watery lettuce that donkey sees, he will immorally grab and be whopped for. And those ragamuffins will never again be able to resist the temptation of sticky sweet-stuff, and they will steal and be sent to prison, and you will be responsible for the whole mischief."

And I retorted that the Reader's cynicism was but a poor, cheap affair—worse than his Arabic. . . . And so it went on, till the sun was near sinking and the street corners all shadow.

Trivial babble! But what a happy sense of comradeship and holiday-making it gave!

When we got to the Square Casphar again, I held out my hand to bid him good-bye.

"Won't you let me call you a carriage?" he said.

But I told him that the tram-car was just starting, and that for the sake of old times I must go in it.

"I will go too," he said. "I have a call to make half-way up the hill."

The sun was setting as the omnibus clattered up. It was a stormy sky—great splashes of purple-red cloud tinging the bay, and crimsoning angrily behind the pointed summits of the Vasques hills. The waves breaking on the sand were red too, and so were the sails of two boats scudding across Médiane. Surf broke over the long black reef at the end of Rassem, and there were broad white marks on the horizon-line. To-morrow will be bleak and tempestuous, but to-day Nature has been royally gracious, and tender and sweet as the scent which floats from orange-groves and rose-gardens.

.   .   .   .

A ravine runs furrowing the fir-covered hill which rises behind the Cosmopolitain. Its sides are woody with ilex, mimosa, and arbutus set among the pines; there is an underlay of heather; and many other wild plants and shrubs grow along the banks. Over the bronze-grey rocks there tumbles a mountain torrent, and along the side of the stream a narrow footpath curves, and turns into the heart of the forest.

This is my favourite walk, and often I spend hours in a shady nook, where a great fissured rock makes a rampart from the road and an ilex dips its branches into a shallow pool, with sandy bottom, and slippery stepping-stones bridging it. The stream steals gently out of the pool, tender-sounding as the clink of musical glasses, then, falling with hoarse murmur over a tiny precipice, it foams and rages among miniature boulders, as might the life flowing in tranquil course, till a great love stirs it to passionate tumult. The sun glints on wet briars, and the soft roar of the water brings an indescribable sense of lonely remoteness from the common world, so that if it were not for the faint rumble of carriages up and down the zigzag, there would seem no connecting link with prosaic existence.

Looking up the dell, the tall columns of the firs blend into each other, and the branches cross and interlace among the blobs of foliage. A palpable resinous scent hangs in the air. The sun sends a ray dancing askant the red-dappled boles; and other rays gleam on the cascade drops, while through the glistening green of pine-needles I seem to see deep into unfathomable azure, as far as Infinity.

Ah! do you know the beauty of those quivering pine-needles drawn upon the great blue concave of this enchanted land?

Here I write and dream—dream out my new love-story.

It is the Reader's pet dreaming haunt too, he tells me. Several mornings we have met and sat by the torrent while he has read from my manuscript, and we have talked over my story—and many other things. But our talk is so wandering and fragmentary, that when I try to remember and write it down, half its meaning has gone.

Maybe this is because so much of its life and vividness lies in tones, looks, gestures, and even in the pauses of speech. So real and great a fact has our fellowship become—for indeed, were there no compact in words, I should still know him for my close and dear friend—that in all my solitary hours I am never without the feeling of companionship. At those times I have the continual consciousness of his eyes searching mine, in the way they do when we talk—gazing straightly, clingingly, piercing barriers, till I realise as definitely as I realise my pulse-beats, the rare electric force which draws our inner selves into relation.

And I wonder within myself, since this pure intellectual friendship is so sweet, what more subtle joy would love itself have to offer. . . . If this be friendship, what then may be the Beyond?

Truly, it does not seem so difficult here, in the perfumed glow and glamour of the Blue Land, to dream oneself beyond the borders of friendship into the consecrated dual life—the love-life in which hearts affined might throb to the rhythm of Nature's music, sense and soul, revelling exultant in sun, and sky, and waving branch—in the reed chant of Pan, and the virgin's hymn of praise to Aphrodite. . . . Ah! I am pagan in the passing hour of spring.

A dream. . . . But how fair a dream!

And all the time the torrent sings its own rich-toned song. And the words of it are those which he read me from a book one day.

"Love! love! There is nothing that endures but love!"

. . . .

To-day he said to me, with that odd shake of his shoulders:

"I should like to ask you a question—tout droit et de bon cœur—comme ça——"

" Tell me what it is."

" Do I dare ? . . . You have written about love: and sufficiently convincingly for most people. Yet I am sure that what I have already hinted at is true. As far as actual realisation of the master-passion goes, you are still a child behind nursery bars. Am I not right ? "

I answered him frankly, "Yes, you are right. I have never loved."

" Your art, then, has been all-sufficing to you? Is that what you have fed your heart upon since early girlhood—the desire to be great? And how has the human emotion been kept pent? Did you make *Naamah* your safety-valve ? "

It must have been something in my face which checked his impulsive questioning, and caused the change in his tone as he added—

" I beg your pardon. I spoke to the artist rather than to the woman."

We had been standing at the shallow where the stepping-stones are ; and now we crossed by them, and began to mount the hill, walking in silence along a side path which leads to the hotel.

At last, he said abruptly—

" Esther Zamiel—I know no other name to call you by—I want to say something. . . . Of course I have seen you go in and out of the Hôtel Cosmopolitain, and naturally conclude that you are staying there. My wife and I are in the villa-annexe. Therefore, does it not strike you that as we are bound sooner or later to discover each other, we might as well declare ourselves at once ? Of course you will command me as you please, but that seems to me logic. I don't suppose it's necessary for me to assure you that your secret is as safe with me as though I had never had the privilege of meeting you in Mr. Brock's office as the ' Reader '; also that I have not even looked at the hotel list."

Then again, all in a moment, there came over me that extraordinary mystic perception which I have had once or twice —the instantaneous mind-flash backwards and forwards, by which I *know* that in some strange incorporeal fashion this man's being and mine are inextricably linked. We looked into each other's eyes, and to me the look seemed a recognition through the mists of æons ! . . . That was my fancy. But, of course, he could have had no such fantastic thought. . . . Yet sometimes I think that he too *knows*. . . .

I said no word. Just then it was impossible to talk out, for some French people had strolled up, and were chattering behind us ; and we weren't alone again till we had passed through the wicket-gate into the Cosmopolitain garden. Then he made straight for a secluded gravelled nook, closed in by dwarf bamboos, where there are seats and a table ; and here, planting his stick in the gravel, he stood facing me.

"Well!" he exclaimed. "This is what I have got to say. Release me from my parole. And this also—my name is Robert Vassal."

And now there was borne upon me the meaning of that fatalistic flash! It seemed to me that my inner self must all along have been aware of his identity with Mr. Vassal's nephew. . . . But how blind, how foolish not to have guessed with my bodily faculties ! . . . For a moment I felt giddy.

"What is the matter?" he asked. "There is nothing so extraordinary in the revelation. I only wonder that you haven't got to know before this who is Mr. Brock's pet reader. Frank Leete might have told you."

"Yes . . . there is . . . it is extraordinary," I stammered, "because I . . . I am Mrs. Vassal . . . your uncle's wife."

" *You !* " he cried in a sort of smothered gasp, and gave me a queer, wild stare ; and then burst into a yet wilder laugh. "And you didn't know?"

"No. . . . How should I know?"

"Yes, . . . of course . . ." he answered absently, staring still.

"Perhaps you wouldn't have cared to help me if *you* had known?" I said.

"Why not? You are Esther Zamiel."

He said the words defiantly, as though he were maintaining a disputed assertion.

"I am your uncle's wife," I said again.

He laughed, the same queer laugh.

"Yes ; you are the wife of Hector Vassal, the millionaire, as they call him. You are the mistress of Grisewood Castle, and of Tregarth, and of the mansion in Grosvenor Street, and of the yacht, and of the Vassal diamonds, and the Lord knows what besides. . . . Yes ; how the lace and the big pearl puzzled me—you didn't notice—that day at Brock's ! Well, you are all that ; and I perfectly understand why you are also a most unhappy woman."

"I am not unhappy—now."

The words came out involuntarily. Did he realise, I wonder, how much he himself has done to mend my lot? He has given me my power of working : he has given me his friendship and sympathy . . . and so I am no longer unhappy.

That's what it amounts to.

He did not answer. I keep seeing him in my mind as he stood, his profile bent, his gaze fixed moodily outward through a cleft in the bamboos, his hands clenched nervously on the crook of his stick. Then suddenly he looked at me, his eyes staring still, but bright and soft, and less wild.

"You have been to me as a star shining in darkness—Esther —Esther Zamiel!" he said. "I hope that the light is not now going to be all quenched."

I stretched out my hand. It seemed to me as though I were stretching it forth to importune Fate, that I might hold fast this thing she was threatening to take from me—this beautiful and noble friendship, the only good gift she has ever let fall into my life. How can I bear to lose it? How can I meekly give up all that I care most for in the world? I have written it, and I am not ashamed. Why should I be ashamed? Are we not friends?

That was what I said to him. "We are friends."

He took my hand and held it in a tight clasp for a moment.

"Yes—friends always, even if we never see each other. For how will it be henceforth with our friendship—our pleasant literary intimacy? That's the trouble. I don't know if this can go on."

We faced each other, blankly and miserably, confronting together, as it were, a common peril. Then I said—

"But a woman . . . a wife is not a slave. I am not bound to submit to dictation that is unreasonable."

"Would it be unreasonable? I am not so sure. A wife has to judge of those things, however, for herself. But it seems to me that in such a matter you would be bound to obey your husband—your lord and master."

"My master!" With all the miles of sea and land intervening, I seemed to feel the compelling force of my master's cold, imperious gaze—that indescribable current of mingled fascination and repulsion, but of entire supremacy, which I have no power to resist. No, it would be useless to strive against my master.

"I am a coward," I exclaimed. "I cannot stand against him. He makes me do what he chooses."

"Is not that perhaps best? Otherwise your life might be harder; and our friendship is certainly not worth that price. Besides," he added, "there is another will to be counted in the matter."

"Another will!"

"My wife's. She has strong feelings on the subject. She regards Mr. Vassal as our enemy—hers, mine, and our son's."

"But . . ." I don't know why there should have come over me a sense of chill and constraint; yet so it was, and I could not go on.

"I am bound to consider my wife's wishes, as much—perhaps more, than you are bound to consider those of your husband."

I had never heard before in his voice the note that was in it now; it affected me strangely; we were both silent. . . . Presently he said, jerkily—

"I must think the thing out. I am sorry that we know each other's names. It would have been better had we remained Esther Zamiel and 'the Reader' as long as might have been. . . . Good-bye. . . . I ought to be back at the villa."

So that is what has happened; and I don't know what to do.

I suppose that according to the ordinary laws of conjugal relationship, I ought to tell Mr. Vassal of my discovery, and ascertain his wishes. But—am I not justified in looking upon our marriage relation as outside the pale of ordinary conjugal law?

.   .   .   .

It is three days since I parted from the Reader in the bamboo arbour. I have not seen him since. He has not been in the garden, nor has he sought me in the ravine. Perhaps he has gone, as he once told me was his habit, on a long tramp to "think the thing out."

Has he told his wife about me, I wonder!

Mione's description of Mrs. Robert Vassal is vividly before me; and she is so real, in my imagination, that I can hardly believe I have not seen and known her—that mad yellow woman, with the fierce yellow eyes, the cameo face, the determined will through all her madness, and the intense love for her husband! Could that have been the splendid love, in its terrible and magnificent possibilities, to which he alluded? I find myself constantly searching the square, and in passing vehicles, or the grounds of the hotel, for a sight of her, but in vain. I know that instinct would make me recognise her were we ever near together. But it is evident that she no longer sits in the Cosmopolitain garden; and the only sign of occupancy I have ever seen at the annexe has been a brougham drawn up, which I know to be that of my own doctor. The annexe has its separate roadway, and a rose-trellis divides its grounds from those of the hotel. Yesterday my doctor asked me if the Mr. and Mrs. Robert Vassal who inhabit the villa are any connections of mine.

I replied that there was a family connectionship, but that I was not acquainted with Mrs. Vassal.

Then yielding to the immense curiosity I feel about this woman, I put to the doctor some trivial question concerning her health, remarking that I never saw her driving or walking. His reticence rebuked me for a breach of professional etiquette.   He never talks about his patients.   " Mrs. Robert Vassal suffers a good deal," he answered, "and she seldom leaves the villa."

.   .   .   .

To-day I received a telegram from Mr. Vassal.   He is with the yacht at Mandour, and wishes me to join him on a short cruise.   Mrs. Raphon, Mione Arathoon, Lady Diana Cleeve, Mr. Paravel the writer, and one or two others, are of the party.   They and the yacht will be here to-morrow.

.   .   .   .

Everything has come back—the terrible oppression of false-seeming ; the weight of sadness ; the shrinking from life's hideousness, and from a galling yokeship ; the gasping, as for very breath, in the fetor of this moral prison.

Here, on the yacht off Mandour, that hateful atmosphere encompasses and stifles me.   But there—beyond the sea and the mountains—there, in blue beautiful Philotis, lies the enchanted garden of peace and purity.

. . . It is a wild night ; there is a mistral blowing ; the wind whistles through the rigging, and the surf booms yonder on the shore !   And I lie in the groaning darkness, panting, yearning, bound.

And something stronger than fleshly fetters, fiercer than the elemental fury, drives my spirit through the wrack and clangour, across sea and land, and over the granite hills, to a fair haven, moonlit, rose-scented, murmurous with tender cooings, and blessed by benignant influences, where troubled hearts may rest from aching and kindred souls commune in safety.

It is he—my friend—who has given me the key to the enchanted garden ; and not man nor devil shall wrest it from me.

I have the dreadful consciousness of a sort of demoniac hatred in Mr. Vassal's eyes.   They seem continually watching me, forcing mine, as it were, mesmerically towards them ; and their gleam gives me a sick frightened feeling, making me as helpless as though I were indeed under the domination of an evil power.   Sometimes I think that look in Mr. Vassal's eyes makes even Mrs. Raphon uncomfortable.   Yesterday I saw her turn pale and wince, when, as she was talking in that way which I dislike so intensely, and which causes me to almost dislike Mione for joining in, Mr. Vassal turned upon her in a savage sort of fashion, and said something in a low tone that had the effect of completely quenching her vivacity.

In the evening, however, some dancing-girls came from Mandour, and turned the deck into a scene of curious gaiety ; and by that time Mrs. Raphon had recovered herself, and Mr. Vassal's humour was changed, and they seemed excellent friends once more as they sat and whispered together through the performance. But it filled me with an unspeakable dreariness—the dance of these bold beautiful girls; and I had a nausea as of the husks the swine do eat.

I have never seen Mr. Vassal in so peculiar a mood as now— or rather, in so many peculiar moods. Perhaps it is the Eastern atmosphere which lends a certain suggestiveness to his talk, and makes so plainly evident the contempt in which he holds women —the Eastern atmosphere too, perhaps, that accounts for his alternating fits of wild geniality and of sullen depression, while again at times he seems devoured by the craving for some new excitement, so that he scours Mandour in search, as he puts it, of a sensation.

This evening at dinner he said that he had found one which had been difficult to negotiate, had cost him twenty pounds, and promised to be almost as exhilarating as a Black Mass had once proved. He asked Mione if she would like to see a Black Mass, at which she shuddered and crossed herself—for, like all the Delmars, she is a rigid Catholic.

"Please don't," she said. "I'm not superstitious, I'm not bigoted, and I'm not exclusive; but I do draw the line at the devil."

"I love superstition," said Mr. Paravel. "Alas! the Reformation killed our superstition, and at the same time it killed our art."

But Lady Diana Cleeve ignored Mr. Paravel's gentle attempt to turn the conversation. She is a mundane-mystic, a clever woman of the London world, and sufficiently handsome and agreeable to be a welcome visitor at Grisewood. Having no orthodox scruples, she plied Mr. Vassal with questions, and he went on to tell of his experience of Eastern and Western sorcery, and of certain magical incantations in which Jewish babies are said to be sacrificed, whereat it was Mrs. Raphon's turn to shudder.

"I can't bear to hear you," she cried. "You must be a black magician yourself."

"Yes, I believe I've a touch of the Diabolist in me," he answered. "It goes with my temperament."

"Temperament!" repeated Mr. Paravel in his musical voice. "Shall I tell you what it is that absolutely rules the world? It is temperament."

Mr. Paravel had been abstractedly playing with a peach, a

half-listening smile upon his mediæval-looking face. Mione says of him that he ought to carry a halo under his arm when he goes out to a party, instead of an opera hat. He is an Oxford don—a man of grave thinkings which are often hidden under a show of æsthetic fantasy; a writer on art subjects, his chosen period the Renaissance, so that sometimes his talk is as an echo of the troubadours, or a waft from the Rose of Chivalry. He interests me in a fashion. Just now he is meditating a new work, of which he has told me the gist; and he is so inwardly absorbed that I have been wondering what his attraction can be to Mr. Vassal that he has been invited to join this yachting party. Yet I have sometimes fancied that Mr. Vassal's tendency towards psychological analysis is stronger than I had imagined. Possibly, however, Mr. Paravel's presence may be accounted for by the fact that he is a great friend of Lady Diana Cleeve.

"I speak of 'temperament' in its English sense," he added, "not in its usual French acceptation—if, indeed, one can define the term clearly enough to give it a sense."

"I should like to know how you define it," said Lady Diana.

"Ah, how ! . . . As an imponderable quantity—a mist, an atmosphere, which permeates, surrounds, qualifies, and binds together an individuality—an unknown something, no more to be analysed than you can analyse animal magnetism or spiritual affinity. A link between body and soul; of the substance of both, and yet neither. Briefly, the essence of the personality."

"In fact," put in Mr. Vassal, "that indefinable something which, according to poets' drivel, expresses love."

"I certainly imagine," answered Mr. Paravel, his face losing a little of its dreaminess as he leaned forward, smiling sympathetically, "that one might pretty safely define love as the point of contact between two temperaments."

"Just as one might define many a marriage as a tragedy of temperament," said Lady Diana, who delights in such discussions.

"That is unquestionably true," affirmed Mr. Vassal, with an acrid laugh.

"And you are quite right," Lady Diana went on, addressing Mr. Paravel, "in what you say about the absolute tyranny of temperament. It is so insidious that we are almost unconscious of it, though as a matter of fact, from the time we get up in the morning till the time we go to sleep at night—and who can answer for the influences that regulate dreams?—every thought and action are governed by temperament. You wonder why a person enters the room in a particular way, and has certain peculiarities of gesture and unaccountable tricks of speech. That person is simply fulfilling mechanically the dictates of temperament."

Mione was gazing thoughtfully out of the saloon window.

"Mrs. Arathoon, what are you plotting?" asked Loseley Allard.

"Your conquest," returned Mione, turning sharply.

"Ah, that is accomplished already," said he gallantly. "When you are present, I renounce art, transcendentalism, and all their works, and yield myself to the minor excitements of life."

"That, anyhow, should simplify existence," said Mione. "I must say, Mr. Paravel, that you booky people seem to me to waste a good deal of time in running round your own tails. Loseley is more practical. He extracts his minor excitements out of his friends—dinners, I suppose, and such trifles—like the street boy pulling periwinkles out of the shell. Now I don't hanker after affinities and 'essences of the personality'—whatever that may mean—and points of contact, and the rest of the rubbish. I like good embroideries—Cretan by preference—and old silver, and hunters, and diamonds, and plenty of clothes—fine batiste, and petticoats with cascades of valenciennes—and the remainder accordingly. My temperament would get on quite nicely if I had money enough to buy all the things I wanted."

"Well now, suppose we start off," said Mr. Vassal. "I see Osman hanging round waiting for orders. You shall take all you can stand of my twenty pounds' worth of sensation."

It turned out that we were only able to stand about ten minutes of it. Before long we found ourselves at the heart of the old town of Mandour, in a mysterious Moorish court open to the sky, flickeringly illuminated by Arab lamps, and with galleries from which white-shrouded heads protruded, and occasional eldritch shrieks issued; below, a mass of evilly excited faces, tom-toms beating, clouds of incense rising, and in the midst of the incense, a saturnalia of bearded ghouls, writhing their unclean limbs, uttering devilish cries, dancing on burning coals, gashing themselves with knives, swallowing scorpions— horrors unnameable—I know not what, for I could look no more. Here was certainly the flavour of diabolism. Worst part of the horror seemed the expression of Mr. Vassal's own face when he turned it towards me, as the other pairs, sickened already, moved to the door. Mr. Paravel had been the first to escape. Mione followed him. Mrs. Raphon glanced at Mr. Vassal, but he motioned her forward with Loseley Allard, and taking my hand, placed it within his arm. He stopped behind the rest, at one of the outer pillars of the court, and made me stand against it, thus shielded from sight of the performance. There was an angry movement in the multitude when it became aware of the retreat of the English party—and a crowd of Mandour fanatics is not a monster to be bearded lightly. Mr. Vassal looked round for our dragoman.

"That damned Osman has got frightened and made off," he said. "This is a meeting of religious madmen, and it might be dangerous to force a way. As a sensation, the thing is crudely brutal. You can keep your eyes shut, though perhaps that might be a pity. They are going to swallow live snakes, and probably one or two will kill themselves before it's over. There should be some excitement in that. Don't shudder; it's only their short cut to Paradise."

I blurted out something wild—asked if he had exhausted all the varieties of sensation, that he must make one in the watching of torture—said that perhaps this was with a view to inventing new methods for inflicting it.

"Oh, by God!" he exclaimed, "you hit the mark. Modern civilisation doesn't give a man much scope for punishing a woman who has made herself a curse to him. One has to remember that he is a gentleman. . . ."

Presently he said in a quieter tone, "I suppose that you look upon me as a sort of devil. . . . You don't answer me, so I'll take the compliment for granted. Perhaps I am. That's the result of marrying for love. . . . A blasé sensualist with a big brain—the modern definition of the devil! And it pretty well defines *me!*"

He turned round and became absorbed in the performance. I imagined that the snake business was proceeding, and with my eyes shut, leaned hard against the pillar—I haven't the least idea for how long. The thrilling hush, then the excited swell and murmur of the crowd, the shrill screams from ghosts above, and the unearthly howls of grey ghouls below, turned me sick. Through the shrieking I could hear Mr. Vassal's cold chuckle. He was amused at the show. But after a minute or two, I knew that he had turned again to me, and that his arm was holding me up, as he fumbled in his pocket for his flask. Then just as everything was going black, the silver cup was put to my lips.

"Drink some," he said; "this thing is really beastly."

I did as he bade me, and the clammy faintness passed. He filled the cup again and took a draught of the spirit himself.

"They've packed the doorway," he said. " But I'll chance

it in a minute. I assure you that if I were the devil, I'd choose a more refined sort of torture for you than this."

After a few minutes he spied Osman the dragoman, and the two manœuvring a passage, got me out. We stood in a dark Arab street out of sight of the horrors, and out of hearing of the yells.

"Please go back," I said. "Osman will take me to the boat."

"No; I've had enough of it. As a sensation, the thing wasn't worth twenty pounds."

He gave an order to the dragoman, who went on, and I was alone with my master. Soon we reached the open space by a mosque, and he told me to sit down.

"Yes, if I were really a devil," he repeated, "I should practise more subtle methods. There's where the dramatic instinct comes in : you ought to appreciate that."

All of a sudden he bent forward and gripped my wrist so tightly that it hurt me.

"And that's why I'm not going to interfere in the least with your sentimental friendship for Robert Vassal," he said. "You can see as much of him as you please; only it's not to be in my house, remember. You may meet him how and where you choose, provided that it's outside Grisewood and Grosvenor Street and my presence. I've no objection whatever."

I stared up at him bewildered, not knowing what to say or to think. And it seemed to me in the pale light which played upon it, that his cold, puffy face, with its glittering eyes and deep lines and satirical smile, did in truth resemble that of a Mephistopheles. Yet the feeling that surged through my bewilderment, my repulsion and terror, was one of intense relief; for the key of the enchanted garden remains in my keeping. Then, what does anything matter? I have always my Friend.

"You didn't expect that grace," he said, ironically chuckling. "Perhaps, after all, I'm not such a devil as you think me."

At that moment Mione's voice called from the top of the flight of steps leading to the mosque, where she stood with Loseley Allard and Mrs. Raphon.

"The battle has been fierce and sanguinary," she cried, "and the list of casualties serious. Mr. Paravel has lost his halo, and Lady Diana her temper; and Loseley has shed his blood in a vain struggle to rescue Aunt Rhoda's pince-nez from the clutches of the Infidel. As for me, I've had enough, thank you, of sensation for one evening. Great Cæsar! you may have all the rest of your twenty pounds' worth for yourself."

Presently Mr. Paravel and Lady Diana appeared also, they

too having retreated to the mosque. Mrs. Raphon hysterically attached herself to Mr. Vassal, and I moved to the other side of Mione. Thus we walked down to the shore, and took boat back to the yacht.

. . . . . .

I am at Philotis again. The yacht has gone, and Mr. Vassal and his party with it.

A cold caught that night at Mandour has kept me within doors. It is chill and rainy; and soddenness and desolation have fallen upon the Blue Land. I, too, feel desolate. I have so wanted to see the Reader, and to tell him that we may continue to meet and be friends. Before leaving I gave the concierge a note for him, to say that I had gone in the yacht to Mandour, and that I hoped he would be still at Philotis on the date of my return, which I duly appended. I thought he would have replied to the missive, or at least, when I did come back, have called to inquire; but there has been no word.

Yet I have always the feeling of his nearness, though now it is as of nearness on the other side of a thick grating. Why should he not have written a kindly line? It would have been natural; it would have been courteous.

Does he wish me to understand that I have over-estimated his interest in me—that in his official capacity of the Reader, I, as Esther Zamiel, a young writer of promise, might have had a certain literary claim upon him, which, knowing me now as Mr. Vassal's wife, he desires to repudiate? Have I, out of my need and longing, been all the time imagining a sympathy that never really existed? Could he have even misconstrued my frankness and my leaning upon him as an ordinary man of the world might misconstrue them? Could he fancy——?

No, I won't write it. The bare thought is ignoble. But as it comes over me—and it will come in spite of myself—I shudder in unspeakable humiliation.

. . . . . .

Perhaps it is that Mrs. Robert Vassal refuses to countenance our friendship.

Perhaps they have left Philotis. The season is ending: the rain is over now, and spring in a great glad burst is upon us: the almond-trees have shed their petals, and the fig-branches are putting forth leaves.

No. I asked Tremlett to inquire if Mr. and Mrs. Robert Vassal are at the annexe, and the concierge informed her that they are still there, but are leaving in a few days.

I cannot let him go out of my life without stretching forth a hand—without at least being sure that we part by his wish. It is right that I should tell him I have received Mr. Vassal's sanction to our acquaintanceship—our "sentimental friendship"!

What made him use that phrase?

And then there is my literary work! He promised to read and give me his opinion of the chapters as I wrote them, as "the Reader" might do. And I have several to show him.

Yet an unaccountable dread of I know not what, holds me back from writing—the feeling that by summoning him I may be invoking the calamitous irrevocable.

.   .   .   .

I have written. Only a few formal lines asking him to call.

.   .   .   .

I waited nervously.... We are now within the pale of the Conventions; and he was ceremoniously announced and ushered in.

Everything was changed, and he himself changed also. He looked worn and ill at ease. His manner was constrained; there seemed somehow a cloud over his face; but his eyes, earnest and sad, were as true lights shining out of the cloud.

He made some banal remarks—about the weather, Mandour, the emptying of Philotis.

"You are going away too?" I said.

"Yes; I've got to be back at *Views*. Ought I to mention that I am the editor of that flourishing journal?.... I'm taking my wife across, and shall leave her at Hyères till one can depend on the weather in England."

Then I exclaimed—and indeed I was deeply hurt:

"You would have gone without saying good-bye to me?"

"I am here. Always the last moment, you see! Is that the artistic temperament?"

I threw off the forced pleasantry as though it had stung me. And his nervous laugh gave place to an expression of almost tragic gloom.

"Forgive me," he said.

"You would have gone—if I had not written. And I wrote, too, before."

"Yes."

"I wanted to say—it seems right—that Mr. Vassal has no objection to our knowing each other."

"Ah!"

He made no other comment, but an odd light came into his face; and then the cloud spread again directly, as though he had been momentarily glad, but was on the whole disappointed at the information. I went on.

"Perhaps it would be best to say Mr. Vassal's exact words—that he had no objection whatever to our meeting, provided it were not at Grisewood or in Grosvenor Street—or in his presence."

"The proviso was surely unnecessary."

"I did not ask his permission; he spoke of his own accord."

"It is strange, isn't it?"

"I don't know."

"Well," he said, "that limits things."

"Yes. . . . But here. . . ."

It was all so jerky. I can't recall anything but bald words.

"Oh, here!"

He sat moodily staring out of the window and saying nothing. I seemed to feel that the invisible barrier between us was getting thicker and thicker, and that I *must* tear it away.

"If you would help me still in my work. . . . Why should it not be as before? . . ." I stammered. "Could I not write to you sometimes?"

"Yes; there's no reason why you shouldn't write—or even call upon me at my office, since I can't see you at your own house. . . . Many of my lady contributors to *Views* do call upon me at my office—if you were a contributor. There's no reason why you shouldn't write," he repeated; "just as Esther Zamiel would have written. . . ."

"And you . . . as the Reader?"

"No." He made a quick gesture. Then he turned his eyes upon me, and said slowly, "I *want* to be the Reader. But don't you see?—it's difficult."

"You said. . . . Perhaps it is. . . ." I went on stammeringly. "Perhaps you think that you ought not to help me, because of what Mrs. Vassal feels about the connectionship with my husband?"

"*You* are Mrs. Vassal." He gave an odd little laugh. "My wife is Mrs. Robert Vassal. No, I haven't mentioned you to my wife."

I don't know why I felt glad. Presently he added, "I mean as Mrs. Vassal."

"But as Esther Zamiel? . . . You said—in one of your letters, I remember—that she had read some of the *Naamah* proofs?"

"Yes—only one or two sets."

"Does she . . . ." I feel always a curious hesitancy in uttering the name. "Does Mrs. Vassal help you with your work?"

"Some years ago she helped me a great deal. That I am what I am, is entirely owing to my wife. Perhaps it is well that I should tell you this. Perhaps, too, I ought to explain that her

claim on my gratitude is all the stronger because, mainly through
anxiety and attendance upon me at a trying crisis of our lives, to
which she was physically unequal, her health and nerves gave
way, and her mind is not now brilliantly clear as it once was.
That is why when the *Naamah* proofs seemed to interest her—
she took them up accidentally—I encouraged her to go on with
them."

" But—you said it was only one or two sets ? "

"Yes—she fell ill again, and has not been able to do anything
of the kind since."

There was another silence.   He played absently with a silver
wine-cup on the table, which is one of the things I bought in the
old town that day we were there together—I wondered if he
recollected it, and how light-hearted we had been.   The thought
of it all blended with the long cadences which the rustle of the
palm-leaves made ; and the same fancy may have been in his
mind, for he said suddenly in an absent way—

"Do you like the sound of the wind ?. . . It seems to come from
such a long way off ! "

" This is a ghastly sort of joke, isn't it ? " he added abruptly,
his dreamy tone changing.

" What ? "

" The whole show ! Life, love, and all the rest.   It really
seems sometimes as though the Demi-urgos had been allowed to
try his hand at world-making, and were laughing in his sleeve at
the mess he has made of things, and at the fine fighting that goes
on among the devils he has set loose in us."

" The devils ! "   I wondered of what he was thinking.

" We're full of them—we writing people.   Good demons and
bad demons !   And upon my soul I don't know whether the good
or the bad are most responsible for the best work we do.   I know
that when I've honestly tried to give the moral excellences an
innings, I've done my feeblest and insincerest work.   And the
other way on, when I've let go the brake."

I made some faint remonstrance.

" No, I couldn't let the brake go altogether," he said.   " Seriously, I'm too great a coward.   Besides, I've built a wall round
myself—a wall of hard and fast obligation—dead-letter respectability.   But it strikes me sometimes that I might be a truer man
and a greater artist if I had the courage to knock down my wall
and strike out for the open."

He got up.

" Talking of demons, my poetic one has been pretty active
lately.   You'll see the result shortly in *Views*."

He did not seem to hear the question I asked about his poem.

"Don't you think," he said, as though he were taking up some previous argument, "that conscience may after all be only a geographical and chronological question? There's not a sin you could mention which I couldn't show you to have been at some time and in some place accounted a virtue. You know that when Herodotus was shocked, and reproved the Scythians for eating their fathers and mothers, they bade him not blaspheme."

He half held out his hand, but let it fall to the back of a chair. "Good-bye," he said.

I got up too and faced him, and I would not say good-bye. I would not let him go like that; and I knew that my voice was choky and my eyes swimming, and I did not care.

"Won't you tell me—what I am to do?" I said desperately.

He leaned over the chair, looking intently at me, and his face softened from its hard, veiled expression, while his voice deepened and shook slightly as he answered—

"How can I tell you what to do—I who am weaker and more doubtful and more ignorant than you yourself?"

"Tell me whether you want us to go on being friends. . . . It doesn't seem so quite."

"You think that I don't care whether I ever see you again or not?"

"I don't know."

"Then I'll tell you that to see you and talk to you sometimes would be just the greatest pleasure I could have in life. . . . So when we are both in London again I'll write to you. I'll write and ask you to do something for *Views*. And you shall come and see me, and we'll talk over the work."

"Thank you. . . . Then I shall wait until you write to me?"

"Yes, that will be best."

"You see," he said, "yours was the true instinct which made you want to keep the art-life distinct from the life of conventions. I like this standing with you outside the walls of the city. We have the whole free wilderness to roam in—the great, grand, poetic wild."

He held out his hand again. I put mine into it, and so we stood with them clasped.

"Esther Zamiel of the Wilderness," he said solemnly. "Not Mrs. Vassal. That name belongs to the City and the Conventions. Esther Zamiel, give me your friendship, and let me give you mine. And we will thank Heaven for that which is the second reallest thing the world holds."

"The second reallest!"

He laughed.

"Never mind grammar; we can keep that for our books There is one thing more real, but it is for the elect souls."

"What is that?"

"Whosoever loves knows the cry of this voice," he said. "Perhaps you will have to hear that voice before you do the best work that is in you; and perhaps you will be happier if you never hear it. . . . Now good-bye."

And so he left me.

.   .   .   .

He promised to write, but he has never done so. It is more than three months since I came back from Philotis, and I have received no communication from the office of *Views*, official or personal.

I have read his poem. He calls it *The Garden of Enchantment!* And while I read, I wondered whether some sort of occult telegraphy had conveyed to him the unspoken words in which during many hours of loneliness I have talked to him as to my other self. I seem to find the echo of them here. And that thought-fellowship of Philotis, instead of lessening with time and distance, has become an uncanny haunting and a bitter pain.

All this while he has been in London. I have read his articles in *Views*. I see his name mentioned in various papers. Our lives seem to run in parallel grooves, yet we never meet face to face.

He was at the first night of Dr. Quintin Glaive's new play. We were in a box, and he sat in the front row of the stalls with the critics. How their faces reminded me of *Claudia!* I saw him talking to Frank Leete, and wondered if he knew that I was there.

And last week I went to hear a debate in the House of Commons, and through the grating of the ladies' gallery I looked down upon him as he sat, his hat tilted over his brows, engrossed in what was going on, occasionally exchanging a remark with the man next him, or scribbling something on a sheet of notepaper, or else animatedly joining in a "Hear, hear." I remembered his having once said to me, "A man wants two interests in life. Literature isn't enough; it's too desky and cramping." My feeling of remoteness seemed despairingly intensified by the sight of him in this place—one of the distinctive crowd of legislators; a man in the world of men, touching, so to speak, the pulse of Great Britain. I remembered what he had said to me about the dead-letter wall of respectability he had built round himself; and as I watched him bowing in this House of Rimmon, I asked myself what affinity could he have with Esther Zamiel of the Wilderness, that he should leave his gods to worship with her in the "great, grand, poetic wild"?

Alone! yes, one must be alone—alone on the broken spar, drowning out of sight! Alone amid the crowd applauding you —supposing they do applaud, which sometimes they do not. . . .

My old mood has come back to me. I am filled with the nausea of life's falsity. The world seems unreal, and people all wear grinning masks; and that sense of loneliness in a vast alien crowd becomes at times intolerable. The thrill of human sympathy and of fellowship with other women, and with little children, and with living, growing things, which stirred my heart at Philotis, has never quickened it again. All the companionship I know is that of a ghost—the grey ghost of Kassis; the ghost of a friendship which was but falseness and illusion too.

I snatch at straws of distraction. Last night I let a man make love to me; and afterwards I went through agonies of self-abasement at the desecration of an ideal. It strikes me with a shock of terror that there is another side to my own nature, which I have never understood, though I have dimly felt it. I realise that the exaltation which seemed all spiritual may take subtler lower forms, may lie in the wail of a violin and in the clink of a zither; that it may lurk in the scent of ball-room flowers, in the sparkle of champagne, in the movement of a waltz. Love! What is it but exaction and withholding; squandering and beggary; ecstasy and revulsion! The essence of it uncertainty; the core of it regret. And friendship? . . . A mockery.

Mr. Vassal is fishing in Norway, and afterwards will be yachting till October. One of the servants fell ill and died of typhoid fever, caught in the London house. The drainage has been condemned, and the place given over to workmen. So I have taken rooms at the St. Cyprian Hotel; and there is no reason why I should not receive the Reader there if he cared to come and see me.

I have written to him, and he has replied excusing himself from coming, with a certain conventional insincerity which hurts. Oh, it hurts. . . .

FROM
ROBERT
VASSAL
TO
ESTHER:

My dear Mrs. Vassal,—Your note was a pleasure to me, and I thank you for not having forgotten one who has but an unworthy claim on your remembrance. I am afraid, however, that I must postpone the further pleasure of talking to you about the *Views* story, and other more or less interesting subjects, for a little while at least. In the first place, my time is not my own after two o'clock; and though I have occasional bits of leisure, I never know whether or not I can count on them. In the second place, my wife, who is very ailing, goes to Germany immediately, and my movements depend greatly on her state of health; it is probable that I shall accompany her.

Please forgive my apparent insensibility to a flattering invitation, and don't let it lose me the privilege of seeing you at some convenient opportunity. Three things, of which I know something, cannot be explained in set phrases—Eton, the British constitution, and the life of a journalist-politician. The last is my plea for grace.

With my best wishes, I am ever sincerely yours,

ROBERT VASSAL.

BOOK VII

*" Love is not altogether a delirium, yet it has
many points in common therewith.   I call it rather
a discerning of the infinite in the finite, of the idea
made real, which discerning again, may be either
true or false, either seraphic or demoniac, inspiration
or insanity."*

<table>
<tr><td>WRITTEN
BY
ESTHER
VASSAL:</td><td>A THING has come to pass, so blessed, so altogether unlooked for, that I scarcely know if this be the world of yesterday, or a new universe in which all the old fashions are changed.</td></tr>
</table>

Now I have heard the cry of that Voice.

Yesterday, when I got here, London was grey with creeping mist and dank with the chill of late September—a city of autumn gloom, and of hopes withered and dead as the brown leaves which fluttered down upon the pavement and were whirled away by the gusty wind. This evening the mist and the drift have gone; the sun sets golden and glorious behind the trees of the Park; the hopes that seemed sapless have put forth in one night miraculous blossom and fruit, and London is London no longer but a magic city lying fair and radiant mid the glow and glamour of the Enchanted Garden. For the universe is revolutionised all through the revolutionising of a man's mood, which brought me yesterday, as I sat forlornly in the darkling evening waiting for lights, a note that had been forwarded from Grosvenor Street.

This was all :—

OFFICE OF " VIEWS," September 27.

MY DEAR FRIEND,—Always keep your true friendships in repair, said the rude but otherwise excellent Dr. Johnson. Are you in town, and where? And if at the St. Cyprian Hotel, may I come and see you?—Yours ever sincerely,

ROBERT VASSAL.

.   .   .   .

It was bewilderingly formal at first—and he didn't seem the same man quite—was better groomed, more conventional; the frock-coat gave a suggestion of London buckram. . . . There was the usual autumn questioning, and the answerings thereto— conversational road-making: the weather, the doings of the past season. . . . That sort of thing didn't make much difference to him, he said. He was debarred by the circumstances of his life from taking part in the social whirligig. . . . But as for society! There was only one kind of society worth having—meaning good talk. "And after literary society," he went on—and then came the worried smile and absent mane-toss—"I prefer the diplomatic. One broadens out there. Lawyers are too worldly, doctors are too scientific, politicians are too one-sided, actors are too boisterous, musicians are too stupid, and mere drawing-rooms are too dull. . . . That's why nobody, not even Quintin Glaive, can write a society play. 'Clever' dialogue is so utterly untrue. To be natural it must be idiotic."

The theatres had their turn.

Suddenly, jerkily, "You are not looking well. The festive tread-mill, I suppose. That social wear and tear does more harm to a constitution like yours than any amount of work. It is called relaxation—which is just what it isn't."

I said that I had been working a little as well as playing a great deal.

"So I saw—and read. How voluminous you are becoming. Your five volumes make an imposing show on my shelves. But *Naamah* remains still the beloved affinity. . . ."

A pause.

"I envy you your absorbing attraction to story. For myself, I'm beaten by a stupid versatility. It's not laziness, it's not culture—the terrible word—it's a fatal perversity, which prevents me from becoming a popular novelist. . . . Well!

'Oh, British public, who may love me yet. Marry and amen!'"

He got up, fidgeting, and looked steadily at a photograph for more than a minute. A desolation was creeping over me, like unto the desolation of that last parting at Philotis. Had he come just for this? He turned abruptly back and stood, his eyes probing deep down into me.

"No! . . . you are looking over-tired. Take care—play *is* work, my child."

Then . . . How did it come about? I cannot tell. He took my two hands in his, and, as his sad-happy eyes looked into mine, and his deep shaken voice sounded in my ears, all the formality and strangeness and jerkiness vanished. The pain and humiliation melted into joy, and there remained no more of bitterness, only sympathy unquenched and content inexpressible.

"Little woman," he said, "I'm like the children. *Please* I want to come home. I've missed you; I've wanted you; I've *longed* for just a look at you."

And then . . . It was as though a spirit went from one to the other of us, kindling both our hearts. Quite suddenly he drew me close to him, pressing my hands against his breast and bending his face to mine, and we kissed each other.

And his own words were fulfilled: for I knew the cry of that Voice; and the bridge which God has built between heaven and the lower earth was shown unto me.

.   .   .   .

He poured out all his heart to me, and I mine to him. He told me that he had loved me always, from the very beginning, even when he had found himself looking forward to Esther Zamiel's letters and pondering upon why he should take so deep a personal interest in what was after all but a branch of his trade. He said that he too had the feeling of kinship æons back; that he too had dreamed first at Kassis of an ideal friendship. But he had become afraid, he said, as he had yielded to the charm of our companionship—afraid because of the demons within; afraid because of the dues already owed; afraid because of his own Laodicean nature, which made it impossible for him to render in justly-balanced measure either to Cæsar or to God. So he had fought with his demons. And when defeat threatened, he had doubled round the fork of the Y, as he phrased it, and had taken refuge within his wall of dead-letter obligation, justifying his cowardice, in going back from his compact as the Reader, by disingenuous excuses, for which he nevertheless despised himself. Then he had got to know in some occult fashion that he was doing me harm. It was borne in upon him that our bond demanded truth from him to me, even though this should mean renunciation. So, in an uncontrollable impulse, he had broken down his defences, and had resolved that, come what might, we two should stand, were it but for an hour, face to face, soul to soul, out in the open—beyond the City and the Conventions.

All this he told me haltingly, in mingled exultation and compunction, with a certain blended recklessness and solemnity.

"And now that I am with you face to face," he said, "now that we are really alone together in our wilderness, I know that it is not to be for one little hour, but for whole lives; and that here we shall find refuge for our hearts, and our hope and salvation. . . . For I love you, Esther, with the truest and best part of me; and if you are dearer to me than anything in the world, you are highest to me above it. There shall be no clashing with the Cæsar dues. We'll keep this thing apart and holy. Do you understand?"

Yes, I understood. There was no need for assurances. Our hands clasped in unspoken pledge. And we talked on—he saying dear and tender words that somehow I can't write in cold black ink, for they are holy.

Oh, I want to be good. I want to be worthy of his noble love. I want to love God. I want to make people happier. I want to write beautiful books. I want to live a beautiful life. . . .

He has gone. I watched him disappear among the trees in the golden sunset. But it is only till to-morrow. . . . He will come again to-morrow.

And I sit here, dreaming, dreaming, in the after-glow of my great happiness. . . .

From a mirror near, my own face looks out at me; and I don't seem to know my face, for there is a radiance upon it. Am I indeed gracious and sweet and lovely?

Those were his words; and because they were his words, it is not vain and foolish to treasure them.

My love! my love! I do not treasure them in vanity. I love myself only because you love me.

And as I sit dreaming, it is as though your living presence— no grey ghost of Kassis, but *you*—in warm flesh and blood— filled the vacant chair. And your tender, troubled gaze never leaves me.

Dear eyes! I shall always see you—so loving and so sad. Why are they so sad? . . . Dear lips! I shall always feel your kiss. . . . Dear lips of mine that are consecrated!

.   .   .   .

It is the renewing of youth—his treasured words also. We live in the hour; and for seven days shall know neither past nor future, for we have snatched a week from Time and Fate.

We never speak of the duty that lies afar. There seems a tacit agreement between us that no allusion shall be made which could break the poetic spell. So that in all our tender familiarity, of which the wonder and the joy deepen hourly, there is a certain reserve that I respect as I would the sanctuary of an alien worship. Why should I murmur because in our Palace of Bliss there must always be a locked chamber. Could I have it otherwise?

Yet I shiver at the thought of dread possibilities, as at an advancing shadow; and, though it is realised only at moments, I know in my heart that the spectre of a woman stands ever between us—the woman whose strength lies in her love and whose claim no righteous judge could deny; and I know, too, that in any conflict of duty and passion it would be I who should fall, forsaken, and wounded to the death.

But why should I be afraid? There will not be any conflict. Are we not clean of heart and clear of purpose to keep our love but as a green place in the desert—a spring of pure water at which our souls in drouth may slake their thirst?

.   .   .   .

There flash upon him less lurid lights—gleams from his world of men; and the boyish side of him comes uppermost—as when he drops in upon me in friendly intimacy—and there's always such a dash of friendliness, pure friendliness, in the art-comradeship—when he talks literary shop, and scolds me for being too much of a mental anatomist, and for my "gloomy, gormy, death's-head-and-crossbones" views of things generally. How we laughed once over my sentimentalism! And I was a little hurt, till he confessed to being very much tarred with the same brush.

"Here's a lecture that for your pretty sins' sakes, you've got to listen to. It *is* a bad kind of world, dear little woman, but I'm too absolutely care-free and blest in your sweet companionship for the moment—alas! the moment—to bewail it over-gruesomely. Drink; be merry! Life is mortal; the time on earth is short; and death is immortal when you are once dead. That's my lecture, which cometh from the Ancients. . . . And so, pending our joint immortality, I'm going to embalm the humours of 'the local man' in satirical verse for *Views*."

He had come from a suburban political meeting.

"Such a fight! I got them quiet as lambs—chaffed them: made them laugh: and thought of you all the time, and laughed myself at the queer incongruity of my inner vision of you—my Muse and my Egeria, hovering over as grimy a collection of Republicans as ever brayed at a Tory candidate. King Demos rampant!"

"And you quieted them?"

"Held them as sheep before their shearers till I had done. I like that sense of grip upon primitive man. I believe action, and not contemplation, is my *métier*. Really, it often strikes me that I'd have done better—say, waging war in the desert at the head of a tribe of Bedouins, than polishing pentameters in a London fog. What weather! One doesn't need to be a Magian to rejoice in the soft tender radiance of this sun-star which dawned—when was it, Stella?—I can tell the very instant—five by the clock on Tuesday of this same all-blessed week—and here's the *Times* prophesying a fine day on American authority: and the Almighty brings down soot to spite 'em. Bless Him! How He hates Yankee cocksureness!"

I too had my day's tale to tell. I had been to Quintin Glaive, and the Desert had been ordained for my winter destiny.

"Which means—Philotis?" he said.

"Yes, I go no farther. And we shall meet—and that will be well."

I fancied that his face clouded. "Will it be well? Who knows! The inaccessible desert might be a better abiding-place for you, my Esther. . . . Never mind! . . ."

He threw off the momentary shade in whimsical merriment. "So the bells shall go a-ringing for Sahara; but we'll not be parted—no.

> For I'll send you reamses,
> Beyond your dreamses,
> Of friendly nonsense by the camel-post.

The degradation of doggerel, dear! Poste restante. Sandsea. Sharon. C.A. (Central Africa)—where you will be safe enough from me in bodily presence, and the paper-talk shall begin again."

Then, in one of those strange alternations of mood which puzzle me, a sadness fell upon him, and for the remainder of the hour we spent together his tenderness was tinged with melancholy.

.   .   .   .

Now I know the meaning of the vague sweet pain of girlhood's time—the troubled rapture : the uncomprehended yearning. It was love, not art, that I craved always. . . . Or are love and art so interblended that the desire and accomplishment of them are one and the same ?

Love! One has read of it: written of it: jested about it, blasphemed it, denied it! How familiar a word, idea, symbol! And till the hour of initiation, how uninformed by knowledge!

There has come to me a curious awakening of the religious sense : a groping apprehension of spiritual potencies beneath the apparently material. It is as though in the thrill of my being to that of the Beloved, a mystic wire were set vibrating, and flashing along it, through some divine electricity, a ray from the Great Central Sun, lighting its kindred beam in him and in me. Hitherto the word Heaven has conveyed to my mind little meaning. It was impossible to conceive of a condition of bliss in which all needs and aspirations should be fulfilled. Now, in its earthly reflection I discover the Beatific Reality : and I know that this white flame of human love is a spark from the Divine Love, pervading life and nature, as spirit interpenetrates body. So that by the light within, we may perceive substance illuminated, discerning its inner essence, and realising that according to a Law unutterably mysterious we two through love have become one with the Soul of the Universe.

Thus I find the spiritual current of our blended beings pervading all ordinary interests and associations, investing them with an ethereal charm and meaning. And this in much greater degree when the higher enjoyments are concerned, such as books, music, scenery, and the finer emotions. So it is when loftier feelings are stirred that I am most vividly conscious of Robert's influence either in or out of the body—the corporeal nearness, even when unperceived by the senses, becoming in an inward manner more real and intimate.

In this inward manner I was suddenly intensely aware of him yesterday afternoon at St. James's Hall, during the performance of Brahms' Sextet in B flat. Do you know it?—the solemn andante, followed by the rippling scherzo, like a stirring of the sea on a sunshiny day, with always underneath its dancing gladness a sorrow inexpressible, a wail as of drowned dead from the depths? My eyes were involuntarily attracted to a certain part of the hall, and I recognised him by the turn of his shoulders and the tossing of his short curls in that upward gesture of his. I saw him shift posture and glance searchingly back, as though he too had divined our nearness. And as I throbbed to his mood of dreamy unrest, I felt that for him, as well as for me, the stuffy room, the rows of well-dressed people, the grand piano and long sob of the violins, the sea of dark heads beyond the bowed figures of the performers, and the grotesque shapes of the instruments which gave forth their strangely human modulations, were all merged in one vast vague ecstasy of rapture, regret, and longing.

We missed each other in the outgoing crowd, but he was with me nevertheless; and as my cab rolled along, the roar of London grew faint, and my thought travelled swiftly to grey Kassis.

I crossed the Park in the dusk, when the Serpentine bridge was almost empty. Night was creeping up, and lamps twinkled feebly, eclipsed by the red glow of the sky on the water. And just then a hansom rattled by, and *his* face flashed out of it, bathed in the day's dying light.

And I laughed outright to myself in sheer joy.

"Oh, I hope that I may live to be old. Life is so good when one is happy!"

I AM indeed glad to know that I make you happy. How strange it is! And how true and sad and beautiful! Yesterday, doubt, separateness, and misery. To-day, joy untold and understanding perfect. For me too, commonplace realities have become dim, bodiless, and unmeaning. For me too, the world is a glorified dream; the day is steeped in a wondrous peace; the sun shines with a mystic light; and through the squalid London streets there are breathed unknown scents that might be wafted from the Garden of Paradise.

Dear! do you care for that child's story, which long ago I used to read to my little boy, and which comes to me at this moment in all its deeper interpretation? For the lilies bloom now around me, and the bliss of life is chanted by the invisible choir. From the tree of knowledge drop no blood-red tears, but rose-lit stars; and standing beneath it, the fairy smiles and beckons. Have I strength to gaze and not enter in? Can I rest content with worshipping that lovely face on bended knee, and not forfeit right to worship in wildly seeking the forbidden kiss? . . .

I look forward to the future with an awful hope.

.   .   .   .

. . . Last night I walked all the way home across the moonlit Park and thought of you—*you*—*you*—of your unfulfilled possibilities; your heart, which might have found and made such happiness. . . . The broad road was rattling and aflame with carriages; the white moon shone above in its deep blue tent; and the scene seemed an illustration of the noisy gaudy vulgarity of social life and the higher thought and nobler impulses which—the gods be thanked—descend upon us sometimes like dew from heaven. . . .

. . . I often think of that wish of De Quincey's, that a prayer might have the pursuing power which old-fashioned superstition assigned to a curse, and might follow its mark and reach it always. In such case, I should send a prayer to you, to reach you through whatever counter-influences, and bring you health, and repose, and happiness. I would bid you have sweet dreams to-night—and not of me, unless they carry with the thought of me some soothing and strengthening power to make me seem to you sleeping, what I would try to be for you waking. . . . In the fine old words, I pray God to have you in His keeping. The prayer which for half a life had ceased to be anything but a barren formula, becomes a thrilling reality when I breathe it for *you*. Am I too effusive? Forgive me, Esther.

.   .   .   .

  . . . A little line, dearest, sped from my soul. What a wealth of meaning, by the way, that word has—Dearest ! . . . Need one write any more? In one sense, no. But alas ! where there are barriers which cannot be removed, that would not be overleaped, then it is impossible to give the word its fullest meaning, which would make it tell its whole story. . . .

  . . . These hours together, and our frank interchange of ideas, have indeed brought us near to each other—made me feel in a curious sort of way as though we were sharing one soul between us. Is this too fanciful? In truth I love you with soul and spirit, as well as heart. . . .

.   .   .   .

  . . . So you like my little notes—my simple love-notes? And are they then so different from what you are pleased to term my "official" and my "analytical" letter? . . . Who taught me to write them? You teach me to write them. For they are the natural bubbling up of my feelings to you at such moments as I write. . . .

  . . . I wonder if it is from my own immortal works or somebody else's that I gather the phrase, "How sweet and gracious you are ! And how I have done well to love you !" . . . You are my poetry of life ; the ordinary concerns of the world, my prose ; these only touching the poetic when they win your interest. I pass from the prose of existence into its poetry when I come within the faint fragrance which I associate with you. . . .

  . . . I have cast off the mood of depression—the cloud that had been brooding over me since that strange waking dream—my curious dialogue of the two waking voices of which I spoke to you ; one within, the other without—the one a voice of good, the other a voice of evil. Yes, I am nervous and sensitive, and given overmuch to melancholy—at times devoured by melancholy. Though you make me very happy, and life seems indeed dear, there is always still the "inseparable sigh for her"—for *you*. And worse : always the wrench of a divided claim. . . . Perhaps it was because of this that our talk took its mournful turn, and dealt with life's mysteries, and life's oldest mystery after life itself—

death. . . . Alas! alas, Stella! this day is cold and grey—grey in the skies; grey too in my spiritual conditions. . . .

.   .   .   .

. . . I wonder will you be surprised to get this little greeting in the morning. It will be like some loving tone, perhaps, sounding softly in your wakening ear, or like some tender touch upon your cheek. . . . Perhaps you will come to me in my thought to-night—in my half-dreaming thought. And I shall feel your presence and be thrilled by it. . . . A dream! Yes—but let us dream!

.   .   .   .

Some fairy tips your missives fairest fair—which is a blank verse to your intention, or will be a rhymed one if you make a rhyme to it. Just a hand-clasp; one more real being I hope soon to follow. Do you know that I saw you this evening on the Serpentine bridge. You were steeped in the glow of sunset, which had in it a certain tenderness and melancholy sweetness. I can't think of you in glare—odd fancies! But they come.

By the way, look in *Views*. There's a passage in an essayette of mine which *you* inspired. Guess which?

.   .   .   .

The chapter has been delightful—all delightful! And now it is closed, and I shut the book and go upon my way—back from the green place in the Wilderness to the City within the Walls!

Closed! In the real sense it can never be closed, but is always open to be read, and re-read, even if only as some pages of past life. Remember this, if you should feel grieved or hurt —which, alas! I fear may be, when my letters change, as change they must, under changed conditions. Believe that the chapter we have gone through together is real, true, and living in the heart of me—as living, real, and true as my love for you which inspired it.

As to the world beyond our wilderness—the Step we have taken together is perfect peace. But as regards this world, my child—for that same Step—n'en parlons plus. . . .

I have been grinding out "copy" six hours to-day. And I am—TIRED!—Thine,   R. V.

WRITTEN
BY
AGATHA
GRESTE:

I will fill in a gap here.

That was in the autumn, when I came home unexpectedly, and in great trouble of mind. I wanted to consult with my father upon a painful discovery I had made in relation to my husband. Never mind what this was; it's buried now in his grave, and, there's an end of the matter. I allude to it just to show how it was that I came to be at Grisewood Castle for the inside of a week in the October of that year.

Dr. Quintin Glaive was a little mixed up professionally with my trouble. I met him in Paris, where he happened to be spending part of his holiday, and we talked it over there. Dad came to join me in Paris—Mother died that summer—and we had a bad time together—very bad, but more bearable in unfamiliar surroundings than it would have been at home. So it happened that out of the six weeks I was in Europe, only ten days were passed in England.

Esther Vassal would not have had so much of those ten days, but that Dr. Glaive talked to me about her, and asked me to write and propose myself, if possible, on a visit to Grisewood. He did not tell me anything very definite, but I gleaned from what he did say that she had been extremely unhappy, and quite morbid for a time, and though she was better again, and seemed, he said, to have taken a new grip on life in the way of intellectual interest, that she had found out Mr. Vassal was a brute—I always knew it: didn't I, in old days, declare to Esther that he must be one of the wicked Roman emperors come into the world again?—Dr. Glaive went on to tell me that he knew she was lonely, and that he was sure it would be a relief to her if she could disburthen herself to a real friend.

Therefore I did write, though I had not intended to. I was so miserable myself, and in such perplexity—for I had to make a decision on which my whole future depended, and which, when made, was against Dad's wishes and advice, so that it led to troubled discussion and fresh heartburning that I did not feel like going near any of the people I used to know before I married.

Besides, Esther had become such a grand lady! It's no use to maintain that accidents of fortune don't make any difference in friendship, for they do make a difference, if not in fact, at any rate in atmosphere and surroundings: and these cause a certain stiffness, by which one or both of the two concerned are unconsciously affected.

I suppose that was why I did not get really into touch with Esther during those few days at Grisewood. Yet she was ever so sweet and dear—extraordinarily improved in manner from the old time; and I dare say that if I had thrown my arms round her neck, and blurted out all my wretchedness, and appealed to her sympathy, she would have responded by confiding her own sorrows, and would perhaps have told me of the consolation she had found for them. Of course at that time I knew nothing of the intimacy with Robert Vassal. But all the chasm of years and changed conditions lay between us, and I could not somehow bring myself to the laying bare of my wounds in open fashion. Time is needed for free reciprocal outpouring: and so we remained affectionately aloof. She did not even talk to me about her writing. Dad had explained the *Naamah* mystery—which was no particular surprise to me, for I had always believed that there was genius hidden somewhere in Esther—but he had enjoined upon me not to betray his breach of confidence, unless Esther herself started the subject. She did not do so: and I was silent. It was partly because I hadn't read *Naamah*. I had meant to do so, but other matters had engrossed me; and this omission on my part made me guilty and tongue-tied. And— I know it was small and mean, but I did find it impossible to get over the fact that she was no longer Esther Vrintz, the shy half-starved actress, who had been glad to come on Sundays to St. John's Wood to dinner or supper, and read Massinger and Webster, and talk over her ambitions, but Mrs. Vassal of Grisewood Castle and Tregarth, a most high and mighty personage in her way, while I was just the wife of a captain in an Indian regiment, poor, sick, and sorry, with no fine dresses, nor jewels, nor fashionable chit-chat, nor attendants, nor appurtenances whatsoever—the most insignificant member of the big house-party gathered at the Castle.

This insignificance seemed accentuated in an odd way, by the presence of Mrs. Audley Arathoon and Mrs. Raphon, far more disconcerting than that of greater and simpler ladies. such as Lady Cotherstone and Lady Diana Cleebe. and the Bishop's wife, and, even in a lesser degree, young Mrs. Littlewood. Those other two were so very much at home, and apparently so satisfied with them-

selves, apparently also so satisfactory to Mr. Vassal, that they had
the knack of making one feel badly turned out, behind date in
conversation, and, generally speaking, a blot on the picture.   Still,
after the first day or two, I got to like Mione Arathoon, and to be
amused at her frank announcements concerning herself and her
neighbours, and also at the pains she took to conceal any indications that she possessed a heart.   As for Mrs. Raphon, however,
with her big, dark, deceitful eyes, and cat-like manners, underneath which there was always the scratch of a claw, from the first
moment of my acquaintance with her till now, I have thought her
simply detestable.

But to go back to Esther.   It puzzled me a little—the dark
allusions Dr. Glaive had made to underlying horrors in her life.
Certainly one could easily conceive that marrying Mr. Vassal
might mean tragedy of sorts; but—well, perhaps I had lately
become familiarised with tragic conditions in marriage, aggravated
by sordid fret; and I had come to the conclusion that though
money won't mend a broken heart, it provides soothing dressings
for it.   I don't know about being virtuous on five thousand a year;
but it does seem to me that on fifty thousand or thereabouts,
virtue may at least contrive to avoid jarring encounters with vice;
and that the situation once faced. alleviations may be found to
make it more bearable, when, as in this case, the worst sting—that
of a betrayed love—be wanting.

I fancied that Esther, thinking likewise, must have faced the
situation and counted its alleviations, for it did not strike me that
she was in such dire inward distress as to need emotional outlet.
I was not then aware that she had found for the time, at any rate,
a very comforting outlet.

As I write this, I am almost inclined to put my pen through
the lines, so tinged do they seem by my bitter mood of that dark
period; but perhaps it is truer to my feelings of the time to let
them stand.   Later I learned to know Esther better.   Yet, in
spite of the warp in me, I could not help noticing, through all the
mechanical graciousness with which she performed her part, and
notwithstanding the sad expression which is a peculiarity of her face,
an air in her of dreamy content, as though her real self were living
in company of some secret joy in a world apart.   This was the
impression she gave me, far more than that of a woman weighed
down by hidden misery.   At moments she seemed to glow with a
white inward fervour that I could only liken to the sheen of some
fine pearls she often wore.   I thus got the fantastic notion of her,
as of a rare pearl among rubies or other more garish stones.   Mrs.
Raphon, I imagined, might be a cat's-eye—I had seen splendid

specimens in Ceylon—Mione Arathoon, a yellow diamond perhaps; Lady Cotherstone, a rich deep-hued amethyst—one might multiply similes. As for Mr. Vassal—well, I don't know what particular gem is dedicated to a certain baleful Power.

This sounds melodramatic; but really I used to have a feeling as of a bad moral emanation whenever Mr. Vassal came near. That's ungrateful too, for he was especially courteous to me—his least-liked guest. I know that he didn't like me; and as for me, I couldn't bear that bored saturnine smile of his, and the look in his eyes, which seemed to wither up all fresh homely sentiment. I could imagine Mephistopheles looking in that way while he might be watching a game of chess, with men and women for the pieces, wondering within himself whether one of the puppets would be moved by some other motive than the old hackneyed ones with which he was quite nauseated, and so give him the zest of a new interest. I used to see his eyes following Esther about, as if he were waiting for developments; and there was a gleam in them which convinced me that whatever his attitude towards her, it was certainly not one of cynical indifference. Thinking it over later, I came to the conclusion that only one woman had ever roused Mr. Vassal's deepest feelings, and that this woman was his wife. Indeed, I believe that she remained the greatest and the last excitement of his life, and that the only other strong passions of his nature were his hatred of Robert Vassal, and his intense bitterness at having no son to oust his nephew from inheritance.

It has sometimes puzzled me what there was in Esther which appealed in so forcible a manner to certain men and women with whom she came into contact. It was not her beauty, curious and characteristic as that was. There were many women in her circle —Mrs. Raphon for instance—more remarkable for fleshly charm. Nor could it have been her talents, for her gifts were very much under the surface, and so impressionable by her surroundings was she, that anything antagonistic to her own temperament would have the effect of making her shrivel up like a sensitive plant into shy self-conscious reserve. Nor was it a faculty of sympathy; for in this, during her earlier life, she always seemed singularly deficient. I can only define it as some odd personal magnetism —what Dr. Glaive used to call her exotic charm, which she exhaled, as it were, in such manner that one could not help being subtly conscious of it; perhaps, too, as he said, the tantalising suspicion of unsounded depths, and of immense capacities for all the stronger emotions.

The Cotherstones and the clerical set were only two or three nights at the Castle. After them came a London contingent,

including one of Mione's Guardsmen, Mr. Paravel the critic, and
a few others tending towards the more familiar Bohemian type.
It struck me just now that Mrs. Raphon and Mr. Vassal must
have entered upon a new lease of friendship, they were so much
in each other's company; and I remembered some talk I had
heard, before Mr. Vassal's attraction to Esther, of his subjugation
by the handsome widow.   Mione Arathoon, with whimsical petu-
lance, declared herself aggrieved at the transference of attentions
from herself.

"I must own that Aunt-in-law is clever," she said one day to
Esther, while we three were sitting together in Mrs. Vassal's
morning-room.   "I always imagined that when ripe charms had
once palled, their day was done.   But, you see, it's a mistake to
suppose that burned-out fires can't be rekindled.   Rhoda Raphon
understands men better than I do, which is saying a good deal;
for the surest way to learn man in the abstract is not to care twopence for man in the concrete—only, of course, you must make
him believe that you do."

"But if you don't care, Mione, why take the trouble?" said
Esther—serenely unconscious, I thought, of Mrs. Audley's
insinuations.

"Because it annoys me to be left out in the cold," answered
Mione.   "And now-a-days you're only valued for the number
and variety of your admiring appendages.   That's why I cultivate
Guardsmen. . . . Esther, I don't believe that you paid the slightest
attention to my remark about burned-out fires?"

"I suppose you mean that Mr. Vassal used to admire Mrs.
Raphon—you have always told me so—and that now he has
begun to admire her afresh.   That is not so surprising."

"Yes, it is—on the burned-out-fire theory.   But it appears
that if you grovel long enough before the ashes, and blow flattery
hard, you'll set the sparks alight at last. . . . It annoys me as much
as being out in the cold myself," Mrs. Arathoon went on, "to
watch Aunt-in-law, at her time of life—though I'm bound to confess that she wears her years jauntily—blushing and squirming,
and protesting that nor Melchisedec, nor Mahomet, nor Don Juan
himself were comparable for wisdom and seductiveness to Hector
Vassal, Esq., of Grisewood Castle and Tregarth—millionaire, a
detail—of the ancient house of—— By the way, Esther, have
you ever found out the true facts about that unseemly ancestor
who married the lunatic?"

We laughed—there's nothing to do but laugh at Mrs. Audley
Arathoon's thrusts; but Esther looked uncomfortable.

"I thoroughly enjoy digging up the bones of that ancestor,"

N

Mione went on, "and discreetly pelting the greatest of the Cæsars with them. There's a doubt, isn't there, as to whether he wasn't an illicit Vassal altogether? It was 'cute of him not to begin starving the poor heiress-wife till she had given him a legitimate heir. And how did she contrive the Curse, Esther?—was it a dying malediction, or does the ghost walk?"

Esther flushed and paled quickly, as she has always had a trick of doing if moved about anything.

"There's no ghost, Mione. Please don't talk about the Curse; we don't like it."

"But if there isn't a ghost, anyhow there is a Curse?"

"They say so."

"And I've heard that since it was laid on the house, no Vassal has ever prospered in his love affairs. Well, we'll drop the subject. At any rate, according to Aunt Rhoda, Mr. Hector Vassal beats the record in woman-charming. It's a pleasing piece of information; but when it begins with curried prawns at luncheon, pauses with the coffee, and starts afresh with soup at dinner, it's apt to produce yawns."

"You are malicious, Mione."

"I'm jealous—that's it. The truth is, I used to find Mr. Vassal good company. Reformed rakes always are—the scent of the roses clings round the broken vase—and now he's bored with me. I've done all my tricks, and there's nobody here to help me invent new ones; and I really can't play the fool without a gallery. Don't give me away to Aunt Rhoda, Mrs. Greste. She'd tell Mr. Vassal, and that would be too humiliating."

It was just then that Tremlett, Mrs. Vassal's maid, came into the room with some Philotis embroideries, for which Esther had sent to show Mrs. Audley Arathoon.

Looking back on things, certain trifles in connection with this woman stand out, though at that time I only remarked her as the means of throwing an unexpected light on Mione's character. Mrs. Audley Arathoon spoke to her kindly, praising the reparation of a piece of embroidery that Tremlett had made. She was a dark, repressed-looking woman of middle age, who must once have been extremely handsome, and was now the model of a trustworthy lady's-maid. When she had gone out, Mrs. Audley turned off from family matters to chiffons, and presently observed incidentally to Esther—

"Did you know that Tremlett had a daughter?"

"Tremlett? No; she has never been married."

Mione gave her shrill little laugh. "Can you imagine the impeccable Tremlett straying? It's true, though. I've had a soft feeling for the woman—I used to dislike her before—since last season, when I saw her half mad with grief by the girl's bedside. The poor thing had been run over, and was lying stunned."

"I think you must be mistaken," said Esther. "I remember that last summer Tremlett told me she had had a niece run over, and asked if she might go and nurse her. That is what you are thinking of."

"The niece was her daughter," emphatically replied Mione. "Tremlett doesn't know that I know it, and please don't enlighten her. I heard her with my own ears imploring the doctors to let her stay with the girl because she was her mother. The wretches had been talking about the rules of the hospital."

"But how did you come to be in the hospital?" asked Esther.

"Oh!" said Mione, with a slightly embarrassed air, "I happened to be reading to an old woman in the ward. Tremlett didn't notice me. I knew her."

"Why, Mione, I didn't know that you went in for that kind of thing."

"Slumming, child-rescue, and the rest! Oh, I do, when I've got nothing else to amuse me. I'm like Mr. Vassal, always hunting a sensation. I never hankered after a colossal fortune," she added, in an off-hand manner, "because I should feel bad eating ortolans and knowing that a few streets off there were people starving. And I shouldn't at all relish the bother of providing them with dinner."

That speech of Mione's made me begin to like her. Later on, I found that she did an immense amount of charitable work in an odd secret way, and that flinty frivolous Mrs. Audley Arathoon was a sort of guardian angel in certain unsavoury quarters of Westminster and Southwark.

The next day, Esther told me that she had spoken to Tremlett about her daughter.

"I thought, you know," Esther said; and her voice trembled a little, suggesting that she might have private reasons for feeling strongly on such a subject, "that the girl may be living an unguarded life; and that, if she is pretty, wrong might come to her, of a terrible kind. . . . And then it seemed so sad that a mother and child should be separated in that way; and I thought how easy it would be to help Tremlett, who is a good dressmaker, to a home of her own, and a business in which her daughter might be with her."

I remembered at the moment that trait in Esther Vrintz upon which I have commented, and that I always regretted—a kind of insensibility to the needs of others, so that it used not to occur to her to do any of those little helpfulnesses which may come within the scope of women, even of small means. It interested me to see that her nature had to some extent broadened and sweetened—for more than one tiny incident of the sort had struck me ; and I wondered if the change had come through the possession of wealth, a result which does not always follow.

"But it was of no use," Esther went on. "Tremlett did not take my suggestion at all kindly. She answered, almost excitedly, that she did not want any one to interfere in her life, and would not admit that she had a daughter. Her manner makes me sure that there must be some sad story behind it all, but of course I can't do anything in the matter against her will."

Another small circumstance impressed the affair still more upon my mind. Esther asked me to take a turn with her in the grounds. She was considering a question from the head-gardener as to the uprooting of a certain rhododendron patch ; and her inspection of this led us past the windows of a library-smoking room, which she told me was Mr. Vassal's business sanctum. On our way back from the rhododendrons we saw the outer door of this room open, and Tremlett emerge from it, apparently deeply agitated. She escaped by a side walk, leading to a back court, and Esther was turning also, I fancied to avoid the windows, when Mr. Vassal, standing at one of them, tapped upon the pane to call our attention, and made a sign that he would join us.

His face through the glass, with its impassive sardonic look, brought back my grotesque notion of him as a maleficent genie setting emotions working for his amusement, and grimly watching results, as though human nature were a sort of moral roulette-wheel, and there was a cold-blooded satisfaction in counting how the numbers came up.

He stepped out to where we stood, and accompanied us to the end of the terrace, which makes quite a long walk. Esther said scarcely a word, but he talked the whole time, making various polite remarks to me about the shortness of my stay in England, and his regret that I should not be able to pay Grisewood another visit. And then he deliberately—I know he did it deliberately—turned the conversation on to army scandals, and the inexpediency, supposing a man were unfortunate enough to incur such scandal, of absenting oneself too long from England.

"Two years, Mrs. Greste," he said, looking at me from between his puffy eyelids. "That is the outside time in which one should lie *perdu*. In two years the British public forgets *any* crime. After that it has an unpleasant knack of fancying it ought to find out whether there ever *was* a crime, and, if so, who did it. On the other hand, it's the greatest mistake to stand up and face the music. If you stop and let yourself be knocked down, England never forgets you have been knocked down, and never forgives you for it. But *filer* quietly over to Boulogne for three months, six months, a year—according to the magnitude of the offence—then get yourself well tailored, go to your club, shake hands with all your friends, ask after everybody as though nothing had happened, and you'll be the best fellow in the world, and nobody will recollect that the papers ever said anything unkind about you."

Fiend!

After that he turned abruptly to his wife.

"You saw that Tremlett had been with me. She is distressed that you should have discovered an unfortunate episode in her early life, in which, I assure you, she was more sinned against than sinning. She is the daughter of an old family servant, Mrs. Greste, and therefore I know her history. Might one ask, Esther, how you came to find it out?"

Esther told him in a reluctant, nervous manner, which made me uncomfortably conscious of strained relations between the pair, not looking at him, and faltering when he inquired blandly what motive she had had in desiring to establish Tremlett in business.

"I had no motive—except that I thought I should like to do a little good."

Mr. Vassal's sallow face puckered in an evil smile, and the lines about his eyes and nostrils seemed to describe a pattern like that upon the back of a poisonous spider which I have seen in India.

"Mrs. Greste," he said, with his cold little chuckle, "do you know that if Satan wanted to start a scheme for disorganising and demoralising the lower classes, he'd take a philanthropic, philo-beast, sentimental, slumming woman with religious convictions and plenty of money, and set her off on 'doing a little good.' And, Gad! how Satan would grin over her efforts to give the poor starving creatures honest employment and reform their characters! Half of them would be hanged, and the other half would have twins!"

You say that my letters are meagre, formal, and infrequent! I plead guilty to the arraignment, and have no excuse to offer. Did I not warn you? I have been going through one of those mental crises we talked about, and now at last dare to write to you. Three days' solitude, granted through the intervention of compassionate fate, has been to me a salutary experience, utilised for thought—thought and self-examination. I gat me to a lonely forest inn and fought things out—a pretty sharp conflict. Here, not now alone—though exhausted and shaky as from a kind of ground-swell after a nerve-tempest—there's a simile for you! —I'm getting well. "Here" means at five minutes' boat from pretty, academic Bonn, in the middle of the beauty of these particular seven hills, looking towards the golden west, and face to face with Roland's historic tower; and with enough bustle among country-folk, enough assortment of country-trippers, enough large and varied traffic upon the great, still highway, to keep one restfully amused.

It is a soothing occupation, this "vaguing" in the glorious mid-October Rhineland, with the mighty Swiss air rushing straight at me from the mountains, on the swirl of the broad river. This is after a brief imprisonment in an Alpine valley—'entièrement inaccessible aux courants d'air,' as I once saw Engelberg described, by way of recommendation, in a medical advertisement. . . .

I can give you no address, but will write later.

.   .   .   .

Now in Florence, I lose myself in the meshes of Italian magic. Truly in this city one might make a lifelong home. A very centre of what remains of history and of art, giving a delicious sense of refinement and rest, which contrasts beyond words with the rampant vulgarity of modern England—literary and artistic England most especially. . . . The London papers, as far as I have glimpsed them, have roused in me a chastened amusement, to be corrected at the Pitti. . . .

What shocks me most in England, and makes me despair

of her intellectual future, is the absolute decay of humour, which that vile old Carlyle brought in with his involved phrases and Brummagem Germanisms. . . . A touch of humour would make the last London lion-taming phase as impossible as it would be in France—the only country where divine laughter, even in the midst of her gloom and abasement. still falls like rain upon the lower earth, and which alone shattered the ranks of the Salvation Army, by laughing it out of the midst of her. . . .

But there, I'm grumbling; and that is not my vein after all. and certainly not the vein in which to write to so sweet a correspondent as you. But I'm taken by that Southern demon, a chill, and I'm sick with many cares. My heart and years are wearied out, dear one, and even to your sweetest self I cannot write a long letter. . . . I have been keeping self-dissatisfaction at arm's length with casinos, cafés, theatres, and such-like, till I found myself wildly wondering how such a life can amuse anybody. With any number of resources against boredom, I do resent being bored. But I grow analytic—rather in your line, my lady; and if I didn't know how fond you are of mental anatomy, should be afraid of boring you in my turn, past pardon.

. . . .

. . . "Lettres à une Inconnue, par un Homme de Lettres. Deuxième Série"! And by the way, what is it that gives your letters just that tender caressing touch that seems to belong to you, and to which my heart leaps forth in answer? Did you begin to think that pleasant paper-talk of ours was a thing of the past? Faith, I did. Somehow I could not and would not write and sadden you with morbid complainings, when I could write in no other mood in the Valley of the Shadow I have been passing through. But I send you herewith a mad versicle, which will show you that my flexible-steel nature is thawing from its deadly frost. And my own Fiction-geist began to-day on its own account, and I don't think is failing me quite yet. Till it started I was fearful. Fifty—and I'm getting to that—sounds so witless.

I leave this place alone to-morrow, and, before settling down to *Views*, shall give myself a week in Paris, which, sad as she is, and in spite of the garish vulgarity of the Second Empire, that went far to ruin her charm, remains ever "la ville ou on peut le mieux se passer du bonheur."

BOOK VIII

" *Prove yourself; and if you are afraid, go back with the East-wind who brought you hither. He is about to fly home now, and will not be seen here again for a hundred years: the time will seem to you like a hundred hours, but it is a long time to be tempted. Every evening when I leave you I must say to you, 'Come with me.' I must beckon with my hand; but do not follow, for with every step your longing will grow stronger. You will come into the room where the tree of knowledge stands: I sleep under its sweet-scented branches—you will bend over me, and I must smile; but if you press a kiss upon my lips, the Garden of Paradise will sink into the earth, and be lost to you for ever. The keen wind of the desert will whistle round you, and cold rain will fall upon your head; care and sorrow will be your lot.*"

BITTER—sweet! And do I already scent revulsion? What it is to lie awake through silent hours! To long and wait and pray for the letter that must surely come to-morrow—the letter which will stifle doubt and assuage pain. ... And the stroke of the morrow makes it to-day; and livid dawn steals in like a warning wraith through the curtain's chink. Then the morning's packet is brought. And hope leaps up in the eager scanning, and sinks fainting in disappointment.

.   .   .   .

Philotis once more! Blue sea, dancing sunbeams, palms and roses, and glittering white domes against the purple hills!

All night in the train which whirled me through France, I lay awake watching the moon high in heaven, and the bare flat fields as they rushed by with their sedgy pools, and here and there the lines of spectral poplars. And all day and night at sea, content lapped me, and my beating heart rested in the thought that to-morrow I should see you, my dear.

For he is at Philotis—with his wife. Is she mad now, I wonder!

I wrote to him at the Club, as he bade me, telling him of the day of my arrival. The hour of the mail packet he would know. There would be nothing extraordinary, it seemed to me, in his coming that afternoon, or even after dinner, from the Annexe to the hotel. And yet a certain anxiety mingled with the joyful expectation. How could I help remembering one balked meeting when he had been "suddenly called away" . . . and the restraint of his later letters—letters so unlike those of the golden week? And then the perhaps intentional missing of me in Paris!

.   .   .   .

The day wore on; he did not come. Carriages rolled to and fro in front of the Cosmopolitain; there were carriages in waiting at the Annexe entrance.

It struck me that the villa had a different look, and I remarked this to Tremlett.

"That's likely, ma'am, for it's much livelier now," she answered. "Mrs. Robert Vassal never had visitors."

"Why, is not Mrs. Vassal here this year?"

"No; hadn't you heard, ma'am? It's a Russian Grand-duke who has it this season."

The sun set behind the Vasques hills; and a pink after-glow spread over the sea. By-and-by the lights of the French town came out; and one large soft star beamed palely, while the reflection of the after-glow yet remained. Then all the solemn blue became gemmed with stars and lamps, the rumble of carriages ceased, and the night was a sobbing desolation.

Nor next day was there word or sign, though he is in Philotis, for Tremlett saw him in the town.

I am frightened. Must it be always so—always this heart-hunger and sense of mutilation when we are spiritually apart? For I seem to know intuitively that he is stiffening himself against me. And I chafe my wound with the old cynical saws— that a love returned is a love lost; that the woman's idolatry is the man's indifference.

.   .   .   .

It is the third day, and he has come.

We stood holding hands; and our eyes flew to each other— his fierce and tender, while his face was moved like the sea after a storm.

He made some inarticulate sound and released my hands; and we sat down, he a little distance from me, a chill impalpable barrier between us.

"I am sorry I could not come sooner," he said. "Yesterday I was prevented. We are a long way off—on the other side of the town."

"You had the Annexe several years!"

"Yes, but we had been wishing to change; the traffic of the hotel makes it noisy."

We talked conventionalities—the weather; my autumn occupations; his travels; politics; books; his *Views* essays. . . . It was all constrained, artificial; and I felt that I must speak out or choke.

Suddenly he moved nearer, and took my hands again; and the deep note was in his voice.

"Are you glad to see me?"

"Glad!... But this is horrible! We are not ourselves; and I can't bear it. Remember I'm only a weak woman, and don't be hard on me."

"I hard!... hard on *you*!" He laughed tremulously.

"Why do you laugh?"

"I suppose because I'm so happy in being with you. . . . Because it's the first time I've ever heard you put forth the plea of being a weak woman."

"You make me realise the misfortune of such weakness."

"The misfortune of loving me?" he asked sadly.

"The misfortune of being utterly dependent on you, so that it is you who make the world glad or wretched for me. . . ."

He looked down upon me with a tender, faintly humorous, miserable, and altogether *man's* look.

"Little woman! It won't do. . . . You've been crying, making yourself sick with crying. . . . Why?"

And then I poured out impetuously what was in my heart.

"Why should I be ashamed that you should know it, since it is true? My whole life is bound up in you. I am *you;* and everything is *you.* You are in the sky and in the sea. You are in the scent of the roses and the sound of the wind. And yet you are apart from them; and they are only unreal things after all. Nothing is real but you. *You* give the dreamy glow to life. *You* cause the pain which seems to rise up out of the very face of the rocks and to strike one from the spikes of the pines against the sky."

"My child! This is bad; this is bad. Don't tell me it's like that."

"It was like that yesterday. I drove to the monument at Cape Feurd. And there were the cairn of stones and the rusty iron cross; and Sralta so near and peaceful; and the sunlight of the bay! And *you* were in everything; and everything was sad!"

"It won't do," he repeated more tenderly than before. "You mustn't make things harder than needs be, for both of us. After all," he added, with that funny gesture-laugh he has, squaring back his shoulder and throwing up his head, "although you do call yourself a writing-woman for an excuse, and I'm half a poet, which is only another way of saying that we are a pair of sentimental ninnies, we did agree to try and be sane, sensible humans, as far as our limitations would permit. We can't marry each other, dear, because we're both married already—worse luck. And for your sake as well as for that of others, I'm bound to guard against disagreeable comment upon our—friendship. And you must help me, because I love you better than anything in the world, and because—shall I tell you a secret—whisper it in your ear?—I'm just as bad, and worse than you are. And I walked half-way to the Cosmopolitain the evening you arrived, and turned back, saying to myself that it wouldn't do. And I've been punishing myself ever since. And if I didn't cry myself sick too—well, a man's a man, you know—and not a weak woman!"

And he held my face back from him a little, and our two pairs of eyes met. And he gathered me up in his arms with a sound like a mother's croon over her child.

.   .   .   .

To-day Robert told me the story of his marriage. He told it baldly, jerkily, standing by the fireplace, and now and then taking a stride up and down, as he had done that day in Mr. Brock's office, fighting, I fancied, against an almost unconquerable reluctance. He was in one of his odd, half-reckless moods. . . . I shall try to put down his own words.

. . . "I've got to go back to the financial smash which ruined us and killed my father. So there I was, a young man about town, turned all of a sudden into a starving journalist—otherwise a briefless barrister. I loathed law and loved literature, knowing in essence nothing about it—you remember my telling you in a 'Reader's' letter about my hopeless dilettantism? I was bound to starve, anyhow, being the sport of a perverse demon who wouldn't, or couldn't, knock off a sprightly paragraph or society play, but would cheerfully produce five acts of tragic blank verse, or an absolutely unsaleable philosophical novel. . . .

"Well—after I had been at starvation point for a bit, I found out that I was going blind. . . . Don't shudder, dear! My eyes are as strong now as ever they were before that year or so of blackness. . . . One of my old college pals tackled the business. He picked me up when he was slumming in the East End for a fellow-parson on a holiday, and took me off to an oculist. I must tell you that I had reached such a pitch of pride and destitution that I shunned decent people as if they were the devil—though, as a matter of fact, I came into pretty close quarters with the devil in those days.

"Well, the oculist gave the ghost of a hope—an operation which succeeds once in a hundred times, and the speciality of a great German man, meaning an enormous fee and months of careful treatment—practically a year of night, expensive nursing, idleness, an empty exchequer, and ninety-nine chances against a cure! So I looked Fate in the face, and liked her so little as to make up my mind that when the light went out I'd swallow a dose of prussic acid, and that till then nothing mattered. Brooke shepherded me down to his vicarage, and his mother and sister looked after me, and cried over me because they didn't know how to help me — they were so poor themselves. . . . As if I wouldn't have chosen the prussic acid first! My God! I wish I had chosen the prussic acid. . . .

"There was a girl staying at the Brookes', an orphan, with a little money of her own — between three and four hundred a year. . . . What do you think of a woman crippling herself, reducing her little fortune to a pittance, risking a hopeless, helpless burden on her hands for life—just for love? It's something splendid, isn't it? Something to be grateful for—something to bind a man in chains, and make him feel that his whole body and soul aren't sufficient in payment. . . ."

(Ah, dear Heaven! Think of being *paid* for giving the man you love his life. . . . Will men never understand women — or realise the sort of torture they may unconsciously put them to? Dear Heaven! If *I* had been in that woman's place!)

. . . "She was handsome and interesting — very handsome; quite beautiful — she used to be called 'the beautiful Miss Delmar.' And she was interesting, being so unlike other women. Clever; a little hard outwardly, but with a capacity for feeling that—well, she gave suggestions of drama. It amused me to study her. . . . I—I liked her."

(The yellow woman! . . . Keep me from hating her! Keep me from grudging her—what she *bought!*)

"Yes, I liked her. . . . I let myself go. . . . I never dreamed of that brilliant creature caring for a poor blind devil like me. . . . But she did care. . . . She cared . . . odd, isn't it?—intensely.

"Oh I liked her—she attracted me greatly. That wasn't what I thought most about, though. . . . I sold myself. . . . Good Lord! That's the truth. . . . I did her an awful wrong. I sold myself out of mean sordid selfishness—for the chance of getting back my sight. I was afraid of blackness for ever; I was afraid of the prussic acid. Life began to seem sweet when I knew I'd got to leave it. And the sunshine was gladdening, and the earth lovely. . . . It was my cowardly weakness, which has been my curse every way, all through my days. . . . Can't you realise the immeasurable debt of loyalty? . . . And that wasn't all. I believe there is some fiendish law of compensation, by which what is given to one must be taken from another. She was my scapegoat. Her life was a martyrdom to me, who couldn't recover for endless months, though the operation proved a success, and the cure, as far as the eyes went, was complete. But for a long time I wasn't able to get any spring at all for a mind gone to hopeless waste; till, all of a sudden, my intellectual faculties came back—the stronger, it seemed, for that fallow-time, and I pulled myself together, worked, and made a literary hit. Then, when I was fairly started, she broke down. It was the stress of anxiety, in the first instance, during that year of black suspense, and the waiting on me hand and foot, when she was quite unequal to it, and I should have cared for her. Her mind gave way entirely; they didn't think it would ever come right. But we pulled her through that Valley of Darkness, and every year she has improved, till now her attacks are comparatively rare ... and I've managed to prevent the world from knowing much about it. ... Glaive and the rest say that if there's no return of the acute phase, no grief or sudden shock, she may in time get back her old brilliant wit and keen intelligence and common sense. ... Now "— He gave a passionate gesture, was silent for a moment or two, and then burst out impetuously—" Now it is a dead level of lucid imbecility—has been ever since the rational interval I told you of, when I thought she was beginning again to take an interest in real literature. ... But for a long time I haven't been able to rouse her to appreciation of anything higher than the shop-girl class of novelette—' *Araminta and the Fortune-Teller and the Wicked Earl*'—you know the sort of brain-poisoner—no, I don't suppose you do. ... And when I remonstrate, she lectures me seriously on my own want of popularity with the multitude, and tries to feed me on that stuff. *Me! Me!* I'm obliged to tell you—I can't stand it; I must have it out. ... But do you think I don't know how disloyal I am—how base! That poor martyr! And all the suffering for my sake—the wrecking of herself that *I* might steer safe into port. There isn't a day or night that I'm not weighed down by shame and remorse. But think of it, I'm like a forest beast chained—the only outlet I have here, to walk miles and miles— when I can get away; and that's only by convincing her mind, through her poor loving heart, that I need air and exercise—or that I've got to carry on my work. ... At home there are *Views* and the House. ... She was always ambitious; she wanted me to make a name. ... And I'm freer when the boy's there. ... I wish you could see him. He understands in the most marvellous way. And devoted to his mother—I'm very proud of that boy. ...

"But I want more—more—more. And I want to be alone— oh, alone!—Since I can't have the dear dual solitude ... I crave for the loneliness of the desert—for even a Trappist cell. To live my own life! To break away mentally and bodily! Oh the joy of it! ... I'm driven to tell lies—to invent petty excuses— when she is logical enough to take excuses in—to take anything in, but the necessity for *me*. ... Imagine what it is to be hanging round all day in that stifling feminine atmosphere—listening to the ghastly astrological babble humouring the poor foolish fancies about myself—a portent in the flight of a butterfly; an evil presage in the face of some passing woman!

"And then to think of her as she was—the strong reasoning power—where has it gone—isn't that enough almost to make one disbelieve in a soul?—the love of good books, the mental companionableness of her. . . . And I reminding myself always that by every law of honour and loyalty my heart and life are vowed to her, and her only——"

He walked up and down between the table and the window, with hands locked behind his back, an odd intent light in his eyes, and his chin a little forward, with the sun catching the curl upward at the points of his hair, and the ripple on the wave where it was brushed back from his forehead.

"And the worst part of it is that I don't know whether it's worse or better since I've cared for you. Sometimes I think you've been my salvation, sometimes my——"

He pulled himself up abruptly, shocked at the pain in my look which I could not hide.

"I've hurt you! Poor little white troubled face! what have I done? Oh, are we men all brutes, that we don't know how to treat the women who love us, and whom we're not worthy to love!"

.   .   .   .

It seems so stupid to be sitting here all through the long night. . . . Yes, I will be brave. It is death in the soul, but I will face it. . . . When I saw him torn and tortured, I cried out, "Go back to the duty which holds you in stronger chains than your love for me."

How can I fight? What weapons can I use which would not be of Satan? "Give me up, and let me go," that's what I said; "I am strong enough to bear it."

He answered, "Very well; it shall be as you wish." His face became cold and white, and he left me with no other word.

After he had gone I stayed very quiet. The hours went on. . . . It is all over! That is the only distinct thought which shaped itself for a long time. . . .

By-and-by I began to feel light in the head, and very tired. Odd fancies rose up out of the nothingness. It seemed to me that I was in a deep, dark valley, choked with poisonous fumes, so that I could not move nor breathe. Then through the giddy blackness a silver ray seemed to pierce, and in a strange inner way I saw high above me pure snowy heights, and white forms floating in a golden glory. And I knew that if I could but reach the heights the choking oppression of misery would be lifted, and

that angels would minister to me.   I knew too, in the same
inner way, that this silver beam was the ray of renunciation ; and,
as I struggled towards the light, it seemed as though for one
moment of time my soul were liberated from trammels that had
held it bound.   A great peace fell upon me, and I heard a Voice
within saying, "Passion is the grave : Love, the resurrection.
Purify your human love that it may become one with the all-
consecrating Love, and so shall you be free and blessed!"

But the suffocating cloud wrapped me round again, and the
ray vanished.   I got ready for bed.   Something had risen in my
throat, and I had a queer sense of being strangled, but I did not
want to cry. . . . Tremlett went on brushing my hair mechanically.
. . . I felt quite stupid.   By-and-by I slept.   I dreamed a curious
dream—that I was out in the bay, drowning in deep water.   The
Vasques hills towered grim and gloomy on the land side, and all
the sea was dark, till suddenly the moon shone out, and showed
me Robert standing by the shore watching me.   Somehow in
my dream, his face seemed to change into the face of my master.
I stretched out my arms, imploring him to save me ; but he shook
his head and smiled a wild, cruel smile : and then the waters
engulfed me, and I awoke.

I thought it must be morning when I awoke, but it was only
the moon which made my room light, and when I looked at the
clock, I saw that my sleep had lasted just an hour.   I got up. . . .
And now I am sitting here—thinking, thinking.   It is as though I
had thrown my whole substance into a swiftly running stream and
were watching it being borne out to sea—lost for ever and ever.

The pain! . . . It's not mental : it's physical—stabbing my
heart and making me gasp and writhe till there comes the relief
of a sobbing fit. . . . Such odd little things blend with it—the
green pot of carnations, the glint of silver on the dressing-table,
the pattern of the wall-paper, the sputtering of new-lighted fir-
cones—I have made up the fire, for I felt very cold.

Oh, the tiny remembrances, the little intimacies and their sweet
sting !   He said the other day, that I did not understand olive-
wood fires, and we kneeled together on the hearth and put on fir-
cones.   The convent-bell is ringing in the new day. . . . I must
not let him see how unhappy I am.   Surely I have gone through
it now—the death-throes of renunciation !

.   .   .   .

He flashed past me in town this morning, driving with his
wife—I have seen *her*, and it was the impression of a moment—
tragic, eerie, haunting.   She must have been very beautiful !

.   .   .   .   .   .

Dear Heaven ! How happy I am !

Quite unexpectedly he stood there trying to seem as though there had been no gap of despair between this and our last meeting. And the laugh and shoulder-shake—pathetic, shamed, lion-like, dolesomely whimsical—went so strangely with the worn look of his face and the terrible sadness of his eyes.

" I had an uncanny foreboding," he said, "that you would have paid me off in my own coin, and that I should find you departed for Quintin Glaive's desert—you told me, you know, that we were never to meet again—and then what would have been the end of the idyll ? Elegiac, perchance ! For seest thou not, my child," he went on in tragic banter, "that when the Mountain (that's me) can't come to Mahomet (which is you), and Mahomet (that's you) defies the proverb and runs away from the Mountain (which is me)—why Mahomet and the Mountain aren't likely to meet : and broken hearts and tombstones may very probably result ? Dearest ! don't you *know* that I couldn't do it, even if I wanted ? And that's the truth of it. It's too late now for heroics : I couldn't give you up, if I tried ever so hard. . . . Lord ! what fools we mortals be ! Forget our last talk, when I said things that were base, and tried to make my- self out a sort of caged lion. It strikes me, dear, that—

> ' Humble pie is wholesome meat,
> Good for some of us to eat,'

and that such intellectual vanities are to be avoided. It strikes me too that I must have been a loose hyena more like. . . . And as your humble slave is not altogether a bad fellow by nature, he hopes that those roarings may be forgiven him, on the under- standing that he never roars in like manner again. . . . And, O Esther, my star, my dear. There's no use in trying to pretend. . . . I love you. . . . I love you."

Forgiven ! The pain and struggle were over, and our hearts beat together once more.

.   .   .   .

Robert tells me that he is working at a set of articles for *Views*, about the old Moorish towns and ruined eyries of the seaboard hills, and sometimes he is absent for several days tramping the mountains.

Yesterday, on his way back from the Katkas, he came upon me at Kassis. We met at the brink of the old grey keep, and together wandered away from the mosque down the sunny side of the slope, where olives grow on terraces built up in heat-baked walls and shadows lie black and mysterious, and where there is nothing to remind one of the French and Eastern life of the village.

We came to a tiny plateau—a nook where the wall took a curve behind us, and the olives above, slanting over it, canopied this wildly odorous chamber of Nature's fashioning, while a low lattice of roses screened the outer edge of the terrace from the jessamine and violet garden lying several feet below.

A gnarled old olive-tree opened its split trunk, making a sort of cave arm-chair, its sides clean, warm, and sinewy, its cushions dry moss, its curved roots giving arm-rests. I curled myself close within the tree's embrace, and he, on a root-stool, sat by me.

How lonely it was! In the whole world there might have been but him and me, and the mating birds calling to each other.

A breeze came in gusty swells—a softly ardent wind from the glowing sea, that tossed the pale sides of the olive-branches uppermost, while the sun played in tender frolic upon the leaves, changing their pallor into smiling radiance—a daring wind that parted asunder the rose-petals, unveiling the blossoms' core, so that the sun might kiss at will, and the bee wooing with his deep musical drone, might enter for sweet-feeding.

The sense of source-life was in the air around us. I leaned against the unbarked heart of the tree, and its vigour of running sap seemed to course through my limbs. Gazing upward, I could see white clouds moving swiftly in the blue dome, as might Nature-spirits who were rejoicing in the great mother's plenteous bounty, and bearing to her pleasant tidings of the fulfilment of her laws. The warm rays caressed my face, and the earth magnetism thrilled me with tender gladness.

Then as I turned in sympathy, involuntarily Robert's eyes met mine, and in them that exquisite trouble, that infinite yearning which the very air distilled. Our hands clasped. Mystery of soul and sense affinement—that mutual conquest and mergence into each other, through mere touch of loving hands, of two separate human individualities!

"Strange, strange!"

"What is strange, Esther?"

"Tell me. . . . From the first your touch thrilled as no other touch had ever done. . . . Tell me . . . was it so with you too?"

"Always! Thus did I know that I loved you. . . . Ah, dearest . . . with your little wistful face and its baffling charm. . . . And your smile seems to say 'Come with me.' . . . And why may I not follow—into Paradise? . . . The joy of life is round us : the roses are blooming in our wilderness. . . . Love ! love ! . . . how sweet they are . . ."

The roses of Kassis !   The roses which cannot fade ! . . . He gave me two : they are white and red.

˙ I drove back alone to El-Meriem : and yet I was not alone. His ghost-self sat by my side ; and dear, sad, happy eyes shone on me in answering pledge.

.   .   .   .

. . . I cannot sleep.   It is early morning : the Muezzin-call has sounded, the convent-bell has rung, and the nuns are praying ; and as I lie awake, I praise Heaven and count my beautiful hours one by one.   So I tell my beads of happiness and offer up my *Magnificat.*   I keep my rosary enshrined in my heart's most secret place, and when I am an old woman it shall serve me in the last Act of Adoration.   Ah, grant me more beautiful hours ! Grant me more beads of happiness !

. . . I hear the faint, full, distant murmur of the sea.   For a long time have I been sitting by my window watching the dawn break.   First, the moon looked down very large and wan—and wanner yet, as the horizon softly lightened.   How pallid the curving roads seem, and how sharply defined the delicate tracery of the mimosa-tree with its plumes of gold, and the fronds of palms and spikes of aloes !

The moon has vanished, and daylight creeps into the room. I watch it dimming the fire-glow.   The olive-logs are hissing and sputtering, and making an odd quivering noise like the sighing of a living creature.

.   .   .   .

. . . Will he come to-day ?   This is the burden of the hours which breathes in the cadences of the love-song that some Neapolitans are singing on the terrace of the hotel—they come every morning to sing to the Grand-duke. . . . Then when the song ends and the tinkling of the mandoline stops, my heart's longing beats a more jocund measure to the chaffering of birds and insects, to the pawing of impatient horses on the gravel, and to the colloquies of waiting coachmen.   Then in another key, whimsically pathetic, I hear it in the uneven rustle of the palm leaves, and it seems to cling caressingly to the luxurious atmosphere fanning me.   The breeze bears it in waves of perfume— the scent of roses and freesia flowers ; and everywhere and in everything is the refrain of that wonderful chant, the reflex of that mystic joy. . . . And so I brood, lapping myself in the warm glorious peace.

But the chill shadow advances, and the spectre hand clutches icily.

Tell me—are you happy too? Shall you be sorry to-morrow? Are you sorry to-day?

No, you are not sorry yet, for I should surely know it, and the knowledge would be agony. Not for one single instant am I alone these hours. Ever is that living ghost beside me. Though I cannot see you, your presence is vividly near and persistent. I stretch forth my hand and clasp an invisible hand. Flesh and blood could scarcely be more real.

Dear, do you remember how we spoke of my fantastic notion —you said it was fantastic—that in human love lies the clue to Nature's sublimest law, the law of duality working through the worlds visible and invisible? And you smiled, and talked of mind currents, and brain vibrations, and sympathetic nerve-cells, when there seemed no means of explaining the curious and constant coincidence of thought and feeling between us, which we have tested so often. Then you smiled yet more tenderly, and called me "dear visionary" when I confided to you my intimate belief that one day there will be given to regenerated humanity the secret of a stupendous force, which must have been before the Moveable Powers were established, and shall endure when they have ceased to be. You said—do you remember?—that there must indeed underlie the monogamic ideal in the mind of man, some great natural truth—a truth quite independent of theological doctrine, the significance of which in the scheme of human evolution, we could only as yet dimly discern.

And your smile grew sadder and more unsatisfied as I went on to tell you of my vague wonderings about that divine Force, sheathed in flesh ; and of how it seemed to me that through Its strength the bonds of matter might be burst, and the spiritual selves of those who love be delivered from their prisons of body, and be free to hold soul-converse at will, independent of time and space.

Ah, when shall the Messenger arise to preach the "one man and one woman" ideal, and to proclaim aloud the gospel of sacramental marriage? Does not the Voice cry now in the wilderness?—*our* wilderness, *our* grand poetic wild !

Fancies ! fancies ! . . . How may I grasp them ; how express them ! Am I indeed touching the borders of that exquisite life ?

Are they so foolish then, my fancies ? Is it because they are

so foolish that you have not come to-day? . . . But are you not
certain to come to-morrow!

.   .   .   .

Three to-morrows have become to-day! And all blank.
Where are you? Why do you not come?

You should not let me think that you are sorry.

.   .   .   .

Four days since Kassis.

.   .   .   .

It is very strange that he does not come. . . . "Very strange,
very strange." . . . I don't know whether I said the words. They
kept repeating themselves stupidly all the time as I walked into
the town. Everybody and everything seemed to throw them back
at me in an odd, dazing way—the leprous beggars whining as I
passed, and the washerwomen at the fountain, the soldiers, and
the tattered Arabs, the stiff well-dressed people carrying prayer-
books—there is a memorial service or something at the Protestant
Church, I remember—how coldly righteous and vindictively
virtuous they look, these Englishwomen!—the carriages going
along, the villas and by-ways leading up to the pinewoods, the
boulevard and ficus trees, and the band playing—all mixed up
with that parrot iteration "Very strange! very strange!"
It has been raining, and there are little pools on the road.
How sickly the datura smells, and those asphodels in that bit of
waste garden! . . . There would come a choking feeling, and then
it would go on again, "Very strange! very strange!"
There's a mistral blowing; the bay is steely blue; and the
frise of rock at Rassem's end shows a long splash of foam. The
olives look ghastly as the wind turns up the leaves, and there's
no sun to-day to kiss them.
I saw you. You stared out for an instant from the window
of a closed carriage. I was coming out of the Crédit Lyonnais,
but you did not see me. You had a lady with you all muffled in
furs—light sable. Women with sallow faces and yellow eyes
should not wear light sable—it only suits dark people like me.
The fur came up round her chin, and her eyes shone above
it. . . . Yes, yellow-grey eyes, hard like topazes—and fiercely
bright!
There was a portmanteau up beside the coachman. You
were going to the station, I suppose. . . . Very strange!
It is cruel to leave me like this without a word. . . . Your eyes
had a hunted look. Are you afraid of me? Why do you run
away?
. . . This room is intolerable—so hot—all closed up. . . .

And the scent of the freesias, and those yellow roses! . . . Perhaps it's the pain that's stifling me!

I am very cold. My teeth are chattering. . . . I wonder who the lady is that the concierge said had called and left word she would come to-morrow. . . . Very strange!

I hadn't noticed the card. It's Mione.

Will he write to me to-morrow?

.   .   .   .

Mione has been on a yachting cruise, but not with Mr. Vassal, who she says is coming to Mandour later. She has left her friend's company, and is waiting a day or two for one of the big steamers which put in at Philotis. I asked her why she preferred it to the yacht; and she answered that the truth was she had been bored on the yacht.

"The true truth," she went on in a burst of confidence, "is that my host of the yacht, who dangled after me very pleasantly for a bit, and of whom I had thought better things, has suddenly developed a tragic devotion. I'm not a paragon," said Mione, "but really, though you mightn't suspect it, Audley and I have a code of morals of our own; and we do try to act on the square by each other. Well, I didn't think it would be acting quite on the square to accept diamond bracelets, and listen to amorous declarations, while Audley is swallowing Count Mattei's globules and drinking boiling water at home."

I don't know what made me ask Mione if she thought it wicked to care for a man who is not your husband.

"That depends on the marriage contract," she replied. "I've got a prohibition clause in mine. Besides, I see the absurdity of that sort of thing. It begins beautifully in Platonics, sentimental diaries, and heroics all round; and it ends very nastily in the Divorce Court."

"Mione, tell me—have you ever loved any one?"

"Good gracious!" Mione gave an uncertain little laugh, and went on vigorously closing up the envelopes she had been directing.

"Oh dear! what a dreadful nuisance Christmas is; and I wish Christmas cards hadn't come into fashion. However, I've got some mild amusement out of mine. I've sent Aunt Rhoda Raphon a nice little religious book entitled *Plain Paths for Pilgrims' Feet;* and I've written under it, *High-heeled Shoes for Limping Sinners.*—She complains of corns and refuses to wear anything but the Louis Quinze cut!—And I've sent my father-in-law a fraudulent cheque drawn on the Bank of Peace and Goodwill. And what a nasty shock Caliban will have when he discovers that the cheque isn't genuine. I drew it for a reasonable amount!"

"But, Mione, you haven't answered my question?"

"Haven't I? What was it?—Did I ever love anybody—any man, I suppose you mean. I certainly think it's rude to put personal questions; but if you really want to know—I once did. Only, when I married Audley, I buried my skeleton—otherwise my platonics—decently in the family vault, and the defunct Delmars—the Arathoons haven't yet accomplished a family vault —take precious good care it shan't get out and worry me."

Then she was silent for a few minutes; and I wondered if Mione had ever kept a note-book, and if she had any comprehension of the Religion of Love. Presently, however, she was her flinty self again.

"Oh, why can't I find disinterested Guardsmen who will dangle for nothing? Why do I never come across those high-minded Society heroes one only sees over the footlights, who reel off epigrams and platonics as fast as Wilton's man opens oysters? Where do these prodigies lie; and where do they hide in the noonday, as the psalmist hath it? . . . Why don't you laugh?" asked Mione. "You look as though you were in a dream; and I'm sure you haven't heard half the clever things I have been saying."

Yes, Mione is right. I am in a dream; but the dream is a nightmare.

"I don't believe that you are ill," Mione continued. "Tremlett tells me you hardly cough at all now. It must be that you are moped. Now I'm going to shake you up. You've got to come with me to El-Meriem to-morrow, where I've a commission to buy scent and oranges; and I shall take you to the Club dance in the evening."

.   .   .   .

We went over the scent factory and had luncheon at the hotel. Afterwards we walked to the Cours, where there was a band playing, and where Mione met some friends, with whom I left her.

I strolled down to the Cathedral, having a superstitious fancy that if I were to put up a prayer at that side-altar before which I had kneeled the day after my first meeting with Robert at Kassis, Heaven might be gracious to me and lighten my darkness.

So I prayed in the dim side-chapel with my face upturned to the thorn-crowned Image. No spoken words came forth, but from its very deeps my soul cried, "Give unto me my heart's desire!"

Was the supplication impious? And will it be by the curse of a granted prayer that I shall be answered.

Is God mocked of His children? As I kneeled a certain beatitude crept over me, and that ineffable sense of oneness with Robert. Truly, in this incorporeal communion might be found an argument for the soul's eternal existence. If there were certainty of the life after death, and of the companionship of our loved ones, then, verily, the grave would be as the portal of Paradise.

My cry went up, and was answered speedily.

The consciousness of Robert's nearness became overwhelming; and I seemed to hear his voice, low, anguished, saying "Esther!" I rose from my knees and turned, searching the dimness in a trembling awe, fearing and yet expectant. I had not far to seek. He was standing at an angle of the recess watching me. It was himself, not his ghost. The movement he made towards me checked words rushing to my lips; and for a minute we held hands silently.

How plainly I could see that he had suffered! His face was worn; his eyes were sunken; and there was a streak of grey in his short brown beard.

"You have been praying?" he said. "Tell me what you prayed for?"

"I prayed for the granting of my heart's desire."

"And that?"

"I longed to see you again—and my prayer has been answered."

"Answered indeed! Two days later, and a miracle would have been necessary. I go back to England to-morrow."

"To-morrow! You were going without a word?"

"It would have been better so. Partings are too hideous."

We were speaking almost in a whisper. He still held my hand. Presently he said solemnly—

"Esther, don't pray for the granting of your heart's desire, in any bodily sense. Pray for me, if you will—that I may be given strength to stand firm. Pray that my love may avail to keep your pure womanhood unsullied to the end. Pray—and that would be far best—that you may come to despise and forget me. . . . I am going to leave you, that you may say that prayer."

For a moment or two we stood, close, yet held apart, as by the clashing of spiritual swords between. Then he cried hoarsely—

"Esther, don't look at me with that dumb despairing appeal in your eyes. I can't stand it: it haunts me through days and nights when I am away from you."

"Are you going to leave me like this?" I asked.   "Say that you will see me again. . . . Say that you will write."

"No. . . . Yes, I will write.   Forgive me, Esther."

And he was gone.

I sank upon a seat and covered my face.   I don't know how long I sat there.   The blistering burning feeling on my cheeks and hands made me know that I must have been weeping scalding tears.   I got up, all dazed; and then I saw a woman standing almost in the same place as where Robert had stood—looking at me.

I had seen the woman twice before, but never near or upright. She is very tall—-wasted as a skeleton—I could tell this through the long mantle trimmed with light sable that covered her.   She is like nobody whom I have ever beheld.   Her Greek features seem refined to an extraordinary clearness and tenuity, as by an inward devouring flame.   That flame leaps out of her yellow-grey eyes, which would mesmerise me, I think, if I stared at her. Though they are so different, they remind me somehow of Mr. Vassal's eyes.   Her face, except for the interior illumination, is like the face of a dead person. . . . But how beautiful!

She made an abrupt gesture, stretching out her thin hand glittering with rings—a nervous aristocratic hand—and one of the rings forming *his* name by the initial letters of the stones composing it.   Ruby, opal, beryl, emerald, ruby, topaz!   I can't imagine how at such a moment I could have taken in these details, but the thought was clear in my mind that this must have been her engagement ring, and it struck me as inartistic.   So intense was the passion in the woman's face as her eyes met mine, that for an instant I fancied wildly she was going to strike me.   But presently all the fire went out, her pallor became ghastly : she pressed her hand against her heart as if she were in pain, and staggering a little, moved along the aisle to one of the benches.   Through the uncanny animosity with which she filled me, I felt a stab of deep compunction, for I guessed that she had witnessed my meeting with Robert, and in the emotion written on our faces had read our secret.

I would have gone near, and asked her if she were ill and if I could help her, but I dared not.   It would have seemed almost like offering her an insult.   I waited, and after a few moments she got up and left the church by a side-door.

Mione's laugh sounded at the entrance ; and she came in with her friends and inspected the place, making the regulation bob as she passed the high-altar.   Later on, she said—

"If you had stopped in the Cours, you might have had a

dramatic meeting with your husband's hated heir. The Robert Vassals were there. He left her on a bench : and then, I think she must have been afraid I was going to speak to her, for after a bit she got up and followed him. I really should have liked to ask her whether that Influence had come along yet. The woman gives me the creeps. There isn't the smallest doubt that she is out of her mind : her eyes have such a wild way of glaring at you. As for him, he has altered extraordinarily since I saw him last. The Delmars certainly seem to have an unhappy matrimonial effect ; I must warn Audley."

Mione wanted me to drive to Kassis, but I persuaded her to make another excursion. Her friends went with us. It was all part of the nightmare. And so was the Club dance.

It is not ended ! It *can't* be ended. . . . All through the dark hours, his longing drags me as by red-hot chains. . . . " Esther, Esther ! " he seems to be calling.

And I lie bound and tortured—arms stretching vainly to empty space : lips seeking lips that are illusion.

It is to-morrow that he leaves Philotis.

.   .   .   .

From my balcony I watched the boat steam out. But perhaps he has not gone in her. And if not, he will surely come.

. . . The carriages have driven up and away—the Grand-duke has been giving a tea-party at the Annexe. The musicians on the terrace have packed up their instruments. . . . The sun has touched the Vasques hills.

. . . Now the beacon on Cape Feurd is alight, and the stars have come forth.

Dull dead despair ! He is gone.

.   .   .   .

How well I get to know the awakenings after these sleepless nights—the maid's knock rousing me from that confused doze which dawn brings : the tinkling of the electric bells in strokes of two, and the jingling of the market omnibus starting for town : the bruised feeling which is soothed by one's cup of coffee !

The look of the furniture is a jar, and the pattern on the carpet an irritant. Sometimes there comes over me a fantastic wondering whether the emotions which have flowed forth in these hotel rooms, do in truth leave their impress within the four walls to afflict sensitive occupants. For nothing, they say, is ever lost ; and the ripple of a sigh must roll on through space to eternity. If that be true, I shall feel sorry for my successor here.

I gave him his chance of freedom. I was prepared. I

offered myself to him for a burnt sacrifice to his conscience. Why didn't he know his own mind then and settle accounts? I could have borne it—before Kassis.

But what is misery when one comes to reason it out? It has no relation with outside existence; it does not alter one single fact of the substantial world; it exists but in one's own morbid consciousness. If one could forget, it would cease to be.

This is only a nightmare. Wake up! wake up, Esther! The sun shines; the sea dances; the harlequinade goes on; the laughing old earth whirls round just the same; the Garden of Paradise is nothing but a fairy-tale after all. Wake up! wake up, and work!"

    .   .   .   .

I shall write a story about Tourmestral. Yesterday, from the Cours at El-Meriem, I looked up at the castle on the crag, and made up my mind that at last I would go and see it. So I sent this morning for a carriage; and though the concierge told me there was snow on the Katkas, and that the English are waiting for settled weather to make their expeditions, I set off all alone, and am here.

Such a queer old-world place, and such a wild drive right into the grey heart of the hills! Past the campagnes and orange farms, the French cabarets and Arab coffee-houses; past the pine forest and the grotesque-looking monsters of cactus plants round the gourbis, and the patches of wild onion spreading out tufts of fleshy leaves, with the blue flowers yet unsheathed. Past the last string of camels, and the last herd of goats; right into the Mestral Gorge, where the green river foams between high precipices, and where the road winds round barren mountain-sides spread with speckled grey and black rocks, and showing here and there huge streaked boulders leaning to each other like monoliths of some ancient temple. And there's Sralta close ahead, every furrow distinct, except where his hump is wrapped in cold grey haze.

"Eheuh! eheuh!" the driver shouted, as he rattled round the curve of the zigzag, where there was only a low parapet between us and the river five hundred feet below—not a pleasant road to travel with mettlesome horses on a dark evening. Now we saw Tourmestral jutting out on its pinnacle at the head of the gorge; and it's hard to tell where the natural rock ends and where the fortress begins.

And there was the Chemin du Paradis drawn in wavy lines on the face of the cliff, losing itself in the shadow of an elephantine rock which overhangs the Mestral Pool.

The sun gleamed out fitfully all the time, and an icy wind from the Katkas made me shiver; but I like these keen blasts, which numb the gnawing heart-pain for a space. The carriage passed under a broken arch and into a tiny square, where there is an old stone fountain with a bench, and round it some sickly palms. A high white wall closes one side of the square, and in it is set a carved door painted green. From the other two sides narrow streets dip unevenly down, like the streets of the old town at El-Meriem, only that here there is no trace of Arab occupation. I remember having heard that the De Cayrols had re-colonised the village, which is now inhabited by some ten or fifteen families, not counting a few monks.

As I walked round the square I got glimpses of crumbling steps, battered doors, and cavernous interiors from which, at sight of the carriage, there rushed out small packs of queerly-dressed children, then a couple of sturdy peasant-women in blue blouses and short skirts, and then a grand-dame with a crimped cap and a distaff.

"Madame wished to see the Château?" suggested the driver, who was unharnessing his horses by the fountain and tying on their nose-bags. Then one of the peasant women, pulling an iron bell-rope, flung open the green door in the wall, and I was in the outer court of the old palace.

Have I ever seen Tourmestral in a dream? It has an oddly familiar look. In truth, I seem to myself to have lounged before now in these Moorish courts, with their slender spiral pillars and pointed arches painted in green and gold. I seem to know the sculptured fountain and the orange-tree hanging over it; and the funny little French custodian, with his crumpled, winter-apple face and apologetic smile, is like a dream-man too. But perhaps that dream is only caused by the strange medley in the place of orientalism and mediævalism; for the contents of a Breton château which, starting from the feudal ages and ending with the Second Empire, has grown its furnishings with the centuries, have been emptied into a Saracenic palace, and the effect is queerly bewildering.

The only part that isn't a jumble of incongruities is the harem court and the rooms opening off it, which, with their dark narrow recesses and raised platforms, where the eunuchs used to sleep, are quite unadaptable to European domestic requirements. And the harem garden! Was ever such an opium-dream hermitage—

if only one might never awaken from that voluptuous slumber!
High stone walls enclose it, draped with roses, wistarias, bougainvillea, and all manner of heavy-scented and gorgeous blossoms.
A fountain trickles wooingly, and round it a carpet of shadow
and sheen is stretched beneath old gnarled orange-trees, which
spread their cool green canopy hung with golden fruit. . . . One
ought to hear the bulbul here. . . . I have a vision of gazelle-eyed
Arab women in tinselled trousers and gauzy haiks reclining on
silken cushions, nibbling sweetmeats, and sipping sherbet out of
jewelled cups. . . .

No, I shouldn't care, after all, to dream in that garden; it is
too enervating, too suggestive of the Moslem's houri-paradise.
Poor little honey-fed prisoners! Did they ever feel, I wonder, as
I have sometimes felt at Grisewood, when they peered through
their loopholes at the world—the only world they knew—going
and coming in the outer court? There's one loophole in the
corner, higher and wider than the rest, with a stone seat beneath
it, and a view of the valley and road winding up to Tourmestral.
Was this, maybe, the perch of the Dey's favourite wife, who loved
her lord perhaps and watched eagerly for his coming; or who
hated him perhaps, and shuddered through every rosy limb in
dread at his approach?

All the while, as he led me along, the custodian chattered.

"Ah! unfortunately, visitors are not many at Tourmestral;
though, since the road was improved, carriages with English and
Americans come up sometimes from là-bas. It is the magnificent
collection of Damascus tiles which attract the connoisseurs; there
is nothing to be seen of such an antiquity, even in Philotis. . . .
And there are interesting possessions of the De Cayrol family—
Madame may be assured that the bureau in the late Marquise's
boudoir is a genuine Pompadour. It is a pity that the present
Marquis, though he once came as far as Philotis, had not the
enterprise to visit the Château. . . . Madame will find everything
in excellent order; though, it being some months since the summer
tenants departed, the garden has been perhaps neglected a little.
If Madame should desire to rent the Château for a few weeks—it
is permitted to place certain apartments at the disposal of persons
of consideration—a piano and other comforts might be brought
from là-bas. Mademoiselle Marthe would have pleasure in making
the ménage for Madame. Wood, it is true, is a little dearer
than in town, but what of that! For food, a sheep is killed once
a week, and there is poultry in abundance; and is not the
Mestral trout famed all round Philotis! . . ."

Yes, Madame thinks within herself, it would not be disagreeable to pass a spring month here, away from the glare and bustle of the Cosmopolitain.

At last the dream-person bowed himself into retirement, and I set myself to remembering where I could have seen a face like his. . . . Ah, now I have it! I used to notice him at the entrance to the café in the square at Kassis, where he would stand bowing—in the old French days of the place, when I was a child.

. . . I have eaten my little luncheon of pistolets-fourrés and fruit, and have wandered about the garden. Not the harem-garden, but one made in terraces below the castle front—a garden which has lichen-grown balustrades, and a sun-dial, and curious massive excrescences at the terrace corners, like miniature watch-towers, which command the whole spreading panorama of valley, river, and grey scarped heights.

The wind sweeps from the Katkas, stabbing like a knife; and to escape it I have come down some flights of grass-grown steps to a little court closed in by a high parapet, with broken pilasters and the ruins of a grape-trellis. . . . But even here the wind has found me out. It swirls round the castle in fierce gusts; and the sun, which all day has been shining only at intervals, is quite hidden now by the grey scud driving along from Sralta.

An icy rain lashes my face, and there are white feathers floating round. I start and shiver—less from the cold than from the superstitious shrinking which unexpected snow always causes in me. I don't know why it is, but I am afraid of snow. . . . Now it makes me think of *Claudia* and of my marriage day. . . .

As I went up the steps, back to the castle, there appeared upon the second terrace a form blurred by the mist, the sight of which made my pulses slacken. . . . And then my heart beat fast —fast, in a great gush of gladness.

He did not recognise me at the moment, but moved slowly as though to meet a stranger. But when I stepped forward he knew me, and bared his head, while a wonderful white light of joy shone out from his face through the mist and the falling snow.

He took my hand and put it within his arm, and saying, "Come in at once," hurried me through the whirling flakes to the entrance of the castle. He led me into a sitting-room—a sort of library, with a big empty fireplace, and bookcases all round it, in which there was nothing Moorish except the tiles lining the window recesses. He held my two hands, and looked at me long and earnestly.

"I am glad to see you!" he exclaimed. "Oh, I am glad to see you!"

The custodian, who had followed us, stood in the doorway bowing and apologetically protesting. Robert went to speak to him, and then I noticed the tiles, which are beautiful; and somehow, blending with the pattern of them, came the thought that of course the custodian must suppose we had arranged this meeting. What did that matter? What did anything matter now?

Robert came back to me, and the custodian advanced, still smilingly protesting.

Monsieur and Madame might command him. Monsieur already knew the resources of the Château, for it was not so long since he had spent a night at Tourmestral. Fires should be lighted immediately in the bedrooms, and there would be dinner at Monsieur's orders. Happily they had killed the sheep yesterday.

"He has been telling me that he is afraid you are weather-bound," Robert said. "It may stop snowing, but he doesn't think so; and any way, it would be dangerous for you to attempt getting back to El-Meriem in the dusk. Don't worry over it, dear; everything is all right."

Then he turned again to the ex-innkeeper, who was looking so exactly as my child-memory had him in his doorway at Kassis. I wonder how he came to be the De Cayrols' bailiff.

"Yes, please, a fire here at once; and some hot coffee, if Mademoiselle Marthe would be so good—I know these people," he said, as the custodian bustled off, "and can answer for Mademoiselle Marthe's coffee. . . . Are you cold, Esther? Has the snow wetted you? What should I do if you got your cough back again? Dearest, were you mad, to come up here on such a day?"

He talked on mere commonplaces, with the intention, I knew, of putting me at ease.

"I explained to the man that I am a relation of your husband's," he said. "It is the simple ironic truth, you know; and if you are going to be benighted, they'll look after you all they can. I brought him a letter from De Cayrol—whom, oddly enough, I met in Paris the other day—instructing him to give me the run of the library. I understand there are some interesting Arab manuscripts, which I want to overhaul. Do you know that my *Views* series has caught on tremendously. I'm going to do an historical article upon Tourmestral, and have tramped up, with my camera and a quire of foolscap, for the purpose."

He took off my cloak, brushing away the snowflakes, and tucked me up in a fur rug, while the olive-logs sputtered to a blaze. Then, when the coffee came, he poured me out a cup and made me drink it steaming ; and all the time as he chatted he fussed about the room, pulling forward chairs and tables, and giving it an inhabited look, with a feminine knowingness that set me laughing in spite of the strangeness and after-taste of pain. But it is always like this with us when we are together in a natural way for ten minutes. No matter how strained the situation, it becomes homely and delightful, and we are at peace in our souls. . . . Till the ghost hand clutches us anew.

" I know now," he said, " why I had such an overwhelming impulse to make tracks across the hills for Tourmestral. Sympathetic brain-cells and nerve-currents at work again ! "

" I thought you had gone to England."

" Yes, but I have come back. My wife is ill."

The dark look came into his face, and I felt the ghost hand moving nearer.

" It's a sort of nervous illness—her mind has been upset again. . . . I can't do much ; and she doesn't seem to care about having me by. . . . I find a relief in walking the country. As soon as she is well enough to travel I shall take her away. . . . But don't let us talk of troubles. Since Fate has given us this hour unlooked for and unasked, let us at least be happy in it."

The cloud passed. This was not the racked, remorseful Robert of the Cathedral, but Robert dear and tender of the golden London days. There stole over me a gentle warmth and a sense of extreme well-being. The fire blazed up, and threw pleasant gleams upon the old furniture and brass mountings of the bureaus and bookcases. He had settled me in a big chair at the corner of the hearth, and placed himself on a lower seat by my knee. Outside, the tempest blustered, and thick flakes of snow blotted everything—a winding-sheet maybe for a dead conscience ! . . . But here within, all was rosy glow and great peace.

He leaned his head against me, and I heard him murmur ; and stooping, asked him what he said.

" Dear, it is good to rest for a little while." And I felt the quiver of a man's deep-drawn sob. . . . " O Esther," he whispered, " if you could know the temptation that comes over me to give up everything—everything for you and happiness. But—it is my curse that I have a conscience."

Ah, the dead conscience ! Not dead, but only drugged !

I laid my cheek against his, and my bosom yearned to him with a yearning, in which blended at once the tenderness of mother and of wife. The deep wells of love in me brimmed and overflowed, drowning everything in the passionate longing to comfort him, because of his long struggle and his force outworn: the longing to be one with him in his defeat, which was in truth—angels defend me, if the thought be unholy!—in very truth it seemed, the triumph of my womanhood. . . . That womanhood pleaded for him and for itself. I yearned to be his in the abyss as upon the height; his in the evil rather even than the good; his—in the man's weakness rather than in the poet's strength.

*   *   *   *   *   *   *

Dawn after the irrevocable: and darkness, the angel-haunted abyss, dividing two worlds. . . .

It is a new sea which I behold from my turret window, stretching out palely luminous; and a new earth revelling in splendid life; and a new heaven, in which the sun as a bridegroom from his chamber comes forth rejoicing.

"Awake, Esther!" triumphant Nature seems to cry. "Awake and be glad. Dream no more nightmares of doubt and parting. Awake to imperial reality. For the throne is ready, and the crown wherewith your king shall crown you!"

And there, within the great rayed Arch it lies—far from life's sombre fret; beyond dominion of the people's gods—that conquered realm, where love is law.

BOOK IX

"' What have I done?' he cried. 'I too have sinned as Adam sinned—and Paradise is lost.' He opened his eyes: a star that shone like his lost Paradise was yet before him in the heavens. It was the morning star."

Gone the wild enchantment. Closed the gates of Paradise. Back to the City and the Conventions.

There was a telegram awaiting me at Philotis. To-morrow Mr. Vassal will be here.

We dined together at the table-d'hôte—my master and I. He would have it so. It is the first time I have dined downstairs. Every one stared at us, as we sat at our little table apart. Did they notice the mocking sneer which was masked by his elaborate courtesy?

He is in his demoniac mood of Mandour, and there's something in his manner which frightens me.

Last night I awoke shuddering from a dream of a great cold boa-constrictor strangling me in its coils. The electric light was turned on; my master stood there at the foot of the bed watching me, his dark eyes gleaming out from between their puffy lids with an expression in them which made me cry out in terror. He came a little nearer. I had the feeling of the snake about to spring, and there was such fierce hatred in his eyes that I thought he must be going to kill me. But he laughed and said—

"Don't be frightened. I was only looking at you, and thinking what a very beautiful woman you are." And he turned away and went out of the room.

I got up and tried to get to the door and bolt it; and then the staring electric light seemed to grow bigger and to be coming down upon me, enveloping me in a cloud of dancing stars. I remember nothing more, till I awoke shivering and found myself upon the floor, with the light still burning. To-night I have locked and bolted all the doors.

We have been to the great ball which the Governor gives to the Sheiks. My master commanded me to accompany him, and to look my best. He asked Tremlett what dresses I had here, and ordered me to put on the white brocade and the diamonds; and he himself chose my bouquet, which was white too. The Grand-duke complimented him upon my bridal appearance.

Hate sat between us in the carriage as we drove home; and again I had the gruesome fancy that presently a dagger would flash out and stab me, or that strong iron arms would gird me, and smooth cold hands grip my throat, and that I should be crushed and strangled, as by the snake of my dream. But there was nothing except the quivering suspense of silent terror, and of an aversion that seemed supernatural in its intensity.

When we had mounted to our salon, he just held open the door of my bedroom for me with a formal good-night, and asked if I would not like some iced soda-water.

Mr. Vassal has left Philotis.

*   *   *   *   *   *   *

It has come a knife-thrust after a kiss. I was not prepared.

I had not seen Robert for several days. He looked changed, aged, tempest-ravaged: the tortured ghost of the lover of Tourmestral.

I seem to hear my own pitiful questioning. . . . What had I done? . . . Was he angry with me? . . . Four days ago we had been utterly happy!

"Utterly happy!" Oh, the discord of his laugh! "Happy with conscience drugged and the sword dangling! . . . But we *were* happy! My God! we were happy!"

He spoke in hard jerks, standing opposite me with his arm on the mantelshelf, and his gaunt face, which had my doom written in its rigid lines and staring out of its hunted eyes, pushed forward, as if to give emphasis to the sentence he was about to deliver. He would not touch my hand, nor offer me the slightest caress.

Thinking it over since, I know that he forced himself to be cruel, because he was afraid to be kind. One moment of wavering and the floodgates would have burst. Passion would have swept all before it, and he would have stood irretrievably committed to the sacrifice of what was even dearer to him than his love—the heritage of good repute he should bequeath to his son, and the life-owed fealty to a woman who had rescued him from worse than death—a woman whose influence over him had always been immensely dominating—a woman whose absolute devotion and dependence upon his affection must appeal to every chord of loyalty in his nature.

Yet though I know this—knew it in the very rack and wrench of the throe—I have asked myself whether that terrible law of reaction after desire fulfilled, and which so often poisons the relation of man and woman, may not now have been faintly in operation.

... "Fate does not give happiness like that gratis, Esther. The bill has been sent in and has got to be paid. ... I've something to tell you ......"

Blur.... And the sentences stand out.

... "My wife is aware of what my feelings are towards you. ... And" (very slowly, like ice-drops falling) "her demand is that we never meet again."

Never—meet ... again! At first I hardly grasped his meaning. He repeated the stroke—made me know that the end has come, that the legitimate has conquered, as it must conquer in the long run.

... "She saw us in the church at El-Meriem. ... She has divined—or discovered—Heaven knows how—not the whole truth, but enough of the truth. ... Enough to have caused her illness— the mental derangement. ... Her mind is clear again now. ... Yesterday there was a scene—an agony. ... I am confronted with the alternative of leaving her, who was my saviour in need —to die, perhaps, in a madhouse—and of forsaking you. ..."

"You have chosen?"

"Yes, I have chosen."

No need to ask the decision. *She* stood there, claiming her own—the yellow woman, the mad woman!—in her strange beauty, with the glittering eyes that in spite of me drew him where she would. The wife, who had law and righteousness to defend her,— and ranged in her support, the compelling association of years of wedded life; of good and ill fortune borne together; of joys and sorrows shared, and of all the dear everyday cares and tendances. ... And beyond all, and in forefront of the host, that champion to whom nature had given right and sword—the son who was hers and his. In face of human bond and fact, my mystic sophistries shrivelled like dead leaves before a wind-driven flame.

Deep in my soul the fire kindled, but then to no avail; for the flame of truth was quenched by a wave of jealousy, that surged over me, flooding my heart with gall, and I could think only of myself, outraged in my most sacred faith, forsaken, betrayed.

I am. a wicked woman, stricken low in punishment, and left desolate.

It is these sentences of his, rising out of the blur, which give me back in their hideous selfishness the bitter words I said to him.

. . . "Esther, don't be cruel . . . don't say such killing things. . . . If you could know the torture I suffer ! . . . How can I desert my post? How can I join my life to yours, when there's an impassable wall between us?"

The cry pierced me, awaking the old tenderness. I would have thrown my arms about his neck in loving penitence and begged for pardon ; and then, as always, had our hands and lips met, there would have been peace and healing. But if that had been, he would not have been able to leave me. And he knew it, for he drew back with a gesture of repulse.

"No—I cannot."

My breast stiffened to stone.

. . . "Yes, there's a wall between," he said. . . . "It has always been there, though we have tried to blind ourselves to the fact. You think we have been happy ! But we have only caught as at the skirts of a garment, and the living reality has passed us by for ever. You think we have known the higher joy, but that was impossible, when we chose the lower place."

"I . . . chose . . . the lower place ! . . . Do you realise the sting of that?"

He gave a little shiver. "No, I was thinking only of the truth of it. . . . Esther, have it that I am abjectly base. . . . Where's the use of fine pleading? You can't forgive me !"

My pride rose in fiendish revolt. I challenged him to speak the whole truth. I said that which it shames me to remember— I will be honest in my degradation. He stood there perfectly grim, misery in his eyes, but with his lips set and hard, as though they were carved out of rock. . . . Oh, the irony of that silent condemnation ! . . . So my Paradise had been but the ante-room to his hell; and my love, which I had fancied the ideal to him of all spiritual good, was no more than temptation incarnate, loathed now in the hour of revulsion. What had been my triumph was dishonour to his sight. In his heart of hearts he held me no higher than the companion of his worst self.

And he denied nothing.

"It will be easier for you if you hate me," he said. "I admit that I have been weak—abominable. It is my punishment that I make you suffer. But bad as that is, wretch as I am to you, I am not destroying you so wholly as I should be destroying another."

"Then—it is that other whom you love with your truest affection?"

"She is my wife, and the mother of my son."

"You have always loved her?"

"Yes " . . . He seemed dazed; the words dragged out of him.

"You never loved me in the way that I thought?"

"No. . . . Perhaps not in the way that you thought."

"And I was never . . . the nearest . . . the dearest?"

"No. . . . You were not the nearest."

"And Tourmestral?"

He gave me one wild look and stiffened to iron again.

"I *will* know. . . . Give me my cup of humiliation in full measure; let me drink it to the dregs."

Oh yes, that is the way with us people. The cup must be drained—and more than that, worse than that, the dregs must be analysed.

"You know," . . . he stammered, . . . "there are things a man *can't* say."

"Not even to a woman who has lowered herself beneath his respect?"

The mad bitterness overswept me.

"Don't," he said hoarsely. . . . "I have told you . . . I cannot bear it. . . ."

He turned abruptly from me, and went towards the door; he seemed to stagger. There was a screen before it, which hid him from me. I did not hear the door open. When I followed him, I saw that he was hunched up against the panels. I put my hand on his arm, but he straightened himself, as if shaking me off.

"Are you going away—never to see me again?"

"Yes—I'm going away."

"Where?"

"To India . . . California. . . . What does it matter? But out of this place—to-morrow."

"Come and speak to me."

He came back, and we faced each other, he leaning forward, his hands clutching an arm-chair; and I remembered, as one does remember such things at moments of crisis, that this was the same chair over which he had leaned that day a year ago, when he had bidden me good-bye in this place, and had pledged me in everlasting friendship. . . . And with the recollection, it became relentlessly clear that his true self had indeed never willingly consented even to the friendship bargain. For I thought of his early avoidance of me, and of his variable moods later, and knew that there had been conflict as far back as that innocent beginning.

And now!

I half kneeled against the chair and gazed up to him in despairing and futile appeal. He would not look at me. His eyes were fixed brightly, staring into vacancy; his face was drawn and grey, and though we were close enough to have clasped each other, the iron wall divided us. For a long time he did not speak. Then, still staring at blankness, he said slowly—

"There never—never was such a love."

"It is murdered."

"You think so. . . . Very well; that is perhaps best."

"You leave me nothing—*nothing?*"

"No," . . . he smiled strangely, "I leave you nothing! . . . You don't understand now," he went on, in an odd far-away tone, "but you'll understand one day; and you'll know that it's only the body which has been murdered, and that the spirit of it can never die. . . . It was never what you thought it. You had a transcendental-material idea, which isn't in accordance with man's nature and with life as it is. . . . And I have been wicked, and untrue—in one sense—to myself and to you, and have committed a wrong that no tortures of regret can expiate. . . . But there are two things you must never say or think. One is, that I don't love you : the other, that I have ceased to respect you. . . . Good-bye."

He laid his hand on mine, which, as I kneeled, rested on the chair a little way from his. An impulse made me put my head down and draw his hand to my cheek, and my lips across it, as I used to do. If there had been tears left upon his hand, they might have softened him; but I could not cry—then.

And the old magnetic thrill of contact had virtue yet. Never for one single instant have I lost the ghost-impression of that touch. I knew that he bent down over me ; and it seemed as though billows of passionate feeling were clashing and dashing round us. I knew, too, that one moment of yielding, and our lips would have clung together, and we should have entered the haven of reconciliation. But he would not yield. He took away his hand, and stood a few paces from the chair.

"Good-bye," he said. "I don't want you to think that I shall be utterly unhappy."

I laughed out. If only he had not carried with him, as his last memory of me, the echo of that laugh!

"Oh no—that is not what I shall think."

"Because," he said, with a deep break in his voice, "whatever you may think or feel, my love for you was a beautiful thing, and the good of it will remain, and you will know it."

He came back for one second, and touched my head, and was gone.

.   .   .   .

And I, Esther of the end of all, look back upon that passion-poisoned Esther of the years that are gone, and from the tear-stained pages of this little black book, beyond, to the Other Side. The past is past: the sin is sinned, and the cleansing is done!

For passion is the scourge with which God chastises His children. Only when soul and sense mingle may it serve its true uses ·as Heaven's scourge-stick. To the earth falls that which is earthy; to the Spirit mounts the spiritual.

Wherefore should I weep for my blindness, now that the end is here, and that God is justified of His instruments? Why should I grieve now because I was not great? Since now I know, what then and later I only fitfully guessed, that if my love had been the true, grand thing we dreamed of at the beginning, it would have lifted me out of my contemptible egoism. I would have said to him, even so late, repeating his own words, " Dear, we will keep this thing apart and holy." And gently and lovingly I would have bidden him go and pay his debt. Bravely together we would have buried deep the body of our love, clasping hands once in sad, solemn farewell over its grave. Then we would have gone our ways, never to meet again, maybe, in the flesh, but to be one eternally in the spirit.

BOOK X

" Now I go whither thou hast sentenced me, whither 'tis said the road is common, where oblivion is the remedy for those that love.   But could I drink it all, not even thus could I slake my passionate longing."

"MARTYRDOM expiates everything. Suicide is no expiation."

I read this in a book yesterday; but I can't take in its sense; it seems all wrong somehow. . . .

Things look so strange up here at Tourmestral—things within and outside one—all blurred and distorted. . . . And everything is like a painted picture—nothing real anywhere. The valley, and the river, and the cold grey hills! What are they but a drop scene? . . . And the people too—that funny bowing innkeeper, and the peasants and the monks—they are only people walking about in front of a drop scene. . . .

• For the Garden of Paradise went down—down, when the Prince clasped the Fairy in his arms. And the keen north wind blows over it, and there's nothing left but the reflection in the clouds; and that's what I'm looking at. . . . Nobody wants to climb up the road to Paradise—now.

It's all wrong. . . . " Martyrdom expiates everything ! " . . . But you see, even being burned alive doesn't last through years and years and years—and go on after you are dead, and blacken with shame a poor helpless innocent, that never wanted to be brought into this cruel world—that has got no right to be in the world. . . .

"Suicide is no expiation ! " That isn't true. No . . . not when there's no other possible way out of the tangle. . . .

Shall you say it's cowardly—"not great, dear ; not like *you*." Oh, darling . . . I can't go on any more trying to be great. I'm nothing but a weak, wicked, self-deceived woman . . . all nonsensical play-acting talk—till it came to doing a big thing ; and then I wasn't big enough for it. . . . I couldn't touch the part—as they used to say in Bohemia.

It seems odd—those words of my mother's. . . . "Esther, all your trouble in life will come from not loving enough." . . . And see ! It has come from loving too much. . . . And yet Mother was right. I have been hard and self-bound, blinded by my morbid egotism. I have wandered in the dark seeking a clue to the spiritual life, and only for a very little while finding it in my love for you. . . . Now I have lost the clue, and all is dark again —suffocatingly dark.

If I could but write to you—if I knew—if I dared. If I might but ask you to forgive me for the sake of the beautiful beginning, and of the good that will remain—you said it would remain.

The pain! the pain! . . . Billows of it . . . oceans of it, drowning my soul. Drowning . . . they say it is an easy death to drown. . . .

I can't get away from the pain. I walk—down the Chemin du Paradis — up again. . . . Down to the black pool of the Mestral, which has no bottom. Nothing that went down there would ever come up again; it would keep a secret well.

There's no other way. I've gone over it all — reasoned it out, till I'm giddy. . . . Sometimes I've thought of taking ship to Borneo, Patagonia, Yucatan—what does it matter where, so that it be far enough—of burying myself in the forest Mr. Littlewood used to describe to us. . . . But Mr. Littlewood would be sure to find me; he'd want to come scraping again at his buried cities; and he'd tell Addie, and Addie would tell Mr. Vassal. . . . And besides, even if I escaped from everything else, how could I escape from myself, and from that which should come after? . . . How could I escape from the ghost?—you ghost that I try and talk to, and make understand. . . . And I cannot; and you *will* not hear. . . . Shall you hear me and understand when I come to you without my poor body, which will never worry you nor make you angry any more?

.   .   .   .

There's a carriage winding up the zigzag, a long way off—winding up the hills from the Mestral valley. . . .

Only a little black spot, but creeping steadily, slowly, surely every minute nearer. In less than an hour it will be here.

The yacht lies off Philotis: my master has come for me.

I wanted to write you such a long letter. I've tried and tried, and torn up so many sheets, and now it is of no use. I had thought that I would send the letter to Dr. Glaive to give into your own hands. . . . Oh, do you know now? You had never thought of *that*.

And you see, don't you? There's no other way.

.   .   .   .

Of course, I know where I am. It's my cabin in the yacht; I remember everything. . . . That was only a ghastly dream, the notion I had of being penned in a slave-ship—down below water-mark; and the sounds I fancied clanking chains and groans of prisoners, were only the heaving of the anchor and creaking of the timbers and wind in the rigging when there came on a storm.

Oh, such dreadful dreams! Why did you send that horrible negro, with the weals on his face—you know—to hinder me from calling out to you? Laying his great fat black hand on me—pinky-red it was, inside—Faugh! Laying it on my lips—my sacred lips. . . . You shouldn't have done it. You *might* have trusted me.

Of course it was you who sent him. Who else could have known where to find him—just at the corner of the stair street and close to the Bab-el-Ouestani—outside the Arab coffee-house, where we sat that day? Why, of course you know.

Did you *want* to drive me mad? And if I go mad or die, how will you ever understand? . . .

But I'm not mad now. This is my own cabin. Yes—didn't I choose that stuff for the hangings? . . . And I had that picture painted for the panel at the foot of my berth—I told you how I thought it would help me to sleep, and keep the bad things away. . . . You know the original quite well—in Venice—but we never could agree about Carpaccio. . . . And do you remember telling me that I was like St. Ursula when I was asleep?—as young and sweet and good and happy—that was what you said. But I wasn't dreaming of my martyrdom . . . then.

"Martyrdom expiates everything. Suicide expiates nothing!" . . . But why *don't* they open the porthole?

I *am* half dreaming. . . . This is a prison, you see. They've tried me, and found me guilty, and condemned me; and I'm to be executed . . . but not till afterwards. . . . That's the law. . . .

Oh, why *won't* you open the porthole? Can't you remember I never could live without air?

My master won't trust Tremlett now; he's watching me in-stead. . . . That's because there must be a jailor always in the condemned cell—night and day. . . . You see, of course, if there wasn't, and they would open the porthole, I should be free—quite free. Free to go to you and tell you. . . .

But, if you won't talk, what is the use of your sitting there beside him staring at me like that? Let Tremlett come, if there must be two. . . . Not *you*. . . . Don't you understand that you really will drive me mad? . . . Sitting there so close, and staring—staring. . . . Are you afraid that I shall scream it all out; and are you trying to stop me with your eyes? Because you're only a ghost, and you can't say anything. And besides, we never wanted

words to make each other know things. . . . Oh, you ghost, go
away and don't torment me.   Can't you trust me enough for that ?
If Tremlett hadn't watched me, you'd have had no need to be afraid.
. . . I never told you that she watched all the time.   She watched
me going down the Chemin du Paradis, and showed me to my
master, so that he knew where to find me.   How should I know
that there was another road—much shorter—at the top of the
gorge ? . . . *You* never told me about it. . . . You said there was
only one road to the Garden of Paradise, and that nobody ever
climbed that path alone. . . . But I had to come down alone !

I know that the gates of heaven were shut fast that day, and
the ramparts manned. . . . Great walls of livid cloud behind the
ashen crags !   *We* think they're clouds, but they are the fortifica-
tions of heaven, and they only become clearly visible when some
wicked presumptuous soul goes too near and tries to enter before
God calls it.   Then the angelic warders shoot out their lightnings,
and the poor soul is shrivelled and blasted for ever and ever.   *We*
think that's nothing more than a thunderstorm ; and some of us
pretend that we're not frightened.   But you'll understand better
now that I tell you. . . . For when one has gone down the Road
from Paradise all alone, you come to know things you never
knew before.

But I didn't get the truth properly into my mind then.   I was
thinking of such foolish, trivial matters.   Fairy stories !   Fancy
that !   It was looking down into the whirlpool—such a small,
sluggish eddy ; not a dramatic whirlpool, which ought to roar and
rush and swallow you up quick and give you no time to think
nonsense—it was that which put Hans Andersen's Seamaid into
my head. . . . You are so fond of Hans Andersen. . . . Do you
remember how she swam through the whirlpool to the Witch's
home, and let the Witch cut out her tongue, and gave up her
beautiful voice, and chose pain sharp as a two-edged sword—
just for the sake of winning the Prince's love and gaining an
immortal soul ? . . . And it was all wasted !   For the Prince
married another woman, and she didn't gain an immortal soul !
Wasn't that foolishness to be thinking, while I watched the
scum upon the pool go round and round—the dirty yellow
scum, all mixed up with dead leaves and broken bits of stick ?
I threw in a little twig—and then another and another. . . .
They swirled round so slowly—round and round, getting swallowed up at last. . . . And I thought of how my hair would
look, spreading out in long twirling things like snakes, with the
horrible scum getting into it. . . . And I thought how badly the
stale spume would smell and the rotting leaves. . . . And I never

could bear bad smells. . . . Then I got down quite close, and looked into the water, where the eddies circled in ; and there was your face—not quite clear, but the eyes shining. . . . I wanted to wait one little minute, till the face got clear and the eyes looked into mine. . . . For I knew that when once we should look straight and true into each other's eyes, you would understand. . . . Now I'm telling you exactly how it was, so that you may know it wasn't my fault, and that I *did* mean to be great. . . .

Then that was my master speaking. . . . " Esther, you shouldn't stand so near the edge ; you might fall in, and you'd find the water very cold." . . . And as I heard his voice, it seemed to me as though a great white bird fluttered its wings close over my body and drew me up into itself, so that I could feel its warm life thrilling through me and turning me giddy. . . . And I thought this was the White Swan of Death. . . . And then everything became dark. . . .

It was only that I fainted : and I have fainted many times before—but never quite like that.

BOOK XI

*" This is a great mystery, but we are animals
in time and space; and by time and space and our
animal nature are we educated."*

GHOST! ghost! why do you sit there always with those blank eyes and immovable lips? Are you stone-blind and deaf, or is it that you *will* not hear? Do you know that I am pleading to you day and night for comfort and counsel in my dire extremity? Or is it only in the Enchanted Land that spirits may commune in bodiless freedom? Have you no word for me here, in this evil house, with the curse of hate upon it?

I am not wrong in my head, though they act as though I were. I know all that goes on around me—why they have brought me back to Grisewood, and who are the people that come to see me, but are never allowed to be with me alone. I know the meaning of the rector's smile, which used to make me think of a sympathetic cod-fish; and what is in Mrs. Wargrave's mind, though she can't say it out before my master, when she nods her head so impressively that the parting shows all along it, and purrs gentle platitudes about "woman's noblest mission."... And I understand why Mione has put aside her little worldlinesses for the moment, as she yawns over her crewel-work—such a grotesque inconsequence is Mione, in her frilled petticoats, and silk fripperies, and Paris hats—and I know why she had that pitying shocked look in her eyes when she kissed me good-bye.

"You are in trouble, Esther," she said. "I am certain of it. And I'm not hankering after confidences, for I'm not sure that I like them. But I want you to remember that though I am supposed to be a flint, fit for nothing but throwing off conversational sparks, I can do a good turn for a friend, and hold my tongue for ever afterwards. Mind that—if the time ever comes."

Yes, Mione. You can't help me now; but I will remember if the time should ever come.

Oh, of course I understand it all. My reasoning faculties work well enough as far as outside things go. Yet there's a mist upon my brain sometimes, like the dark cloud that used to settle over Sralta before snow fell; and it darkens my inner eyes, and has blotted out my landmarks, so that I go astray, as I wander alone in the wilderness—*our* wilderness!

How else could I doubt you, dear? How else could I fancy, as in those black hours I do, that your love for me was never true love at all—never the irresistible union of souls that I believed it, but only on your part an attraction of body, an idealised sentiment, created largely by my need? For I see that what one fancies a need of you, in one you love, goes far to shape that one's relation to you. . . . You were "the Reader;" and I was "Esther Zamiel" the writer, whom you fancied you might help and mould intellectually. You had a generous wish to throw open the Art-temple to a neophyte, for which I thank you. And maybe my morbid type, tainted with genius—which I know is how doctors like Quintin Glaive would classify such women as I am—appealed to the poet, and to, perhaps, a strain of the decadent in you. . . . But all the time your most real self did not waver from the allegiance your heart had first sworn, so that, while to me you were the one foreordained mate and spouse, I to you was only the poetic distraction of some idle months—only——

No ; I will not say it—I cannot say it. . . . For it isn't true. . . . Ghost, tell me that it isn't true !

Leave me my rosary of happy hours. Let me still cherish my sanctities. Echo back to me my *Magnificat.* . . . Have I not passed through the gates of the Enchanted Garden, and been taught of the gods ?

   .   .   .   .

No, dearest, I am not mad—not mad now ; nor wanting any more to kill myself. Never since that strange dream—was it only a dream of the night ?—when you came to me and held me close—close. And I whispered in your ear. . . . And now you *know.*

Yes, now you know.

And you can never alter it. Never, even when we are dead and cold, and no more than bodiless shades, can you forget that once we loved in the dear human way.

We talked it out, the two souls of us, that night. And you made things clear to me which had been dim before. . . . Yes, I will wait, and bear, and hope, as you have bidden me. The rankling doubt has gone ; it melted away in that dream-kiss which awoke me, it seemed so real. You love me ; we are each other's. Who can tell what the distant years may bring forth, though the near years be owed ?

Owed ! Ah, for us that is the word of the enigma. You have made me understand. You have awakened the sense of justice in me. The long-back Past, the far-off Future—both are ours, our very own, our timeless birthright, of which none may rob us.

But the Present! That is not yours, nor mine. While *She* lives, it is owed to *Her*.

She bought it with her love, when she rescued you from blindness and despair.

So we talked the whole thing out in the silent darkness—we two souls.

No, you need have no fear. Could I requite your love by bringing ruin, perhaps death, into your home, and dishonour and remorse to share your bed and your cup? "Doer must suffer" —where have I read those words? *I* am the doer. *I* was the tempter. It was I who importuned Heaven. . . . Ay, and I exult in the ill-gotten boon, even though it has brought upon me the curse of a granted prayer.

But, alas! I am in sore strait, and the waters have risen up over my soul.

.   .   .   .

Last night I went to my master. I cannot tell what impulse drove me. I felt that I could endure the suffocating suspense no longer. And so I crept downstairs, with the frenzied idea that I would make one daring appeal for release from the horrible falsity of my position, and for permission to leave Grisewood. I thought that at least I would force him to break the ghastly silence there has been between us, and that then I would implore him to inflict upon me any punishment that he pleased, so that I, and I only, were the sufferer.

He was sitting alone in the library—for Mr. Arathoon, who has been with him, left the Castle yesterday. I opened the door so softly that I had time to watch him unobserved from the threshold, as he leaned back in his arm-chair, smoking, his eyes fixed broodingly on space.

What is that element in Mr. Vassal which, whenever I step within the outer wall of his personality, quenches my vital force, and turns me into a bundle of quivering nerves, played upon by some irritating and overpowering influence? Never was the oppression more strong upon me than last night as I waited, while he sat there, silent and solitary, amid the rich furnishings of the place, these seeming all to speak of race, wealth, and possession, so that I was seized by the fancy of him, as an epitome of Vassal traditions and Vassal supremacy, resistless now in the effect it produced. There he sat, each detail of his appearance deliberately perfect—his well-cut evening suit, the uncannily-striped flower in his lapel, even the silk mesh covering his high instep. And the whole square shape of the man—the massive iron-grey head, the Cæsar-like face, lined and old, and

marked with many a fierce impulse and many an angry thought,
all giving out that distinctiveness, that something mesmerically
coercive, which make Mr. Vassal a complex power with which
it is impossible to reckon. Suddenly his glance flashed at
me from out of the ivory mask that he rarely takes off in
my presence. He removed his cigar, saying not a word, and
rose politely, sitting down again after a moment. He let me
advance, smiling slightly, as though he were gloating over my
abasement.

The entreaty which had framed itself so eloquently died on
my lips. I halted, stammered, crouched on a settee; our faces
fronted as if we had been foes measuring steel.

For an illuminated minute I got the feeling of having, as it
were, lost touch of my own identity, and was dazed by the
appalling doubt as to how much of me, in my deeds and speech,
had been real woman, how much an artificial duplicate, a theatric
double *me*, for whom my fancy had, to its thinking, cast an
appropriate part in the drama of Circumstance. Do mad people
have this curious sensation of being momentarily outside themselves? They say so. Or is it a foretaste of the death-con-
sciousness that is supposed to reveal one's naked self, shorn of
psychological trappings? . . . By that supernatural flash of insight
I seemed to see myself, through all my relation with Mr. Vassal,
a sort of stage-person reciting lime-light heroics, in which I had
persuaded my mind to believe; a creation of my own disordered
imagination; a neurotic growth, to which my dramatic tendencies,
my literary outpourings, my sickly self-analysings had served as
might so much hothouse fuel to one of Mr. Vassal's over-stimu-
lated exotics. And as in a glass, side by side with the tricked-
up puppet, I seemed to behold the flesh-and-blood actuality for
which the Creator had intended me—a creature faultful indeed,
but of wholesome human sympathies, imbibed at Nature's fount,
and thus becoming elementally one with sunbeams and raindrops,
earth-mould and great-hearted living things, as should true women,
and mothers to be, of men.

And then, my memory gripping further and faster, so likewise,
it seemed to me, had been my earlier relation with the Reader.
Exaggerated sensibility and a distempered egoism—what but
these had been at the root of Esther Zamiel the writer's existence? Not even in my love—the one overmastering emotion
of my life, which had gone farthest towards dragging me out
of my unhealthy self-absorption—had I been grandly simple,
wholesomely human. . . . Do not my little black cahiers bear
witness against me?

I know it. . . . Yet even now, how can I help analysing my intuitions? That is ingrained in us writing-women.

Yes, it was true. I had looked at my lot with warped vision. I had been given my chance, and had not taken it. Life's realities had faced me for the first time on my marriage morn. Had I then resolutely torn away the swathings of morbid sentiment, and loosed the spontaneous clean-breathing earthling in me, that other fiercer animal might have been won by it to docility, and marriage have become a better thing for us two sinners.

A universe in a tear! The moral tragedy of generations upon generations of erring humanity, contracted into an extremest spasm of self-abasement, as one guilt-stricken soul stands for a second of time face to face with the all-revealing Absolute!

Oh! must one needs go down into the abyss of suffering to find truths of our mortal nature which shall lift us within reach of truths beyond mortality?

Is it that a double lock guards the human mystery; and that to open this door, one must possess, not only the key of love, but also the key of sin?

.   .   .   .

The natural instinct, so long sleeping, awoke and cried out. I flung myself before my master, not caring what should happen, so only that I might be real. Something of those words I have written, and of the remorseful feelings that were stirring me, came brokenly from my lips, as I made my petition. It was the litany I had never before framed even in thought; the confession of a soul convicted; the plea for compassion of one wrong-doer, to a fellow-sinner. . . .

Was he moved by it? . . . A sense of unexpected forces set free in the air between us, made me fancy so. I looked at him. He was bending forward, his eyes strained, and the muscles of his hands, which gripped the chair-arms, standing out in knots. Never before had I seen that expression upon his face. All the anguish of Apollyon expelled, was in it. Instinctively I understood, that only to strong men who have loved, despaired, and glimpsed heaven hopelessly, can come such a look.

Yes, truly, must this man, if but for a moment, have soared into touch with the higher passion. . . . I know its mark—I, Esther of the Tourmestral Dawn!

"There has been one woman in the world whom you have loved with your whole heart, beyond all others," I cried—I was thinking of Robert Vassal's mother—"one woman who has shown you what love may really mean. . . . For her sake, have pity on me."

His face slowly changed. It was as though the emotion in it were being drawn down deep into his being. When he spoke, his voice had a curious concentrated ring.

"Yes," he said, "there is one woman in the world whom I have loved with my whole heart, beyond all others. One woman who has shown me what love may truly mean—though not in the way I would have chosen. That woman is—yourself."

His eyes seemed to accuse, to judge, to condemn: and my conscience faintly cried, "I am guilty."

He went on.

"I loved you passionately—and as purely as was possible to a man of my temperament, in whose grim experience women had been either odalisques to be bought, or else cold-blooded world-lings and sexless pietists. In you I thought I had found, as yet undeveloped, those capacities which form the rare and perfect woman—dormant capabilities of feeling, which I believed that the intensity of my affection would rouse into energy, and that so I should gain that late-won happiness I had always in my best moments dreamed of and longed for. I loved you with a devotion which, had you not repulsed it loathingly, would have made me your slave till death instead of your hated master."

"I am guilty!" my conscience cried yet louder. . . . Where were the sophistic advocates that, in my own mind-communings, had vindicated me so glibly? Gone. Dumb-stricken. . . . We were alone—eye to eye—we two, who in law and natural fact had been made one, under an honourable obligation by which the very pillars of society are held fast. . . . None might reckon the count between us. A wrong had been done; an ordinance had been broken; and that heart-piercing Ray made it relentlessly clear to me that no specious arguments of mystic morality might avail to gloss over the breach.

On which side does the balance of wrong lie? Again my conscience answered. Coarsened, smirched, even debased as this man might have been, he had loved me, and, according to his own lights, had meant loyally. . . . He had seen in me his hope of regeneration; he had married me, taking me from, as he had expressed it, the slums of a theatre, and had put me into a high place, and bestowed upon me worldly advantages such as in my wildest dreams of success I could hardly have looked for. No matter that it was not these advantages which had weighed with me. I had accepted them, and had given nothing in return but repellent toleration and grudging obedience. Then, knowing the secret bitterness of his life, had I not added the doubly distilled drop, to poison the years left him? Could I, had I schemed

with the most malignant intent, have plotted to surer purpose?
But in counter-plea to my hysterical self-arraignment, memory,
shudderingly active, brought me back through long vistas the
sense of that rushing train: of my master's face close to mine . . .
of the snow blurring everything. . . .

"I know of what you are thinking," he said, in that same
indrawn voice. . . . "It is that my love was a base thing at which
you did well to recoil. . . . Do you not now understand human
nature sufficiently to know that all love of man, as man, for
woman, is two-thirds mere material attraction, which must be
equalised before the intellectual third becomes a governing force?
Some men are more adroit than others in masking the beast, and
that's all the difference there is between what romantic women
call the higher and the lower love. . . ."

His words rang an echo from my own dark hours of doubt;
and the serpent-suggestion bit with a poisoned fang. Yes, trace
alike to its root the love of poet and profligate, and is it not true
that each stands planted in earth-mire? Clothe the fairest soul
in an uninviting garment of body, and would it seek its twin to
any completion? If the hands had never clasped, would the
spirits have spoken?

"You know that there is a point at which mystic and materialist must meet," he said, as though answering my unspoken
thought. "Dress up Nature in whatever idealistic sentiment
you please, she remains Nature still. At least I have been honest
in my materialism. Did I ever pretend to you that I had been
a saint? Your friend, Frank Leete, knew enough of me to have
explained that to you. One doesn't visit Bohemia for the sake of
going to church. I have had an insatiable curiosity to explore
life to its core; and I think I may say that I have gauged sensation to its material milligramme—what is existence worth but the
amount of experience one gets out of it? Be human first—and
then a philosopher. . . . And I've known all the time, that there
lay a supreme, ethereal, and elusive emotion, still beyond the
milligramme—a something so rare and exquisite that one might
almost be deluded into imagining it outside the sphere of earth—a
very justification of immortality—a something which I discovered
in my boyhood's love, and lost through treachery, in the grasping—
which I found again, intensified, when I met you in Frank Leete's
drawing-room, and heard the note of passion in your voice when
you recited the Duchess's speech to Antonio.

. . . "What is it?" he went on, in a dreamy fervid manner, quite
unknown in him, and which impressed me extraordinarily—"that
strange and baffling emotion—wholly transcendental, and yet, as

dependent on matter as the electric spark to which the carbon thrills. For, not all the brainless logic of the spiritualists, can prove after all, that when the body dies, an emotion lives after it. . . . Yes, what is it? . . . The point of contact between two temperaments—do you remember Paravel's definition? Love in its dual perfectness—the pearl which a ploughboy may claim and wear, but which is not to be purchased with all the gold in the Mint. . . . That's what I have failed to buy—money down notwithstanding. That's the treasure common to humanity, of which I have been doubly defrauded. Have I not cause to hate those two men, the dead and the living—father and son—who have robbed me of my birthright?"

The passion in his voice was a revelation of the man. Out of the depth of new knowledge that had come to me, I spoke wild words. He took up my self-denunciation.

"No, you did not know; you *would* not know! You found yourself too late. . . . Oh, the tragedy of temperament! . . . That was indeed a true saying! . . . And the grimmest part of it all is that I'm not a fool in reading women: and up to a certain point I read you. . . . Did I not know that all the time there was something in your nature akin to the monster in me—a dear, sleek, caressing beast, lying asleep under all that vitiated romanticism and those shuddering-detestation airs? . . . Yes, if you had not infuriated and embittered me, flaunting your aversion, I could have taught you that a man may love a woman with all the body and the brain of him, and yet not have made a compact with the devil. . . . God! I believe that I *am* half a devil since I've hated you—I take such a queer hellish delight in making you suffer. . . . Perhaps, after all, I shall get more satisfaction out of my hatred than I ever got out of my love. . . ."

He rose abruptly, almost spurning me in his passion. I remained crouched there, quivering, bruised down to the deepest fibre of me. I heard him walk the room with heavy perturbed tread, and then pause . . . and pace the floor again—and pause once more.

When at last I looked up, he was a few feet away, gazing at me, the veins in his temples swelled like cords, as though in some mighty inward struggle.

He walked deliberately to a table where decanters were set, and poured some liqueur out of one of them into a glass. Coming close, he bent over and put his arm round me, underneath my shoulder—his muscular arm that felt like iron in its firmness. With great strength, and yet with great gentleness, he supported me to the chair from which he had lately risen.

" Drink this," he said quietly. "I have agitated you beyond what you can bear."

The warm, soft liquid coursed through my veins, bringing me new vitality.

I waited. And again there seemed to me in the air that strange feeling as of palpitating forces let loose.

"Esther," he said at length, and all the hardness had gone from his voice. It was deep and shaken, and its modulations reminded me of those tones which had wooed me in the dressmaker's parlour so long ago. . . . And there was the same indefinable perfume about his clothes—or was it the orchid faintly sickening? . . .

"Esther . . . I don't hate you . . . I love you !"

He stooped near me, one knee resting on the broad ledge of the chair, as he spoke almost in my ear.

"Listen . . . you know more now of life's facts than when I brought you, a girl-bride, to this house, imagining, fool as I was, that because you had been an actress you would also be a woman of the world. . . . Esther, you are very dear to me. . . . I would do anything you wish. . . . I would forgive you—everything. . . . You should go away from here, as you have asked. . . . I would not worry you or come near you till you gave me permission. . . . I would be scrupulously considerate of you. . . . If only, by-and-by, you would accept me again. . . ."

In the eagerness of his pleading his shoulder brushed mine. As I drew back into the angle of the chair, the flame of his eyes seemed almost scorching.

"Esther . . . don't shrink from me. . . . If you knew how that hurts. . . . Lift your lips to mine, and kiss me of your own accord. . . . No, I will not ask even that of you now. . . . Say only that if I let you go away you will come back . . . come back to your rightful position—that which a wife should hold in her husband's house, and her husband's heart."

It was creeping over me, his irresistible magnetism.

"I cannot. . . ." I try in vain to make the words audible.

"Think, I have never in my life before stooped to plead so to a woman. Do you know what it costs me? . . . It is the last time. . . . Consider before you refuse. . . . I would be generous to you. . . . I am an old man now. What if I, too, have learned a lesson ! . . . I would be very generous—to you—and to yours. . . .

. . . "Esther, I told you that my methods are subtle. . . . I told you that there's something of the devil in me. . . . You know it. . . . Don't goad the demon. . . . To-night, once and for ever, I offer you the chance of crying quits. . . . Then, give me your lips—of your own will. . . . And that kiss shall seal the act of oblivion."

Again he waited. I put up my hand feebly—a shield from his eyes.

"Is that your answer?"

At last my dry tongue found power of articulation.

"You know . . . what it is that makes it impossible."

"Have I not said that I would be generous? I can keep my word, though it is not a light thing that I would promise. All I ask is that for you, as well as for me, there shall be no backward looks. Think again. . . . I offer you the chance of rebuilding your life on a new plan—the past left behind you. . . . And it is not only your life—and mine—which are in your power this night; but another life too—that of your child. . . . I will provide liberally. You need fear no vindictive revenge, no reproach. . . . Unnatural as it might seem, what you look upon as the bar dividing, might be in reality the link to join. I am not an ordinary man, nor are the conditions of the case ordinary ones. Not only is a great inheritance in question, but, by a strange Nemesis, I have here the means of avenging a bitter injury—of at last carrying out a purpose, sought for over forty years. It has pleased the Powers above to make me the subject of an ironic jest, but I can give Fate back her own coin. My enemy's sword has pierced me, but the wound is not vital. I have strength to pluck out the weapon and to turn it against the thruster."

A grisly jest, in truth! Fine sport they must be having on Olympus! I laughed hysterically.

"Oh no," he said, his voice changing and becoming harshly metallic. "*You* need not chorus the mocking gods!"

He drew himself back, crouching as it were, while he watched my face.

"Well? . . . I have put the choice before you. Which thing is it to be?"

The minute he gave me seemed an eternity. His excitement had apparently burned out. I knew, however, that it was at white heat.

"I am awaiting your decision."

"I cannot . . . I cannot. . . . You say that you understand women. Then you must know that there are things which are impossible to a woman—*impossible!* You talk of human nature! It is Nature herself which forbids."

"You say so!" He spoke impassively.

Then I poured out supplication and self-reproach in broken phrases that seem to sound on yet accusingly. . . .

. . . "Oh, you are generous—more generous than I deserve.
You are greater than I ever guessed. . . . But be greater and more
generous still, and in pity don't ask of me what would degrade
me in my own eyes more than I am already degraded. . . . Yes,
it has come over me—the truth. . . . You make me bare to my
sin. . . . I see now, at last, what a hard, selfish woman I have
been. I see how I must have exasperated you—if you loved me
as you say—as I never understood till to-night. . . . I see my
cold ingratitude. . . . Even though I did not care for you, I should
have remembered that you gave me everything you could, getting
nothing in return. . . . And in spite of pretending to myself that
I despised worldly things—still, I married you. That was the
worst wrong I did you."

"No," he replied, "I exonerate you upon that charge."

"But it is a just one. . . . Then . . . there is something which
I cannot disguise from myself. . . . What you said is true. . . .
Delude myself as I would, it could not alter the material fact. . . .
The weakness which shocked me in others was all the time in
myself. . . . I was the tempter—when I ought to have fled from
temptation !"

"That," he said sarcastically, "is the law and the prophets."

. . . "My whole life with you has been one hideous mistake—
from the beginning !"

"It is not too late to rectify it."

"Yes, too late—in the way you wish. . . . Our marriage is a
dead thing. I hated it—I killed it."

He urged me still—sternly forbearing. I pleaded on desperately.

"Anything—anything but that. I should feel that it was the
offence against the Holy Ghost. . . . I know that I have sinned
against you, and against the law, in breaking my marriage oath.
. . . I know it now. . . . But there's just this excuse for me . . .
I *did* love, with my whole heart and soul. . . . I made a religion
of my love. . . . I *can't* dishonour it."

"A religion of what? . . . In the Decalogue it is called by
another name."

His gibe gave me courage to defend my heart's sanctuary. . . .
Once more I appealed to him in passionate disclaiming. I
entreated in frenzied despair.

Let him inflict any punishment upon me that he pleased.
I would bear it meekly. I would lead any life he might choose.
I would obey him to the letter in all the duties he should com-
mand of me. He would find me patient, unselfish, cheerful.
I would try to anticipate his every wish. . . . He would have my

gratitude, my respect, my affection. . . . I would be his devoted daughter, sister, slave. . . .

He checked the flood by an impatient gesture.

"Enough," he said. "All that means nothing to me. Your obedience I shall command; the rest is balderdash. I want no daughter, nor sister, nor slave. It is my wife that I want—the woman who is, and has always been, the one woman in the world to me, and whom I must either love—or hate. There is no half-way post. . . .

. . . "Understand," he went on, "from this night forth, you will indeed live the life that I choose. When there are people about, you'll take my cue. When I strike up the tune, mind, you've got to dance; otherwise, there'll be no intercourse between us, except what is absolutely necessary for the preservation of a decent appearance. I'll have no scandal. . . . Now—good night."

There was exceeding bitterness in the low laugh he gave as he went out, shutting the door behind him. It was as though he too, perforce, echoed the mocking gods.

BOOK XII

" Benoni, Son of my Sorrow! "

"On the 29th of October, at Grisewood Castle, Woodfordshire, the wife of Hector Vassal of a son and heir."

This was in the first *Times* I took up, after landing at Marseilles, when I came back to Europe a widow.

There is no need for me to say anything about my husband's tragic death, the news of which had met me on my arrival in India, eleven months before. I am taking up the thread of Esther Vassal's story, not telling my own. And, in truth, there are some calamities which change for one the whole face of the world, and may not be put into words.

Mione Arathon told me that before the boy's birth Esther's mind was quite off its balance, and that she had to be carefully watched during the voyage from Philotis to prevent her from throwing herself out of the porthole. Though she got over this phase upon the return to England, Mione's description of her own first visit to Grisewood sounded sufficiently pitiable.

. . . " Really it was a most uncomfortable spectacle, and gave me a horrid shock. And I've had so many shocks, that I ought to be getting used to them. I got one the other day when a woman I believed in confided to me that she had a lover. They always do confide" (Mione discursed a bit). "They say it makes them feel easier in their minds. To be sure, this woman was angry with the man, who was showing symptoms of desertion and talking about marriage. . . . Still, they do mostly confide . . . except Esther."

"Except Esther!" I was indignant at Mione's flippant inference.

"Oh, well, you never know. The quiet women are always worst. 'I like 'em to howl; it's the sulky ones that go under.' That's what an army surgeon said to me once, talking of the wounded after a battle. Esther doesn't howl, and she has gone under."

" Oh, don't say that."

" Well, you'll see. Perhaps she has come up again. Babies
are wonderful buoys when a woman gets into deep water—I don't
mean a pun. If you want to know really what I think, I can't
help a suspicion of some bad business behind it all. Nowadays
one isn't supposed to swallow even Bible miracles; but I must own
to a terrified faith in Mandour black magic."

Mrs. Audley crossed herself, and went on to relate some queer
adventure they had had in Mandour, and to declare that Mr.
Vassal had confessed to being a diabolist.

" I am convinced that he has offered sacrifices to the devil, in
order that the detested nephew may never reign at Grisewood;
and this weird infant is the result. Esther wouldn't have gone
mad for nothing."

" Oh, surely not mad ! "

" Well, not exactly raving, but a sort of melancholy. She
would sit for hours never uttering, tearing her pocket-handkerchief
into little strips, or plucking at the fringe of something, and all
the time staring—staring with those eyes of hers, which seem to
have got the wild Delmar look in them—only she isn't a Delmar.
If *I* had gone mad there'd have been some sense in it. . . .
Then Mr. Vassal was in such mortal dread of muddling up his
devil-sent revenge, that he couldn't be induced to quit watching
her, to make sure that she didn't inadvertently throw herself out
of the window. So he sat staring too. And then there was a
nurse in uniform—a sort of keeper person, popping in and out.
And there was Tremlett like a chastened Gorgon, in an embroidered apron, hovering round with smelling-salts. . . . And a
rainy summer ! And the churchyard cedars for a background !
Ugh ! it gave me the creeps, so I wrote to Audley to telegraph
that he had got the gout and wanted me back immediately."

.   .   .   .

Of those days Esther never afterwards spoke to me, and I
don't know if she kept any definite recollection of them. My
impression is that they remained always in the background of her
consciousness, an unspeakable horror ; and of one thing I am
certain, that though Esther Vassal lived on through the horror a
changed woman, it killed Esther Zamiel the novelist. There
appeared no other book by the author of *Naamah ;* and I remember how at the time, people wondered over the extinguishment of
that new light in the world of fiction, and deplored the cutting
short by death, as was supposed, of a promising career. But
those who knew the secret of Esther Zamiel were faithful to their
trust ; and when, years later, Mrs. Vassal took up her pen under

her own name, no one identified her work with that of the literary comet of a bygone season.

I showed the notice in the *Times* to Dad, who met me at Marseilles; and he was much interested and excited, not having heard that such an event was impending.

"The house in Grosvenor Street has been shut up, and I fancied that they were yachting," he said. "I have seen nothing of either of them for months. Of course, this accounts for old Vassal not having turned up lately at the Roscius. I wonder how Robert Vassal feels about it. Well, the desire of Hector's life has been granted him at last, and much may it profit him! Anyhow, I'm glad for her sake," Dad went on. "This puts her into an assured position. I have always felt a little guilty in having delivered her over so entirely into the hand of the enemy. It was disagreeably suggestive, that refusal of his to make a marriage settlement."

Dad despatched a congratulatory telegram to Grisewood Castle, which was becomingly acknowledged by Mr. Vassal, just as dear Dad, in the catholic exuberance of his sympathies, had sat himself down to indite condolences to Robert Vassal, the dispossessed heir.

"Damn!" he cried, tearing up the sheet. "One can't run with both the hare and the hounds!" And he went off to the Roscius instead.

When he came back I noticed that he seemed troubled, though he did not tell me why. Presently I saw him drumming absently with his empty pipe on the table, and heard him murmur softly to himself; and then he asked me to look up the quotation, "Life is a comedy to those who think, and a tragedy to those who feel." For, he said, he wasn't quite certain whether it was Horace Walpole who was the author.

Dad never could be happy till he had verified any quotation that occurred to him.

We had begun to gather together strands of the old working life; and though I could not as yet go to any first performances or enter into general society, I tried to be as cheerful as I could, and not to let the shadow of my widowhood darken Dad's home. For a grief does not become any the lighter for pulling a long face; and at least one need not lay the burden of it on those who love one. So I put my back to the wall and fought my foe; and by-and-by, in the daytime at any rate, the enemy retreated, and I was able to throw myself, with an interest that daily grew more real, into Dad's literary occupations—correcting his proofs, doing a little easy novel reviewing, consulting authorities for a biography he was writing, and taking a curious pleasure, after eight years of the vapid life of an Indian regimental station, in the once familiar atmosphere of books. Truly, there is a nostalgia for Bohemia; it is born in the blood, and one can never get away from it. That was how I gradually became a writing-woman too, though, of course, in a far less degree than Esther Vassal. Besides, at my husband's death I was left very poor, and there were drags of which I did not want to say anything to Dad; and so I was glad to be able to earn a little money.

No answer came to the letter of congratulation I sent Esther, which hurt me unreasonably, for I ought to have considered that she would probably be some time in recovering her strength, and would no doubt be inundated by congratulations from a host of friends, which she would feel bound to acknowledge. But no, that was not quite the cause of the hurt. The real sting lay in the fact that she had not taken any notice of me in my great trouble, when sympathy from her would have been dear, for I had always been—even when I did not properly know her—deeply attached to Esther. Now I jumped to the bitter conclusion that worldly prosperity had spoiled her, and made her heartless and forgetful of former friends. In this I realised later that I had done her great injustice.

It was in the beginning of December that I nerved myself to pay Dr. Quintin Glaive a visit at his consulting-room in Harley Street. It needed some courage to face him, on account of his indirect association with the tragedy of my married life.

As I was admitted, a man passed out, going by me with a hurried lifting of his hat. I recognised him at once as Robert Vassal; and from that day to this I have been haunted by the expression of stony misery on his face. I wondered at the moment if it could possibly be caused by disappointment at the loss of his inheritance, but decided that there must be some nearer and deeper-seated source of grief. Then it occurred to me that perhaps Mrs. Robert Vassal, whom I had never seen, but had understood to be in bad health, might be ill or dying; and, on an impulse, hardly in accordance with a regard for medical etiquette, asked Dr. Glaive the question.

He too seemed strangely discomposed, as though something painful had recently happened. But he was reserved, as usual.

"No," he answered, "I believe that Mrs. Robert Vassal is better than she has been for years. The trip round the world has improved her health, and now—I don't know if you have heard— she is likely to remain in the East. Robert Vassal has thrown up *Views* and the House of Commons, and has accepted the post of British Consul at Mandour."

"Isn't that throwing up a career as well?"

"Perhaps; but Mandour is an important post, and the consulship there practically a diplomatic appointment, which could only be offered to a coming man. No doubt, too, in the Eastern surroundings he will find a fresh literary field; and besides that, it will probably mean his wife's restoration to health."

Dr. Glaive seemed to me to be speaking perfunctorily and with a heavy heart. He leaned back in his chair, fidgeting nervously with his eyeglass, which he fixed in his eyes, tightening the brows over it, and relaxing them suddenly, so that the glass fell— a trick of his that I knew, and which indicated that he was perturbed in mind. Suddenly he said—

"Have you seen or heard anything of Mrs. Vassal of Grisewood?"

I answered that I had heard nothing about her beyond what the *Times* had told me, and that I had been a little wounded by her silence.

"Don't be hard on her," he said, leaning forward earnestly. "You are the only true woman-friend she has in the world; and I know that however self-absorbed she may have seemed, she does care for you and appreciate you. Be kind to her, if she will give you the opportunity. Go and stay with her, if you can make it any way possible."

"Surely," I said, "she needs me now less than ever. But you know that I would do anything—anything that was in my power— to help my friend. I don't know what it is about her that makes me feel as I do for Esther."

"Yes," he said, "she has a curious, in some ways inexplicable, knack of inspiring affection in those who get below the surface of her nature."

He was perfectly silent for a few moments. Then when I asked him if he could give me any news as to her present condition, he replied abruptly, that he had had nothing but the most formal communication from Grisewood, and changed the subject, beginning to talk to me of my own affairs, with that delicate sympathy and comprehension which make him the good physician he is, and, so much more, the good friend.

When I got home I found Dad ruminating with a letter spread out over some proof-sheets before him--a letter in a hand that I knew, on thick notepaper, with a neat heraldic emblazonment.

"You see, it's from Vassal of Grisewood," said Dad. "We are invited to the christening—a gathering, he says, of his own and his wife's oldest friends, to celebrate an event which all must regard as productive of moral and material satisfaction. Odd way, rather, of putting it! Here's something for you, Gagsie, enclosed."

He handed me a note from Esther, which was pathetic in the quavering formation of its letters, and the little bald sentences of which it was composed.

"DEAR AGATHA,—Please will you come—as a great favour to me. I did not answer your letter, because I could not. I am better now. Please come to your old friend,   ESTHER."

"I don't want to go," said Dad. "I don't like the country—especially in December."

Dad's eyebrows took the curve, and his eyes gave the peculiar twinkle with which he always heralds a scholarly paraphrase.

"In fact," he went on, "I love the unspeakable *urban* solitudes, and the sweet security of streets."

"But all the same," he added, after having smoked a pipe, "I *ought* to go, and I'll go."

. . . .

So we went. Out of tune as I felt for the atmosphere of Grisewood, and for the society of Mr. Vassal and of his friends, I could not find it in my heart to refuse Esther's request, remembering too what Dr. Glaive had said to me. I wondered if he were going to be of the party, since, surely, dating back from *Claudia*, he might be counted as one of Esther's oldest friends. I learned afterwards, however, that he had been invited and had declined the invitation.

No, it was impossible to refuse, for something told me that it was indeed my old friend forlorn Esther Vrintz who appealed to me, and not Mrs. Vassal of Grisewood.

Snow was falling when we arrived, the first snow of the season, and the gaunt cedars outside the Castle looked as though they were dressed in their winding-sheets. I had never seen Grisewood in mid-winter, and it struck me as indescribably gloomy. But, in contrast to its forbidding exterior, the large inner hall, which was then the usual winter lounge, seemed full of life, light, and merry voices as we entered it out of the white dimness of that December afternoon. I don't know much about great English houses, but the hall in Grisewood Castle has always appeared to me one of the most noble and picturesque interiors possible to imagine. I am told that the oak carving is noted all through the country; also the massive proportions of the fireplace, and of the supports to the gallery, which runs round on each side of the splendid staircase. Then there are paintings worth a king's ransom, as we story-tellers put it, supposing indeed that kings were ransomed nowadays; and suits of armour and wonderful bronzes and porcelain and tapestries, and I know not what besides, rare and valuable.

A fire of logs was blazing in the majestic chimney, the tea-table at an angle with it, and brass stands in front, holding all manner of hot cakes; and at each corner was a red-lined basket, from which crawled a sleek dachshund, while a glorious yellow collie got up from the rug and made a stately advance towards us, gazing up into my face with brown eyes that reminded me of Esther's. There was a number of people collected round and about the hearth, and Mr. Vassal, in hunting costume—several of the men had evidently returned from the day's run—stood with his back to the fire, towering above the Bishop of Wood-chester, who was contemplatively stirring his tea. A gentle, unassuming bishop, with a kind quaint face, as wrinkled almost as the episcopal gaiters upon his lean legs, and in as distinct anti-thesis as could be imagined to Mr. Vassal, who looked more vulture-beaked, more fleshily saturnine, and more imperially domi-nant than the mind-picture I had kept of him from my last visit of over a year back. I had, too, exactly the same feeling of an unwholesome moral exhalation as he shook hands and gave me his stiffly elaborate greeting.

For some minutes I did not get sight of Esther, and had time to glance round the party. There was Mrs. Raphon, in a gown trimmed with yellow fur—I think it was a kind of otter—looking extremely handsome, and Mrs. Audley Arathoon, a fashion-model from New Bond Street, whom I heard remarking in an audible undertone to a Guardsman she had in tow, "Now, Sir Jock, it is really too great a strain upon my nerves watching you to see that you don't disgrace yourself. Do recollect that you are *not* to tell that story to Lady Cotherstone, because you'll shock her, and then silence and consternation will fall upon us, and my hair will begin to uncurl, which would be unbecoming."

There were some people I did not know, and some I did know, having seen them at Grisewood during my former visit, such as the Heseltines, and Littlewoods, and Lord Cotherstone, who, I was told later, was to be a godfather—the other, of all persons, being Mr. Arathoon, the solicitor. I think that Mr. Arathoon, with his Jewish nose, his sleek fair beard, his red lips, cold grey eyes, and soft false voice, is personally even more obnoxious to me than his sister, Mrs. Raphon.

Then there was a little London group, in which I recognised, from the *Punch* cartoons, an ex-Minister of the Cabinet, and a certain Lady Diana Cleeve, whom I knew of as friend of Dr.

Glaive, and a great admirer of his plays, and Loseley Allard, of the Foreign Office, whom Dr. Glaive calls the Parasite, and with whom I used to act in private theatricals years ago, when I was a girl; and a little way off, talking to Sir John Willoughby, the member for Woodchester, Mr. Paravel the critic, whose elderly stained-glass face seemed to belong to another world altogether. It was an odd, interesting party, larger than I had expected; and I felt shy and out of keeping in my mourning, and wished I had not come.

"Mrs. Vassal is showing Lady Cotherstone our new orchid," said Mr. Vassal. "She will be here in a few moments. Audley, will you ask your wife to give Mrs. Greste some tea? Excuse me, Bishop, the muffins are behind you."

The Bishop moved, and made me welcome.

"You have not been long back from India, Mrs. Greste. I had the pleasure of meeting you here last year, just before you started. I hope——" And then he was reminded, no doubt by my garb, of the sorrow that had befallen me, and stumbled in his speech. Mr. Littlewood came sympathetically forward, and there were "how-do-you-do's" from Mrs. Audley Arathoon and the others, and the babble went on.

"Addie and I were nearly taking passage from Naples to Marseilles by your boat," said Mr. Littlewood. "We should certainly have done so had we known you were on board. But Addie is such a bad sailor that she funked the Mediterranean."

"The Mediterranean can be a terror even between Corsica and Marseilles," filled in somebody, with what Dad calls the macadam of conversation, and Sir Jock drawled—

"The worst of a short voyage is, that you don't get the comfort of quarrelling with your fellow-passengers, because you haven't had time for the excitement of making friends."

"Or for establishing a proprietary right to your deck-chair," remarked Mr. Littlewood.

"Oh, when I take my passage, I always make a point of finding out how many unattached ladies there are," observed Loseley Allard. "Once I discovered there were to be nine, so I provided myself with ten deck-chairs, had my name printed big on one, and distributed the others among the damsels. Then I was pretty comfortable."

"Nine unattached damsels!" commented Mr. Vassal. "I once made a voyage to the Cape in company of one, and I was extremely uncomfortable."

"Was the damsel pretty or plain, young or middle-aged,

stupid or agreeable?" questioned a Willoughby girl. "And what did you talk about?"

"She was young, beautiful, and conversational; and first of all, we told each other everything that had ever happened to either of us. That took a week."

"Not more?" murmured Audley Arathoon.

"Then I invented thrilling misdemeanours, which carried us through the second week. The third seven days I was so mortally bored that I contemplated getting the captain to marry us, and committing bigamy for the sake of ten minutes' excitement."

Mr. Vassal walked slowly to Mrs. Raphon's side as he spoke, and stooping to say something in a low tone, stroked admiringly the fur on her sleeve.

And just then some one came in with Lady Cotherstone from the conservatory—some one I knew, and who yet was strange to me. A pale woman in clinging black velvet, looking taller than she was by reason of her thinness, with haunted brown eyes and a mechanical smile, and, what was stranger than anything else, a broad streak of white hair spreading from her forehead over the top of her head, while all the rest was still its old brown. . . . And this was Esther.

My start unnerved her. There seemed something dreadful in the quiver that passed over her face, disturbing its gracious rigidity.

She came close, not offering to kiss me as she had always done before, but holding my two hands, and staring into my face in an odd, frightened way.

"Don't," she whispered. "You mustn't upset me. . . . I'm not quite strong yet. . . ."

I murmured a few incoherent words, for I was too shocked and bewildered to say anything I ought to have said. She smiled a wan little smile.

"It's my white hair. . . . Being ill has made it so. . . . You'll get used to me." . . .

She gave her hand to Dad, and thanked him for having come.

"For I know you don't like leaving London in the winter. . . . And Griscwood is so terribly dreary, and so cold—outside. Indoors one *can* keep away from the snow. Isn't it curious that there should be snow now—for my little child?"

There was an indescribable intonation in her utterance of these words, "My little child."

"Why! not curious at all, Mrs. Vassal—but seasonable.—A green Yule—you remember the proverb?—seasonable and fortifying to the youngster," said Dad, with the dear, big, tremulous laugh which always means that his soul is moved within him.

"I congratulate you. . . . I congratulate you . . . with my whole heart."

"Yes . . . yes . . . thank you. . . . And you must come and sit by me close to the fire, and Mione shall pour you out some tea. . . . And you'll tell us about the new plays. . . . Oh no, he won't have muffins, Mr. Allard. . . . You see I have remembered the buttery scones you used to be so fond of. . . . And you know Lady Cotherstone, don't you? . . . Dear Lady Cotherstone, this is my great friend Mr. Leete, and his daughter Mrs. Greste, whom you met here last year . . . " and so on.

Oh yes, *Claudia*. I seemed to realise somehow that the actress-training was being turned to account at last. And as Dad says, it is a big part—that of the Mistress of Grisewood—and takes a lot of playing.

And while I sat there in the shadow of Mione, silent and depressed, and a little bewildered, the shifting groups and the scraps of dialogue became somehow, in my fancy, bits of a scene in the kind of play that Loseley Allard calls tragedy in trousers.

"Snowing heavily!" said one of the hunting men. "We were just in time, master!"

. . . "A thirteen mile p-point in twenty minutes! . . ." from Lord Cotherstone.

"Nonsense!" cried the eldest Miss Willoughby, who was in her riding-habit. "You mustn't expect a rational person to believe that."

"Any more than you must expect a rational person to believe that Littlewood jumped Stratton's Brook," put in the master, with his heavy guffaw.

"'That wasn't St-t-ratton's Brook, Miss Willoughby; it's a m-mile higher up," said Lord Cotherstone.

"Oh, well, it runs into Stratton's Brook," said Miss Willoughby.

"And Stratton's Brook runs into the Wyn, and the Wyn runs into the German Ocean. So, on that reasoning, it is clearly proved that Mr. Littlewood jumped the German Ocean," observed the Bishop, giving a gentle clerical laugh.

"And he's cramming muffin down his throat, and can't defend himself," exclaimed Mione. "Mr. Littlewood, what *are* you sitting on? You might be one of those creatures on toadstools 'mid nodings on.'"

"Oh, I've got a little more on, really, Mrs. Arathoon, than when I did sit on toadstools in the forest of Yucatan, before Addie took pity on me. But I'll go now and find a chair."

"And tell Audley that he has flirted long enough with your wife, and that I want him to come and put Flapper through his tricks. Oh, you needn't be jealous. Audley's flirtings are quite harmless. He doesn't talk much to his adorations, but he likes to know they're there. . . ."

"Sad business, that of the Rathdowney smash," said a hunting man. "Everything up for sale—all the family pictures. Portrait of a lady, portrait of his grandmother, and the rest. Poor Rathdowney!"

"Poor Rathdowney!" echoed Mr. Vassal. "He lived beyond his income for thirty years, had a ripping time, and has now gone to join the Immensities. He was a prosperous sinner! To give the devil his due, Providence has been kind to Rathdowney."

"Of course you know the place has been bought," said old Lady Cotherstone. "Inskip, the Woodchester lawyer, told me this morning as I was gettin' into the train. For a hundred thousand! I didn't ask him whether that included ancestors. What is it to be turned into?—silk, cotton, or what other dreadful thing?"

"Lamp oil," said Mr. Arathoon. "The coming man owns a petroleum spring in Texas."

"Oh, really! Petroleum! How very curious!" and Lady Cotherstone turned with chilling vagueness in another direction. Her face assumed, however, an expression of intelligence at the approach of the ex-member of the Cabinet.

"You're just the person I'm looking for," she said. "The Duke wants me to get him the straight tip about politics, and *you* can give it me."

"Well," said the ex-Minister after a reflective pause. "you can tell the Duke we're coming in, and that there will be no foreign war after all."

"I'm glad to hear that," remarked Sir Jock. "Then I shan't be buried in Bulgaria without a tombstone. I don't mind being decently potted, but there is an ignominy in a nameless grave."

"The English do love a scare about a foreign war," put in Lady Cotherstone. "We're always screamin' out to foreign nations, 'Look here, our ships won't float; our cannons burst; our bayonets crumple up—there's no deception. Come along and judge for yourselves.'"

. . . "I'm told there's to be a new wing built at Rathdowney, and that petroleum is going to make the county hum," said Mr. Littlewood on the other side.

"How Woodfordshire will grovel!" exclaimed Mione. "I don't know which amuses me most—to hear a Yankee pay compliments, or to see human nature grovelling before a millionaire."

"The Yankee for choice," put in Lady Diana Cleeve. "Their patois is so quaint, and they never *can* get our names right. I had one lunching with me yesterday, and when he went away he said, 'I'm married to just a lovely wife—from Kansas city; and I'm much obliged for your hospitality, Lady Cleeve; and we shall have vurry great satisfaction in returning it.' That's what I call putting things on a square footing. . . . Mr. Vassal, I've come to tell you that Cosmo Paravel is quoting Dante to your wife, and that you'd better go and look after her."

"Thank you. . . . But I'm not afraid of Dante."

"Nor of Mr. Paravel?"

"Nor of Paravel."

"Lady Diana, I observe, divides humanity into four classes," said the ex-Minister—"men, women, politicians, and—Paravel."

"It appears to me that you give politicians a prominent place," retorted Lady Diana.

"I put them, you see, below women."

"Below women! What a concession! I shall tell that to Mrs. Vassal; it seems an appropriate moment. If her husband won't fly to save her, I must."

Presently Esther came to me.

"I am going to show you your room, Agatha: you are to rest before dinner."

Then I noticed, what struck me still more forcibly later, that though Mr. Vassal seemed to be aware, even at a distance, of his wife's every movement, he always turned away when she approached, ingeniously avoiding speech with her. Also that she never addressed him, nor looked at him, but was much less tactful than he in covering the omission. She went with me up the great staircase and along the corridor to my room, talking hostess-trivialities all the time in a nervous, rapid manner, quite unlike that of the old Esther, so that I longed to say, "Surely we are not now behind the footlights."

As she was leaving me, I asked if she would not take me to see the son and heir.

Then again the painful quiver passed over her face.

"No; no . . . not this evening. . . . And the nursery is a long way from here . . . in another wing. . . . To-morrow . . . I couldn't now—and get through dinner. . . . You see," she went on, collecting herself, and speaking with a strained artificiality, "I'm obliged to be so very careful not to break down. It takes such a long time to recover from an illness . . . and a little thing upsets me. And I have my duty to perform to Mr. Vassal's guests."

I went deliberately to her, put my arms round her neck, and kissed her.

"Yes, darling, and you are quite right not to class this person with Mr. Vassal's guests—or Mrs. Vassal's either, for that matter; for I'm the guest of my old girl-friend Esther Vrintz, whom I love dearly. And I've come to Grisewood because *she* asked me—come in my sorrow, to rejoice with her in her joy."

"O, Gagsie! ... Oh, I *was* sorry for you ... I was ... I was. ... .Oh, I know he was all the world to you ... and I would have written. ... But I couldn't, indeed, Gagsie ... then. ... I was so unhappy myself ... and I——"

The poor thing, trembling all over, clung to me for a minute or two, gasping the words out between her sobs, which she tried in vain to stifle. ... "O, Gagsie dear ... don't ... don't. ... You *mustn't* be kind to me. ... I shall forget all I've got to do— just like Claudia ... and something dreadful will happen. ... I mustn't think about myself. ... Don't, Gagsie dear!" ...

She broke away from me, as a knock sounded at the door, and Tremlett appeared, a phial and a glass in her hand.

"My mistress ought to take her drops, if you please, Mrs. Greste: it is now past the hour, and Mr. Vassal has sent up, ma'am, to ask if you would kindly go down presently."

"My drops!" cried Esther with a wild little laugh. "Oh yes, Tremlett, my drops. I need them, for I'm very shaky still. Give them to me, Tremlett."

She took her dose from the maid and drank it. No doubt it was some strong restorative, for after it, a faint dash of colour came into her face.

"Thank you, Tremlett. Please tell them to let Mr. Vassal know I am coming."

The maid left us, and Esther stepped close to me again, look-ing into my eyes wistfully for a moment, and then laughed once more—that strange laugh.

"Yes, I must go back to the show and dance my steps— dance to Fate's fiddling. ... Do you remember that line, Gagsie —it came into *Claudia*. ... Oh yes, the actress-training does help one along a bit!" ...

.   .   .   .

We were all assembled and waiting in the drawing-room before Esther appeared.

"Do you know what is keeping her?" said Mrs. Audley Arathoon. "I went into her room the last thing before coming down, to beg as a personal favour that I might not be sent in to dinner with you, Sir Jock."

"Why this thusness?" asked Sir Jock.

"Because if I sat next you, I shouldn't have a rag of reputation left for the Woodfordshire canonesses to tear into tatters. . . . Well, I went to Esther's boudoir, and there was the greatest of the Cæsars, issuing his imperial command that she should put on another gown. He didn't consider black brocade and old Venetian point sufficiently festive for the occasion."

"And Griselda obeyed?"

"Meek as a lamb! All I can say is, that I—*just wouldn't.*"

"Don't you ever change your gowns to please your husband, Mrs. Arathoon?" artlessly inquired Mrs. Littlewood.

"Oh dear no," replied Mione, "I change them to please other people's husbands."

"Well, really," bleated the youngest Miss Willoughby, "if I were a man, I think I'd want my own wife to be what I liked to look at."

"If you were a man, dear, you wouldn't look at your own wife; you'd look at other people's wives," returned Mione. "The true art of marriage is——"

She stopped. The door had opened to admit Esther, and behind her the butler, who announced dinner.

"The true art of marriage is—?" repeated Sir Jock, offering his arm to Mrs. Littlewood.

"To be continued in our next," said Mione, taking that of Dad; and I heard her say, "Our dear Esther looks quite bridal, doesn't she, Mr. Leete?"

Yes, she was all in white, and her little head, set bravely back, supported the famous Vassal tiara. I noticed the sombre blaze in Mr. Vassal's eyes as they inspected her from head to foot, and the flash of steadfast courage—the first I had seen those brown orbs emit—as she lifted them to his for a moment. I asked myself if it were motherhood that had changed the lamb into a lioness.

At dinner, I was too far from Esther to be able to see or hear anything that went on in her neighbourhood. In the drawing-room afterwards, the ladies were discussing the decoration of the table, which was of tea-roses and violets that had been procured from Philotis.

"But it's nothing to the font," exclaimed Mrs. Littlewood. "That's a dream of myrtle and white carnations, sent over expressly from Philotis. You should have come earlier, Mrs. Greste, and you would have helped us in decorating the church."

"O Esther," Mione broke in; "do you remember the fields of carnations and roses that day when we went to El-Meriem? But I heard afterwards that the snow had come down right over Kassis, and had cut them all off."

Then Esther seemed to be speaking somnambulistically, so unlike itself did her voice sound.

"Yes . . . the snow came down over Kassis. And the roses were all blighted and dead . . . all dead!"

She was forgetting her part, and gazed helplessly round as Claudia might have done waiting for a cue. At that moment the men came in; and somebody—Lady Diana Cleeve I think—said:

"O Mr. Vassal, do tell me—was it your notion to order all those lovely white flowers especially from Mrs. Vassal's birthplace?"

"Certainly: do you like the connection of ideas?"

"Why, I think it is the most charming compliment I ever heard of from a husband to his wife."

"But nobody except Mr. Vassal could have thought of any thing so delightfully romantic," chimed in Mrs. Littlewood.

"A mere sentiment!" said Mr. Vassal, in his ironic manner. "And at my age I might well be ashamed of it."

"Do not say a mere sentiment," exclaimed Cosmo Paravel, his deep poetic voice ringing out reprovingly. "It is sentiment that never palls—the one thing that brightens our future, soothes our present, and reconciles us with our past. To those who have nothing to hope and nothing to enjoy, sentiment still offers happy memories."

"Hear, hear!" exclaimed Sir Jock.

"Worthy of a man and a Briton!" murmured Loseley Allard.

"And now, Mrs. Arathoon, after that, your continuation of the true art of marriage," said Dad.

"It is to keep the carrot dangling in front of the donkey's nose," replied Mione. "I know I am vulgar; but when Britons take to sentiment, they need a corrective."

"I must cap that by something that was said at my dinner-table the other evening," remarked Lady Diana. "A young man defined love as passing up wine and waiting for it to come down again—and marriage, he said——"

"No, no—Anti-climax!" cried Loseley Allard.

"The carrot takes the cake!" said Sir Jock.

Ah! what tragic nonsense it all seems now, with the later lights upon it.

Mrs. Littlewood began to play, which started new combinations; and some persons listened, and some did not. She never minded. Half the charm of Addie's music lay in the way she made it blend with what was going on around. . . . I heard the Wargraves and some Woodchester clergymen discussing Mr. Vassal's presentation of £2000 to the Rescue and Reformation League, towards, as Mr. Arathoon put it, the foundation of a cottage-home for children without visible fathers. Then Lady Diana and Loseley Allard set going a conversation-game, which provoked ringing laughter, and from which I shortly retired. I had the uneasy sense of being no more than a spectator in the drawing-room comedy, and might have said with Dad—and Teufelsdroch, "We looked out on life with its strange scaffolding, where all at once harlequins dance and men are beheaded and quartered."

The room is a large one, and has many nooks and recesses, and if one is placed out in the cold, socially speaking, there are always the gracious Gainsboroughs to smile consolingly. I was wondering whether those peerless ladies had belonged to the original or pseudo-Vassal stock, when I became aware that I was sitting, wedged in by a palm and the curate of Fincham's back, close behind my host and Mrs. Raphon, whose conversation, though it was carried on in an undertone, I could not help hearing. No doubt he had been telling her that she was looking well— which was no stretch of fact—for she answered :

"My friend, I can't return the compliment. These domestic joys don't agree with you. You have aged ten years in the last six months."

. . . (I lost the beginning of the sentence). "At a certain stage in the descent," he said, "the drop comes suddenly."

"Do you mind?" she asked.

"Do I mind! Is it ever an agreeable discovery that the big throb of life has stilled for you, and that it takes a sensation of considerable poignancy to stir the languid pulses to a quick beat?"

"I can't help thinking," she replied, "that over there, you are providing some one else with a pretty poignant sensation. I don't pretend to unravel mysteries, but if that isn't a soul in torture, I don't know the signs of suffering."

Mr. Vassal's gesture, of which I was darkly conscious, made me certain that the momentary stoppage of Mrs. Raphon's swaying fan had indicated Esther.

"If so, the soul has chosen its own particular corner of hell," he answered grimly.

There was a buzz, for just then the curate became suddenly aware of me.

"Oh! I beg your pardon. I fancy that Mrs. Littlewood is looking at me and wants me to find her music."

His back removed, I caught a glimpse, past the palm, of Mr. Vassal's countenance, with the dying fire of its bleared eyes, and, to my exaggerated fancy, the death-clutch mark upon his loose jaws and flabby indented cheek. One might well conceive here, the craving for some vitalising emotion to set the enfeebled nerves tingling once more, even though toll might have to be paid for it on the other side of Acheron.

"What did you do it for?" Mrs. Raphon said, a wild note in her half-whisper. "Where was the charm? One could see from the beginning that she abhorred you, and that she only married you for your money. It must have been a powerful attraction on your side. You never paid *me* the compliment of hating me."

"I pay you the greater compliment of desiring your friendship."

She gave a bitter laugh.

"A convenient label for—ashes!"

"Let me put down your cup," he said.

As they moved, I got up too, and the grouping of the scene shifted. Lord Cotherstone had the centre.

"I s-say, Mrs. Vassal, we ought to see our godson. How can we do our d-duty properly to-morrow, if we none of us know the object b-by sight?"

"Hear him!" cried Mrs. Littlewood. "Fancy insulting the hope of Grisewood by calling it an 'object.'"

"Or an 'it!'" retorted Lord Cotherstone. "But he can't be anything else, can he, B-Bishop, till he's a Ch-Christian?"

"I think," said Mrs. Raphon, "that the object ought to have received us in the hall on our arrival."

"Of course!" exclaimed Dad. "Mrs. Raphon has an eye for situation. Carter-Blake couldn't have stage-managed a finer close to Act IV.—the peace, goodwill, happy-ever-conclusion! Such a background—the oaken hall, baronial hearth, properties in keeping, ancestral portraits"—Dad waved his hand comprehensively. "And, 'curtain!'—our host here, the grand old English squire, presenting to us the long-desired heir of the house! Where was your dramatic instinct, Esther—I beg a million pardons, but old habit is strong—to have missed such a telling effect?"

"It is not too late," said Mr. Vassal, with a curious smile on his face, and a fierce gleam shooting in Esther's direction from his serpent-like eyes. "The child shall be introduced to you now. You will allow me?" And he turned more directly to Esther, with that formal courtesy which Addie Littlewood calls Grandisonian, and rang the bell.

Esther had risen from her seat, white and agitated, and seemed about to make a protest, but no words came.

"Oh! it's a shame to disturb the brat!" said Mione.

But, still smiling, Mr. Vassal commanded the butler to convey his compliments to the nurse, and request that the infant, well wrapped up, might be brought down to the drawing-room.

"Let the greatest of the Cæsars be obeyed!" breathed Mione, "even though it kill the child!"

"Yes, it is a shame," murmured Addie Littlewood. "You never saw such a quaint misery. I doubt their rearing it."

"Poor little dear!" said Mrs. Heseltine. "Surely by now it's tucked up and fast asleep in its bassinet."

"And it won't have on its lovely lace robe," said Mione, "for I saw that taken off and folded up, and the creature put into common cambric."

"*You!*" cried Mrs. Littlewood. "You don't mean to say that you have been to the nursery?"

Mione nodded shamefacedly.

"And I couldn't induce you to come and see *my* boy tubbed!"

Mione nodded again. "No, but your boy is a baby, and I don't like babies. And this baby is a phenomenon, and I like phenome—na!—That's right, isn't it, Mr. Paravel? One has to mind one's grammar when there are critics hanging round."

Everybody laughed. I felt pretty sure, however, that Mione had cried over the phenomenon, for on a private voyage of discovery to the nursery on my own account, I had met her coming out of the door with red eyes which she dabbed with her pocket-handkerchief, saying that a cinder had got into one of them in the train.

Presently the double doors were thrown open, and, preceded by the butler and followed by two footmen, a portly and dignified personage in a silk gown entered, with a magnificent white silken-embroidered and swansdown-bordered mantle hanging over her arms.

Esther, white and trembling, made a step towards her. "My little child!" I heard her say almost below her breath, a sound wafted as might have been an angel's benediction. But Mr. Vassal, stepping between, intercepted her movement, and she retired into the background.

The nurse halted under the central chandelier, in front of Mr. Vassal, who stood straight and tall and imperious, with outstretched arms upon which she placed the babe. The men and women gathered round, bare shoulders and jewels glittering, and the gentlemen's gilt hunt-buttons shining, as all pressed forward beneath the lamps, to get a sight of the infant. But its mother, still as a statue, kept quite away by the window.

I too hung back, for I had seen the child before.

The nurse unclosed its wrappings, arranging a fold of the cloak so as to form a shield for its eyes from the light. But Mr. Vassal mercilessly swept the mantle back, and there from under the swansdown peered a pair of uncanny eyes, below a bulging forehead and out of a wee misery of a face, which seemed to give the spectators so great a shock that no one said a word.

Mr. Vassal held up the pitiful thing, regarding it himself fixedly for a moment; then, looking round upon us, always with that strange smile—

"Let me present to you"—he seemed to pause—"my son and heir."

There was an inarticulate murmur. Then Dad came to the rescue, with a tremble in his voice as he said—

"For me, alas! life is now all retrospect!—a phrase I have heard used by Cobden. But from nursery recollections, Gagsie, my dear, I should say this is a remarkably intelligent little fellow. And I hope" . . . here Dad faltered—"I hope he will grow up to be an honour to his father's name . . . and . . . a comfort to his mother. . . ."

"God bless him!" said the Bishop.

All the time the babe never uttered a sound, but stared with its supernatural eyes.

"You haven't told us yet what you are going to call him," said Lady Cotherstone. "Hector, I suppose?"

"No. He will be given the name of his"—again Mr. Vassal made a slight pause—"his great-grandfather—Robert."

Then suddenly there was the clatter of an overturned chair, and a dull thud. And as we turned, it was seen that Esther had fallen in a dead faint, her head against the velvet curtain at the window.

Mr. Vassal thrust the child, which now began to wail eerily, into the nurse's arms, and there was a rush to the window.

"Has any one smelling-salts? . . . Water. . . . No, give her air. . . ."

Lord Cotherstone parted the curtains and flung the window open, and the shock of a flake of snow which drove in by the casement from the storm outside, roused Esther, and she came to shivering.

But the next day she was so ill that Mr. Sergison had to be sent for, and she was unable to be present at the christening, or at any of the following festivities in honour of the heir.

WITH my child's birth, the oppression of fear was lifted for a while. For there is one place into which Hate may not enter—that Holy of Holies where a mother watches over her newborn babe.

So for a few weeks kindliness was my nurse, the world shut out, and my little child lay cradled on my bosom.

It was such a tiny atom, smaller, frailer, more piteous than ever babe had right to be. Yet it seemed to me that the wee body was charged with some sacred regenerative force, by which my passion-poisoned being might be cleansed and healed. Dimly I felt this then : I know it surely now.

My little child! Was this the answer to my prayer at El-Meriem? Was this the granting of my heart's desire? It had come to me, the gift of this mysterious new life, born of bliss and anguish, from out that love-region beyond the gates of dawn—the dawn which had arisen upon my Paradise.

Herein I found the sign that, in His vast humanity, God pitied and pardoned the human error; and while taking from me the joy wrongfully clutched, by right another's, had bestowed upon me this boon for my solace and redemption. As I gazed on my little child, I began to realise in shadowy fashion that God is in the All—in the evil as in the good, in the darkness as in the light : working through darkness to light, through evil unto good, through flesh unto spirit. Clearly the truth shaped itself that love is the language in which its Maker speaks to the world. Had I not learned that love has many cadences—symphonious as the choiring of seraphs, in near flight from heaven ; harsh, with discordant notes of pain and vain longing, as the song descends earthward? And yet I knew that through my love and anguish, and even my sin, I had come within speech of angels. . . . In the eyes of my babe, I seemed to behold a shadow of the Divine-human—That which is outside law, because all law is therein comprehended, linked to the world by love and pain, so that where love and pain are, there stretches the Cord Invisible.

On the third day after the child's birth, when slight fever was upon me, I had the vision of a stairway to heaven, with radiant spirits floating on either side, and I myself mounting between them to the glory of the dawn, a little child leading me. Other visions I had, too, that day and night, but none so beautiful. Then it seemed as though the babe's lips, clinging to my breast, were drawing out of me, in living streams, those morbid thoughts and feelings which from the beginning had put me in conflict with my lot—the egoistic art-yearnings, the false faith, seeking vain gods, the futile fret of all that was unworthy in my love. I did not understand then, as I came to feel later, that these things had been necessary for progress upward. I had only touched the borders of that knowledge, in dim realisation of the oneness of the Divine with all human experience—even with that which appears to be evil, since without evil there can be no good.

Now for the first time in my troubled life I felt my fingers close on the clue to the king's palace. And that clue which I had believed was in love of woman for her mate, I found now in love of mother for her child.

Art! Love! Motherhood! But the greatest of these is Motherhood!

.   .   .   .

The remission of pain was only for a time. Hate lurked menacingly still outside my chamber door; and as I grew stronger, and life took up its march to the tune of Fate's piping, the old dread came back upon me—that terrified fascination which forced me to do my master's bidding unquestioningly—the old obedience in which now was mingled penitent submission to a punishment earned. The hardest part of the punishment was that it separated me to a great degree from my child.

For that seemed Mr. Vassal's chief object. I was forbidden to nurse my son; and on this point the doctors also would admit no parley, so that I was doubly helpless. I might have been a royal lady claimed by court pageants and state cares, so inconsiderable were the dues maternity was permitted to exact. It was almost only by stealth that I could get a little while alone with my baby.

The child was installed in a wing of the Castle apart from mine, with a retinue of nurses and maids and men, and all paraphernalia befitting the future monarch of Grisewood. No longer did he seem my own, the living gift Heaven had bestowed upon me, to draw sustenance from my bosom. He was the heir of the Vassals, in whom I had little part or property. And there were streams of visitors and great doings at the Castle; and on

all occasions Mr. Vassal exhibited the same cold courtesy, and
was sardonically benign to guests and tenants, while to me he never
spoke, except, as he had said, when it was necessary for the maintaining of a decent appearance.   He played his part grandly, and
forced me to play mine—entrances and exits, and speeches to his
cue ; and ghastly jigging to his fiddling. . . . Oh, it was a brave
show—with, all the while, the skeletons rattling in our ears, behind
the gilded background.

WRITTEN
BY
AGATHA
GRESTE :

IT was commonly declared in Woodfordshire that Esther Vassal would never rear her child, and people pitied Mr. Vassal for the terrible disappointment which they thought would inevitably follow upon the fulfilment of his wish for an heir. Nevertheless the child did live, though it cannot be said to have flourished.

A poor pitiful little heir it was ; and as Dad put it, had Robert Vassal, the nephew, been inclined even now to raise money upon his expectations, the Jews would probably have managed it for him. But nobody heard anything of Robert Vassal in these days, except indeed, when his name adorned a leaderette, or appeared in the occasional column of "Our Mandour Correspondent." This at one time happened pretty often, for diplomatic trouble had arisen in regard to the Sheiks, and the British Consul at Mandour had been turned into a sort of Envoy Extraordinary and entrusted with certain negotiations, that he had discharged apparently to his own credit and his country's satisfaction. Once there was a report in the newspapers, afterwards proved incorrect, of his having fallen into the hands of a hostile tribe of the desert, from whose clutches it was supposed that he would not come out alive ; and it was Esther's uncontrollable emotion upon reading this news, which gave me the first definite clue to her life's secret history. The truth flashed then upon me as such truths suddenly do, with a piercing certainty ; and though no words ever passed between us which could directly confirm my intuition, I *knew* all the same, and I am sure that Esther knew of my knowledge. This intuition on my part altered greatly our relation to each other. It strengthened our friendship, imparting to it a peculiar sacredness, enabling me to understand things that had perplexed me before, and to give a silent sympathy, which I think was a comfort to her in her lonely sorrow. For she must have been terribly lonely. Even I did not realise for a long time how lonely, since several years elapsed before I was admitted to Grisewood Castle upon a footing of complete intimacy. In the earlier days, when I was merely one among other guests, we spectators, who came and went in continual relays, looked on at the play as it proceeded duly staged and mounted, Mr. Vassal never forgetting his lines, and Esther following suit with hers, hardly one of us suspecting that it was a mere theatrical performance at which we assisted. For myself, I had from the beginning a dim realisation of the tragedy beneath the laughter ; but it was not till the chief actor began to grow a little weary, and to lose grip on his part, that there came to be undress intervals into which my stayings at the Castle were allowed to lap. Then I saw what no ordinary visitor was permitted to witness, and gained sufficiently clear indications of the battle between two hatreds waging in Mr. Vassal's breast— hatred of the unfortunate little heir, and hatred of the dispossessed nephew ; the two hates balancing each other, and keeping the machinery moving and the situation from collapse.

I could now more easily comprehend Esther's meek sub- mission to a system of restriction in regard to her intercourse with her son, that at first appeared to me unjustifiably tyrannical. It was pathetic to watch her seizing opportunities for spending an hour in the nursery, and, when the child ailed ever so slightly, coaxing the head nurse—who was a hard disciplinarian, engaged to obey orders, and invariably chosen by Mr. Vassal himself— persuading her to take rest or exercise, and to leave her in charge of the child. The nurse was so unwilling to do this, that I cannot help thinking Mr. Vassal must have made much of his wife's mental trouble before the boy's birth, and had thus estab- lished a reason for the method of espionage he adopted. No doubt, too, Tremlett had been properly primed. I hope I am not uncharitable, but I could never believe that Tremlett was really as devoted to her mistress as her manner would have led outsiders to suppose.

Poor Esther ! Sometimes at night I would hear a step outside my door and would find her stealing along the corridor to Master Vassal's wing, and then she would excuse herself by saying that she had awakened fancying she heard the boy scream—which was an impossibility. But the nurses had told her that he often started up from his sleep about midnight crying violently, and this expectation would arouse her, and she would go and watch surreptitiously for a few minutes by the child's cot to assure herself that all was well.

Then when, as rarely happened, Mr. Vassal went away for a day or two, she would contrive to send for Mr. Sergison, and cleverly work him up to the delivering of a medical ordinance that the boy should have carriage exercise or some such thing, and there would be, of course, no plausible reason why he should not accompany her on her drives. Of course, too, when the child was really ill, she could not be denied the nursery; and this was a pretty frequent occurrence, especially during his teething time. Once when he was about two years old, it was never expected that he would recover, and prayers were offered up for him in the village churches, and physicians were summoned from London—Dr. Glaive, at Esther's urgent request, among them. I fancy it was owing to him that the child did get well. But when we talked it over afterwards, he shook his head sadly, and told me there was such evident tendency to brain trouble, that he should always be anxious on the boy's account; and that he had strongly impressed, both on Esther and Mr. Vassal, the necessity, as the child grew older, of keeping him under the healthiest influences, and of avoiding cerebral excitement and exposure to the sun. But after this, and until he was about five years old, little Bobby did seem to throw off his infantile delicacy. The weird look left his face, and his forehead lost, to a great extent, its bulging appearance. Though he was always shy, strangely dreamy, and given to curious imaginings, so that he lived as it were in a world of fantasy and it was difficult to tell when he was inventing and when relating fact, he was a forward and intelligent child; and probably if he had been brought up in a gamekeeper's lodge or a fisherman's cottage with romping brats of his own age, he would have falsified Dr. Glaive's gloomy anticipations. But it was his misfortune that he was born to inherit a fortune.

As the boy increased in stature, he gained in beauty. His hair was fairer than his mother's, and had a tendency to curl at the points, growing back in half-moon shape from his forehead, and standing out in a kind of aureole. His skin was extraordinarily transparent, the blue veins showing through its ordinarily waxen whiteness, though he had a trick of flushing at a word or look to the most exquisite rose-petal bloom, that again faded almost as quickly as it had come. His head had the fault of seeming a little too big for his body, but his limbs were straight and daintily formed, and the features very regular, like and yet unlike his mother's, while his eyes were especially lovely—wistful and earnest, with long dark lashes, and this peculiarity, that whereas one was luminous grey, the other was half grey, half hazel.

Notwithstanding the anxiety he caused her, and in spite of the gruesome atmosphere, to be felt rather than described, which his presence near, and such slight intercourse as he had with Mr. Vassal, brought about, the child was, I am certain, Esther's greatest joy, and the most beneficial influence her nature had ever known. It roused in her a womanly sympathy in which she had formerly been wanting, and made her more tolerant of things and persons she disliked, and more ready to take life from the point of view of others and less from her own.   This was noticeable in the way she bore with Mr. Vassal's bitter humours and taciturn gloom, and in her patient acceptance of her lot as he ordained it. Often did I marvel how she could endure uncomplainingly the ironic coldness of his manner, and go through, with such effort at cheerfulness, the social duties he heaped upon her.   Once, before I got to realise the situation, I said something of this kind—for I am taking up unevenly the threads of these years, as my recollections unravel themselves—advising her, in a moment of undue expansion, to rebel against some irksome demand Mr. Vassal had made, and to which her health was at the time hardly equal.   It was, I remember, that she should play hostess in a yachting trip to Monte Carlo and other places, among a gay company, totally unsympathetic in ideas and occupations, in which some of the ladies were not unstained in reputation—a prolonging of the tragic farce, which meant also a long separation from the child. But this was part of Mr. Vassal's new system.   Formerly he had preferred to yacht on his own account, and to divert himself at foreign gambling resorts, independently of his wife.   Now he always desired that she should accompany him in his pleasure-seekings.   I often wondered about, and never discovered, the reason for this freakish wish to have her in his train.   I must have delivered myself pretty freely upon the subject of Mr. Vassal, for Esther's reception of my strictures did not encourage me to repeat them.

"Gagsie—you don't know—" she exclaimed, in much distress. "I must beg you not to judge Mr. Vassal so hardly.   There's a great deal that I cannot explain to you ; and so it is better for us not to talk about what you fancy is his unkindness, but which I have truly deserved."

I protested a little, but she only blamed herself the more ; and I could not help thinking how like Esther it was that she should go from an extreme of self-exculpation to one of incrimination.   She was never evenly balanced.   Perhaps in this lay some of her curious charm.

"You see," she said, "Mr. Vassal married me when I was poor Esther Vrintz, with no idea how to perform the duties he had a right to expect his wife would fulfil.   I never tried to learn anything, or to please him in any of the ways he would have liked.   I just gave up when I found I wasn't equal to things, and grew utterly morbid and wrapped in my own selfish broodings. Dr. Glaive knows that, and how unhealthy my mind became. . . . Everything went wrong—and—well, never mind, Gagsie ; you must understand without my saying. I've got to make up now for the bad things I have done, in the best way I am able. It's no use your telling me I should rebel, for I never can; and it isn't mere weakness. My mind is fixed that I must do every-thing—even the smallest thing Mr. Vassal wants. And there's nothing—unless it involved some dreadful wrong to Bunchy; and then I should—yes, I *must* stand out whether it would be of any use or not—but, short of that, there is *nothing* Mr. Vassal could require of me that I should be justified in refusing."

"You allow him to do Bunchy a wrong already," I said, "in keeping the child so much away from you."

"I've thought of that," she replied; "it's part of my punish-ment. If Bunchy were as ailing as he used to be, I should be different, and they'd have to drag me by cart-ropes to make me leave him. But you see how wonderfully better he is now; and Mr. Vassal spares no pains nor money in getting trustworthy people round him, and in giving him every comfort and advan-tage. There isn't a little boy in England so splendidly arranged for as Bunchy."

"Simply because he is the heir of Grisewood," I said.

Esther coloured, her flush reminding me of the evanescent rose in Bunchy's cheeks. There was nothing more to be said. Whatever the motive might be, the little heir of Grisewood was as sumptuously provided for as though he had been a prince; there were just those things wanting in his bringing-up—his mother's companionship, a father's love, and the free gifts of Nature, that many a cottar's son has in generous measure.

I said no more to Esther; it only pained her, and I knew that she would defend Mr. Vassal. No obligation rested upon me, however, to respect Mr. Vassal's feelings, and I took an opportunity of letting him know Esther's view of the matter, and how much I admired her loyalty. His chilling reserve rebuked my presumption. But somehow I fancied that he liked me better for what I had said; and it was certainly after this that I became a more frequent visitor at Grisewood. If he did not suggest the invitations, it was at any rate clear that he did not resent their being given.

Another thing that used to puzzle me in the first year or two after her child's birth was the absolute extinction of Esther's literary ambition. Of course, long before that, I had read Esther Zamiel's novels, and had felt that they certainly justified their success. Peculiar, slightly unhealthy, and mournful to despair as was their tone, as to the power of them, there could be no manner of doubt. The critics had been safe in predicting that with years and experience she would go far, and I was surprised also to find how much more deeply she had read and thought than I ever imagined. What surprised me most, however, in the novels, was the almost unconscious revelation they gave of a fund of passionate feeling one would hardly have associated with the exterior woman, and which I then put down to aberrant genius rather than to temperament. It seemed to me a sin that such literary power should be wasted, and I urged her to resume her pen.

Not to any purpose. The far-away look came into her face—the look which troubled me; and all I could get from her by word of mouth was—

"I can't write now; Esther Zamiel is dead, and will never come to life again."

"No, no," I cried; "she is not dead, but sleeping. The time will come when she must awaken and do better work than she has ever done."

"The time will come!" Esther repeated in such a strange tone, and with so wild a look, that I was startled. "Oh, perhaps you are right . . . perhaps you are right, Gagsie; and Esther Zamiel will really awaken—awaken to the roses and the sunshine, and to the song of the torrent and of the wind among the palm-leaves. . . . And she will write beautiful books — such beautiful books—because they will be true."

She was trembling with agitation as she turned from me abruptly and left the room.

But later on, she wrote in answer to a letter of mine again attacking the subject, and recalling to her our girl-talks and her early ambitions.

. . . "I wish I could make you understand, Gagsie; but I can't—any more than I can make you understand why I feel bound to act in some ways as I do——Perhaps, as you say, Esther Zamiel will awaken some day.

"But I had a great, great shake—about which I cannot tell any one, and which was in a kind of way connected with my writing-life. It brought me to the conclusion that my fancy, which I had welcomed with such joy, was in reality a source of danger-fostering tendencies it is now my duty to repress. For I believe that we writing-people are a race by ourselves—slaves to a temperament, as Mr. Paravel would say; and I don't think the temperament is one to make ourselves or others happy. . . . Not you, Gagsie, or your father—you are not of the type—though you are writing-people. You should give thanks to Heaven, dear, for it. Oh, I hope that my boy may not be of the type either. But I fear—I fear!

"Sometimes still the old egoistic, analytical mood seizes me, and I can't help, if anything moves me greatly, putting it down, just for relief, as I used. It seems to do me good, and I lock the book away and try to forget. Then, too, I have a vague purpose in my scribblings, which perhaps you may know some day. At all events, if I should die first, you will find that I have left you a certain tin box in which are stored a bundle of note-books, and the legacy—if you choose to accept it—of carrying out my wishes in regard to them.

"*Naamah* was the outcome of morbid emotions pent within me and cankering. Probably I should have gone mad if I had not written it. But the phase has passed. I am like a bird which can only pipe one note, and not till my life has rounded itself into harmony—I live on that hope—shall I ever sing a true song."

I seemed to read in these last lines a distant allusion to the freedom which, in course of nature, through Mr. Vassal's death, would permit her to live her own life; and the notion jarred. Afterwards I divined her real meaning, which was something quite different.

.   .   .   .

I used often to wonder over the thoughts of little Bobby Vassal — or Bunchy, to use his mother's fond, foolish name for him—and how he would have summed up things generally—supposing that he could have found expression for the feeling which must have underlain all his childish philosophisings, that he was not as other boys are, nor his parents as the parents of other children whom he knew.

Poor wee Bunchy! His wistful face and small sad existence were ever an affliction to me; and he was continually in my mind, whether I was in London or at Grisewood. As I write now, I glance backwards and forwards, haphazard as it were, jotting down impressions gathered from the child's prattle and from what I saw myself of his life; impressions, too, of what I learned more indirectly from Esther and the people round him.

Not that Bunchy knew many boys with whom to compare himself, for Mr. Vassal did not encourage playmates, and the child's opportunities were few of contrasting his own lot with that of his neighbours. But there was the Rectory near, with its big brood, each of which was far in advance of Bunchy in size, if not in years—a household that gave him an occasional glimpse of what a love-illuminated home may be, where father, mother, and children dwell together in the bond of amity. Then there was the small Littlewood, the idol of Fincham, who was only a few months older than Bunchy, and who was often brought over by Addie when she came to luncheon at the Castle, while Bunchy would be in his turn invited to play with Horry at Fincham when the Littlewoods made their periodical August and Christmas visits. I fancy that precocious Bunchy used to ponder a good deal on the happy freedom of the Rectory boys and girls, and to note enviously how they joked with their genial father and chaffed their sweetly serious mother; how they were never afraid to say anything that came into their heads, or to enter their father's study uninvited; and how they flew into passions and committed naughtinesses, and were often reproved, and sometimes punished; but how it was an understood thing in the establishment that the sun must not go down upon wrath, so that no matter what the offence, it would be wiped out during the half-hour between prayers and bedtime by father's and mother's forgiving kiss.

And the same with Horry Littlewood, who was always getting into scrapes on account of unlawful dealings with his father's properties, and audacious tricks played upon that rather precise gentleman. I have seen Bunchy stand in amaze when Horry, having gone a little too far in his mischief, had called down parental anger upon his flaxen head, and would then stand shamefaced but resolute, to plead, with fearless eyes looking straight into his father's face, "Dads, me sorry. Please, Dads, forgive Horry for Mumsey's sake." And Bunchy must have marvelled greatly to find that the plea was unanswerable, and that Horry the artful would invariably be forgiven, caught up, and smothered in kisses "for Mumsey's sake."

In the wildest flights of his imagination—and Bunchy had an innate and hereditary tendency towards fiction—the little fellow could never have conceived the possibility of such a thing happening to himself, or of his mother voluntarily bringing about any kind of familiarity between him and that awesome being before whom every inhabitant of Grisewood quailed, and whom he would not dream of calling anything but Mr. Vassal, if indeed he ever dared to address him. What else should he call him? He never heard his mother use any more intimate term. Once, I recollect, Bunchy astonished Mrs. Littlewood, who was playing upon Horry's feelings with the threat that Dads would not kiss him if he were naughty, by solemnly remarking—

"Bunchy got no Dads. Where's Bunchy's Dads?"

"Why, good gracious! child," exclaimed Mrs. Littlewood, "Mr. Vassal is your Dads, and I am sure that he is very devoted to you, and that he kisses you ever so often."

But Bunchy shook his weird head.

"Mifter Vatt'l not Dads," he said. "Mifter Vatt'l never kisses Bunchy."

I heard Mrs. Littlewood relating the episode, which seemed to puzzle her a good deal, as not fitting in with preconceived theories. She softened her perplexity by surmising that it must be difficult for an old man who had never had children to accustom himself all at once to baby ways, and went on to suppose that it must be gout and age which had so changed Mr. Vassal, who, she said, was certainly not the delightfully genial and polished old gentleman he used to be. If Mrs. Littlewood had been as much behind the scenes at Grisewood as I came to be, she would still further have revised her former conception of its master, and would have admitted that by no manner of reasoning could Bunchy have fixed a tender appellation on to that stern old man with the alarming eyes and the ghoulish smile. In fact, as the little boy artlessly confided to me, Bunchy felt certain in his own mind that "Mifter Vatt'l" must be one of those ogres or magicians, with tales of whom, one special nursemaid was wont to enliven the hour when the head nurse was at supper, and Bunchy waited broad awake till "Muvvie" stole up from the drawing-room after dinner to bid him good-night.

"Muvvie" was at these times usually richly dressed and sparkling with jewels, for Mr. Vassal could not bear to stay at the Castle unless it was filled with guests. He seemed possessed by a demon of restlessness and an insatiable craving for amusement—a craving nothing would satisfy, since nothing really amused him. Often I would ask myself if there could be in the world a more melancholy spectacle than this wicked, worn-out old man who had survived his capacity for enjoyment. No one knew for a week together how long he would remain in any place; and Esther was obliged, or believed it her duty, to follow everywhere at her lord's beck, leaving the boy, who was seldom taken even to London, in the care of his governess and nurses.

It could have made very little difference to Bunchy whether the house was full or empty, for he was very rarely brought into evidence. Only one or two of those more intimate visitors, such as Mrs. Raphon or Mrs. Audley Arathoon, would make a call on the forlorn little hereditary prince in his own quarters; and then, as I once heard, Mrs. Raphon would report on the little fellow to Mr. Vassal, after a fashion that made the old man chuckle evilly, and the mother wince notwithstanding her wonderful self-control. The child hated Mrs. Raphon, but of "Auntie Mi," as the two settled between them he should call her, he was oddly fond. It amused me to see how tender Mione was to the boy when nobody was looking, while, if any one else was present, she would make bright, biting remarks, and bless Providence for having denied her the over-rated boon of children. She never forgot to bring Bunchy a present, and would spend much time and thought on the selection of some peculiar toy which she thought would amuse him, and which his mother would not already have procured.

Occasionally, too, the Willoughbys and Cotherstones and others of the Woodfordshire neighbours would dine at Grisewood, and ask that the boy might be sent for. Then he would be brought down, "a quaint misery," which was how Mrs. Littlewood still described him, beautiful as he had grown, in his velvet suit and Vandyke collar, his fair hair brushed into shining filaments like the tassels of Indian corn, his slender form shrinking involuntarily at the sound of Mr. Vassal's voice, and his large, frightened eyes sending nervous glances towards his mother, from whom the length of the table separated him, and who, in a pale agony, would sit silent and constrained till the signal was given for the boy's departure.

In Bunchy's estimation, as I used to glean from his baby prattle, "Mifter Vatt'l" was the one infallible deliverer of edicts, and the embodiment of all that was most to be feared in the universe. In child-fancy he used to class "Mifter Vatt'l" and the devil together. Of God, Bunchy was not so much afraid, for in the teachings and prayings of their scant hours together, Esther had given him the notion that God loved him and wished him well, as his mother loved him and wished him all good, though the opportunities for showing this were limited by outside fate. Also he got the idea that God was sorry, just as his mother was sorry, for the existence of a Power of evil, before which Bunchy must tremble, but which it was his duty to regard as a painful necessity in the divine system of education. If Bunchy pitied himself and his mother, for—he scarcely knew what, except that it was somehow connected with this Power of evil and "Mifter Vatt'l"—he likewise deeply pitied God for having been obliged to create "Mifter Vatt'l" and the devil. Thus, following the sequence of ideas, as he trembled in spirit before the power and influence of Satan, so he trembled in bodily presence before the power and influence of Mr. Vassal. Whenever he caught sight of that personage in the gardens or stable-yard, or on the staircase or along the corridors, Bunchy shuddered and escaped. Alas! he could not escape when the freak took Mr. Vassal, as it sometimes did in the desperation of his boredom between the house-parties, to have the boy down at the *tête-à-tête* dinners or the meals at which I made a third. It was worst when husband and wife were alone. Then Bunchy would sit in his high chair between the two and quake all through the gruesome feast, which no doubt he contrasted with those occasions when he had come down with Horry to dessert at Fincham, or had assisted at the cheerful Rectory meal. It had seemed a matter of course that there should be a fire of affectionate raillery between Mrs. Littlewood and her husband, and even the old Heseltine pair, while the adoration of Mrs. Wargrave for the Rector made them appear more like lovers than a prosaic elderly couple. I can fancy how Bunchy reflected upon the fact that in the gardener's cottage and the head-keeper's lodge, where he was sometimes taken by his nurse, the same happy domestic relations prevailed. His poor little mind must have been strangely confused by the condition of things in his own home, where, as a rule, when they were alone together, the master and mistress maintained towards each other a grim silence, broken perhaps in presence of the servants by the utterance of some formal commonplace. Bunchy must have noticed that his mother avoided looking at Mr. Vassal, and never of her own accord addressed him, but would sit pale and nervous, smiling occasionally at the child in a wild, forced manner, or saying some tender word to him, which Mr. Vassal's sneering laugh would quench. Sometimes Mr. Vassal would break in with some sarcastic question about the boy's doings, or would suddenly burst into angry abuse of a dish served, or of somebody present or absent who had incurred his displeasure. For as days and ailments gathered upon him, his self-command weakened, his temper grew more capricious, and he would succumb to gusts of unreasoning passion, at which times he did indeed seem more fiend than human. Under the stress of rage his reserve towards Esther would be broken, and he would snarl at her like a savage beast, making the boy shrink and shiver in terror, while the poor mother, growing whiter every moment, would at last piteously implore that the child might be sent to his nursery. But that Mr. Vassal would not allow, and when his fury reached this point it usually began to abate, and he would content himself with the hurling of ironic speeches of which the child could not have understood the drift, but which, he must have felt, were as knives piercing his mother's bosom. The tears would gather in his eyes; he would give a little convulsive sob; and Mr. Vassal would gibe at him for being a baby, and then, filling a glass with strong wine, would bid him drink it, finding amusement in seeing the little fellow's pale face flush and his timidity vanish. To my delight, on one of these occasions, Esther got up like a goaded lioness, and gathering the child in her arms, marched with him out of the room. I don't know what happened after that—to judge from my poor Esther's face, it must have been something very terrible. The next day the house filled anew, and later Mr. Vassal dragged her off to Homburg. Anyhow, as far as I saw, Bunchy did not come down to dinner again.

With the failing of Mr. Vassal's powers, things changed somewhat and became easier, and his system was carried out less rigorously. He had an efficient co-operator in Tremlett as long as she remained at Grisewood, as far as watch and ward went. But, oddly enough, she seemed to have a liking for the child, and when Bunchy was tiny, one of his favourite amusements was to play in the workroom with her reels and coloured balls of silk, and apparently she enjoyed his company. But Tremlett went away, and a new maid came, who did not care for children, and would not let Bunchy watch her preparing those beautiful gowns in which he loved to see his mother arrayed.

Tremlett, impassive and reserved to the last, never told any one why she gave up service or where she was going. I know that she rejected the sum of money which Esther offered her as a parting gift, but we heard of her some time later through Mione Arathoon, who, when on a country-house visit, discovered Tremlett set up in a dressmaking establishment in the neighbourhood, and evidently in very flourishing circumstances. I have always wondered what was the true history of Tremlett.

BOOK XIII

*" Naught but the greatest struggles, wrongs,
defeats, could make thee greatest. No less could
make thee."*

BENONI! Son, not of my sorrow only, but also of my joy!

Life was bitter, and the way I had to walk steep and stony, but the hand of my little child upheld and guided me to within reach of those greater Hands which, as I mounted from my valley of shadow, were stretched forth to help me.

For in truth, and, as I believe, through the regenerating influence of my child, I became dimly conscious of a Power outside myself, assisting my feeble efforts, not only in the soul-struggle towards a nobler faith, but in the performance of everyday duties and in commonplace deed and speech, acting as a deterrent from ignoble thought and selfish impulse. This sense of a mystic guardianship may be looked upon, perhaps, as merely a vivifying of the old-fashioned mystery of conscience, and is no doubt familiar to all who endeavour to walk, however haltingly, the spiritual road; but to me it became something much more—by slow degrees a reality indescribable, but so intense that, upon lying down to sleep, I would commit myself to the unknown Servers in a fantastic yet ever-deepening conviction that my dream-life was thus purified, and my dream-body turned into a vehicle for the learning of spiritual truth.

I fancied, maybe at first too rashly, that, by means of this other-world governance, my love for Robert became gradually rarefied and elevated. Though it remained always an abiding consciousness permeating my whole life, time lessened the active torture of those earlier months of separation. His thought had still strength to pierce space and draw to him the immaterial part of me, but the almost bodily pang as of severed flesh, the torment of unavailing longing for his touch and presence, grew less and less insistent. It was as though Nature's law had fulfilled itself, and as if the child, descending like an angel with healing on its wings, had delivered me from a spell, at once rapture and agony.

    .   .   .   .

One night of Spirit-illuminated experience I remember, as

Jacob might have remembered the darkness of Peniel, when there wrestled with him a Man until the break of day.

It was a strange mental cataclysm, disproportionate perhaps to its immediate cause. For children with a morbid taint have been born in all time to even sane and sound parents, and boys have lied and been punished by a night of solitary imprisonment without madness or perdition ensuing therefrom. But in the spiritual being of each of us, the seed of an upward growth may be sown when we know not of it, and the blossom open in an hour of storm, when God's sun seems farthest from us.

As my babe began to grow into boyhood, I discovered in him and grieved over small signs of moral aberration, due, I was aware, in great degree to physical conditions—a nervously strung temperament, a frail physique, and all those baneful pre-natal influences, producing cowardice and deceitful propensities, which caused me nevertheless the deepest distress, and at times well-nigh broke my slow trust in a Providence working for ultimate good.

Remembering Dr. Glaive's advice, I did my best that the boy should lead as simple and natural a life as was possible. I did my best also to conceal from Mr. Vassal his tendency to tell stories. But one day he was convicted of a fault about which he lied flagrantly; and when the matter was brought to Mr. Vassal's knowledge, Bunchy's sentence was that he should be confined for the remainder of the day and the night, in a turret-room away from his nursery, and that neither I nor his governess nor any of the servants should go to him.

Almost for the first time I broke through my rule of strict obedience, and remonstrated and entreated. Mr. Vassal made the concession that a maid should sleep in a small room next the turret-chamber, under orders, however, that she was not to speak to the boy or enter his presence unless there were danger of his suffering seriously through fright at being left alone. To me the restriction was made absolute. The maid and the boy were locked up in the turret together, and, short of breaking open an iron-bound oak door at the head of the staircase, access to that part of the house was impossible.

The turret, which contained two bachelor chambers, and was only used when the house was full, lay above the oratory leading from my own sitting-room. There through the oak ceiling I could hear the patter of my boy's little high-heeled shoes upon the parquet, as he ran up and down in his helpless anger. Then I knew that he must have flung himself upon the ground, and the muffled sound of his sobs and weak cries of "Mother" pierced down into my heart, till I could bear the pain no longer, and ran upstairs in defiance of my master's orders, resolved that I would speak to my darling through the door, and tell him that I was below and that he was not to be afraid. But it was when I reached the corridor at the head of the stairs that I found the iron-clamped door fast, and knew that I was further away from the child than I had been in the oratory. So I went back and listened and waited. And as night crept on, I lacerated my heart in picturing the timid, sensitive creature suffering in the darkness, with the black cedars swaying and groaning in front of the turret windows, and all the dismal sounds of darkness preying upon his nerves—lacerated myself unreasonably, for I should have known by his screams if he were really in terror, and he did not scream, he only sobbed in querulous grief.

I too sobbed in lonely misery and fear of things supermundane. A blackness fell upon my soul and a horrible doubt, so that it seemed to me that there was no God to protect and comfort those who trusted in Him, and that the pallid Christ, who looked down upon me now with the same tortured smile which had mocked my anguish upon that long-past winter morn, was not Saviour but victim, whose last ineffectual cry had, eighteen hundred years back, rung the knell of a God-forsaken humanity.

All night I remained in the oratory, pacing the narrow space or huddled on the ground at the feet of that ivory Symbol of a world's deliverance—or of a world's despair. Yet though I was crouched there in the body, and alive with my bodily senses to every faint murmur overhead, it seemed to me at moments that I was in reality dead, and that in the spirit I was standing at the firmament's edge, with illimitable space spreading in dense darkness before me. Not space as I had imagined it, still, empty, and ethereal, but a vast eddying blackness, a turbid, unknowable sea, in which the sin-stained soul launched upon it might find no bath of oblivion.

And the circle of my own being was, as it were, contracted into a meaningless span, that held not hope nor faith nor consolation. Gone the fable of redemption by pain. Gone the myth of a celestial Energy, working through Love's mystery to the reconcilement of flesh and soul. Gone the dream of a divine transmutation of the human into the spiritual: of passion into the higher love. It seemed to me that I had come to the end of the human tether. Natural Law must be obeyed. Beyond, all was blank futility. The Wheel of Life must go grinding on. Effect must follow Cause, and in its turn become Cause again, and sin and heredity must produce their appointed result. I had brought the child foredoomed into the world, and, by a mistaken reading of the code of duty, had placed him under the influences most prejudicial to his moral development. Where was the use of having acquiesced in my fate, accepted my punishment and lived my life? Could falseness ever lead to good? Would it not have been nobler to stand by the truth, to have braved the world and risked the consequences to myself and those dear, leaving Nature to adjust her own balance of right and wrong?

Looking back, I seemed to see in my supine driftings of the past, and now, in the character of my son, the operation of that fatal weakness which, since the day of my *Claudia* failure, when I had submitted to the domination of Circumstance, had been my curse. With this doubt came, too, a paralysing doubt of the purity of my motive in yielding myself to punishment and recognising Mr. Vassal as the earthly agent of a higher Tribunal. Was it indeed the wish to spare others shame and suffering, and not rather expediency and a sweet, selfish, quenchless, hope that had lain at the root of my obedience? Had the renunciation been complete? Was there not even now, lurking deep in my innermost heart, the expectation of reunion at some near or distant day, when death had cancelled vows and broken fetters?

Oh, let me cling to that last anchor-truth—truth to my own soul. Even if there be no God, still let me be true!... And if God lives on in heaven, how can He open His gates to falsehood?

It must be wrenched away from me, that enticing, terrible hope—that secret longing, never expressed in form of words or definite thought, cherished only in dreams of the night, and banished by waking fancy—the dear longing for warm hands clasping, for living lips clinging, for the joy of Tourmestral once more. . . .

Out of the thrilling silence I heard the child call weakly. . . .

. . . And Mother couldn't come to you, darling—Mother, who gave you life, yet was powerless to keep trouble from you—Mother, who brought you sorrow-weighted into this unloving world where there was no place for you. Oh, lonely, tormented baby-soul, struggling too on the verge of that black immensity—comprehending nothing but that destiny was cruel!

. . . And Mother's arms tied and bound, so that they might not stretch out and fold you safe! Mother's heart weeping tears of blood, but helpless to comfort you in your weeping! Oh, my baby, my little innocent baby, what had we done to God, you and I, that this wicked thing should be?

No, injustice could have no part in the design of a beneficent

Creator. God did not exist. . . . It was only a great Wheel, revolving, revolving for ever and for ever. . . .

To what purpose?. . . . Could the Wheel turn endlessly on to no intent? What became of the human lives lashed upon it, to revolve with it and to disappear? Why—if all were but blind law, dead matter, crumbling into nothingness—why evil, why good? Why the eternal conflict?

Then, with my baby boy's smothered wail sounding in my ear, by one mighty effort I sent my soul outward from me; and it strove and wrestled with the Self, as might Jacob have wrestled with the Man of Peniel. It strove and wrestled that the child might be delivered from the burden of my sin. For it seemed to me that in this moment I had reached that acutest stage of the spirit's travail, when personal desire is expelled once and for ever, in the all-mastering prayer for another's good at whatever cost to the Self.

And in the extremity of the throe, I cast myself forth upon the Infinite, crying voicelessly into the immensity—

"O God—if there be a God—punish me only, but spare the child. Take everything from me. Let me bear any torture that seemeth well to Thee. But keep the boy good. . . . O God—if there be a God—keep the boy good."

Then I offered up my last and dearest sacrifice—the tender hope that had lain close and warm by my heart—which had been verily a nearer part of myself than bone of my bone and flesh of my flesh.

"O God, I will renounce my love for ever and ever! . . . Dear God, for the child's sake, accept this sacrifice. God, if there be a God to hear—hearken to this my vow. Of my own will, I will never see my love more. I will die and never kiss his lips again. I renounce all—all—utterly. . . . But give me the price, dear God! Give me the price."

I know not what mighty angel came to me out of the heaving infinity. It may be that God's Hand was then stretched forth upon me. . . . As I lay at the foot of the altar my consciousness went. I could not tell whether I had fainted, or whether I had slept, and in my sleep had been carried to the Beyond and shown the Great Glory. . . . There are no words in which to phrase the Unspeakable.

When I awoke there was nothing that I could recall— no dream; no beatific vision; no utterance of the Divine. . . . But I *knew*—knew with the certainty of one who has beheld his Lord face to face—that God *is*, and that in His love is our being. . . . I knew that my prayer was answered, that my sacrifice was accepted, that truly all would be well with the child.

.   .   .   .

When the turret-room was opened, and I went to my boy, he was lying dressed upon an old-fashioned settle at the foot of the great canopied bed. His little limbs were curled up in an unnatural attitude; his curly hair was matted, and his face was white as marble, puckered and stained with tears. I approached him in dread, but he was sleeping tranquilly. As I kneeled down by him, kissing his damp curls, his hand, his eyelids—a tear plashing upon his cheek awoke him, and he started and stared at me with frightened eyes, which lost their wild look when he recognised his mother. The thin arms went up round my neck; the little body heaved against my bosom. . . . "Muvver!" he kept repeating in his baby accents. "Oh . . . Muvver!" and sobbed gaspingly, while I hugged him close and soothed and wept with him.

I carried him to my own bed, sent away the nurse, and sponged his face, and undressed him, and straightened his disorder; and then, when I had him safe within the cool sheets, I cuddled him in my arms and fed him with hot milk and bread. He ate the food hungrily, and the convulsive movement of his chest ceased. The nourishment seemed to clear his dazed brain, and to give back remembrance of the punishment, which had been lost in his dreams. He clenched his small hands in helpless resentment; his brow flushed and his grey eyes gleamed as he cried passionately, "Bunchy *hates* Mifter Vatt'l."

And the tragic incongruity of it all—the ill-dealing of Fate, not now to the child and to me, but to our enemy, whose hand lay heavy upon the boy, smote me, bringing piercing condemnation of myself. Again, as during those illuminated moments in which I had gazed upon him before making my last appeal, I pitied Mr. Vassal, and beheld myself as the wronger rather than the wronged. Upon that chaos of thought and emotion, out of which during the night a new spiritual sense seemed to have evolved within me, strange lights flashed, now as then, clarifying the inner deeps; and every word, detail, and gesture of that scene with my little child rises up, marking an epoch of soul-experience never to be undone nor unwritten.

"O Bunchy, my darling!" I cried, stirred by the new compunction. "You must never say that—never! never!"

The expression of my face seemed to startle the boy; he gazed at me earnestly, with all the anger gone from his eyes.

"What for, Muvver?"

"Because it's wrong. I cannot bear it."

"What for, Muvver?" he said again, wonderingly. "Did you have punishment too?"

"Yes," I answered. "When Bunchy is naughty and tells lies and gets punished, Mother is punished as well; and it hurts her just as badly as it hurts Bunchy."

The child's look widened.

"Why is 'oo punished?"

"Because you are my baby, and a bit of my own self; and everything that hurts you hurts me too. For God gave you to me to make me good—to make me learn love and obedience through teaching you to love and obey—first God, and then those—who are appointed over you."

"I know. My parents and guardians; that's what Nana says. Muvver, is Mifter Vatt'l 'pointed over you too?"

"I must obey him and do everything I can to please him, because he is my husband."

"But you never please him, Muvvie. He's always cross. . . ." The child waited, wistful and curious. Presently—

"Husbands is farvers too; isn't they, Muvvie?"

"Sometimes."

The boy thought deeply for a minute.

"Nana says Mifter Vatt'l is Bunchy's parent and guardian. Is parent and farver the same thing, Muvvie?"

"Yes, the same thing."

"Then why does Bunchy never say 'Farver' to Mifter Vatt'l —same as Horry and Brucie Wargrave? Why doesn't Mifter Vatt'l never kiss Bunchy?"

Oh, what could I say to my child? How could I answer him but with wild remorseful kisses?

"Muvver, was 'oo very naughty, and did 'oo tell lies to Mifter Vatt'l for him never to speak to you—only when he punishes?"

"Oh, my baby, don't torture Mother with your question-ings. . . . Oh, you know that you have been very wicked, Bunchy!"

"I know, Muvvie . . . I'se always wicked. I'se always telling lies. Something makes me. . . . And God hates Bunchy like Mifter Vatt'l."

Then all the passion of pity and pain and mother-love and newly quickened faith thrilled up in me, and spoke by a Voice which seemed like the voice of One outside myself. As the quivering cadences come back, I know them not for my own utterances, but rather for the words of One who bore me up when the billows of doubt went over me—of One who comforted my forlorn soul, even as I now strove, in broken interpretation of the language, to comfort the bruised heart of my little boy. Maybe the words were beyond the baby-brain's comprehension; but who can say that the baby-soul did not hearken and understand!

"No, God cannot hate," the Voice said, through my halting speech. "Could *I* hate my baby-boy? Do *I* not love you—love you, my baby who was wicked and was punished? . . . And think, dear sweet! Mother's love is only big enough to hold her boy—and—and just a few of the people in her life who have cared for her. . . . But God's love is great enough to hold the whole world, and the stars that are worlds too, and every man and woman and child in every world that ever was and ever shall be. . . . God loves you, baby-man—loves you—loves you, and will always love you, for ever and for ever. Mother knows it. . . . Last night God told her."

"In a dream, Muvvie?" the child murmured. "In a Bible dream?"

"God spoke in Mother's heart, and made her understand. . . . God showed Mother that His love holds *everything*—the world and the stars and her love and the angels, and even the spirits of evil. For God doesn't want the spirits to be evil. . . . And He grieves over them—as He grieves over your badness and mine, little Bunchy. . . As I grieve, in my way, which is so very small a way compared with God's way—when my boy is naughty. . . . For oh, my baby-man, that's the sorrow of it all—that we can't care in God's way till we have had sin in us and round us, and have conquered it through love, and have changed it into good. . . . God means everything and every one in the end to become good. . . And this may be His way of helping the spirits of evil, whom He cannot make pray and turn to Him of themselves, because of their evil. . . . He gives *us* the task; He teaches *us* to turn to Him in our great trouble, when sin scourges us and torments us sore. Then, at last, we are forced to join our will with His. So we show the evil spirits, by our resistance of them, the knowledge of good. . . . And that's how, when we fight the sin that is in us, we are helping God to fight the sin that is outside of us. . . .

"That's why we must never hate any one, even though people may seem unjust and cruel. . . . For that is shutting our souls against love, and taking away the hope of turning evil into good, and of helping God and each other. . . . It's taking away the power of prayer. . . . And prayer is love—nothing else. Not the saying of words—like 'Our Father'—it's much—oh, much more than words ! .. And not the wanting to be good for our own sake, or even for the sake of goodness itself ; but the being good for the sake of helping God and others. .... It's letting all our heart go away from ourselves in effort and yearning, till our love joins the great river of His love—the river that waters the world. .... Sometimes our earth-love flows in strong, clear streams, and sometimes in shallow brooklets, and sometimes in fierce, muddy torrents that storms have fouled. .... But even this love— if we pray for it—finds its way to God's river at last, and becomes purified before it reaches the Sea."

My child's eyes, big with awe, and bright with gathering tears, gazed up into my eyes that were brimming. And in the lucent orbs I seemed to see reflected the whole mystery of love and life. .... A catch came into his breath, his lips trembled, and suddenly a great sob shook his small frame. He hid his face against my wet face, and, with his arm clutching my neck, whispered between his sobs—

"Oh, dear Muvvie, don't cry. .... Bunchy loves Muvver. .... Bunchy will help Muvver. ...."

MRS. LITTLEWOOD was not the only person who commented upon the change in Mr. Vassal. Woodfordshire in general began to wonder and talk, and to rake up ancient history in the shape of that Vassal heiress, who had been weak in her head, and had died a tragic death. Perhaps there was, in fact, a twist in Mr. Vassal's brain, or it may have been that as age and infirmities gathered upon him, he became careless about tying the strings of his mask, so that it dropped occasionally, giving lurid glimpses of the real man who had always been underneath, though so cleverly hidden. No doubt, some persons who did not belong to Woodfordshire, and had known Mr. Vassal under other conditions, had long ago suspected the horns and the cloven hoof. Dad was one of these; so, I am sure, was Dr. Glaive; and so also, in a more intuitive fashion, was I myself. Therefore, their manifestation did not come upon me with any great shock of surprise. I was far more interested in watching the development of Esther than the deterioration of her husband. She was immensely altered too. So much in appearance, that any one who had merely known her casually, ten years before, would hardly have recognised her. But though she had lost the beauty of youth, and that especial flower-like charm, it often seemed to me that she had gained much more than she had lost. Her pretty dark hair was now almost white, and all the old flashes of enthusiasm and inspiration were gone. Her eyes were deeper and more steadfast, her smile sweeter, and her expression had no longer the touch of querulousness. There was in her manner a repose and gentle strength, also a strange humility, which seemed to create round her an atmosphere, felt, though it was impossible to define it, by all who approached her, and quite outsiders remarked how much more sympathetic and kindly she had grown. Formerly she had never troubled herself about the sufferings of the poor, going out of her way to avoid the sight of anything disagreeable. Now she took an active interest in village charities, in old women, and hospitals, and almshouses, and was doing good work, not exactly on the lines of the Rescue and Reformation League, but in an unostentatious and quietly practical manner of her own, among girls who had gone wrong — in whom, alas! notwithstanding the Cathedral and the League, Woodchester abounds. It was not generally known that the establishment for the making of embroideries and fine linen and fair needlework, in the High Street, was a private enterprise of Mrs. Vassal's for the employment of these unfortunates, who when they entered there left not hope behind, but found the slate sponged, and no record against them. I, however, had a good deal to do with the workings of the place, and can bear testimony to her ministry. I know, too, that though she was the wife of a millionaire with servants, horses, and jewels galore, and all the rest of the show in marching order, her charities were not altogether easy to manage, and involved some self-denial, for she had no income under settlement, and, except for what she had made by her two books, no means at command except the personal allowance arranged for her at the time of her marriage.

To go back to Mr. Vassal, who isn't such an agreeable object of contemplation—a bad fall in the hunting-field was put forward by his friends in Woodfordshire as the excuse for his unsteady nerves, his violent outbreaks of temper, his curious treatment of his wife and the boy, and the neuralgic pains that made him so restless, and for which he was continually being sent to foreign waters. But whatever excuses the county might find, it could not forgive him for scoffing at the Church he had once delighted to honour : nor could it forgive the sort of society he collected upon occasions at Grisewood. Dad isn't given to arbitrary social distinctions, and is rather apt to class mankind generally, according to Elias' ruling, into two races—the men who borrow, and the men who lend—he himself belonging distinctly to the lending race. But even he, with all his Catholic toleration, did not approve of the company at the Castle, especially when it became theatrical. The Roscius was to him sacred ground, yet he was wont to say, "Of actors—outside the Roscius—I will quote my Shakespeare with a difference, 'I will trade with them, write for them, criticise them, but I will not eat with them, drink with them, nor pray for them '"— which only meant that he had been invited to meet at Grisewood a certain eminent member of the dramatic profession—a French actress, of whose introduction into county circles he had not approved.

It certainly seemed a queer premonitory symptom of the decay of Mr. Vassal's powers, that he, who all his life had paid strict homage to the respectabilities, should now take a freakish delight in defying them. Woodfordshire rose at last in revolt when the Cotherstones, Willoughbys, and others were asked, and went unwittingly, to meet that same fascinating ornament of the French stage, and two ladies whose ill renown had penetrated even the Cathedral Close. And more deadly insult to Sir John Willoughby and the Tory squires of the party was the presence of a certain Radical atheist, whose private life and public utterances had made him a stumbling-block and stone of offence to Church and State. Unfortunately this gentleman's name had been figuring freely in the papers of late, so that even in the unenlightened Midlands there was hardly one person among the county families who, on being confronted with him, would not inwardly have cried "Avaunt!" One might perhaps except in the connection, placid Mrs. Heseltine, who never read leading articles, and knew as little about Radical politicians as she did about the French drama. Though a little shocked at the actress's free application of carmine, she swallowed her as a foreign possibility. Neither Lady Cotherstone nor Lady Willoughby, however, would allow her to swallow the atheist. The position did not admit of immediate explanations, and it was not till after dinner that she turned her mild blue eyes upon me in mystified inquiry. "But, dear Mrs. Greste—you come from London—do tell me who *is* this dreadful Mr.——?" Perhaps it's safer not to mention names, but really you might as well have asked just then, "Who *is* Prince Bismarck?"

As soon as the ladies had returned to the drawing-room, Lady Cotherstone ordered her carriage, but before departing she found an opportunity to expostulate with her hostess.

"My dear," I heard her say, "what does this mean? They've been telling me queer stories—Inskip the lawyer's at the bottom of them—but I put that down to spite. To-night I believe it all. Is he going off his head?"

Poor Esther smiled drearily. "No, but Mr. Vassal is in bad health, Lady Cotherstone : it's a great thing for him to be amused ; and these people distract his mind from his sufferings."

"Then he should start a private theatre—he's rich enough. But he needn't ask the actors to dinner. At any rate, he needn't ask *us* to meet them."

"You would forgive him, dear friend, if you knew how his illness preys upon him."

"I see. Drugs—morphia and all the horrid business. That sort of thing does weaken the brain. Neuralgia! A bee in his bonnet! It's what I've been saying to them all. I'm ready to blacken my soul with excuses, if it will do any good. But I don't see how we *can* dine here again. My dear woman, can't you prevent him from asking such people to the house?"

Esther shook her head. "No, I'm afraid not." And there was something in her tone that made Lady Cotherstone look at her, I thought half curiously, half compassionately.

"A bee in his bonnet!" she said again. "There was something, wasn't there, a long way back—or is it the Delmars?—one forgets. Or is it just that he is breakin' up? Such a pity. And Grisewood used to be the pleasantest house in the county. To be sure, that dreadful Mrs. Raphon—I never could understand the attraction towards those Arathoons. Of course that's at the root of Inskip's ill-nature!—and that pretty young Arathoon woman, who hunts and dresses and says startling things—they were always a little incongruous. But there was the Bishop, dear man! and really good political people I could quote to the Duke. As for these creatures!... And they're *known*. There's no deception about it. They are an insult; they are impossible!"

"Yes, they're impossible," assented Esther.

"I'm glad you see it. But of course you would. Can't you put your foot down? Can't you reason with him?"

"I'm afraid I can only obey him, dear Lady Cotherstone."

"That's the mistake you have made all along, my dear. Obedience is all very well. But when a man has a bee in his bonnet! And I used to hold him up as a model to Cotherstone! Yes, he must be breakin' up. He walks unsteadily. I know the signs."

"And you can feel how terrible it must be for such a man as he was—to face decay!"

"It's what we've all got to come to. But we don't all outrage society in consequence. Well, I intend to use the privilege of an old friend, and as soon as the place is clear I shall drive over and give him a bit of my mind. And I'm sure Mrs. Greste will agree with me that he deserves it."

. . . .

Lady Cotherstone was as good as her word. She gave time for the doors and windows to be opened, as she put it, in order that Radicalism, Atheism, and Impropriety might leave no bad fumes behind them; and then she got driven over in her yellow chariot to deliver her mind to Mr. Vassal.

Esther was not at home, having gone to her shop at Woodchester, but I was hanging round arranging flowers; and anyhow, the old lady only wanted to see Mr. Vassal, and had herself shown in straight upon him, in the inner hall, where he had established himself. He was sitting in his big chair with a screen behind him, and a little table by his side covered with papers and wicked French novels—I once took one up and opened it, and that was quite enough for me — and though June sunshine streamed in through the diamond panes and there were bowls of roses all about, a fire of logs was burning on the hearth, and the old man shivered slightly every now and then, as though his blood ran cold and languid. He seemed now to have a hatred of being alone, and I fancy that he preferred the hall to the library, because here he came more into touch with the life of the house. To-day there was little enough, for all the guests had departed and new ones had not yet come. Only Bunchy, attracted by the litter of flowers, peeped furtively in at the outer vestibule, and catching sight of the dread-inspiring figure in the chair, ran swiftly away. Somehow Mr. Vassal, as he sat there with his fierce eyes gleaming from over his book or paper at any sound that caught his attention, made me think of one of those old, bloated, uncannily marked spiders one sees lying in wait for unsuspecting flies. His limbs had a shrunken look owing to his huddled position in the great chair, and his head seemed to have grown larger, while his face was yellower and more deeply lined and broader about the jaws, giving the effect of a faint leer. That smile, which was a caricature of his old bland expression, always caused me a disagreeable jar when I looked at him, and I think it jarred also on Lady Cotherstone. She must have observed too, as I did, the slight staggery movement in his legs when he rose to greet her, and a touch of hesitancy in his speech, less apparent as he got himself under control.

"Don't let me disturb you," she said. "Yes, I know that your wife is out, but you're the one I want to have a little talk with to-day. I am sorry to see that you don't look quite so well as you did the other evening."

Mr. Vassal gave a more accentuated travesty of the old smile.

"Ah, milady, it's not your sex only that's at its best after sundown. Cheerful company, and champagne, and pink-shaded candles help a good deal, don't they, to soften the ravages of time?"

"Well, at all events, you provided yourself and your neighbours with cheerful company—not to say exciting company—when I dined here. A little too exciting for us quiet-going Woodfordshire folk! And that's exactly what I've come to talk to you about," said the dowager severely.

I judged it seemly that I should retire ; but from the vestibule where I filled my vases I could hear the murmur of the lady's discourse, which seemed long and eloquent. When I went back, which I did at the sight of butler and footman bringing along silver trays with tea and covered dishes, and waited for the urn to boil, quieting the clamouring dachshunds meanwhile with bits of biscuit, Mr. Vassal was speaking in his husky drawl.

"Poor ladies! You are very hard upon them. Let me assure you that they have all the Christian virtues—perhaps excepting one—and you know the Magdalen became a saint! Could even you, my old friend, declare safely that there was only a *perhaps* between you and salvation? Have you a 'perhaps'? and what-is it? Or are you too good?—too good to have any comprehension of the trials and temptations of your weaker sisters! Beauty is a trial. And admiration of man is a trial. An inadequate income is a trial! Diamonds are a temptation— when they can be bought with a smile—I am quoting dear old Frank Leete, Mrs. Greste. Just imagine, milady! If you hadn't been lawfully entitled to wear the Cotherstone diamonds—and first-rate water they are—mightn't you have been tempted—just to smile? But forgive me. Who would have dared to tempt you— to smile? No, you have been too good. You have never strayed within even bowing distance of temptation."

Lady Cotherstone drew herself up stiffly.

"Really! Mr. Vassal."

"Oh, really, you must let me have my little say, now that you have had yours. And you gave it to me pretty hot, you know. But I'm so glad that you have formed such a high opinion of Mrs. Vassal. You will admit that she is beyond all danger of contamination. Pray take my word that I do indeed entertain for her all the respect her conduct and character have merited. Let me beg you to put the question to her—it might ease your mind. And aren't you a trifle illogical?—you extremely good people so often are. Why should your efforts in the Rescue and Reformation line be confined to streets and penitentiaries? Why shouldn't they be extended to my drawing-room. It really isn't altogether the fault of the victims that they are handsome and well-dressed and agreeable. Provvy—as dear Frank Leete says—may have had a hand in that."

Mr. Vassal's laugh sounded too like a travesty of his old cynical chuckle. Lady Cotherstone, as she took her cup of tea from my hand, glanced up at me with a doubtful and yet enlightened expression.

"And there's the other point," Mr. Vassal went on, and after the brief pause, that odd hesitancy in his enunciation struck us both anew, for the dowager gave me a second sharp glance in which there was a resigned knowingness, and her lips framed the words, "A bee in his bonnet!"

"What did you say?" Mr. Vassal asked, poking his head forward, his wicked old eyes giving more than ever the suggestion of an alert tarantula. "No, I'm not going to change my politics. Tell Cotherstone he needn't be uneasy. I don't care a twopenny damn about politics—excuse me, I swear on precedent —you remember the old duke?—but I do care a great deal about having the tedium of an hour lightened; and that's just what my friend the Radical does for me. He almost amuses me. Think of having come to this for a man who once lived his life to the quick! Ichabod indeed! To be—*almost* amused. The greatest good the universe now holds for me!"

"My dear old friend," Lady Cotherstone cried, genuinely distressed, for there was a mournfulness in the old man's tone that touched even me a little, "it's very sad to hear you talk like this. Amusement isn't everything. One may be growing old and have outlived one's worldly enjoyments, but there are other things—there are the home interests and duties, and ties of family, to bring one satisfaction at the last. There is your little boy— the heir you always wanted. You should feel thankful to Providence, instead of abusing it, for having granted you your wish."

"So I do, egad! So I do, milady!"

Lady Cotherstone shrank visibly at the sound of Mr. Vassal's sarcastic merriment. "Oh, don't laugh like that!" she exclaimed.

"Why not? There's an ironic humour about Provvy's ways which appeals to me. It's so—human."

"You sound rather blasphemous," said the old lady. "I think you must have been catching the infection from your Radical friend. That isn't what we expected of you, Mr. Vassal, whom we have always looked upon as a pillar of the Church and a staunch upholder of the old traditions. How is it that you have so changed?"

"Forgotten my part, milady—that's what it is! He! he! he! —amusing, ain't it, to think how all this time I've made you believe I wasn't acting? Not up to my old form now, though, and obliged to withdraw from the business. The world's a stage, you know. . . . I've been a fine player in my time. Ask Mrs. Greste; her father's a dramatic critic; and she has seen through the trick. Cleverer than all the rest of you. . . . Do I shock you? You shouldn't grudge me the fun of shocking people—the last little excitement that's left me in these lean days. . And now I'm going to let you into another secret. Your Woodfordshire stage isn't the only one I've played on; and some of my favourite rôles haven't been so strictly decorous, that I could have performed them under ecclesiastical patronage. No, I never was what my dramatic friends would call a one-part man. I've squeezed the juice from the big orange, and done my best to get my money's worth out of the show—before the green curtain drops, and the fiddles stop squeaking, and the lights are turned off, and there's not even supper at the Roscius to follow—nothing but the long sleep."

"'There's the awakening, isn't there?" said Lady Cotherstone with an uneasy little laugh, "and we should all of us like to know what that's going to be."

"'The awakening! Ah, dear lady, shall I tell you what I think about that? Don't betray me to the Bishop and old Wargrave and the rest of 'em, or they'll be starting a special Rescue and Reformation League for me all to myself. There will be no awakening, my friend. And when I go to sleep all that will happen is this—I shan't hear my man coming in with the hot water—no, nor any last trump calling me before the Judgment throne."

Lady Cotherstone said to me when she went out that she should never forget the tone in which Mr. Vassal uttered those words, or the look upon his countenance as he leaned towards her from out of his high-backed chair, his hands held in a curve like the crook of talons before him, and his shoulders raised in a shrug.

Just then a sun-gleam through the window struck upon the faded crimson of the screen behind him, and shed a sort of demoniac glow upon the evil deep-lined face with its hard protruding eyes and grisly grin.

Well can I imagine how to the well-intentioned God-fearing dame that picture of Mr. Vassal must have been as lurid revelation filling her with an indescribable repugnance and alarm. She got up hastily and took her leave.

TIME had aged and changed us all. And I had given up play-writing, and was beginning to wish almost that doctoring would give up me, having come to the unsatisfactory conclusion that though science may advance us somewhat in the matter of bones, and fevers, and indigestions, we doctors are not likely to get much forwarder in the field of brain and nerve till there is granted a new revelation.

I was tired, too, of society, and women had ceased to interest me—except as cases. Women, that is to say, who invited me to their parties and did me the honour to confide their emotional troubles to me when they visited my consulting-room. But there was one woman not to be classed with these, for whose confidence, indeed, I had always hungered, and who had never really given it to me ; one woman of whom I saw little in these later days, but who held ever the sceptre in my kingdom of poesy, and remained always enshrined in my imagination as the ideal of fair and gracious womanhood. Yes, though sorrow had robbed her of her bloom, and her genius had suffered eclipse, and in spite, also, of the disillusioning certainty borne in upon me one dreary December day seven years back, that I could not hope to occupy in her life the position even of trusted friend and adviser.

Need I say that this woman was Mrs. Vassal. Imagine, therefore, the shock of surprise it gave me to have her card laid one morning upon my table, and to know that she was waiting her turn to see me.

I shall never forget her appearance as she entered, leading by the hand her little boy. It must have been four years since we had last spoken to each other—not since I had been sent for to consult with Sergison and the Woodchester doctor upon the case of the child, of which, at the time, I had thought gravely. Apparently too gravely. For in the intervening years I had not heard anything from Mrs. Greste—my informant, as to affairs at Grisewood—of the trouble I had then feared.

Mrs. Vassal was greatly altered. Her hair had become a soft, silvery white, which contrasted strangely and becomingly with her still unlined face and shining brown eyes. Those eyes, always her chief beauty, had lost, to a great extent, their pained, absent expression. Sad they were still, very sad, but it was as the sadness of Fortitude compared with the haunted melancholy of Despair; and while all the pathos and much of the tragic suggestiveness of her face remained, it had acquired a sweet and steadfast strength which made its expression seem entirely different.

She told me that they were in London for a short time, in order that Mr. Vassal might undergo a treatment by electricity prescribed for him by an eminent specialist, and that she had taken advantage of the opportunity to consult me about her boy, in whom a certain hysterical tendency had been causing her uneasiness. She had felt, she said, that I, having previously attended him, and knowing something of her own constitution and former morbid twist, might best help her to counteract a similar bias in her son.

I gave my attention at once to the medical business on which she had come, asking her no questions about herself beyond such as concerned the child, and finding a refuge from the rush of memories and emotions that assailed me, in the professional shell, now so habitually cast round me that it had become almost a part of myself.

There was an indescribable grace and sweetness about the little fellow, and he had a furtive, appealing glance, quickly averted, that I thought curiously pathetic; while his limpid, mournful eyes roused in me, to an even stronger degree, that sense of fatality which I had always somehow associated with the eyes of his mother. Yet they were not his mother's eyes.

He was a slender-formed, fragile creature, with that exquisitely transparent complexion, sensitive to the faintest ripple of feeling, which is so sure a sign of constitutional delicacy. From his mother's account of his progress after that illness during which I had seen him, he appeared to have gone on from the early dentition period more favourably than I had anticipated. But latterly, with the change of teeth, no doubt, he had fallen back; and all the particulars she gave me were symptomatic of the mischief I had inwardly prognosticated—the restless nights, with their sudden screaming fits, the frequent headaches, the nervous susceptibility, as well as certain moral and mental indications, among them the exaltation of the imaginative faculty and disposition to falsehood.

The examination, to me a painful one, was over, and I handed her the prescription I had written. Then she said, with a slight hesitation—

"May I send Bunchy to his governess, who is waiting to take

him back to Grosvenor Street, and stay and talk with you for a few minutes—that is, if you don't mind my taking up so much of your busy morning?"

"My time is yours," I answered, "for as long as you are willing to command it. The longer, the better I shall be pleased."

"Thank you," she said simply.

When due directions had been given, and the child was gone, she looked into my face with her deep, earnest eyes, and said, her voice trembling a little—

"That is like my old friend."

"A friend whom you have sadly neglected in these past six years," I answered, and almost started at the sound of my own agitated laugh. Then, as leaning over my table I gazed into the troubled brown eyes, still so softly luminous, a wave of exceeding tenderness and of exceeding pain swept over me, and I could scarcely keep a calm demeanour. The sorrowful joy in my look must have touched her, for she made an impulsive movement of her hand towards me, and said, in low, vibrating tones, which recalled that one outburst of confidence at Grisewood after her critical illness—

"I shall never forget. . . . And you know . . you know . . . you can guess . . how hard it has been. . . . If I have seemed ungrateful, it is that I have looked upon you as a dear and true friend, who would understand . . . and forgive . . . without words —words that were impossible for me to say."

For answer I put out my hand and clasped hers as it lay on the table near me. Her touch thrilled through my whole frame, and any bitter thoughts I might have nursed melted away in the sweetness and the implied pledge of that contact. No speech was needed, and in truth I do not know how long we remained thus, our hands clasped. Presently she withdrew hers, and began questioning me more closely and confidentially about her son. I told her that the boy was very neurotic, and just at the age when trouble might be expected—trouble which should be dealt with by both physical and moral means. Even now, I explained, he should be made to exert some control over his imagination, and should be taught that there was a world of fact to which he belonged, and beyond that, a world of fancy to be governed by his will, and kept at present, as much as possible, in the background. I gave her the practical advice in regard to treatment and diet which is usual in such cases, adding that if, after such extra care, the child still suffered, drugs would be required, and a course of baths might possibly be of service. I did not add what I greatly feared—that the child was too delicate to grow up, but would probably die of some cerebral inflammation before he was fourteen.

"Now," I said, "let me talk to you about your own health, though it is a long time since you have consulted me as a patient."

"I have quite got over my old chest delicacy," she answered, evidently trying to rouse herself from her absorption in the boy. "Indeed, I have nothing to say to you professionally about myself; and is it fair to keep people waiting for anything else?"

"There's no one waiting; you came late; and if there were, it wouldn't matter—unless you would let me come and have a talk with you this afternoon at your own house instead."

"I am afraid it wouldn't be very satisfactory as far as talking went," she replied. "Mr. Vassal does not like me ever to leave him."

"He is no better?"

"No. Dr. Sutcliffe has told me the truth. He will never be any better; he will get worse and worse; and it will become more and more dreadful as the days go on."

"Yes, I know that it must be dreadful; and I can only feel deep pity both for him and for you," I said. "From what Mr. Leete and Mrs. Greste have told me, I understand the nature of the malady."

"I have been trying to learn all that I can," she said presently, "so that I may help as far as is possible. But I can do so little—of course he has the trained attendants—I can only sit there and be ready if he wants me. At first, what he cared for most was seeing people and being amused by actors and dancers, who used to come and go through their performances before him. Oh, you can't imagine any more ghastly kind of revel! And he himself realising the mockery of it, and making cynical comments which told of such emptiness and despair. And nothing that anybody said was of any use. It was like the voice crying 'Peace, peace,' when there was no peace to be found."

I could but murmur such words of sympathy as came to me. She went on, evidently getting relief from speaking—

"Now he cannot bear that people, his women friends especially, should see him. The pitiable object that he is—you can fancy it. There seems no way of lightening the hours except by reading aloud—reading continually. And the only books that interest him are French novels—novels that are horrible. He will not let me read anything that is not wicked. And that seems more dreadful to me than anything—to be letting his soul sink down deeper into blackness. And one longs and longs for power to lift it up nearer the light."

The note of fervent pity in her voice moved me deeply, remembering as I did the misery of her marriage.

"I can give you only one consolation," I said. "It may not last very long."

"Dr. Sutcliffe has told me—a year perhaps; perhaps less. No one dares to put things plainly to him. I have tried, but from me he will not bear it. I am sure that he fights against the thought of death. And there are storms of anger which come with the hopeless effort to make himself understood, and which are terrible to see. . . . And that ghastly, half-open mouth!" . . . She gave an involuntary shudder. "It is more harrowing than I can describe. Oh, I would do anything, anything, if he could be spared the mere bodily humiliation; that's what he feels so keenly . . . Dr. Glaive . . ."

She leaned forward, and my hand again clasped hers.

"It's the state of his mind that so troubles me. Can you not give me some comfort? As the body wastes—even though there may never have been belief in things spiritual—does not the soul awaken at the last? It is so awful—oh, *you* must know how awful —to watch a fellow-creature going down like that, unshriven, into the grave."

I could not answer for a moment, for indeed my heart was sorely racked by her appeal. There was tragedy unspeakable in this grim picture she had drawn of the dying sensualist, but there was pathos more utterly touching in the unconscious revelation she made of the great change that had been wrought in herself. I found something well-nigh divine in her compassionate yearning, which struggled with and almost overcame her physical repulsion; and in the suppression through years of pain and self-discipline, of her own passionate individuality, with its artistic egoism and rebellious cravings for exquisite experience, its sensitive refinement and wayward pride—the very faults which had made up its dear and unforgettable charm, all merged in human fellowship and commiseration for him whom she had once hated.

"You are a noble woman," I exclaimed, "to have forgiven so utterly."

She winced as though I had touched a nerve.

"Don't. . . . Oh, can't you understand . . ." she began piteously. "It . . . it's not the forgiving . . ." She faltered as a child might on the verge of tears. "When one has been down oneself into the darkness, it is such a small matter to forgive. . . . He too had—much to forgive. . . . Don't speak any more of what is past between him and me. Let it be forgotten."

"Perhaps that is best," I answered. "Yet, I repeat, you are a noble woman."

There was silence, in which turbulent thoughts seemed to take form and press us round like an invisible army; and it needed an effort of will to disperse them. I resumed with difficulty, and in a studiously matter-of-fact tone—

"And now about yourself—speaking as a friend, since you won't let me talk as a doctor. You have given up writing?"

"Writing Esther Zamiel's novels? Oh yes, altogether."

"I confess to a feeling of regret—a more personal one than that of the general reader. For wasn't it by my advice that you began the work?"

"Of course—I owed it to you—in the first instance," she replied.

"And it answered its purpose at the time, in drawing you out of your Slough of Despond. Well, anyhow I'm proud of being partly responsible for *Naamah*."

"Yes," she said, and added impetuously, "as you are responsible for *Claudia* and for my giving up the stage."

"No," I rejoined emphatically, "I am not responsible for what led to your marriage. Don't deprive me of the consolation you yourself gave me. Don't you remember?"

She looked at me vaguely, as though she had not quite taken in my meaning.

"Don't you remember telling me that your fate had been decided for you by the chance words of a stranger?"

"Ah!" She gave a little gasp.

"A stranger outside the theatre, you said, whom you heard condemn your *Claudia*. I know that you afterwards came into touch with that stranger. He was Mr. Brock's Reader, and your husband's nephew, Robert Vassal."

I had spoken with a purpose, but was not wholly prepared for the effect of my words, and blamed myself for having been cruel. It was as though the utterance of that name, and the emotions it roused, had swept her in one swift rush out from the valley of calm shadow on to tempest-torn heights into the glare of lightning and the crash of storm. Her breast heaved, and the tender memory of youth transfigured her features, making her face tremulous as that of a girl, while her eyes, fixed far beyond my own beseeching gaze, became dewy soft and deep, so that I hardly dared to break the spell of bygone associations.

"I wanted to talk to you about that friend—the friend of both of us," I said. "Because he wrote to me, not very long ago, from Mandour, to ask if I would give him news of you."

She came slowly to herself again, recalled as it were, from another world; and the gleam her eyes now shed upon me was like that of the moon shining through rain-clouds, so chastened was its pathos.

"He . . . wanted to know?" she said, almost in a whisper.

"If you were well . . . if you were happy?"

"Happy!" She smiled wildly. The gleam faded; and the rain-clouds made a veil of tears, which for a few moments fell silently.

"Tell me," she said at last. . . . "I am shut out from the world—*that* world. I never hear of anything that happens to him. Tell me—is he doing well at Mandour?"

"Yes; the appointment was an immense success. The position of British Consul at Mandour is really more important than that of Minister at many a small Court. You must have read of his mission into the interior, and the reputation it brought him?"

"I saw that he had been made a K.C.M.G."

"That mission was of greater diplomatic moment than outsiders imagined," I said. "I had this from a member of the Government; and the same man told me that he doubted if any one else could have carried it through. Probably it is the poetic faculty which gives him insight into the Eastern character. Yes, Robert Vassal will arrive, as they say. On the whole, I fancy his career has lost nothing through the giving up of Parliament."

"Oh, I am glad of that. And his work has gained. The last book of poems seemed to me beautiful."

Yet it hurt me, the inflexion on that word "beautiful."

Then she seemed to hesitate, but added after a little pause—

"I hope that Mrs.—I suppose I ought to say Lady Vassal now—is in better health than before they left England?"

"I believe that she has taken a new lease of life—has developed quite a talent for foreign diplomacy, and has seconded him ably. Her mind has recovered its tone—as I predicted. She is enormously interested in the whole Eastern show—makes excursions with him into the desert, and is great friends with the Sheiks. Some one who met them at Mandour last winter told me that you would hardly know her; and that it is quite easy now to imagine that she had once been called 'the beautiful Miss Delmar.'"

Again there was a silence, which I broke.

"I was going to answer his letter to-day, though I had little news to give. It seems a strange coincidence—your having come just now—after these years. . . . And, what shall I say to him about you?"

"Say that I am well." It was the old vibrant voice that answered—that voice which had thrilled through me on that winter's day at Grisewood. "Say that my life is more peaceful than it used to be; and that I have work to do—though it is not Esther Zamiel's work. Tell him that Esther Zamiel died . . . died . . . in the wilderness. . . . Tell him . . ." She quavered helplessly, and recovered herself. . . . "Did he . . ." she whispered; "did he ask about the child?"

"Yes, he asked if the child were a comfort to you."

She made no reply in words, but bent her head down, and I saw her body contract and swell in a stifled sob. Then suddenly she looked up at me, and as her wild wet gaze met mine piercingly, the secrets of our souls seemed bared.

"There's something I have often wished to tell you," I said. "But somehow I have never found the opportunity; and I did not like to write. . . . I did write once—after your boy's birth; and you gave me no answer."

"I don't remember," she answered dully; "I can't remember anything about that time." After a pause she said, "What is that you wanted to tell me?"

"I was not sure whether you would care. . . ." The words came haltingly. It was so hard to phrase the communication, and I doubted still if I were doing wisely in making it. . . . "I think you might wish to know. . . . Soon after the child's birth was announced . . . I had a visit—in this room—from Robert Vassal. He had come over straight from Mandour."

She gave a low cry, and again hid her face. I could not look. Instinctively I knew that she was thanking Heaven for the solace my words had brought her wounded heart; and I felt almost as an assassin might have felt, having withheld this knowledge from her in all these years.

"I had written—I told you—and had got no answer, except from Mr. Vassal, who said that you were recovering slowly, and expressed great satisfaction at the birth of an heir. That was before —the visit I spoke of. . . . I showed the letter to Robert Vassal. Later on, I wrote to him all that I was able to glean about you from Mrs. Greste and Mrs. Audley Arathoon."

There was absolute stillness for several minutes, except for the sound of Esther's breathing. Then she rose from her chair, speaking composedly, though the words seemed to be brought out with difficulty.

"Thank you. . . . That was—quite right. . . . There was

nothing more to tell. . . . Thank you . . . thank you. . . . And now I must not keep you any longer."

She laid a little folded paper on the table.

"For God's sake," I cried, "let me for once feel myself a man and not a machine!"

She smiled, her strange, sweet smile. "Thank you; thank you, my friend," she said again. "I will bring my little boy to see you by-and-by. . . . And you have given me such comfort. . . . I think you must know what great comfort you have given me. . . . And my friend . . . you will know too—without words, always in the future, that there is no one I trust as I trust you. . . ."

I took her ungloved hand in mine.

"Do you remember promising me many years ago that you would let me help you if it were possible, and that you would rely upon my friendship and upon my discretion?"

"Yes. . . ." But I saw by the far-away look that she only dimly remembered, and no doubt the more vivid experience of a later time had effaced the pale record. "It was at Grisewood," she said, "before——"

"Before you became Esther Zamiel. And now, as you say, Esther Zamiel is dead. But my—regard for you remains as strong and fervent as in those old days, and as ready to respond to your call, if you ever choose to make one."

I raised her hand to my lips and kissed it—it seemed to me then, as a soldier vowed to the death might kiss the hand of his queen; and an impulse for which I can never account, made me say—

"Esther"—it was the first time I had ever called her by her name—"I want to tell you—here—now—that I understand you —that I reverence you—that I—love you. . . . Good-bye."

' "Good-bye!" she repeated, the word strangled by a sob; and left me.

WRITTEN
BY
AGATHA
GRESTE: IF I have said some hard things of Mr. Vassal, I
am sorry for the necessity that was upon me to say
them ; but I don't repent the saying, and I can't
make myself unsay a syllable of them—no, not now
that he is dead. Even when he lay dying I could
not make myself feel differently about him ; and all through the
times when Esther seemed to wish me to be with her in the sick-
room, I never lost that sense of an evil moral exhalation such as
I used to have in the splendid days when he played host at Grisewood. My desperate longing to rush out and gulp in draughts
of pure air, made me wonder the more how Esther could endure to remain as she did, hour after hour, at the side of his
couch, reading or patiently watching, ready at his slightest beck
or call.

Which is a figure of speech ; for he could make no movement
except the faintest flicker of the eyelids, and no call ever came
from the distended mouth, in which the paralysed tongue lay,
visible sometimes feebly writhing, but unable even in his most
frantic attacks of rage to give forth speech. He used to have
terrible accesses, when the savage beast in him seemed literally
to beat against the bars of its flesh prison, so that the eyes would
blaze out of the mask-like face, and there would come horrible
guttural sounds from the throat, ending in a paroxysm of coughing and suffocation. It was all very terrible ; but Esther never
shrank. Since the day upon which the doctors had told her
plainly what the end was to be, she had taken her place with a
quiet persistent heroism, and devoted herself as far as was possible
to alleviating his sufferings. It took some time before he would
submit to her attendance. At first, while still able to command,
he would morosely order her to a distance. Then, till speech
failed him entirely, he found amusement in making her the butt
of his cynical gibes. But after a while, as his helplessness increased, he grew to accept her ministrations, and in a freakish
way to depend upon them, giving when she was absent distinct
signs of impatience for her return.

Esther has since talked to me of a fantastic theory that used to weigh upon her—a notion she had, that intense desires and tenacious purposes have the power of individualising themselves, and may thus become spiritual agents for man's temptation and hurt, or for his advancement along the heavenly road. She believed in the Scriptural idea of demons of darkness inciting to foul deeds, and in guardian angels preserving and aiding. But these, she said, were for the most part no denizens of heaven or of hell, but the thought-shapes which men and women unconsciously create and send out from themselves, to people those unseen regions where the world's destinies are wrought. She always declared that the legend of a curse upon Grisewood Castle had full foundation; and was haunted by the feeling that Mr. Vassal's vindictive hatred of his brother in the first instance, and of his nephew afterwards, increasing with the years, and gathering vital force from the two lives—her own and her son's—with which it became linked, had taken superhuman form, and that there was in truth a fourth and maleficent presence ever hovering where they three sat together.

Certainly one of the later traits in Mr. Vassal which I most detested was the malevolent interest he got to show in Bunchy. He seemed to gain a morbid pleasure from having the child near him. Bunchy made him remember and *feel;* and I think he enjoyed the sensation, as he might have enjoyed sticking pins into a deadening limb. In the beginning, Esther made no opposition to the boy's being brought into his room, and there for an hour or so at a time, they three, and the Spirit of Hate, and I, who looked on, would abide together—the pale sad child not daring to occupy himself, sitting motionless in his corner, his eyes irresistibly drawn to the invalid couch, from which that torpid form with the burning gaze watched him incessantly. Mr. Vassal seemed to realise with a malignant satisfaction the mesmeric horror he produced; and as the boy, in a kind of fascination of terror, after shudderingly withdrawing his eyes for a moment, would turn them back again, the other eyes from between their flabby lids would glow yet more fiercely, and the revolting guttural chuckle would make my blood run cold. Esther has told me that she too felt herself overpowered by the uncanny horror; and after a few days of this torture, finding that it was having a very injurious effect upon Bunchy's nerves and bringing on the alarmed wakings from sleep and distressing screaming fits, she absolutely refused to allow the child to be brought into the sick-room. This was the occasion of one of Mr. Vassal's most violent accesses, but she bore it with a patience that seemed to me sublime. White to the lips with agitation and with the strain of opposing him, she waited till the worst of his fury was past, and then pleaded and remonstrated with pathetic fervour.

"I will do anything—anything else you want of me—anything that could give you a moment's ease or comfort," she cried. "I would cheerfully cut off my right hand for that—indeed, indeed I think I would almost die for you. ... But don't ask me to hurt the child, for that I can't do. After what Dr. Glaive told me, I couldn't run the risk of harm to him—even if it made you happier to have him near. But I don't feel it's that. ... I don't feel that it makes you any happier—and you wouldn't want to hurt him, would you? You have been very generous—don't think I don't feel it. And now that everything is nearly over—oh let there be forgiveness at the last. And do believe what is the solemn truth, that nothing in the world would make me go against your wishes, except that one thing—my duty to the boy."

The child did not again appear, but the mother sat on—her beautiful face and head with its white hair and deep eyes and steadfast sweetness of expression, so strange a contrast to the grotesque mask set against the cushions opposite. All that Mr. Vassal seemed to care for now, was having her there and hearing her read. And she would read on in her soft voice, with its old organ vibrations and dramatic intonation, as in the *Claudia* days, guided as to when she should stop and in her choice of the subject by the flicker in her listener's eyelids and the contraction and dilatation of his pupils, a language she had learned to follow. She used to try and read to him sometimes books which were poetic and ennobling, but he would have none of them; and so she would have to go back to the coarse witty French novels in which he had always delighted; and the ghastly incongruity of their humour with the dying man's situation makes me shudder now as I remember and write. It is not a pleasant subject to dwell upon—those last days of Mr. Vassal.

But Esther went through them, like one possessed of more than mortal courage. I know that she fought as with the arch-enemy against the sickening aversion that sometimes almost overcame her. She fought because she knew that this was the thing she must conquer—that here was the penance she had to accomplish; and because, as she said afterwards, something within her made it clear that now was being waged the last battle in her nature between the Powers of Darkness and of Light, between the Spirit of Love and the Spirit of Hate; and that as Love gained or lost in the contest, so would God's Scales be adjusted, and so would it fare with her soul and the soul of the child. She has told me that there was no merit to her in the effort she made, any more than to the castaway who grips the rock and fights the waves till the rescuers arrive.

I have fancied that perhaps some dim consciousness of this working of unseen forces in her, pierced to the yet functioning brain of that dead-alive thing of flesh, hardly to be called a man, whom she tended. He was now unable to lie down because of the difficulty of breathing. Literally there was nothing left living of him but eyes and brain. Sight and hearing remained, but the only sign of physical power lay in that almost imperceptible tremor of the eyelids and shadow-like twitching at the left angle of the mouth—that horrible mouth, stiffened into its unnatural leer.

Near the end I seemed to see a slight softening of the vindictive glare in his eyes, and imagined in them a new expression, one of faint beseeching, which made me think at times that he was trying to ask Esther's forgiveness. She fancied that there was something he wanted done, and tried hard to interpret the futile efforts he made to convey his meaning.

I was on the other side of his couch—she and I being alone with him in his room—when one day she pronounced to him the names of several persons whom it occurred to her he might wish to see. Among them was that of Mr. Arathoon, the solicitor. At sound of it, there came over his face such a despairing ghost of a contortion, that we were alarmed, gave the assurance that Mr. Arathoon should not be summoned, and did everything in our power to soothe him.

Esther kneeled by his side, passionately reiterating her promise that every smallest indication of his wishes should be attended to, and begging him not to let his mind be disturbed by regrets or uneasy thoughts about herself. "If it is anything to do with money," she said, "anything that you are sorry for about me or the boy"—her voice trembled, as it always did when she mentioned the child to her husband—"you know, in spite of everything, that I have never cared for money, and that I should understand better than any one else could, how you had felt. . . . I should know. . . And whatever you had seen fit to arrange, I should be willing to accept ; and even if it seemed hard, I should try to look upon it as," her voice sank, "ordered for my punishment."

Again that wraith of a movement, and a fixing of the wild imploring gaze which was dreadful to behold. It seems to me that in this moment the Spirit of Love must have conquered finally, and that Esther's redemption was sealed. She stooped close over the man whom she had once so dreaded and hated, and clasping the inert form with her warm living arms, she kissed him long and tenderly.

"Oh, forgive me," she cried. "Forgive me for having married you as I did. Forgive me for my cold selfishness and want of sympathy. Forgive me for the wrong I did you. .. And, oh! tell me—tell me if I have made up for it a little in these last years? I have tried—indeed, I have tried . . . and I have suffered. . . . I have been punished. . . . Tell me! Give me this comfort——"

Then as her face still touched his, and while her arms were about him, a great inward spasm seized him, and there followed one of those awful paroxysms of coughing and strangulation—the last.

.   .   .   .

I had got into my head somehow, I suppose from novels and plays, that when a person of great estates dies, there invariably happens a dramatic reading of the will, usually in the family library, with the family lawyer taking the chair, and all the friends and relatives and inimical scions of the house gathered together, ready as it were to group for a "curtain."

But nothing of the sort took place after Mr. Vassal's death. Indeed, I don't know exactly what did happen, for I was with Esther, who had collapsed utterly after the strain of those many past months, in her own part of the Castle, and only heard through drawn blinds the sound of carriages without, and knew but from hearsay afterwards that all the county people, and the chief inhabitants of Woodchester and of the borough generally, and the tenants and representatives from Tregarth, had assembled in force to do honour to the dead millionaire, who was committed to the family vault in Grisewood Church with all pomp and ceremony. Esther did not attend the funeral, but little Bobby, holding his godfather Lord Cotherstone's hand, walked behind Mr. Vassal's coffin as chief mourner.

Naturally Mr. Arathoon also was there.

But there was no formal reading of the will. Later we learned that the original document, of which a copy only was in the possession of Mr. Arathoon, had been searched for at the Castle but not found, and a certain delay in proceedings was caused by the fact that it had been, unknown to the solicitors, deposited with other important papers, not in the London bank, but in that at Woodchester.

Anyhow, the first authentic information Esther received as to its nature was from Lord Cotherstone the co-executor with Mr. Arathoon—to whom the latter had sent a copy.

Lord Cotherstone's intellect was not equal to coping with any legal document, short of its being reduced to spelling-book English, and in the perplexity and consternation which an inkling of the contents of this one aroused, he applied to Mr. Inskip, his own solicitor, to elucidate Mr. Vassal's testamentary provisions.

These, shorn of technical phraseology, and summarised by the Woodchester lawyer in a further document forwarded to Esther, and so perused by me, went after this manner :—

The will was dated on the 28th day of November 1876—when little Bobby was about a month old. After appointing Mr. Michael Arathoon, solicitor, of No. 95 Lincoln's Inn Fields, and Baron Cotherstone of Cotherstone Park, Woodfordshire, to be executors and trustees, it nominated Mr. Arathoon to be the sole guardian of Robert, the testator's only child (thereby, as Mr. Inskip parenthesised it, excluding the mother from the position which nature had assigned her).

The testator bequeathed to his friend, Mrs. Rhoda Raphon, sister of his friend and legal adviser, Mr. Arathoon, the sum of £20,000, to be taken by her in cash or in securities at the option of the executors, such legacy to be free of legacy duty, and independent of any other interest the legatee might have under the testator's will or codicils thereto.

The testator also bequeathed a sum of £5000, free of duty, to Mary Tremlett, formerly maid to the testator's second wife, and he further gave a sum of £5000 to his trustees to invest and hold on trust for Madeline, daughter of the said Mary Tremlett, for life and afterwards, as the said Madeline Tremlett should appoint by her will.

The will then recited the deed which entailed the Cornish estates and the estates in Woodfordshire, and also stated that no settlements were made on the occasion of his second marriage, namely, that with Esther Vrintz. It also recited that his only child Robert would, if he survived the testator, be the tenant in tail of the Cornish and Woodfordshire estates, and that the testator wished to provide his only child with income befitting the owner of these properties, subject to certain conditions thereinafter expressed.

The will then proceeded to give the child the whole of the testator's large fortune which passed under his will, and not by way of entail, but subject to certain trusts and conditions of which the following only need be mentioned here. The investments and moneys were all vested in the trustees of the will, to pay the sum of £1000 a year to Mr. Arathoon as long as he acted as guardian to the child ; and the testator declared that this guardianship should continue until the child reached the age of twenty-five ; if he did so, the trustees were to hold the investments and moneys on different trusts, thereinafter declared (to which reference was made presently). The sole guardian, Mr. Arathoon, was also forbidden to allow the mother to have access to her child, or to in any way control the child's education, bringing up, religion, manner of life, or interests. In fact, as far as the law then permitted, Mrs. Vassal (the mother) was absolutely debarred from any communication with her son, and further to effect this object, the testators provided that the trustees were to pay out of the trust estate £600 a year, by quarterly payments, to the widow, on condition that and only so long as she observed the terms and intention of the will ; and that if in the opinion of the guardian she committed any breach of these conditions, the trustees were hereupon to suspend entirely the payment of this annuity to her, and that she was to take no interest under the will. Provision was then made for the appointment by Mr. Arathoon of another guardian to be bound by the same conditions in all respects, if Mr. Arathoon should die or become unwilling to act longer.

The trustees were also to pay the guardian £2000 a year to expend on the child for education or otherwise, but the guardian was to be under no obligation to account for such expenditure, and might in fact use it as he chose, without restraint.

If by reason of death or for any other reason, the child was debarred from taking any interest under the will, the trustees were to hold the trust moneys for other purposes, namely to pay one-eighth of the whole of the trust funds to Michael Arathoon, solicitor, one-eighth to Rhoda Raphon, sister of Michael Arathoon, one-eighth to Madeline, daughter of Mary Tremlett, and so on, without mentioning Esther. Mr. Inskip quoted a number of other conditional provisions, which I don't think I need set down here.

This is what the whole iniquitous thing came to, as far as it concerned Esther. I've copied Mr. Inskip's words as nearly as possible ; and I've left out a lot that seems immaterial.

Yes, the man was a Fiend !

Mr. Arathoon came to the Castle, but Esther refused to see him. I suppose that he saw Lord Cotherstone, whose honest English heart was sorely troubled and whose letters on the subject, enclosing notes and opinions from Inskip, almost made me laugh sometimes in their ingenuous horror and puzzlement. The delay in finding the original will softened the shock of it all a little, but that didn't last long, and soon there was great outcry in Woodfordshire.

Mione Arathoon was the first to rush down to express her

indignation, assuring Esther of her stanch loyalty, and adding the advice, prompted privately by Audley, that she should take the case into the High Court of Chancery and fight it. That was Inskip's advice also.

"And if you settle to fight," said Mione, "I will stand by you to the whole extent of my Delmar dollars—which perhaps isn't saying much—simply for the sweet satisfaction of spiting Aunt Rhoda, who has got distinctly uppish on the strength of Mr. Vassal's legacy, and of confounding father-in-law's knavish tricks."

And dear Dad was of exactly the same opinion. He came too, deeply distressed and remorseful.

"Oh, I'm to blame," he cried, "I'm abominably to blame. I ought to have insisted on a marriage settlement."

He had been working up the matter with an eminent Q.C., a member of the Roscius.

"But it's perfectly simple," he said. "Of course such an outrage on Nature could never in any decent country be permitted. You must have custody of the boy, and you get it by making an application to the Judge of the Chancery Division of the High Court, for the guardianship of, or access to the child. It is at the Judge's discretion to grant this. As you are a perfectly fit and proper person to have the custody of your own son, and it would be impossible for any one to prove the contrary, the decision will of course be in your favour."

That seemed the general theory. Dr. Glaive, like the rest of Esther's friends, had been consulting authorities, and said that this was the only course open to her. But he was grave and constrained, and I had never seen him look so sad.

Lord Cotherstone naturally espoused Esther's cause, and did not scruple to express himself forcibly on the subject of "that r-rascally Jew." Relations, we gleaned, were strained between the co-executors, Lord Cotherstone being primed by Mr. Inskip, who had his own private grudge against the late Mr. Vassal's London adviser. However, after his first country squire horror at being dragged into unsportsmanlike complications and mixed up with Jews and attorneys, Lord Cotherstone began to take a modest pride in the strategic tactics Inskip advocated, with a view to putting obstacles in the way of Mr. Vassal's testamentary intentions, and of furthering the widow's interests as regards the legal battle that was anticipated.

There being neither hunting nor shooting just then, Lord Cotherstone found an outlet for his energies in the new game, and lost sight of graver doubts which, I could see plainly enough, were agitating his mother's mind, and, on the principle of reflex action, his own also.

"Inskip says, Mrs. V—vassal, that what we've got to go for is delay. You can't be t-turned out, or the boy t-taken from you, till p-probate of the will is granted. That's what Inskip says, and he's a clever chap Inskip, and a m-match for any Jew. Inskip says that the w-way to delay probate is for me as co-executor to m-make objections, and to refuse to make an affidavit. I d-don't know exactly what the affidavit means,—something to do with the v-valuation of the estate, but Inskip will explain when the t-time comes."

Then Esther's pained look would recall him to the more sentimental issues.

"I can't understand it in the least, Mrs. V-vassal. P-pon my honour I can't. L-liver don't account for it— that's what I've said to everybody. There's no doubt that p-poor old Vassal must have been off his head, or he couldn't have done it. He never was the same m-man after the nasty spill he had over G-garvie's Ditch. That horse he rode was a clinking goer, but he had a b-bad trick of stopping short and bucking his fences."

"The will was dated long before that fall," said Lady Cotherstone, who had accompanied her son.

"Then it b-beats me. He always would take his own line, old V-vassal, when he knew the country. A first-rate sportsman, and rode straight ; b-but he wasn't riding straight then. P-pon my honour, I can't understand it."

"A bee in his bonnet," said the old lady. "After that dinner, when he got hold of those dreadful people, I said, didn't I, that he couldn't be in his right mind? My dear," Lady Cotherstone went on, speaking with impressive solemnity, "I should like you to understand clearly that I recognise your devoted care of that poor man, all through his last illness, and that I shall make a point of proclaiming how nobly you did your duty. The whole thing, as Cotherstone says, is a mystery. How could he have made that will just at the time of the boy's christening ! Why, I remember our all being here for it, and his having the child brought down. . . . And your fainting suddenly. . . . But nothing will ever alter my opinion that you have been most cruelly treated as wife and mother, and that it is the duty of all Woodfordshire wives and mothers to support you in an appeal for your rights."

And like Dad, she bewailed the want of a marriage settlement. How could her "people" have allowed her to marry without a settlement? Alas, that one fact struck a blow at the root of poor Esther's moral position. There must have been something wrong.

This was the lurking doubt underlying all the valiant show of partisanship, and disturbing the Woodfordshire convictions. I could see the doubt in people's eyes, I could hear it in their voices, I could detect it beneath the veil of sympathy which shrouded their questionings. To marry without a settlement is, in the eyes of the landed Philistine, to prove one's self outside the pale of British respectability. Sometimes the gruesome fancy would strike me that Mr. Vassal might be looking down from aloft, and deriving a cynical amusement from the county flutter. It was a jest which would have suited his ironic humour.

Ah, heart-breaking as was the situation, one could not at moments help seeing its grim comedy.

They all had their misgivings—every one of them, in spite of their kindness and their protestations, from old Lady Cotherstone to Addie Littlewood and the Canons' wives, they all suspected that there was something vaguely disgraceful in the background of Esther's life, some stigma on her girlhood No one, they said, had ever rightly known her antecedents—which doubtless had been concealed from her husband, and discovered and resented in after years. This, I have gleaned from various sources, was the generally accepted explanation in Woodfordshire of Mr. Vassal's extraordinary will.

BOOK XIV

" *As when a bird bewails her callow brood when
they perish, which, still young, a fierce snake devours
in the thick bushes, while she, kind mother, hovers
over them, shrieking wildly, yet is not able, I ween,
to aid her children, for she is, in truth, herself in
great dread to come nearer to the cruel monster.*"

Mr. Arathoon sat in my master's chair in the library of the Grosvenor Street house, while I opposite, watched and listened and waited—waited that I might fully understand my doom. For in spite of the assurances of Mr. Inskip, Lord Cotherstone, Mr. Leete, and the rest—in spite of the elaborate preparations for attack and siege, the heaping up of obstacles, the lengthening of delays—in spite of Mr. Arathoon's impassive attitude during these past weeks, I felt instinctively that his bland patience was but the cover for deadly weapons in reserve, and that, sooner or later, from his hand the blow which must destroy me would fall.

Beyond some formal written communications, I had had no intercourse with him since my widowhood. He had now asked for an interview, in such a manner that I could not refuse the demand. That, in fact, through all its courteous wording, was the nature of his request.

Hitherto I had met him as the host at Chesham Place, as the guest at Grisewood, as the dilettante man of society. To-day, for the first time, I met him as the lawyer, whom every criminal who was not a client had reason to fear. His manner and aspect therefore struck me in a new light, and for all his conventional politeness, there seemed to be in both something peculiarly sinister. From time to time, as he talked, his eyes gave me a furtive glance —they seldom look at one full: wily and inscrutable, they appeared to be studying me from behind dulled glass. His yellow-grey beard, well brushed and glossy, swept his chest, and lent a suggestion of dignity. His red, largely moulded lips, at once sensuous and crafty, showed disagreeably between the silky beard, growing low on the chin, and the yet finer moustache. As I sat in my suspense, I marked the little peculiarities of his face and demeanour; and in fancy I likened myself to some hapless slave woman, whose only child was in the hands of its capturer . . . my little ailing child, for Bunchy has not been well, and I have brought him up to London that I may consult Dr. Glaive . . . the helpless mother, captive also, who, knowing with the instinct of despair that neither tears nor defiance will aid her, draws in her forces, her very being hanging, as it were, in the balance; and, while simulating an icy calm, scrutinises the features of her foe, in search of some faint sign of manly clemency.

There was none. Mione did well to name her father-in-law Caliban. He stroked his beard in a gentle monotonous movement, while in his purring voice, that under certain inflexions can ring so harshly metallic, he made me a statement of my position.

The statement seemed purposely involved—circumlocutory phrases, used perhaps to soften its severity, perhaps to make my questionings more difficult. When I did question, still with the forced quietude I had imposed upon myself, bidding him not spare me in his answers, the gist of the matter needed little interpretation. It was, after all, only what the summary of the will and Mr. Inskip's explanations had made clear. I was merely a resident on sufferance in my dead husband's house, the guardian of my boy, only until certain legal formalities had been complied with; and when these were fulfilled, I should have no part nor right here nor in the life of my son. Shortly there must come an end to the petty difficulties Lord Cotherstone, in his well-meaning partisanship, was raising. These were but as so much useless flutter, counting for nothing in the real issues at stake—just so many kindly endeavours to gain for me a few months or weeks of the companionship of my child. This was what Mr. Arathoon, affably commiserative, conveyed to me. It was far from his wish that I should be hurried. He had acquiesced in Lord Cotherstone's tactics, had sympathised deeply with the motives that prompted them; it was, in fact, a matter of regret to him that the delays had not been still more extended. But the course of the law, if sometimes slow, was sure; and the time had now come in which all must face the situation.

He emphasised the "all," and, after a moment's pause, added—"the time, in which I, on my side, must tackle the very painful duty laid upon me."

A bitter rejoinder arose, which I quelled before utterance.

"Yet, it appears," I said, "that much has been left to your discretion."

"You mean—— ?"

"As I understand the will, it seems to rest with you whether I am or am not absolutely denied access to my son."

"I think," he said slowly, "that the intentions of the testator on that point are very clearly expressed."

"But you have the power to enforce them, stringently or not, as you should think fit."

"That technically might be a justifiable inference; it is hardly justifiable morally. In accepting the trust imposed upon me by the will, I am morally bound to carry out in their integrity the testamentary wishes of my deceased friend."

"Even," I exclaimed impetuously; and I tried to make him look at me, but he would not—"even if your conscience and your feelings as a man were in opposition to them?"

"Ah, Mrs. Vassal," he said, and there came a stronger note into his neutral tone, while as he spoke he divided a strand of his beard and examined it thoughtfully, "that is a point of casuistry, which raises a totally different question."

There was a silence. Maybe, I thought, in those persistently averted eyes there lurked a gleam of human sympathy. Oh, if I might but find and arouse some kinder side of his nature! Clinging to the desperate hope, I cast away my chill mask and spoke in tremulous appeal.

"Mr. Arathoon—you have never had any children?"

"No, Mrs. Vassal, I have not been so—blessed."

"And so it cannot be quite easy for you to understand how a mother feels to her only child—to realise that my boy is just everything in the world to me—everything—and that it would be far less of a cruelty to take away my life, than to take him from me. . . . You couldn't understand that?"

And it seemed to me as though not I but that slave woman were entreating, and that I could hear outside myself the agitated falter in her voice, and see the longing in her eyes, to force this ruthless captor to meet her gaze— the longing that he would dare to be pierced by the mother-anguish in it. . . . But he did not dare. He would not look. . . . And I still found hope in the reluctance which held his lids drooped.

"But at least," I went on, "though you have never had children, you have been a child yourself. You must know you should know, how dearly a son may love his mother when there have been only the two to hold together and to care for one another. . . . Think of my little boy not much more than a baby so helpless so sensitive—separated altogether from his mother to whom he has clung all his tiny life. . . . My poor little boy. . . . And he is so delicate he is ill now Dr. Glaive has warned me that he mustn't be upset or made unhappy, or his brain excited in any way—he has to be treated and watched over with the most loving care. . . . Think of him given up to strangers! Think how his health—his life may depend upon this. . . . O Mr.

Arathoon, there isn't a judge in England who wouldn't say you were justified in not enforcing too sternly that cruel will. . . ."

He gave a faint little indulgent laugh.

"I am afraid, Mrs. Vassal, that you look at the matter altogether from the woman's and not at all from the lawyer's point of view. . . . Believe me, I am very sorry—sorry both for you and for your son——"

"Oh," I cried, "you would be sorry indeed, if you could understand how heavily my little boy has been weighted—ever since he was born. . . . You know . . . you must have learned something of our life——"

"I know a great deal about your life, Mrs. Vassal. Remember that I was something more than your husband's lawyer: I was his friend. . . . Yes, I know a great deal."

"But there's one thing you don't know," I cried. "You don't know that in his last moments Mr. Vassal's heart was softened to us, and he repented of his unjust will. . . ."

"Really! . . . He was speechless, I believe, for some time before his death?"

"It was in his eyes," I went on—"the penitence, the remorse. —Such an imploring, seeking look. . . . And I thought that perhaps he wanted to see you—that things might be altered; I asked him before he died. And if you could have seen the expression upon his face—of anger—oh, worse!—despair—Yes, Mr. Arathoon, it made me certain that he repented. . . ."

"Surely, Mrs. Vassal, without going more definitely into the case, which would be bootless, that look of anger—or worse—is rather against your supposition."

"He did repent . . . I know it . . . I could swear to it—on my knees. . . . Ask Agatha Greste—she was present. . . . And I begged his forgiveness, and he forgave me—we forgave each other when he was dying. He was sorry; he would have undone, if he had been able, the evil thing that he did. Nothing will ever take that conviction from me."

I know not what else I said. My pleadings poured forth, the surging anxiety sweeping all before it, my heart strengthening its courage by the fact that still the man would not face me. . . . I besought, as for dear life—oh, as I had said, for far more than dear life. For what is my life worth to me without my son?

Then at last his eyelids were raised. He tilted his head back, and contemplated his hands for a moment or two, holding them out before him. A little knotted they were, and wrinkled like a vulture's talons. . . . Murderer's hands, they say, are sometimes knotted that way. . . . It is a sign of cruelty. . . . But Mr.

Vassal's hands were soft and smooth and white. . . . Presently he turned his eyes full towards me, and looked unblenchingly into mine—looked at me for quite a long time without speaking. . . . And my own eyes drooped, and hope fell—dead as though a bolt from Jove had stricken it.

If I had never realised the truth before, I knew now that it was my implacable enemy with whom I had to deal: a man who never forgave and never forgot, and who would relinquish nothing that his greed coveted.

His greed coveted the handling of the Vassal millions during the long years of my boy's minority—Dr. Glaive and others had warned me of that. . . . I knew, too, that my enemy hated me with a relentless hatred—hated me because I had supplanted his sister and thwarted his plans, and somehow come between him and his designs upon Mr. Vassal's money. I read all this with unerring intuition. . . . And I understood also that this was the hour of my enemy's triumph, and that I might expect no quarter.

After a few moments he spoke, remotely self-justificatory, and smooth as honey.

"My dear lady, your reproaches place me in a very painful position —all the more so because they are undeserved. It is my misfortune rather than my fault that loyalty to my dead friend obliges me to take an attitude adverse to your interests. As for what you tell me of your husband's last moments, from your point of view, it is very touching. and no doubt, if one might accept it, would be elevating to one's ideas of human nature. But these deathbed interpretations are apt to be coloured by the emotional bias of those concerned. In any case, power of utterance and movement having failed, no conclusions can be arrived at, and it would of course have been too late to undo anything. But I was better acquainted with the workings of Mr. Vassal's mind than you are perhaps aware. I can answer for the deliberation with which the provisions of his will were planned. I know the feelings and motives which actuated him; and it is possible that were your other advisers and friends equally well informed, their opinion of his testamentary dispositions might be less harsh. I know that during the years which followed the making of the will—even when he was only able to express himself by signs, his feelings had not changed, nor had his intentions wavered. I took pains to ascertain this fact. Were I put on my oath, I should be compelled to state it."

There was silence. He held me dumb as a sheep in the slaughtering-house. Presently he went on—

"Mrs. Vassal, believe me that my sympathies as a man, to

which you have appealed so eloquently, are deeply moved. But that does not alter my moral conviction, painful as it is to say so. I can conceive no loophole for doubt as to my own duty. I am bound in honour and in law, as one of the executors of Mr. Vassal's will and the guardian appointed by him to—the heir of his estates, to carry out what I know to have been his intentions. I am aware that you will consider me inhuman."

A wave of passionate bitterness overswept me. "Inhuman !" I cried. "You do well to use that word, for you are committing a crime against nature."

His manner stiffened to irony.

"A crime, since you call it so, sanctioned by high judicial authority. I might quote to you Lord Cottenham's decision that mothers have no right to interfere with testamentary guardians. Even a mother must submit to the law."

"A mother will submit to any law but that which takes her child from her. She will fight to the death for the possession of her child. That's a natural instinct, Mr. Arathoon."

"Yes, it is an instinct which holds sway in the brute crea- tion and usually in the human kingdom—except under certain conditions."

"Certain conditions ?" The phrase sounded knell-like.

"For example ! Those, under which a mother has to choose between the possession of her child and the ruin of one dearer to her even than her child—the man she loves."

Ah God ! They know how to strike, these lawyer men !

The false purring voice went on, and the words smote me as though they had been cut in metal type and were being printed on my brain.

"Yes, my experience of human nature, which has been con- siderable and varied, shows me the interesting fact that there is one passion stronger in a woman's breast than the maternal instinct. Looking at it from the artistic point of view, for a moment, it's a fact that appeals to me as full of dramatic capa- bilities, even in the nineteenth century. You know, Mrs. Vassal, that I am one-third artist if I am two-thirds lawyer."

I can imagine, now, the sensations of those victims of the Middle Ages, in their contracting chamber of doom. Steadily and surely, mine was shrinking round me. Soon its walls would meet, and I should be annihilated within their stone embrace.

. . . ."No, you might not think that there could be any passion stronger in a woman's heart than the maternal one, but I can assure you that there is. Taking a purely problematical case, let us suppose—shall we say yourself?—confronted with the alterna-

tive of wrecking the public and private life of the one man you
have ever loved, and the sacrifice of such happiness as you would
gain from being the unmolested guardian of your son. Which
would you choose—the child's society or the man's good?"

I felt that I was mouthing dumbly—unmeaning, voiceless
words, which the dry tongue could not frame into audible language.

"I think," he said, "that I might venture to predict. In nine
cases out of ten, the woman would choose the good of the man—
especially so if her choice involved no worldly injury to the child
—no deprivation to him in short, but that of her personal care
and influence. . . . On considering the matter, Mrs. Vassal, don't
you agree with me?"

"I . . . I . . . have not considered. . . ."

The stammering accents of that slave mother of my fancy
sound through the mists.

My enemy's soft voice lashed on.

"It would be worth your while, artistically speaking, to work
it out. . . . I see the situation strikes you. It is old, very old—
classic, in fact Æschylean. But the elemental passions are never
too old, do you think, for modern adaptation? Human nature is
always itself, and is always full of surprises. And love has been
love, from Eden to the court in which Sir James Hannen pre-
sides to-day. *Then*, its ultimate penalty the flaming sword : *now*,
disconcerting revelations and a decree *Nisi*. . . . Yes, conceive the
struggle between a woman's love for her lover, and her love for
her child ! . . . There, dear lady, is a theme of tragic interest imme-
morial. Putting aside graver considerations for the moment, I
fancy you might turn it to profitable account, your own literary
tendencies being so distinctly dramatic. I remember being struck,
in one of Esther Zamiel's novels, by the suggestion of a Greek
parallel. . . . Forgive the digression . . . your patient silence en-
courages me. For you know Greek art in any form is my King
Charles' head ; and here it is again tumbling incontinently into our
legal conversation. . . . I have no doubt you have heard me many
times preaching it to our friends the dramatists—Quintin Glaive
for instance. It would be an improving exercise for some of
our playwrights to contrast that magnificent opening scene on
the watch-tower of Agamemnon's palace, when the beacon fires
burning along the Argive hills tell of the fall of Troy, with a
modern-stage prelude to the homicidal doings of some Belgravian
Clytemnestra, where a French lady's-maid, in a frilled apron,
expounds the family complications to an interrogative valet. . . .
Ah, I see you have no more patience with my artistic maunder-
ings. . . . Pray sit down again ; and we will go back to our legal

point, which is to you of so much more vital import than Greek
tragedy and modern drama—the custody of your son."

I had risen, goaded beyond silent endurance any longer. . . .
The slave-woman's voice, high-pitched in agony, comes back to me,
as though echoed from the walls of the room.

"Will you, then, Mr. Arathoon, let me hear your views as to
the custody of my son?"

"That may take a little time; and you haven't authorised me
to prepare a brief. Shall I assume that I am to instruct counsel,
and sum up the case for you as succinctly as I can?"

"If you please."

"Well then—Your late husband has by his will left you comparatively unprovided for. Of course, as the widow of a man
whose income I may fairly estimate as something over £50,000
a year, the annuity you receive—under conditions—is absurdly
inadequate."

"Don't talk of that; it is nothing to me."

"No, I can understand it is nothing to you—though many
women would consider it a great deal—in comparison with what
you feel the deeper wrong of being denied access to your son.
No doubt, any legal assistance you might seek would have for its
object the gaining custody of your child?"

"I will fight for this—at any cost."

"Ah! Shall I show you the means you may take—and the
cost."

"You are my enemy," I cried. "Are you the right person
to give me advice as to what means I should take to get possession of my son?"

"As well, perhaps better than another, since I am more fully
acquainted with the facts of the case than any stranger could be.
And pardon me, I don't admit that I am your enemy. I am
your late husband's friend; and the inference you draw is hardly
established. I should not presume to offer you advice, Mrs.
Vassal; but for many reasons, it might be well that I and not
another should put before you the legal courses possible under
the circumstances in which you are placed."

He waited.

"Shall I go on?" he asked.

I bowed my head.

"There are two or three courses possible by which the validity
of a will may be called in question. Let us take the most remote
possibility first. A will may be disputed by the next in succession
—who in this case would be your late husband's nephew, Sir Robert
Vassal— on the ground that there is a doubt as to the legitimacy

of the child. . . . This contention would raise some delicate and difficult points—such as presumable access on the part of the husband to his wife—the mother of the child. Also the motive for self-incrimination on the part of the alleged father, assuming that he were forced to come forward in support of the allegation. Now, in a question of the succession to large estates, it is clear that the evidence would have to be overwhelming. We have also to remember that the late Mr. Vassal himself, before a good many witnesses, acknowledged the child as his son and heir. My opinion is that, under the circumstances of the case, a plea of illegitimacy would be absolutely untenable, even were you, the mother, disposed to put such a slur on your child, for the sake of keeping him in your custody, or were Sir Robert Vassal inclined —which is perhaps equally improbable—to raise the question."

I could have laughed outright in frenzy at the implication, so grotesquely horrific. I think I did laugh. I must have made some wild movement. He checked me by his own laugh, blandly deprecatory.

"My dear lady, I was speaking as a lawyer, of legal *possibilities*, which, you observe, I still can hardly admit as possibilities. There is no occasion for that eloquent gesture. Manifestly the doubt as to legitimacy is absurdly inadmissible. Let us go on to the second possibility. . . . The will might be disputed in its entirety, on the ground that the testator was not of sound disposing mind at the date of its signing—shortly after your son's birth. Under that contention, Sir Robert Vassal as next heir would derive no benefit, though, of course, your position and the question of guardianship would assume a different aspect. Were it maintained, the child would still inherit. . . . But—it is a provable fact, that although during the last year or two of his life Mr. Vassal may have failed in intellectual power, he was in complete possession of his faculties at the time of your son's christening. You will remember that pleasant occasion, when so many of us were gathered at Grisewood Castle for the ceremony?"

"I . . . I . . . remember. . . ."

Again I have the fancy of those nearing walls breaking the echo of my voice.

"How unfortunate it was," he went on, "that you yourself were prevented by illness from being present at the christening. I have a painful impression of your sudden fainting-fit the evening before, which happened at the very moment, if I am not mistaken, when Mr. Vassal was announcing his intention of naming the boy— after his great-grandfather—that Robert Vassal whose portrait by Sir Joshua Reynolds hangs in the west corridor. . . ."

"And now we come to the third possible course, by which you might gain the custody of your son, and which is the natural and obvious one to suggest itself in the opinion of any ordinary adviser. . . . You may make an application in the Chancery Division of the High Court, to test your alleged claim to the guardianship of your child, and to invalidate the testator's dispositions bearing on that question. . . . Probably you have been already so advised?"

"Yes."

"It is the course I myself should have advised—under somewhat different conditions. No doubt, on outside showing, the sympathy of the Court would be with you, as a mother deprived, with apparent injustice, of her natural rights. You will understand that the Court in such decisions considers solely the interest of the child. If the mother be an unfit and improper person to have the guardianship of her child, the Court would ordain that it be removed from her influence. If, on the other hand, she were clearly a woman of high moral character and spotless reputation, and the question of religious disability did not intervene—if she could prove herself to have been blameless in her relations with her deceased husband, and that the animus shown against her in his will was without justification, the Court would have strong reasons for deciding in her favour. . . ."

Once more our eyes met—steel to steel: one blade broken.

. . . "But—I am entirely frank with you, Mrs. Vassal—the ordeal through which you would have to pass, in proving an unassailable position, might be an extremely trying one. . . . Reflect! . . . Upon common reasoning, the injustice dealt you seems so flagrant as to be outside the bounds of sanity. A man of Mr. Vassal's stamp and standing does not place this indignity upon his wife—who in the eyes of the world is without reproach—unless he be out of his mind, or unless he has good cause to doubt her honour. . . . We know that Mr. Vassal was not out of his mind. The question of motive therefore becomes important, and might form the subject of searching inquiry. Your past life, the lives maybe of others, would be dragged into the light of day. . . . And—deeply as I should regret the necessity, it would be my duty, as Mr. Vassal's trusted friend and adviser, and the guardian he has chosen for his successor in the family property, to oppose your claim, and to place upon you the onus of showing yourself without blemish. . . .

. . . "Yes, reflect. . . . When large estates are at stake, it is impossible to foresee what side issues may be brought forward—what witnesses may be called. . . . Your former maid—whose parents were, I believe, old servants at Grisewood, and in whom Mr. Vassal reposed especial confidence—as indeed his legacy to her shows—she would be called upon to give her evidence. Also persons in and about Philotis—hotel-keepers, cab-drivers, intendants of some of those old fortified places on the sea-board where you may have stayed upon occasions. . . . Occurrences, probably quite innocent, might be twisted to mean something not innocent. How can one tell! . . . And there is such a thing as indictment for perjury, and trial in a criminal court! Think of your men-friends being brought into the witness-box—Sir Robert Vassal, for instance, whom I fancy you saw a good deal of at Philotis. . . . Dear lady, I doubt if, when it came to the point, you would care to face the ordeal. Under the most favourable circumstances these examinations and cross-examinations are very disagreeable to a sensitive woman. . . . Believe me, it would be a mistake on your part to attempt fighting. I am convinced that if your friends understood the case as well as I do, they would counsel you to submit to the iron law of necessity."

There was a long pause. He was standing opposite me, smoothing his hat with the same movement of his vulture hands as that which had stroked his beard.

"You will not fight, Mrs. Vassal?"

The slow gleam of triumph in his cold eyes maddened me. I cried out, "Do your worst, Mr. Arathoon. I have resolved. I mean to fight. Yes, I will fight to the last extremity. I don't care what happens to me. I will sacrifice everything—*everything*, do you understand? But I will not give up my son."

"The fight will be useless," he answered, "and I think that before you have finished with the ordeal, you will repent this decision."

.   .   .   .

He had left me. I stood alone in the strait pass to which I had brought myself, Destiny before me, with arms outstretched barring outlet. . . . Destiny, whom I had sacrilegiously invoked when I had kneeled before the altar at El-Meriem, and had besought the Lord to grant me my heart's desire.

BOOK XV

*" That which is foredoomed remains from the
olden time, and will come to those who pray for it."*

 SHE was standing in the library when I entered it, looking like a woman petrified by some great calamity. So abstracted was she from outward surroundings, that she did not hear or did not heed the announcement of my name. I had been told on arriving that Mr. Arathoon was with her, and had gone straight to pay my professional visit to the child. After leaving him I had stayed in a little ante-room on the ground floor till the lawyer passed down the vestibule on his way out ; and in a few moments the butler, according me the privilege of a doctor and an old friend, led me into Mrs. Vassal's presence.

He retired, closing the door, and I waited silently. Her back was towards me as she stood motionless before the fire, but I could see her face and form reflected in a mirror between the windows opposite. Her widow's dress and cap intensified the tragic impression her appearance gave, which was of itself sufficiently startling. Her features were strained to rigidity, her lips pressed tight as though she were suffering great pain, while her eyes, wide and dark, were fixed on vacancy in a gaze of indescribable despair. There seemed something fate-driven in her whole aspect and in an involuntary gesture she made with her arms, as though invoking the deity at some prophetic shrine.

I addressed her. She started violently, and turning round, her eyes stared dazedly at me from out of her death-white face. Then slowly a more natural colour crept into her cheeks, though she spoke and still looked like a person in a dream or under the compulsion of some terrible necessity, clearly recognised by herself, but at which now I could only guess.

"My friend ! . . . Oh, my friend." . . . She made a little helpless movement towards me and stopped. "I don't know what to do. . . . I am at the end of my tether. . . . Did you know it ?"

"I know nothing for certain, I can only conjecture. You sent for me to see the boy."

"The boy ! . . . O God forgive me ! I had forgotten he was

ill. . . . I have left him all this time. . . . I must go to him at once."

"No," I said. "He is well enough for the moment without you. Mrs. Greste is carrying out my directions. . . . I will talk to you about him presently. Sit down now and tell me——"

. . . "They let him go out in the sun one of those sudden hot days. . . . The house was all in confusion. . . . I was not attending to him as I ought. . . . The strain." . . . She seemed to lose herself for an instant. . . . "Bunchy never can stand the sun; it makes his head ache. . . . And now it's so cold!" She gave a slight shiver. . . . "Do you think the cold will hurt him, doctor?"

"I am not thinking of the boy just now," I said. "I am thinking of you. Tell me what has happened?"

"Tell you!" . . . She paced agitatedly, going to a vase of flowers and taking out a dead rose which dropped over the edge and flinging it into the fire. "I like to burn flowers," she said in an odd absent way, turning to me with a most strange smile. "It's quick—not a death by inches and moments—and years. . . . My friend!" She seemed to draw in her breath again, and fixed me with her piercing gaze. "I'm fighting for my life—by inches. I'm pushed to the last extremity. . . . They're goading me hard. But I won't give in. . . . No, I won't give in." She gave an excited little laugh, which was half a wail. I led her unresistingly by the hand to a chair.

"Sit down and let me help you if I can." Alas! I felt that there was little which man could do in her aid. "I know who is goading you. I saw Mr. Arathoon going out."

"Oh, great heavens! Was there ever such an impasse? Whichever way I look — blank walls and stones ready to fall and crush me. . . . Not me only. That wouldn't matter. . . . But ruin—ruin—to others. . . . I can't see any escape. . . . I'm tied and bound every way. . . . And I did it myself. With these very own hands I tied my cords—and the child's."

I took in mine the hand which she wrung frantically, and softly stroked it.

"I'm at the end of my tether," she repeated. "I'm at the end of my tether. . . . God has forsaken me. . . . What has been the good of all these years of slow torture? Where was the use of my great sacrifice? . . . I made it for a price. . . . And God has not paid me the price!"

"The price!" I repeated, awed by her low-voiced intensity.

"I have done my part. . . . I said that I would renounce my dearest—my *dearest*. . . . Do you know what that means to a woman, who has never loved but once in her whole life?" . . .

She spoke still scarcely above a whisper. . . . "I made a vow to God. . . . Well—I kept that vow—as far as flesh and blood was able. . . . I have battled with my love as though it had been the most sinful thing—abominable! . . . Even in my dreams I have fought—and awakened weeping! Oh, such bitter tears. . . . Only God knows what my sacrifice has cost me. . . . I made it for Bunchy's sake. . . . I did it that my boy might be kept good and safe. . . . I made a bargain with God. . . . And He has not held to His bargain. . . . Does He want another sacrifice—a crueller sacrifice still?"

"Esther!"

"Yes, I must speak. . . . You shall be my safety-valve—do you remember?—again. . . . I did it for the child's sake. . . . I plucked out my own heart from my bosom and laid it on the altar as a burnt-offering. . . . Wasn't *that* enough. . . . Does He want a man's heart—and more? . . . A man's name and fame and all his household gods. . . . Does He . . . this jealous God of Abraham? . . . Then He shall have what He demands. . . . This also will I do."

"What will you do, Esther?"

"What will I do! . . . I'll proclaim the truth aloud in open court—in the newspapers, before the whole world. . . . I'll blazon forth my disgrace. . . . I'll put shame on the man I love—dearer . . . dearer . . . oh, dearer far than my own flesh and blood. . . . I'll put shame on my son, and take away from him his inheritance. . . . Then I'd be giving it to—Oh, what am I saying? . . . Was there ever so dire a strait? . . . And they say I *can't* do it— that the law won't let me! Won't let a woman—won't let a mother—tell the name of her child's father." She stopped, and quavered off incoherently in a most lamentable laugh.

"And to what end, Esther?" I asked.

"Oh, do you think there's anything in the world or in heaven or hell, I'd do it for—except to save my boy's soul? . . . What would become of his soul with Michael Arathoon for its keeper? And with the seeds in him. . . . You said yourself that he had the seeds in him of all kinds of morbid tendencies—Deceit —who knows what worse! . . . And I'm asked to put my poor sin-tainted child into a serpent's den, that he may suck into his blood and batten upon the serpent-poison! . . . My God! I *can't* do it. . . . I'll sacrifice everything and every one first!"

"And when you've done all that you say, my poor Esther brought public dishonour on yourself, your son, your dead husband; on the man you have loved utterly—and not only on him, but on those belonging to him When you have done all this and have failed in your purpose, since it is almost certain that the law will not support you—What then?" Again she gave a low cry, which was like that of an animal hunted to the death, and clenched her hands together, as she answered—

"I will go on fighting. I will fight for every inch—every week—every hour. . . . I will contest every point. I will not leave my son. They will have to drag him out of my arms to take him from me. . . . They will have to carry me bodily from Grisewood or this house to take me from him. . . . *You* shall help me. There are means. . . . Oh, I know—Doctors can do a great deal, when they're put to it. . . . You would swear that he was ill, and that it would kill him to be parted from me."   .

"He *is* ill."

"Yes, I know. Poor little tender weakling ! . . . And you will make him better. . . . And he will be ill again. Excitement, grief, will make him ill—the consequences would be very serious—*You* said so. . . . Oh, you will manage all that for me. . . . And if it comes to the very worst, there are ways still in which a desperate mother may outwit a lawyer. . . . But it won't come to the worst. . . . The covenant will have been kept to the last letter. I shall have paid the utmost sacrifice that a jealous God could require. . . . I shall have bought my boy's soul—at the price of worse than death "— her voice sank—"to his father !"

"My dear ! my dear !" I pressed her hand, cold and trembling in her agony, to my own beating heart, and through a wet mist, my eyes looked into her eyes, which were hard and gleaming full upon me in reckless self-betrayal.

"Oh, my dear, God's covenants are not as man's covenants ; nor does He always pay the price of our sacrifices in earthly coin."

She stirred slightly, and was silent for a few moments. The dry gleam faded from her eyes, giving place to a look of beseeching suspense, but yet uncomprehending.

"I . . . can't. . . . He has pushed me . . . too far. . . ."

Suddenly came a frightened start. "My boy is ill ? . . . You said. . . . Is he *very* ill ?"

"I am afraid that he is going to be very ill. . . . It is impossible to say yet. . . . I shall know better when I see whether the things I have ordered take effect. . . . My poor, poor dear. . . . Oh, don't cry like that . . . it breaks my heart. . . . I'll do everything that is possible ; in a day or two he may be well again. . . . But . . . Doctors are very ignorant, and very helpless. . . . And it may be—Oh, my friend, if it were that God was keeping His bargain in *that* way ! . . . There are stronger Arms than even

a mother's arms to fold the child safe from harm. . . . You know.
. . . It was written long ago. 'Sacrifices and burnt-offerings Thou
wouldest not . . . but a body hast Thou prepared.' . . ."

.   .   .   .

I fought Death hard for the child, knowing full well, as often
we doctors do know, that Azrael, with whom I measured swords over
the boy's bed, was no dread fiend to be shudderingly vanquished,
but rather the Angel of deliverance, sorrowfully repulsed. . . .
That is, perhaps the saddest of experiences in this body-saving
trade of ours.

It was one day, when, though life still hung in the balance, it
dropped some feather's weight on the earth side, that a man from
Mandour came into my consulting-room. A man whom I had
last seen in this same place seven years back, on a like errand
to that which brought him now—to ask me for news of a mother
and a child.

I told him everything—of the boy's illness—of his mournful
little life as the Prince Hereditary of Grisewood, of his mother's
patient endurance of a burden that might well have broken a
weaker soul—of Mr. Vassal's gruesome death, and the terms of
his will. These, the man knew already; but I told him also,
that which he did not realise—Esther's determination, maintained
more strenuously with each stronger pulse-beat of the child, to
bring the case into Court and, regardless of all possible consequences, to appeal for the guardianship of her son.

He listened almost in silence, only once or twice interrupting
me with a terse question regarding the legal issues, that showed
me, reading as I did below the surface, how fully he grasped the
curious complications of his own position.

Presently he said, using Esther's own expression—

"It is an impasse from which there seems no outlet."

He got up, holding out his hand, and we stood facing. At
that moment, notwithstanding some resentful thoughts which had
come to me unwelcome and unbidden concerning Robert Vassal,
I pitied him from the bottom of my heart.

"Dr. Glaive," he said in an awkward, hesitating manner, and
the husky chest-note told me how much he was feeling, "I think
a great deal has been understood between you and me without
explanation."

I bowed silent assent.

"No doubt," he went on haltingly, "the exercise of your profession has given you an insight into human nature as painful as
it may have been enlightening. You must be accustomed to the

exploring of dark places in men's lives, and to the baring of their secret weaknesses. You know us as unworthy to kiss the dust upon which a true woman treads. . . . Yet, as man to man, there's something I want to say to you. . . . Dr. Glaive, I want to thank you. . . ."

" *You* have nothing to thank me for, Sir Robert;" and I was conscious of the faint bitterness in my involuntary emphasis.

"Yes—for *her* sake. You don't suppose it's for my own? You have been a loyal friend to her. In the hour of her desertion *you* stood by her."

"I was powerless. There was no way in which I could help her. Had there been, I would have done it, if it had meant laying down my life. . . . Shall I tell you why, Sir Robert?" Some impulse made me say the words I had uttered only once before in human hearing, "She is the woman I have loved best in the world."

His fingers gripped mine tightly for a second, and he let my hand fall. There was the same look in his eyes which I had seen in Esther's when she stood—at the end of her tether.

"I have no answer to make," he said. "I have taken everything, and have given—misery untold. You have given your all, and you receive—my thanks."

He threw back his head with a laugh that was bad to hear.

"You forget," I said, "I have had her friendship, and that counts for a good deal."

He moved away, but turned.

"Well—you can only think of me as a cur. . . . But—there's a saying, and *you* should be able to feel the truth of it. . . . A great love means a great comprehension—and that means, a great forgiveness. *She* should have taught you that."

"I know it."

"There was another woman's—sanity—or life—in the balance. You know that well enough—a woman to whom I owed everything."

"I know it," I repeated mechanically.

"Now," he exclaimed, with a kind of wild triumph in his eyes, "the scales are even. . . . Do you know that last year, in the desert, there was just one word from a negro's lips between me and certain death. That would have made things pretty equal. Well, it seems to me that they are equal now, and that we've gone through the great death. *She* shall decide. . . . Whether the boy lives or dies, my course is plain."

  . . . . . .

When I saw the child that mid-day, he had rallied curiously.

Towards evening, however, he had sunk into the state of coma which preludes the end.

For convenience and quietude we had moved him into a room at the back of the house, on the ground floor, between the library and billiard-room, whither I came in and out as often as the professional calls upon me allowed. There I was waiting, knowing that the hopeless battle, in which I had used every weapon with which science could furnish me, must soon come to an end, the man in me rejoicing over the doctor that Azrael had conquered. There Agatha Greste, the best aid doctor and nurses ever had, watched also; and there sat the hapless mother by her boy's pillow, quite calm, the agonised strain gone from her face, and the stillness of desolation upon it. My hand was on the child's pulse, and Esther's eyes were reading my features, not in expectation, but with foreknowledge, when the second nurse entered softly from the adjoining room, and held before her a card, upon which "Urgent" was written, and a few lines in pencil. I saw, as I had already concluded, that the card bore the name of Sir Robert Vassal. . . .

Esther's marble cheeks flushed to an almost girlish rose. From the card she looked at me. Her chest heaved, and there came over her features such a look as I have never seen before or since on face of mortal woman. Her lips moved. I had to stoop low to hear her whisper—

"Could I leave him safely—only for a very little while?"

"There will be no change," I answered—"not yet. I will stay with him."

She bent down, and for a minute or two held her face pressed against the face of the child.

Then, like a black shadow, in her widow's dress, she passed out of the room.

WRITTEN
BY
ESTHER
VASSAL:

Hands clasping: eyes thrilling into each other: hearts mingling: the two souls of us, so long parted, reunited once more!

Had our souls ever been far away, the one from its mate? No. But body is a surer prison than stone walls and iron bars.

This is not a ghost—not the dear banished ghost, whom I had no longer dared invite to the communion of spirit. No ghost! But warm flesh: breathing speech: all the dear human ways. The old gestures—that upward chin-toss: the squaring of the shoulders: the familiar moody stare: the same worried lip-droop. . . . And then the sudden change—eyes, mouth softening —the broadening out of tiny wrinkles: the loving smile—ah, do I not know it! The great glad beam of tenderness, that shines only for me!

"So brown though! So very brown. . . . And one small scar that I was not acquainted with—here, close by the temple. An inch higher, and— It makes me shudder. . . . Was it an Arab of the desert who did that? . . . And grey! . . . Talk of *me* being grey and old! . . . But my hair is silver-white, and Gagsie Greste says it is pretty. And yours!—Why, it's just the pepper and salt that brown hair goes into. . . . And oh, you *shouldn't* laugh. . . . Ah no, dearest, you mustn't laugh. . . . Takes me back to that walk, and the gourbis—and Suliman's wife—and the eggs I carried in my pocket-handkerchief. . . . Dearest, dearest, don't laugh, it's all too sad and terrible. . . ."

"And what do grey hair and wrinkles matter, in the wilderness —*our* wilderness—do you remember? . . . Nothing matters. . . . For you know it's of no use. . . . No use in pretending. . . . We'd only got to look into each other's eyes . . . always. And I'd only got to put my arms round your neck! . . . And where was the sense of fine talk. . . . and all the foolish writing-people's speeches? . . . It was *you* and *I* that were real. . . . Just *you* and *I*. . . . Oh, it wasn't any good trying to fight against Fate. . . . I said so—didn't I say so—at Tourmestral? . . . Oh, darling, darling! . . . We were only man and woman after all—*you* said it. . . ."

"And the roses, dear—do you remember? . . . The Kassis roses. . . . I've kept them all these years — dead, mouldering things! . . . No, I'm not sorry. . . . For all the agony, I'm not sorry. . . . Some day we shall know! It's all a mystery. We were made human. . . . And we've got to learn through our humanity . . . to conquer the kingdom of flesh . . . before the gates of the Other Kingdom will be opened to us. . . . Love is the key. . . . And perhaps, who knows? . . . what the world calls sin. . . . But no true love can be everlasting sin. . . . When the punishment is taken and borne—and we've borne it. Heaven's scourge-stick . . . do you remember? . . . I've thought of that so often since. . . . And when I learned the part—oh, how long ago! . . . And when I said the lines—I didn't understand them the least little bit. . . . Listen. . . .

> "'. . . I have seen—*our*—little boy oft scourge his top,
> And compared myself to't : nought made me e'er go right
> But Heaven's scourge-stick. . . .'"

Did my thoughts find spoken language? I cannot tell. They welled up in my heart : and my hands were clasped in his. . . . No, not in all these ghost years, has it changed or waned or waxed feeble—the ineffable virtue of that touch. . . . It's vital still. . . .

And then he said the words . . . "My wife!"

Can there be on earth or in heaven, music so sweet in a woman's ear as those two human words, spoken by the man she loves?

"It's true," he said ; "you are my wife—you and none other. I know everything—oh, if I had but known before. All that you have suffered alone—when I should have been by your side. . . . Henceforth, whatever comes of it, we stand together—you and I—and the child between us."

The child! Dear Lord, wilt Thou fulfil Thy covenant?

"The child between us," he repeated. . . . "Ah, Love—no harking back now upon the cruel past. . . . That for glad long hours of future nearness. . . . But I have not been quite the cowardly wretch you may have thought me. . . . I was away for many months. . . . I heard nothing till it was too late. I had never guessed. . . . Then I came. . . ."

"Yes, I know."

"I came, prepared to face the world with you, if you had desired it. But—you knew? From what I heard, it seemed my clearest duty to take myself out of your life. . . . I thought it would be best for you and for the child if I kept away from England. . . . You have understood that? . . ."

" Yes, I have understood. . . ."

" Only lately have I realised the cruel position in which you were placed. . . . As soon as news of the will reached me, I came over again. . . . I am here, to stand by you through anything—everything—to support you in whatever you think it best to do."

" And your wife, Robert—who was the nearest?"

His look was heartrending. " Don't—That terrible parting ! . . . You have remembered. . . . Esther, there is not a day, nor a night, nor even an hour in which your eyes and voice have not haunted me. . . . But oh, you knew—you must have known— I was cruel, but it was because I dared not let myself falter. If ever living man went down into hell, that man is I—— You ask about my wife. The face of things has changed. Somehow, gradually, the Eastern climate—all the new interests, have restored her health, and her sanity—as Glaive said. She has all her original grip of life. She is now like her first self—allowing for the years—even her beauty has come back, and she seems the brilliant intellectual woman I married—with this difference. Her love for me got a shock which, though her reason was almost gone for a time, has slowly diverted her affections into another channel, and has concentrated them upon our son. He is his mother's constant companion, her pride and joy. Whatever happens, they would have each other."

A vision of those two—another son and another mother—reigning at Grisewood, rose before me. He went on—

" My son is of age. Everything would be arranged. I have thought it all out. I would give up the whole thing—to him and to his mother. . . . We—you and I—would live out of England. I thought of Japan ; it is very beautiful there and sympathetic, and one can get away from people. Then, when the divorce was granted—that I am certain would be her wish— we could marry. Not here, of course ; but there are countries where it would be legal. . . . If it mattered. . . . All that is a mere nothing. I am yours—till death. And you are—*my wife*."

His arms were round me ; his lips were on mine ; it was the renewing of youth once more. For that eternal moment my prayers, my tears, even my dying child, even my covenant with God—all were forgotten. The Garden of Paradise lay open, and in my ears the bliss of life was chanted.

I was in the Blue Land again. The sun gladdened me ; the warm peace of Kassis enwrapped me ; the roses wafted their perfume; the palm-leaves whispered wooingly; the sea and the wind and the mountain torrent sang the old song—

"Love! love! Nothing endures but love!"

Then, as from the turret-chamber on that night of wrestling, I seemed to hear my boy's call sounding weakly, "Mother!"

It was the last—the supreme temptation: the last wrench asunder of self and spirit. The gates of my earthly paradise closed on me again; but the mystic kingdom lay in all its shining glory, a conquered realm.

Clinging to him, weeping, and yet refraining for my oath's sake from the dear caresses, I told him all, and prayed him to uphold me in that purpose wherein I lacked strength. I told him of the night of wrestling—of the despair which had rent me—of the vow I had vowed, of the renunciation I had made, and of the Covenant.

"God has kept His bargain," I said, "and shall I now go back from mine?"

Awe-stricken, he released me, and our arms fell asunder.

"Come," I said.

He followed me to my boy's room. The nurses were there, and Dr. Glaive and Agatha. They all moved away when we entered; and we were left alone together, he and I and the child.

BOOK XVI

" *Good-bye, my Fancy . . .*

*Long indeed have we lived, slept, filtered, become really
blended into one.*

Then, if we die, we die together (yes, we'll remain one);

If we go anywhere, we go together to meet what happens:

Maybe we'll be better off, and blither, and learn something,

*Maybe it is yourself now really ushering me to the true
songs (who knows ?),*

*Maybe it's you the mortal knob really undoing, turning—
so now, finally,*

Good-bye—and hail, my Fancy! "

FAREWELL, beloved Blue Land, ever dear and sacred!

Once more I look out upon early dawn, and the sea lies so still—so still, Médiane and Rassem sleeping upon her bosom. The old town has not awakened yet. Full and softly golden, the moon sinks behind the Vasques hills, which stand forth tender and pure as risen ghosts in this unearthly blending of virgin day and dying night. Tiny hamlets, far away on the mountain-side, and all the near villages and mosques show strangely in the ethereal light, and the beacon on Cape Feurd dims slowly, and goes out at last as the dawn turns red.

.   .   .   .

Shall we know each other, dear, at once—quite at once—there in the love-realm beyond my second dawn? And will it be the semblance of our poor earth-bodies that we shall wear; or shall we be provided with grand new lustrous shapes, in which we shall scarcely recognise our old selves? Ah, dearest, I don't want you in resplendent robe of cloud and with changed, angelic countenance. I want you in the fashion that I knew. You— your very self, with the worn face I last beheld as it bent over the dead child; you, with the sad eyes and moody brow, the flashing smile and impatient head-toss; you, with all the old tricks of speech and gesture that I loved.

No, give me no formless glory. I want your own hand to clasp mine and your own voice to welcome me. Let us meet, the soiled sheaths cast, but, the spirit similitude of human ways remaining. For they are not lost, those dear human ways, only purified. Surely we shall find them again, there as here, the core and essence of our humanity. That most perfect thing which life gave us, shall of a certainty be yet more perfect in the Beyond, and from the ashes of passion's pyre shall soar the bird of immortality.

Truly, if the first great bridge-builders, Sin and Death, have spanned the chasm to hell-gate, there toils still the mightier builder Love, who rears the arch to heaven.

.   .   .   .   .   .

Do you who read, know what it means to approach the doors of the Shadow of Death; to brush the border of the unknown country; to feel the nearness of those hovering presences of whom the form may not yet be discerned?   Have you ever awakened from slumberings on your bed, filled with a wondrous peace and with the sure knowledge that in dreams you have walked with God's Servers, and have heard their voice, and have been taught by them of His works and ways?   These are the silent watchers and cleansers of our houses of clay, the builders in human material, whose bricks and straw are the unruly wills and affections of sinful man.   These are the priests of the invisible temple, who, when deep sleep falls upon the body, open to the soul its prison gates and reveal to it visions of the darkness.   Therefore, what fear of death should cling to that soul strong enough to break its bars—that soul which, on the wings of a great love and a most poignant pain, ascends to the infinite, and in the place of understanding, receives that inner wisdom which cannot be gotten for gold, and whereof man knows not the price?   There, in that hall of learning, is delivered to this freed soul the mystery of our dual selves, the mystery of sense and essence, of the day and the night, of time and the stars, of space, the ether, and dreams.   There this soul is taught that action is indeed but the shadow, and that not in the gross commerce of everyday existence lies the true tragedy of its passage through the lower years, but on the unseen stage where human destinies are controlled and the signal given. And thus the act-drop falls again and again in the great drama; while the players sleep awhile, to take up their parts anew, having no knowledge of what has gone before or of what shall come after.   So again and again, the tragic mummers stand face to face, and do not discover each other; and they mouth, and strut, and wail, and rejoice, and cannot tell that they are but the old masquers dressed in new dominoes.

.   .   .   .   .   .

The world recedes, and becomes a diminishing picture, exquisite, varied, brilliant still, but unreal as the vivid figures in a painted window, behind which the sun is setting.   And as I wait for the act-drop to fall, I ask myself what, for this poor player who has feebly glimpsed the Other Side, is the conclusion of the matter?   Truly it is written that to save his life a man shall lose it.   I have lost my all and have gained the whole, and why should I repine because bitterness and inadequate return have been my portion here? The seed sown in sincerity and watered with tears must, according to the unchanging law, yield in fulness of time its ripe harvest. The ages still are ours, and it is love alone that endures for ever. Yes, many pages have yet to be written of the book of human emotion ; but I know now, that its last word shall be, not Pessimism, not Defeat, but Attainment.

.   .   .   .

My little, black journals have long given out, and I cannot write now as I did in the beginning. And perhaps after all Esther Zamiel's last book, her reallest book, will be her worst failure.

Never mind ! There will be no Mr. Brock to shrug reprovingly and prate about the critics. . . . And it is the Recording Angel who will make this "Reader's Report."

So, as once upon a time the Reader would have quoted : "O British public, who may love me yet—Marry, and Amen."

THE END